Barbara Howe lives on the third rock from the sun, while her imagination travels the universe and beyond.

Born in the US (North Carolina), she spent most of her adult life in New Jersey, working in the software industry, on projects ranging from low-level kernel ports to multi-million-dollar financial applications. She moved to New Zealand in 2009, gained dual citizenship, and now works as a software developer in the movie industry. She lives in Wellington, in a house overflowing with books and jigsaw puzzles, and wishes she had more time time to spend universe hopping.

T0288780

Reforging: Book 2

Engine of Lies

By Barbara Howe

Engine of Lies

ISBN-13: 978-1-925759-24-2

Printed in Garamond and Goudy Old Style typefaces.

IFWG Publishing International

www.ifwgpublishing.com

Acknowledgement

This book would not have been possible without support and encouragement from my husband, Art Protin, and daughter, Lucy. They never lost patience with me or the story, even when I ripped the second book apart and rewrote it. I also owe Art thanks for the wording of the lock spell on the Fire and Water Offices.

I'd also like to thank Gerry Huntman, Rebecca Fraser, Catherine Archer-Wills, and the others at IFWG Publishing Australia involved in turning Engine of Lies into a real book. A special thanks goes to several friends whose enthusiasm for The Locksmith has kept me going: Letha Etzkorn, Jo Leary, and Kristeen Huey.

In memory of

Sarah D Howe

Who taught me, and many others, to read.

The Frost Maiden

The Frost Maiden is coming. Sparks of news, fanned by hot winds of gossip and speculation, blew outward from the Fire Warlock's path and landed on dry tinder. Within minutes, the Fortress was ablaze with hustle and bustle: castle staff converged on the receiving rooms for visiting royalty to spruce up spotless furnishings and replenish gold leaf showing no sign of wear. Scholars never before seen outside library or dining room dogged their footsteps, demanding attention to frayed hems and stained cuffs. Sven Matheson, would-be Flame Mage, jogged down the stairs with a doorstop of a book under his arm, casting about for spells that would trouble a visiting water witch. Captains of the guard barked orders to subordinates to polish their boots and hone their arms. And do them both at once, now!

I watched the feverish activity with a sour stomach. In the Fortress's thousand-year history, no Frost Maiden had ever set foot inside its walls. What sea change would tomorrow's visit bring?

The crackling rumours met the firebreak of the castle walls and checked. Little traffic flowed between castle and the town of Blazes during the mid-afternoon lull, but the delay would not last long. My fiancé—the retired Fire Warlock, Jean Rehsavvy—had gone to the school for a conference with the Practical Arts teacher. I chewed on my lip. He shouldn't hear the news from a bevy of fire witches with burning eyes, eager to fan the flames with tales of how he reacted, but chasing after the new Fire Warlock to make sure he sent a message might be pushing my luck.

A hand the size of a bear paw landed on my shoulder. I staggered.

"What are you waiting for?" the Fire Warlock growled. "Get down there and tell Jean she's coming. I don't want him hearing some garbled fifth or sixth-hand story. I especially don't want him hearing it from Flint."

"Me? I agree, but couldn't you—"

"No dice." He turned and walked away. "It's your fault she's coming. You tell him."

I hurtled down the Fortress stairs. A boisterous squad of guards at the foot bandying about 'Frost Maiden' and 'Himself' scrambled for cover as I approached. I passed them without comment, and loped through the gate and across the causeway over the dry moat. The school stood on the far side of town, but I could run for miles. Years ago, before I graduated to long skirts, I outran all the boys my age in Lesser Campton.

As if whispered comments about my unfeminine behaviour were not already widespread. I stopped short at the far end of the causeway. The retired Fire Warlock never ran. That august luminary never even hurried. How could I hold my head up if anyone laughed at me—or worse, him— because I was not dignified enough to be his consort? I took a few mincing steps down the road.

Burn it. At that pace, I'd get there next week. Worse, he would ask what was wrong.

A long, swinging stride said serious intent without, I hoped, conveying panic. I gave everyone I met a polite greeting without stopping to chat. Most looked relieved rather than offended.

A survey of the neighbourhood near the school showed housewives and servants unpacking trunks and airing out dwellings abandoned during the siege. High-pitched laughter and childish yells echoed from the schoolyard, but otherwise all was quiet. No knots of people whispered on street corners, no gossips banged on neighbours' doors.

Thank God for that.

Emma Johnson, Practical Arts teacher, met me at the gate on her way out. "He's around back," she said, waving at the school. "Playing with the children, bless him. It does my heart good to see him enjoying himself."

All thoughts of the Frost Maiden flew out of my head when I walked into the schoolyard. In a swarm of howling, running schoolchildren, Jean pelted across the playground, a boy of about ten in hot pursuit. A girl blundered in the way, and the boy grabbed her arm. "You're it."

Jean threw a brilliant grin in my direction and kept running. I gaped for a few seconds, then hurled myself into the girl's path. She careened into me. I pushed her away. "I'm it," I said, and gave chase.

For a few minutes, the words dignity and embarrassment meant little, compared to the pleasure of playing in fresh air on a fine spring day. But too soon, Jean stumbled. He was breathing hard, and his face had gone grey.

I barrelled through the mob, yelling, "Stop. Enough." He leaned on me as I marched him to a bench, and offered no resistance when I pushed him prone.

The children crowded around. "Are you all right, Your Wisdom?" "You don't look so good." "I'm sorry, sir, if we hurt you."

"No one hurt him," I said. "The Fire Office's magic kept him young for a hundred years, but it's gone. His own body has had to take over again, and it's not used to the strain yet. He tires quickly."

Jean smiled at the worried faces. "I will recover, but you must continue today's game without me." He tapped the tallest girl. "You are it."

The swarm scattered, shrieking, and surged across the playground.

"I'll have to remember that," I said. "That was more effective than telling them to go away."

"But perhaps not entirely fair. I was not 'it'." His colour returned as he lay quiet on the bench, watching them play. "Mother Celeste warned against overexertion, but I did not listen."

"And will you listen now? How about a picnic by ourselves? That would get us out of the Fortress to enjoy the spring weather, but still be sedate."

"Would it be?" He looked at me with devils in his eyes. "You and I, alone, when the mere prospect quickens my pulse?"

On any other day, his gaze would have set my own heart racing and my face burning. I gripped the top rail of the bench back with both hands. It was a shame to have to spoil his mood.

"I would enjoy a picnic," he said. "Tomorrow morning, perhaps, we can go south for warmer weather."

"Not tomorrow. That's what I came to tell you. The Frost Maiden is coming tomorrow morning."

The sparkle in his eyes dimmed. "Is she?" He swung his feet off the bench and levered himself upright, facing away from me. He stared up at the curtain wall. "To the Fortress? Why?"

"What do you mean, why? To see you. To apologise, as she said she would."

He gazed into the distance without speaking, as remote as the unapproachable Fire Warlock. I wiped my hands on my skirt, and resumed my death grip on the bench. "Beorn doesn't believe she wants to make amends, but I do."

"So you have said, and I believe she intends to. She is too prudent to lie to a warlock."

"I thought you would be pleased."

"I do welcome a reconciliation between the Fire and Water Guilds, but I would rather she apologised to the reigning Fire Warlock, as one Officeholder to another, than to me as an individual, woman to man."

"But weren't most of her insults directed at you personally?"

"Yes, and that is the rub. Apologies will revive memories of quarrels best forgotten. Many affronts still have the power to wound, and when faced with her regrets, I will have to make apologies for my own shortcomings."

"What for? I've never heard you say one unkind word about her."

"Fault for the rift lies with both guilds, and I am not blameless."

"What could you have done or said that was as nasty as what she said to us in the Earth Mother's Warren?" Her prediction of a near-fatal romance had been a personal insult directed at both of us. Months later I still steamed, remembering. I might have forgiven and forgotten if it had not been spot on.

He interrupted his study of the looming Fortress to glance at me out of the corner of his eye. "Forgive me for not enlightening you."

I made a face at the back of his head.

He added, "And despite my desire to modernise Frankland, ushering the Frost Maiden into the Fortress is not a change I welcome. She does not belong there."

My stomach began to unknot, and I slid into place beside him on the bench. "I thought I was being spiteful for feeling that way."

"Not at all. The Fortress is our unassailable refuge, and we do not want that sanctuary breached. If I must meet her, I would prefer outside the walls, but that would be an unforgivable rebuff to her offer of reconciliation."

My stomach knotted up again. "Jean?"

"Yes?"

"If it's a normal reaction, the other members of the Fire Guild will be furious, won't they?"

He pondered for a bit before answering. "Probably not. I had considered her coming from the Fire Warlock's perspective, not from the stance of the lesser ranks. Only you and I and Beorn are so steeped in the history, and aware of our own limitations, that we understand how vulnerable the Fire Warlock is, and how necessary that refuge. The rest of the Fire Guild will think it fitting, as she evidently does, for her to come here. They will imagine the power on display must overwhelm her, and will jockey for position to watch her grovel. No, you need not fear becoming a pariah for having brought her here."

I relaxed against the back of the bench and breathed a long sigh. "Thank you. Grovel? I can't imagine her ever grovelling. Or letting anything, even the Fortress, intimidate her."

"Nor can I. I certainly never succeeded." He rose and offered me a hand. "If we must—"

A column of fire twice my height erupted in the middle of the playground. The roar echoed off the stone walls of the surrounding buildings. Jean went rigid. Children fled, screaming. Warlock Flint, as thunderous as a storm cloud, stomped out of the fire.

"Why the hell," he bellowed, "is that frostbitten ice witch coming here?"

Jean faced the younger warlock with thin lips and glittering eyes. "Watch your tongue. She—"

"She doesn't belong here."

"You heard Lucinda's story—"

"Yeah, it's all her fault." Flint stabbed a finger at me. I edged behind Jean. "I knew all along she's a traitor. She'll let that harpy in, and—"

"How dare you show such disrespect towards two of our most powerful witches—"

"Two of a kind, yeah, and that kind is bad—"

"Each has, in her own way, proven herself a true daughter of Frankland—"

"You've got no right to let that icicle just march in—"

"Sorceress Lorraine is coming to make peace. Of course we will welcome her into the Fortress."

"Still sweet on her, aren't you? After all this time." Flint's gaze flicked to me, and I backed away. "You think pretty-boy Sven will still want you after Silverpolish here dumps you for her?"

The cords in Jean's neck bulged. "You have outdone yourself this time, you cad."

"So what? You can't threaten me with lightning now."

"You think not? Fool." Jean flashed glowing red, as if lava flowed in his veins. Thunder boomed. Flint recoiled. I clamped my hands over my ears and ran for shelter. A blast roared behind me.

"I beg your pardon for frightening you," Jean said into the sudden silence.

I peeked around the corner of the school building. The schoolyard was deserted except for him. I left cover and went to meet him. "That blast was Flint jumping through the fire?"

His colour had returned to normal, but his eyes smouldered. "Of course. I trust you will not make such ostentatious displays when you master that skill. The smallest burst needed is enough to unnerve a mundane."

"Yes, sir. Did he really think you would have hit him with a lightning bolt?"

He shrugged. "That dolt's mind mystifies me. I could have directed a strike at the far corner of the schoolyard to demonstrate I am still capable, but I am relieved it was not necessary. I should not have lost my temper."

He offered me his arm. An instant later, we stepped out of a small fire onto the causeway at the Fortress's foot. The guard saluted and wished us a good day. I kept a tight grip on Jean as we walked under the portcullis and into the tunnel through the walls.

Jean said, "One would think I could learn to ignore everything that fool says. I cannot fathom why I let him push me into a rage."

"You expect better behaviour from a warlock?"

"Hope for, yes. Expect, no. I would rather not dignify his accusations with any notice, but the issue should not fester between us. Does my former relationship with Sorceress Lorraine trouble you?"

Never, ever, lie to a warlock. With as light a voice as I could manage, I said, "Should it?"

"No."

As flat a denial as I could hope for. No equivocation, no whisper of a lie. "Then how could it? But what did you say about welcoming her into the Fortress?"

Jean's lips twitched. "You should know the most effective way to force a warlock on a course of action he would rather avoid is to order him not to. Stop laughing, girl."

She Throws the Gauntlet

Jean sat at the supper table, brooding over his coffee, long after everyone else had gone. I sat across the table from him, fishing for topics to take his mind off the Frost Maiden, but he met all my sorties with polite inattentiveness. Then René bounced in, demanding we resume fighter training.

Jean's eyes lit, and he rose from the table. "Certainly. I welcome the distraction. A short bout and off to bed. We will sleep better for it."

I stayed seated. "Do you need me? I have a book I want to read."

Jean frowned down at me. "Are our practice sessions so onerous?"

"Didn't I demonstrate I can take care of myself without flaming someone?"

"Your lock was effective, yes, but you had the advantage of surprise. Once the Empire's agents understand what you can do, they will not give you time to prepare. Can you throw a lock on an enemy wizard the instant he threatens you?"

"Well, no."

"Or on more than one wizard?"

"That lock wouldn't be any good, either," René said, "against a mundane with a knife."

My cheeks got hot. "I could flame him. Not enough to kill him, but enough to stop him while I run away."

René's nose wrinkled. "Warlocks don't run away. That's talking like a girl."

My face, even my ears, burned. "I am a girl. I don't want to fight."

Jean's shoulders sagged. "My dear, I too deplore the necessity, but our preferences have little bearing. You are a warlock. The world will not let us forget that. The emperor will set a price on your head, to avenge what you have done to the Chessmaster. You will learn to defend yourself, or you will die."

"It's not fair. Those shouldn't be the only two choices."

"Life is seldom fair, my love, and those choices…" His voice trailed off, and his eyes took on a faraway look. I glanced at René. He shrugged.

Jean refocused on me. "I beg your pardon, my dear. There is a third choice, and I have been remiss in not recognising my duty to you. I offer as justification the fact that it is a choice available to you only if you marry another warlock, and until the war's end that did not seem possible."

"Jean, what are you talking about?"

"Simply that it is my duty now, as your fiancé, and soon, as your husband, to protect you from harm."

"What?"

"To shield his fragile wife—her person, her mind, all she possesses—is a man's most sacred responsibility."

René and I gaped at him. He looked quite serious.

"You will, of course, be constrained in your activities. You will not leave the Fortress except in my company."

"Jean, you can't—"

His voice was crisp with command. "And you will forego other dangerous activities, including jumping through the fire on your own."

I shot out of my chair. "Don't you dare do that to me. I'll damn well learn to fight. I'm not going to sit at home and knit while you're out adventuring, you louse, you…"

His eyes creased into a smile. I stopped. "I've been had."

René said, "Huh?"

I said, "How do you make a warlock do something she doesn't want to do? Order her not to."

We walked together to the practice room, with Jean chuckling.

"Protect me, my foot," I said. "I saved your life, remember?"

"How could I forget? You are not helpless, my love. We would all be ill served if I treated you so, but the freedom to act on your own also permits you to put yourself at risk. Knowing you will, and I cannot prevent it, frightens me."

"I know. I'm sorry, Jean. I'll try harder."

"Thank you."

René said, "If you can't order a warlock around, how's she going to handle that bit about 'love, honour, and obey'?"

"Burn it," I said. "I forgot about that."

Jean threw back his head and hooted. He was still laughing when I flamed him.

The townsfolk began gathering on the causeway at dawn. When the guards opened the gate, they flooded in, rushing to good vantage points on the stairs. By ten o'clock, they packed the unmoving stairs, the open space inside the curtain wall, the ramparts, and the terraces. Only the cordoned-off paths the Frost Maiden would travel remained clear.

We watched the jostling for position from the echoing emptiness of the ballroom. "I'm surprised," I said, "there's no one in here."

"I locked them out," Beorn said. He was, for the first time I had ever seen, immaculate. His mane and beard were trimmed, brushed, and braided. Boots gleamed, opals burned, rubies flashed and glowed. The massive accoutrements of the Fire Office—the ring, the silver and opal belt—fit as if made for him. He stood with his hands on his hips, glowering at the mob. "Wouldn't do for them to overhear."

"You need not worry on that score," Jean said. Like Beorn, he wore black silk trimmed with Fire Guild emblems. With a marble countenance, he turned away and strolled along the row of windows. Flames danced around the phoenix embroidered on the back of his robes. "It is time."

"Yeah," Beorn said. "Come on, Lucinda, let's go." He held the door for me, and the two of us walked out onto the terrace. Heads turned to watch us.

"Now listen up, you," he bellowed. Clapping my hands over my ears did not block his thunderous voice. "The Frost Maiden is our guest, so you'd best not embarrass the Fire Guild. No catcalls, no sneers, no jeers, no nothing. Treat her like you'd treat the Earth Mother. If you don't, I'll know who you are. Got that?"

As one, the crowd roared, "Yes, sir."

"Good."

We rode down the moving staircase without talking. Beorn chewed the end of his moustache. I couldn't fault him for nerves—she'd been Frost Maiden for more than a century; he'd been Fire Warlock less than a week. My own palms were damp, but if I wiped them on my dress, I would ruin the velvet skirt. I clasped them behind my back and straightened my spine. Raised my chin.

Beorn said, "I'm glad one of us can be nonchalant about this."

"What gave you that idea? I'm only here because you insisted I come along."

"It's good to have a hostess along when greeting a female visitor."

"Why'd you appoint me hostess?"

"You're the highest-ranking fire witch, and the only one she's friendly with."

"Friendly? That's a bit of an exaggeration."

"She at least talked to you. She's never said boo to me. Not that I wanted her to."

We walked through the tunnel between the gatehouses and out onto the causeway. Water pooled before us. We both flinched and stepped backwards. The Frost Maiden, in dry and shimmering gossamer blue silk, stepped out of the pool, which shrank and vanished behind her.

We made our reverences, welcoming her to the Fortress. She returned them with a rigid and shallow curtsey. I stiffened.

"Thank you, Warlock Arturos, Warlock Locksmith," she said. Her gaze left us—it had settled on me for no longer than an instant—and travelled up the Fortress behind us. "Warlock Quicksilver is waiting inside, along with the rest of the Fire Guild?"

"We'd've had a riot if we tried to keep them out," Beorn said.

"I daresay it will be highly entertaining," she said. "Shall we go, then?"

Be damned if I would let on entering the Fortress still made me nervous. I gritted my teeth and stepped under the portcullis. She sailed alongside as if she had done it all her life. Beorn glowered at me over her head.

He gave her a running commentary as we rode the moving stairs. She said little; I said less. I eyed her; she looked straight ahead, taking no notice of me. She reminded me, as before, of my stepsister, Claire, but Claire was never so cold. The slight she had given my curtsey rankled. We could never be close friends, but the last time we had met, we had at least not been enemies—or so I had thought then.

We left her alone with Jean in the reception room and retreated to the ballroom. I couldn't stay still. I left Beorn waiting by the doors and circled the room, casting about for something to take my mind off the Frost Maiden.

The only subject that came to mind was Claire. She had been my best friend, once, but I didn't want to see her. The glamour spell she used scared me.

On his deathbed, Father exacted a promise that, as the older and more capable sister, I would help Claire whenever she needed me. When George Barnes brought word, months ago, that she had gone to Gastòn, I had done nothing, even though the news made me go cold. What, in God's name, had Mother Janet been thinking, to let a beautiful girl go to the city by herself? Unscrupulous men of all classes congregated in the cities, preying on naïve women. If she gave her consent to being lured to her ruin, there wasn't anything family, friends, or the law could do about it.

I had reasoned I could not leave the Fortress without the Warlock's permission until I had completed my one year's service. Later, the siege had given me a better excuse. Now I had no justification, and still had done nothing.

Listening to my guilty conscience did not improve my mood.

Beorn was staring at the ceiling and gave no indication he noticed my approach. I stared past him at the gilt-covered double doors and chewed on my lip. My little candle flame could slide under the door. They would be so focused on their conversation they wouldn't notice.

"Don't even think about it," Beorn said, without lowering his gaze. "You'd annoy Jean, and you wouldn't get past their defences anyway."

"You're eavesdropping, aren't you?" Not even Jean could shut out the Fire Warlock. But he had a right to listen in; I didn't.

"I was. I'm listening to the crowd now. They're getting restless." He lowered his head and looked at me. "I listened long enough to discover there are some things even I don't want to know. I have to say, I'm glad you thawed her out. I couldn't take some of the things she's said nearly as well as Jean did."

"Thawed her out? You believe she has changed?"

"Yeah. As far as apologies go, she's doing a right good job of it."

"So why was she so cold when she got here?"

"Nerves?"

"Her?"

He shrugged. "Beats me. I haven't got her figured out yet."

He went back to staring at the ceiling. I returned to circling the ballroom. The opposite of love, the philosophers say, is indifference, not hate; love and hate are two sides of the same coin. They had loved once, and been enemies before my grandparents were born. I couldn't compete with that history. In some way, she still mattered to him.

My actions had moved the Frost Maiden to apologise. Some dark corner in my heart said I should have left well enough alone.

When they finally emerged, two hours later, she was as cool as spring water. Jean swayed.

We would have turned towards the outer doors, but she stopped us. "Please, if I may, I would have a word alone with the Locksmith."

"Sure," Beorn said, "if she's willing." I shrugged. The Frost Maiden and I retreated to the reception room.

"I beg your pardon," she said. "This is not the best time or place for this question, but I beg you to humour me."

I wiped my hands on my skirt. "Go ahead, Your Wisdom."

"When Warlock Quicksilver introduced you to the other Officeholders, he proposed a use for your talent, but you had only begun your training, and did not know if it was possible. That was months ago. Can you do as he asks?"

Did she mean releasing the lock on the Fire Office? "I don't know, Your Wisdom."

Not a trace of warmth showed in her expression or voice. "You do not know?"

I crabbed sideways into the door. "We haven't looked, Your Wisdom."

The Locksmith's Warning

The Frost Maiden gave me an incredulous stare. Her voice rose. "You, a fire witch, have not looked?"

My stomach turned a flip. It had not occurred to me, but now that she raised the question, I found it hard to believe, myself.

"We didn't have time, Your Wisdom," I stammered. "I was still learning about locks before the war, and then he was too busy. Besides, he said it would be years before I was ready."

"Of course," the Frost Maiden said, her voice again cool and detached. "Lack of time, not lack of courage or ability."

The chill her question had elicited disappeared in a surge of heat. How I got through the next few minutes without embarrassing the Fire Guild, I do not know. We rejoined Jean and Beorn, and made our curtsies and bows on the terrace, in full view of the crowd, but all I saw and heard was a red haze and my own pounding pulse.

The Frost Maiden vanished in a pool of water, and Jean let Beorn steer him away to lie down and rest. I flounced into the ballroom to stomp back and forth across the long mirrored inner wall, hoping to regain my composure in solitude.

How dare she accuse me of incompetence? Or cowardice? Me, a warlock. A member of a tribe renowned for our rash, reckless, foolhardy... Scratch that. Renowned for our courage and resolve. Releasing that abomination of a lock on the Water Office had taken both, and it had nearly killed me. Why did she insult me, after what I had done for her?

Maybe she had a point. I was a sorry excuse for a fire witch, if I wasn't curious enough to see if I could unlock the Fire Office.

I stopped and leaned my burning face against the cool mirror. Hadn't

I learned yet not to lie to a warlock, including myself? The truth was, I didn't want to know. The lock I had released on the Water Office was a secondary lock. The intact one holding it together must be stronger than the one I already released. The one on the Fire Office, the bedrock of Frankland's defences, would be stronger yet. Of course I was afraid. What sane person wouldn't be?

I would show the Frost Maiden I wasn't a coward. I would read that frostbitten lock. If I could. Jean tried for decades and failed. I still had a lot to learn about lock theory. It might be years before I could read it, if ever.

I pushed away from the mirror and smiled at my reflection. If I couldn't read it, I could stop worrying for a while. At least long enough to enjoy my honeymoon.

Beorn leaned against the parapet, waiting for me to step out onto the terrace. "What did she say," he asked, "that pissed you off so much?"

"Was it that obvious?"

"Not to them." He waved at the last of the dispersing onlookers. "But I know you better than they do."

I recounted our conversation, and he gave a low whistle. "You sure you're a member of the Fire Guild? Any other fire witch would've flamed her for that."

I glared at him. "If you recall, the previous Fire Warlock warned us never even to think such a thing. The Fire Office wouldn't like it."

"Just saying. You've got as much self-control as most of the rest of us, put together. And she's got a lot of nerve saying that here, of all places."

"But if she knows the Fire Office won't let me hurt her…" I shrugged. "She's right about one thing, though. I should see if I can read that lock."

"I'd been thinking that, too, but I didn't want to bring it up yet. I wanted to let you two have your fun while you can."

The hairs on the back of my neck stood on end. "What do you mean, 'while we can'?"

"Sorry. Forget I said that."

"Forget it, my foot. It scares you, too? Have you had a vision?"

"Not about that. Just a feeling."

"Liar." I searched his face. "You're worried. Aren't you? Have you foreseen…?" My face burned. "I'm sorry. I've been so happy about Jean. I'd forgotten you've foreseen René as Fire Warlock. That means…"

"It means I'm gone." He grinned. "Unless we find another high-ranking fire witch to fall in love with me and get me out of the Office. Not likely. But that's not what I'm worried about."

"What? How can you be so calm, talking about…about your…?"

"My own death? God knows I'm not eager, but look, Lucinda, I come from a family with a long history in the Fire Guild. I grew up wanting to be the Fire Warlock. Failing to pass muster scared me more than a fiery end. I've never had any delusions I'd last any longer than average. René will be at least twenty-five, maybe thirty before it lands on him, so that gives me ten or fifteen years, and that's respectable. Unless…"

Unless someone else held the Fire Office in between. I refused to consider who that someone else might be.

He said, "I wouldn't mind much if I could be sure I'll do a decent job while I hold the Office. I'm scared of going down in the history books as the Fire Warlock who let civil war tear the country apart."

"You said something about that once, but we've had uprisings before without serious damage."

"Yeah, but so far they've always been isolated. Some duke or baron abused his power, and the Fire Warlock and the king bullied both the lord and his subjects back in line. Even with the bad blood between the four guilds, and between the Fire Warlock and the king, they worked together well enough to keep the peace."

"As long as the kings took the Great Oath, they did."

"Right. There's powerful magic behind the bit about being 'king for all the people of Frankland.' Things started going to pot after they weaselled out of that. Now the king's not even giving lip service to the idea commoners should get a fair shake."

I nodded. Long ago, to say someone was as fair as the king was a high compliment. Now, that line was good only for a sure laugh in the comedies put on by traveling players. "Maybe things will be better now the Fire and Water Guilds can work together."

"You think? Maybe if you can work another miracle and thaw out the whole frostbitten ice—"

"Watch your language."

"Sorry. Thaw out the whole damned Water Guild. Her wishy-washy, wiseacre flunkies always cold shoulder me and act like they don't care that the Water Office is busted." He tugged at his beard. "The only way I see to keep the country from going up in flames is to push ahead with fixing the Fire Office, and it's more urgent than Jean realises."

"Doesn't he have a pretty good grasp on the mood of the country, even if he isn't a seer?"

"He does, and he's right; things aren't that bad. Yet. If they keep on at the same rate, we might have several decades. But something's going to happen that makes things worse fast. I just don't know what or when."

The conversation with Beorn was still fresh in my mind at breakfast the next morning. "Jean, are all the problems in Frankland's justice system caused by the broken Water Office? Or are some the fault of the witches and wizards running the courts and handing out the verdicts? They're such cold fish, acting as if they don't care that commoners get stomped on when someone outranking them is at fault."

Jean shook his head. "You are mistaken, my dear. A water wizard cannot help but be aware of the anger and fear his guild inspires. He cultivates a cold demeanour to distance himself from the pain the penalties cause. If he took every unjust decision to heart he would drop dead at a young age."

"Isn't there any way to work around the flaws in the Water Office?"

He grimaced. "You are not aware of the lengths the Water Guild already goes to, to mitigate its shortcomings."

"Oh? Tell me about them."

"I cannot, my love. They are Water Guild secrets."

I frowned at him. "But you know."

"If you become Fire Warlock someday, you will learn of them also. I cannot tell you." He scowled past my left shoulder and didn't respond to further questions.

He shook off his preoccupation after breakfast, giving his full attention to the task before us. We followed Beorn through the fire in the Fortress kitchen into an octagonal room with sofas surrounding a central fire pit. Sunlight and frigid air streamed in through floor-to-ceiling windows in each wall. He flicked his wand, and the windows swung shut. I walked to the window in the north wall to admire the desolate beauty of Storm King's caldera.

On my previous arrival at the aerie, no barriers obstructed the steep drops in front and behind. I had suffered from vertigo until Jean had surrounded us with unwindowed walls. Strange that a sheet of glass should make me feel secure.

I stepped backwards, away from the window. "Jean, are the walls and windows real, or illusions?"

"Real? What is the nature of reality? The warm sunlight touches your skin, not the cold mountain air. You cannot deny something blocks the breeze."

The solid, heavy sofa blocked my retreat. I swung over the back and onto the seat in a move that would have horrified a deportment teacher. "Right. That something might be magic, you mean. I'm not budging off this sofa."

Beorn guffawed. "What's it matter? You're not going to notice where you are anyway."

"Thanks for that reassurance. Is there any chance I could sleepwalk while I'm in a trance?"

Jean squeezed my shoulder. "None now, my dear."

"Good." I lay down full length and found a comfortable position. "I'm ready."

In a few minutes, I saw only with my mind's eye. I could have been in a cave underground for all it mattered. To anyone watching, we would have looked like three layabouts, sleeping the day away. Beorn's snapping, guttering bonfire and my dancing candle flame followed Jean's steady lighthouse beacon as it dived into the thicket of spells, following the path he had worked out long ago to reach the lock at the centre.

Even with his aid, it was tedious. Both of us got distracted and lost, but as we approached the centre a growing sense of the original locksmith's presence made it easier to focus. We reached the lock—that lock that had defeated all Jean's attempts to read it for decades—and it unscrolled in my mind on the first touch.

Earth, Air, Fire, and Water agree
To let the fire within the Locksmith, me,
Draw on their power that none may find,
On this Token of Office the spells that bind.
Whichever power releases the lock, I swear,
Shall face my hidden terror there.

If that fool witch hadn't been dead for a millennium, I would have torched her. Then I asked what it would take to release the lock. A lightning bolt struck a yard from my feet.

I fell off the couch onto the stone floor, crying and shaking. Jean picked me up and held me, murmuring into my hair. I sobbed into his shoulder, until I calmed enough to talk.

"That wicked, wicked witch. Did she think she would live forever? Or that the Office was perfect? What was wrong with her?"

"Hush," Jean said. "Tell us what you have found."

I quoted the spell to them and described the lightning bolt. No one said anything for a while. Beorn, his face white, tugged at his beard. Jean paced with his head down, his hands clasped together behind his back, fingers twitching. After two circuits of the room, he paced on out through the closed window. That settled one question. I no longer cared.

I said, "I'm getting a bit tired of risking my life in the service of these infernal Offices."

Beorn said, "You and me both."

"Oh, Beorn, I'm so sorry. I didn't think—"

Beorn's eyes rolled heavenward. "That the bit about the hidden terror might be aimed at the Fire Warlock? Thanks a lot. Your long-ago twin—"

"Don't call her that. I despise the woman."

"—Seems to have had a mean streak. But that wasn't what I meant. I don't like you risking your life, either. I'd rather risk mine than yours. That's what I'm here for."

Jean did not return for some time. We watched in silence as he stood, motionless, on a point of rock, silhouetted against empty sky. When he left his rocky perch and rejoined us, he sported a set jaw and furrowed brow. He sat facing me. Beorn cleared his throat, and Jean shot him a questioning glance.

Beorn said, "I never heard of anyone drawing on another person's power to create a lock, much less four of them."

Jean said, "As this lock secures Frankland's defences, requiring all four Officeholders to agree before making changes is a sensible precaution, although I do not understand how it is done either.

"The last clause, however." He shook his head. "Perhaps she expected to hold the Office first. Perhaps she intended to make repairs in her own lifetime, rather than leaving the Office untouched for a thousand years, or perhaps she believed she would live forever. No one had yet tested the Earth Guild spells for holding off aging with such power at their disposal. They did not know two hundred years is the limit of human endurance. Even the Earth Mother must retire, usually well before then.

"But threatening dire consequences to anyone unlocking it was both paranoid and short-sighted, as they gave us no other way to repair the Office. Assuming such a level of perfection is arrogant in the extreme. When we rebuild it, we must make it easier to repair."

When. He wasn't going to let me out of it, was he? Drown the man. And he said he loved me.

He leaned forward, locking eyes with me. "My dear, I offer you my apology. I failed to anticipate such a hellish lock."

"Hellish is right. This is a stronger lock than that abomination on the Water Office, and releasing that one almost killed me. There's no way I can survive unlocking this one."

"There is a way. A path not without its own dangers, but with rewards as well. I have never suggested this to another wizard; to suggest it to a witch appals me, but…"

"Jean, what are you talking about?"

"Lucinda, my love, you will learn to tap into Storm King on your own, and call down the lightning."

Fire and Frost

"Call down the lightning," I bleated. "By myself?"

Beorn's colour had come back. He blanched again.

A ghost of a smile appeared on Jean's face. "That prospect appears to terrify you as much as the lock does."

"It's the same problem, isn't it? Dealing with more power than I can handle."

"Exactly. You will build up to it, to direct and channel the power without it touching you. When you are able to channel power from the volcano, you will also be able to channel the power needed for this lock. It will take time—years, perhaps a decade—but we have time. We need not panic now."

More urgent than Jean realises. I didn't dare look at Beorn.

Beorn said, "Didn't the Great Coven forbid the Guild Council from teaching anybody because it was too dangerous?"

I dug my nails into the upholstery. "Did you have to say that?"

Jean said, "It was a recommendation, not a prohibition. They thought we would never need it, since the Token of Office channels the energy for an untrained warlock."

Beorn said, "I'd wondered how the old warlocks learned to do it in the first place. Do you know?"

"I do not know how the first lightning-wielding warlocks came to do so. As far as I can determine, the key ingredient in the chain of warlocks leading up to Fortunatus, and the forging of the Token of Office, was the tutelage of an older, more experienced master. Attempting it alone was then all but suicidal. Even with a master's guidance, in the five hundred years before Fortunatus, a third of those attempting it died."

"A third?" I yelped. "And you want me to do it?"

He held up a hand, palm out. "Patience, my dear. I would rather you did not need to, but if you must, I am a better teacher, and you a more willing and patient student, than most warlocks. Also, since that time, the warlocks of Thule have developed spells making it somewhat less dangerous."

Beorn and I chorused, "Somewhat?"

Jean's eyebrows arched. "You should both understand the theory. It is not possible to eliminate risk—not, that is, and still perform any meaningful action."

"I guess not," I mumbled.

Beorn said, "So you're going to Thule on your honeymoon?"

Jean smiled. "I have longed to visit Thule my entire life—I would go there without such a good reason. We need do nothing more, for now, than the exercises I have subjected Beorn to."

"Jean," I said, "Have any other women learned to call down the lightning?"

"The records we have from before the forging are fragmentary, at best, but from what we know of the original Locksmith, she must have."

I subsided, grumbling only a little. Six months earlier, I would have fainted at the suggestion, but I had since fallen under the lure of powerful magic. Some non-rational part of me I had no control over pricked up its ears and drooled. If that wretched woman could do it, so could I. I might even forgive Jean for demanding it from me.

Besides, as he said, there was no point in panicking now. There would be plenty of time later to panic.

"Why did you insist I come? You and Jean can tell the other Officeholders about the lock. You don't need me."

"I'd rather you told them yourself." Beorn ducked through the door. He banged his head twice in the short tunnel to the Warren, despite walking in a half-crouch. When he stopped swearing, he added, "Besides, when I called the meeting, the Frost Maiden said she wanted you both there."

"Jean, I understand. But why me? So she can have another go at disparaging me?"

"She may not intend to," Jean said. "The victim of an evil spell, such as the one the Frost Maiden was under, needs time to recover, and I doubt

24

she will ever lose her penchant for sarcasm. She was on her best behaviour when she came to the Fortress, but as her comment to you demonstrates, we cannot expect that to continue. I am not eager for this meeting either."

His hard eyes and rigid posture had already conveyed that. None of us believed one encounter could overcome a century's friction and distrust. I walked into the amber chamber with butterflies dancing a jig in my stomach.

Mother Celeste's cheery "Welcome, friends," calmed my nerves a little, but I had barely begun to answer her questions about our honeymoon plans when she greeted someone else over my shoulder.

I turned and met a blinding smile. I almost called the woman wearing it Claire; I had never expected to see such radiance or hear such cordial tones from the Frost Maiden. She showed no signs of scorn, acknowledging the Fire Guild contingent with impeccable manners, and introducing me with all honours to the young woman with her. A tall brunette with deep-set eyes and an aquiline nose, Sorceress Eleanor, the Frost Maiden's apprentice, looked as if she would be more at home in the Air Guild.

She said, "Did I hear you say you're leaving Frankland on your honey-moon?"

"Yes. There are places I want to see, and Jean has a list of people to visit—governors, heads of state, and so on he has already been corr-esponding with, discussing governance and, uh..." Better not say jurisprudence—they would be offended we were stepping on their toes.

"That will serve us all," the Frost Maiden said. "We are hobbled by our lack of experience with other governments. Enchanter Paul is the sole Officeholder who has travelled outside of Frankland."

"And I was concerned more with trade than governance," he said. "I never considered that anything might change here."

"I correspond with many of those same men and women," she said. "They have valuable insights into many subjects. Do not let Warlock Quicksilver neglect the opportunity to discuss jurisprudence."

My mouth hung open. "Uh..."

"What about staff?" Enchanter Paul said. "I can suggest several members of the Air Guild who could be of service."

Jean, deep in conversation with Mother Celeste, looked up and frowned, but let me answer.

"Thank you, but we've been bombarded with fire witches and wizards begging to come along as valets and secretaries and maids. If we chose from the Air Guild instead of the Fire Guild we'd never hear the end of it."

"You may have a sizable group." The Frost Maiden's eyes sparkled. "Let me offer you the services of a water wizard from my personal staff, to effect the safety of your ship."

I recoiled. "Dear God, no."

She stiffened. Her eyes flashed. "Oh. You prefer a water wizard who still believes our two guilds to be at war?"

"No, ma'am," I stammered. "I meant we won't travel by ship. We'll jump through the fire."

Her eyebrows drew together. "As far as the New World? Is that possible, even for one who can call on power from the volcano?"

"Certainly," Jean snapped. "Via the Faroes, Thule, and Ultima Thule. The whole world is within my reach."

"Oh." She gave us each a jerky nod of the head. "Then of course you will do so, for no warlock would board a ship unless dragged on in chains. Forgive me my faux pas." She turned away and sat on the far side of the room.

The Air Enchanter coughed. "Shall we get down to business then?"

My cheeks burned and I forced a smile. Somehow, I managed not to bare my teeth. Angry at being rattled, I slumped in a chair in a corner, as far away from the Frost Maiden as possible, with Jean and Beorn between us. Beorn chewed on his moustache and gave her a dark look.

The Frost Maiden sat, as before, facing away from Jean. "I understand the Fire Warlock called us together to further discuss rebuilding the Fire Office. I have a suggestion to make before we address that question."

Beorn tugged at his beard, but shrugged. "Go ahead."

"I took little part in the earlier meeting when Warlock Quicksilver proposed to disassemble and repair the Fire Office. I reasoned I needed time to consider what he had said before offering an opinion. In truth, the blight on my Office kept me at odds with everything the Fire Warlock said simply because he was the Fire Warlock. Now that abomination of a lock is gone, and I am free to say I concur with the need to fix his Office, and we should proceed with dispatch, but without haste."

Jean's eyebrows rose. Enchanter Paul frowned. Beorn settled back in his chair with a deep sigh. I watched the flashing lights of her ring and steamed. We ought to fix the Water Office first, but she would never admit it was broken.

"However," she said, "I do not agree with the plans he laid out for making repairs. The Fire Office is the most complex of the four. It is too dangerous to start there."

Jean's face was an unreadable mask. He and Beorn both started to respond, but she held up a hand. "Please let me finish. I plead with you, nay, beg you, to start by reforging the Office of the Northern Waters."

My jaw dropped. Beorn's eyes blazed. Mother Celeste looked thoughtful, and nodded, as if the idea was not new to her.

The Frost Maiden said, "None of you will argue with my assessment my Office is the most flawed of the four."

Beorn muttered, "Hell, no."

She shot him a cold glare, then turned away. "If my Office is repaired, the urgency to repair the Fire Office shall abate. Is that not so?"

Yes. Oh, yes. But I would have to unlock the Water Office. I didn't straighten out of my slump.

Beorn said, "Yeah, I'd think so. I like your idea. We don't know what will happen when we unlock the Fire Office, or what we'll find under the lock. It would be safer to start with one of the other Offices. We can't survive without the Fire Office. Even if we took the Water Office apart and couldn't put it together again, Frankland would survive without it."

Mother Celeste said what I didn't dare voice. "And be, perhaps, in better shape for it. Certainly no worse."

The Frost Maiden turned her icy stare on Mother Celeste. "And I will be the first to rejoice when the nobility takes over the administration of justice, and show the common people a bias they have not so far dreamt of."

Mother Celeste winced. "Now dear, you yourself said it was broken."

"That does not mean I thank anyone else saying so."

Jean paced the length of the room, frowning. "Several aspects of this suggestion concern me. One is the time needed to analyse the spells constituting the Office. Deciphering the spells in the Fire Office took me decades. How many years will it take to probe the Water Office?"

"A thousand, give or take a few."

Jean's head snapped around. "I beg your pardon?"

"The analysis is already done." Her smile showed flawless teeth. "My predecessors never considered absolute secrecy as important as yours did, and with far fewer of us, and orderly transitions, nothing has been lost. The first Water Sorceress recorded the spells, and each of us has studied them and suggested revisions. I have been awaiting an opportunity for most of my tenure, and am as capable of rebuilding the Water Office as she was of creating it."

Jean's voice was courteous, but his eyes smouldered. "I do not doubt that. However, I am not so sure we can afford to fix the Water Office without also fixing the Fire Office, and fixing the Fire Office first will give us more options for dealing with the trouble that will arise."

Beorn said, "You sure about that? I'm worried about commoners rebelling. If the Office claiming to dispense justice really did—" The Frost Maiden shot him another icy glare and he checked for a moment. "That ought to calm things down."

"It would shift the pressure elsewhere. It would appease the commoners, but the nobles would fight with every means at their disposal to retain the power and privileges they now enjoy. Without help from the king, I see no way out of this tangle not involving bloodshed."

The silence stretched out as Jean continued his measured pacing. At length Beorn growled, "It's a damn shame the king's favouritism for the nobility is so barefaced."

The Frost Maiden's nostrils flared. "We cannot pressure him into taking the Great Oath. The sole action we can take against the royal family is to murder one of them—and we cannot warn them to change their ways." She glared at Jean. "The injustices the Offices maintain are not entirely against the commoners."

He glared back. My stomach tied itself in knots. The Water Office was broken, but interference from the Fire Warlock had inflamed the situation. How many of Frankland's problems could be traced back to incompetence or negligence in the Fire Guild?

Beorn said, "Putting things off won't help. Let's get on with fixing one or the other."

The Frost Maiden gave him a brilliant smile that didn't reach her eyes. Echoing my thoughts, she said, "I am glad the new Fire Warlock is willing to set things right, since a Fire Warlock was responsible."

Jean went livid. "I will thank you, Your Wisdom," he ground out, "for not insulting the people you are beseeching for help." He turned on heel and stalked to the door.

She sailed after him. "Jean... Your Wisdom... I did not mean—"

He strode through the door and yanked it closed behind him. I flinched, anticipating a loud slam, but it closed with a mere snick, leaving her staring at it with a rigid posture and splayed fingers.

"I meant Old Brimstone, not Quicksilver," she said. "I have wanted to make amends, not offer further insults."

Deep in my chest something burned, unappeased by her distress. Every guild has its secrets, but to have a water witch expose one of ours...

Mother Celeste sighed. "Jean was too quick to take offense, but it's no surprise, after you sniped at him for so long." With an arm around the Frost Maiden's shoulders, she coaxed her back to her seat. "You must be more careful what you say to him."

"You are right. I realised he would take offense even as I spoke, but I could not dam the flow of words."

Enchanter Paul said, "Don't worry. Warlock Quicksilver and I often disagree, but I acknowledge he is both rational and fair-minded. He'll calm down, and realise what you said isn't true."

I must have made some reflexive movement, for my chair scraped on the hard amber floor. Five faces turned towards me. Through clenched teeth I said, "He wouldn't be so angry if it weren't true."

The Frost Maiden's eyes bulged. "He told you?"

"No, he didn't have to. It's in Gibson's *History of the Office of the Fire Warlock*."

"In Gibson's? Impossible."

"No one in their right mind would blame Jean, but it infuriates him that he can't fix the damage his predecessors have done."

"What damage?" Sorceress Eleanor said. "What are you talking about?"

"The fifty-seventh Fire Warlock, Old Brimstone, was the last from the noble class, and he had no conscience. He told the king he didn't have to take the Great Oath."

"Oh, that," the Frost Maiden said.

"Oh, that?" I echoed.

"Yes, I should have realised what you meant. Before Old Brimstone's intervention, no one suspected the king did not have to swear to treat all the people fairly. Or, one would hope, the king thought it a good idea.

Now the kings know it is not required, and have no interest in taking it."

"I thought the king found out himself," Beorn said. "Gibson says it was the Fire Guild's fault? Drown it."

I gave him a dark look. "Yes. You should read Gibson, too. You might learn something."

His disconcerted expression dissolved into a half-hearted grin. "Don't have time. Besides, I've got you and Jean and Sven to tell me what I need to know."

I glared at him. His grin got broader. I turned back to the Frost Maiden. "But if you didn't mean that, what did you mean?"

She grimaced. "Old Brimstone was also responsible for the nobles', er, dirty little secret."

Sorceress Eleanor flinched. Beorn's grin vanished. "Oh, my," Mother Celeste said. "That more than justifies Jean's fit of temper. Lorraine, dear, you must apologise again. Grovel if you have to."

"Yes, Your Wisdom, I shall."

I said, "What dirty little secret?"

A Model Fire Warlock

Everyone in the amber room swivelled to stare at me again. Mother Celeste said, "You don't know?"

"If I did would I be asking?" I should have waited and asked Jean or Beorn in private. Someday I would learn.

Mother Celeste started to respond, but the Frost Maiden stopped her with a hand on the Earth Mother's arm. "A moment," she said, subjecting me to an intense stare. I returned the stare. For an instant, fire blazed in her eyes. I recoiled, shaken, but her gaze was now speculative, and as cool as ever. I couldn't imagine why I had thought I saw something fevered.

She turned and glanced, first, at Mother Celeste, and then at Enchanter Paul and Beorn. Each, in turn, nodded. "No, Madam Locksmith," she said, "It is better you not know this secret."

Was this her idea of a joke? She didn't smile; her eyes didn't sparkle. Mother Celeste turned away, shaking her head. Enchanter Paul said, "I must agree with Her Wisdom." That traitor, Beorn, wouldn't meet my eyes.

The burning in my chest grew. "You can't be serious. I have a right to know secrets involving the Fire Guild."

"Of course you do, dear." Mother Celeste attempted to sooth, but recognising magic in her voice fanned the flames. "But in this case—"

"In this case even the junior water witch knows something about a Fire Warlock I don't. That's not fair."

"I know," Eleanor said, "to my sorrow. Be grateful you don't."

"But I'm a warlock! I want to know—"

"I am sorry," the Frost Maiden said, "but we have decided. Paul, shall we continue this meeting or adjourn until another time?"

"If you can't trust me to keep a secret," I spat, riding over the Enchanter's reply, "why do you think you can trust me with unlocking the Water Office?"

She shook her head. "Trust? My dear Locksmith, it is not a matter of trust. You are the very model of a fire warlock: insubordinate, headstrong, nosy, and you take appalling risks—"

The burning in my chest became a bonfire. "I've had enough of your insults," I said, and followed Jean out the door, closing it behind me with a savage little click.

Jean was calling down the lightning from the rim of the volcano. Thunder rumbled across the balcony outside the Fire Warlock's study, where I danced on coals, sending jets of fire cascading down the mountain wall. If René had seen this display, he would have agreed I could produce a killing attack, when the occasion called for it.

I would learn to call down the lightning on my own, too, to give adequate expression to my rage. Acknowledging I had demonstrated I was, as she said, insubordinate, headstrong, and childish to boot, only added fuel to the fire.

But first I would insist Jean teach me to walk through the fire on my own. What a pitiful excuse for a warlock I was, unable to follow him to the aerie to tell him what had happened.

Members of the Fire Guild, particularly warlocks, have a well-deserved reputation for nursing anger as if they are not whole without it. Jean and I are not typical in that respect—neither of us holds grudges for long, and our rages burn out soon. God help me if I ever did carry a grudge—I had only to study Warlock Flint as an object lesson in what I didn't want to become. When Jean joined me on the balcony an hour later, we had both regained enough control to talk without spitting sparks.

I said, "She claimed she didn't want to insult you, and she wasn't lying. She seemed pretty upset."

Jean's eyes flashed. "Giving her the benefit of the doubt is difficult. I came down from the rim because the meeting is over, and Beorn will return soon. Why are you here, my love?"

"She insulted me, too." My face burned as I related the contretemps over the noble's secret. His eyes widened. When I finished, he stared into space, frowning.

"Jean, what's the secret? And why was she rude to me? She owes me something for what I've already done… Jean?… Jean, are you listening to me?"

"I beg your pardon, my dear. Yes, I heard you." His stare carried an expression of speculation so similar to the Frost Maiden's that I took a step backwards. For a moment, his eyes were cold and calculating, not those of a hot-blooded fire wizard. Then the moment passed and his eyes were as warm and vital as ever. I must have imagined they had been otherwise.

He said, "Consider other interpretations. The spell that entrapped her may still affect her habits of speech. If we assume she meant no insult…"

"What other interpretation is there? What she said hurt."

"You are a paragon of a fire warlock—determined, inquisitive, brave, and respectful of justified authority, but intolerant of tyranny and incompetence. Is that not true?"

"Yes, but—"

"How different is that description from the one she gave?"

"The traits you listed are good ones. But you have a point."

His lips twitched. "Consider our own guild members; Warlock Flint would describe you in less flattering terms."

"You haven't told me the secret."

He shook his head. "Not now. Beorn is here."

Beorn emerged from the tunnel rubbing his head. He held up a hand to forestall questions, and ushered us into the Fire Warlock's study. "You have got to see this." He flicked a hand at logs sitting ready in the fireplace; the fire roared. Another flick of the hand, and in the flames my image stormed out of the Earth Mother's amber room.

The knot in my stomach reformed, tighter than before. I turned away. "I don't want—"

Beorn grabbed my shoulders and yanked me around to face the fire. "Yeah, you do. Shut up and listen."

The three witches and two wizards were all on their feet. The Frost Maiden hurried to the door. "Madam Locksmith, I did not mean—" The door closed in her face.

Beorn snarled, "Then what did you mean, you frostbitten—"

Mother Celeste turned on him. "Sit down and shut up. Rubbing her fur the wrong way won't help calm things down." Beorn backed away, muttering to himself and blowing out through his moustache.

The Frost Maiden shook off Sorceress Eleanor's hand. "I did not intend to insult her. Truly, I did not."

Enchanter Paul said, "The Locksmith's reaction was out of proportion to the slight, certainly, but—"

"Out of proportion, my arse," Beorn said. "For a fire witch she's been doing a first-rate job of keeping her temper. She's been simmering ever since the Frost Maiden called her an incompetent coward the other day."

The Frost Maiden's head snapped up. "I what? I never—"

"You did, and don't deny it. I wasn't happy about it either."

Mother Celeste said, "I wondered what was the matter. All three of you from the Fire Guild were on edge from the moment you walked in today—"

"Were they?" Enchanter Paul said. "I didn't notice."

Mother Celeste's eyes rolled. "Yes, Paul, they were. I'm not surprised Jean and Lucinda reacted the way they did."

"They seemed no more upset than any member of the Fire Guild ever is in my presence," the Frost Maiden said, "but that is evidently their reaction to me. Still." She glided across the room and came to a stop before Beorn. "Please explain your ridiculous assertion I offended the Locksmith. You were referring to my visit to the Fortress?"

Beorn glowered and started to respond, but Mother Celeste shouldered her way between them. "Stop," she said. "Lorraine, are you trying to make the score three for three?"

The Frost Maiden bridled. "I am not."

Mother Celeste yanked on her arm and spun her around. "Then don't talk to him. No," she said, holding up a hand to the snarling Warlock, "I don't mean we won't find out what this is all about. But even under the influence of that spell she didn't often snipe at Jean when he wasn't around—"

"I say nothing at all about or to the Fire Warlock if I can avoid it."

"Then it will be safer if she talks to me rather than to you, and if she takes the time to think before she speaks. Sit down and stop trying to intimidate her; it just annoys her."

"Humph." Beorn backed into the corner and sat with his arms crossed over his chest, glaring. Sorceress Eleanor wrung her hands and rocked on her heels. Enchanter Paul looked equally unsettled.

"Now tell me," Mother Celeste ordered the Frost Maiden, "what you think happened."

"Yes, Your Wisdom. And thank you. After talking to Warlock Quicksilver for two hours, I requested a moment alone with the Locksmith, and after her concurrence, I inquired about the lock on the Fire Office. She reacted like a schoolgirl caught unprepared for a lesson. I was too drained from my audience with Jean to pursue the matter further then, as I had no desire to embarrass the Water Guild by collapsing in the Fire Guild's stronghold."

"She almost did," Sorceress Eleanor said. "She arrived back in the Crystal Palace and fell into Sorcerer Charles's arms. We put her to bed and she stayed there for the rest of the day."

The Frost Maiden rewarded her with a cold stare. "Thank you for that revelation." She turned back to the Earth Mother. "If I had anticipated the Locksmith's reaction I would have waited for another occasion. I did endeavour to reassure her I thought no less of her for not having made the attempt."

Beorn surged to his feet, barking, "But she said Lucinda—" Mother Celeste poked him in the ribs with her wand, and he subsided, sputtering. "Well, I don't know what she said exactly...I didn't hear it... Something sarcastic, anyway, about it couldn't be because she was afraid. Lucinda, that is. Like hell. Course she's afraid—the one she already unlocked almost killed her. She'd be nuts not to be scared."

The remaining colour drained from the Frost Maiden's face. Sorceress Eleanor steered her to a chair, and she sank into it, clutching at the arms. "I did not intend any sarcasm. I stated a simple fact; I do not doubt either her courage or her ability."

Beorn gaped. "But you said she didn't have—"

She snapped, "No, fool, I—Oh, dear."

Beorn sported a lop-sided grin. "If you're trying to offend me, too, you'll have to work harder than that. Go on."

An answering smile flitted across her features. "Thank you."

Mother Celeste let out a deep sigh. "Thank God. There's hope yet. Now, go on."

The Frost Maiden said, "I cannot fault the Locksmith for nerves. She is too intelligent to not be afraid. Courage is the ability to act when one is afraid, not the lack of fear, but a warlock would not understand that fine distinction." Beorn snorted. She frowned and massaged her temple. "Oh, dear."

Enchanter Paul said, "When every other sentence you utter sounds sarcastic, Your Wisdom, you shouldn't be surprised when someone takes everything that way. And your description of a model warlock was not, shall we say, complimentary."

"Some of us," Beorn said, "Are proud of being all those things she called us."

Mother Celeste glared at him. "Then why did you lose your temper when she said it? Oh, be quiet. They are true, but only half the story."

"The words I said," the Frost Maiden said, "were not the ones I intended. I meant to reassure her. Frankland would not have survived without warlocks like her to protect us."

Beorn muttered, "God help the poor sod who asks you to cheer up his old, sick mum." Mother Celeste jabbed him again with her wand.

The Enchanter frowned. "How can insubordination and risk taking be construed as vital to Frankland's interests? I suppose she'll behave herself, however, under Warlock Quicksilver's thumb."

"Oh, him." Celeste, Jean's bosom friend, sniffed. "He's more likely to encourage those traits than otherwise."

Beorn said, "And he's got more sense than to order another warlock around."

"This does not bode well," the Enchanter said, "for the success of this venture. Perhaps it's just as well she isn't here, because I want an answer to a question the Locksmith raised. You said it wasn't a matter of trust, Your Wisdom, but how we can rebuild the Water Office if we can't trust each other? Do you trust the Locksmith? And if you can't take an honest answer," he said to the growling Fire Warlock, "you may leave."

"Not now I won't."

"For Heaven's sake, Paul," Mother Celeste snapped. "Couldn't you have waited until the Fire Warlock left?"

"No, Celeste," the Frost Maiden said. "It is better that he hears my answer." She sat motionless for a few seconds, staring at the wall behind Enchanter Paul's head, while Beorn glowered. "Do I trust her? What exactly do you mean by trust? Do I trust that she can unlock the Water Office? It is my impression she is as capable as the original locksmith, but her abilities in that branch of magic are so far beyond my own ken I am not a competent critic. Warlock Quicksilver is a better judge than I."

"Yes, I respect his judgement on that score," the Enchanter said, "but that wasn't what I meant."

"Did you mean then, do I trust her to meekly follow orders and do what I tell her to do, no more, no less? Heavens, no. She is a warlock!" She held up a hand to forestall the Enchanter's interruption. "Or do I trust her to set aside her own comfort and do what is needed for her country, risking pain and possible death? Yes, Paul, I do. She has already demonstrated intelligence and commitment. These are what we need, Paul, not blind obedience. If she were biddable, I would not be here today discussing the subject with her, or with any warlock.

"You were not there when she released that foul lock on my Office. If it had not woken me, she would have died. She performed a heroic feat, alone, for someone she hated, out of the conviction it was the right thing to do. How could I not trust her?"

I staggered away from the fire, shaken out of my self-control. I had steeled myself for a merciless answer, but this was so far in the other direction I was stupefied—and bewildered. This woman, my former enemy, had paid me a higher compliment than I had ever imagined possible.

Jean's eyebrows rose. "This is Sorceress Lorraine, head of the Water Guild?"

Beorn said, "Yep. Not what we expected, huh?"

I looked up at him. "If she trusts me, why wouldn't she tell me the secret?"

The two men exchanged glances. Beorn said, "You won't believe me, but she paid you a compliment."

I glowered, but he was not lying. He believed what he said.

Jean said, "You heard what she said to Enchanter Paul. She asserts she trusts you, and she does not change opinion on a whim." He stroked my cheek, then rested his hand on my shoulder. "Forget about the secret, for now, my love, and treasure her commendation."

"Why are you sticking up for her? You didn't want to go to that meeting either."

"About that," Beorn said. "Mother Celeste made me promise to chew you out. She said as young as Lucinda is, she has some excuse, I have less, and you don't have any. She said you knew about the aftereffects of black magic and should have made allowances instead of acting like you wanted to be offended."

Jean's head drooped. "Guilty as charged. I have for so long wanted to bring about change in Frankland, and now it has come I find it hard to credit. What kind of a reactionary am I?"

"A human one," Beorn said. "There's more. Watch."

"But Paul," the Frost Maiden continued, in a voice holding enough passion she could have been in the Fire Guild, "that begs the question you did not ask. If not now, when? We have a locksmith of such calibre as has not been seen in a millennium, a sitting Fire Warlock, and the second ever retired Fire Warlock, who comprehends the Fire Office better than anyone since its creator.

"If we do not take advantage of these talents now, will their like ever come again, even in another thousand years? Will our successors praise us as the second Great Coven, having the courage and talent to fix the flaws the first Great Coven left? Or will they curse us for having let the opportunity slip through our fingers, so they must watch without hope as the nobility turns into a bunch of slobbering idiots and all our best young men and women flee a country no longer worth living in and caring for?

"Paul, that is the choice we face. We must, at least, fix the Water Office, and we must fix it now."

The Frost Maiden Loses Her Cool

The word 'now' has a different meaning to someone who has lived a century and a half than it does to a young woman of twenty. When the Frost Maiden said, "We must fix the Water Office *now*," I clutched at Jean's arm and yelped.

The image of Beorn in the fire barked, "Can't be done. Not now. She's not ready."

Mother Celeste patted his arm. "She doesn't mean tomorrow."

The Frost Maiden said, "I meant within the next decade. Enough time for the Locksmith to become adept, but soon enough we do not risk either her or Jean dying of old age."

My knees buckled. I sat down on the floor with my head in my hands. A decade. Time enough for my pounding heartbeat to return to normal.

In the fire, the phantom Beorn described the lock on the Fire Office. "It'll be years before Lucinda can handle that lock. If the one on the Water Office is anything like it…"

The Frost Maiden said, "The lock on the Water Office will be a trivial matter, given the great friendship between that wretched fire witch and the first Water Sorceress."

Beorn scowled. "Yeah, you're right, it'll probably be worse. On the other hand, the Fire Office protects the other Offices, so maybe they weren't so paranoid about them. Fortunatus, at least, expected we'd have to make changes someday, and put in spells to deal with the other Offices being temporarily out of commission."

"A rational warlock? That's as—" The Frost Maiden winced. "Never mind."

"As rare as a fire witch wearing pearls? I won't argue with that."

She blinked at him. He grinned.

She shook her head. "It will be safer if I express my apologies to Quicksilver and the Locksmith in writing. Celeste, could you persuade her to read the lock on the Water Office under your supervision? Once she has recovered her temper, of course. She will listen to you when she would spurn me."

"Of course, dear. What a pity there is still such tension between the two guilds. Jean hunted for a locksmith for decades, but I had no idea you were anxious, too."

The Frost Maiden grimaced. "I was not."

"But you said—"

Her voice took on a bitter rasp. "My intellect was prepared, not my emotions. I have known about the Locksmith for months, but I would not dishonour my predecessors and ask for the Fire Guild's help. Only now, with that foul lock gone, has the pain our people suffer touched me. Only now does my heart, as well as my head, demand the mockeries of justice be stopped." Her face was flushed, her breathing ragged. "I have never cared for the sobriquet Frost Maiden, as if the sum of my duties is as the king's executioner, but the ice encasing my emotions kept it from wounding, and made it, perhaps, appropriate. Now, every use is a dagger through my heart."

Mother Celeste squeezed her hand. "I'm sorry, dear."

Beorn walked over and patted her shoulder. "Steady there." The Frost Maiden's head jerked around. He snatched his hand away.

Her voice quavered. "A Fire Warlock comforting a Water Sorceress. The world is coming to an end."

Above me, Beorn waved away the images. "Paul and I talked a bit about what it would take to rebuild the Water Office, mostly to give her a chance to get control of herself again, but that's all that matters."

Jean took a deep breath then let it out with a long sigh. "It is magnanimous of her to offer further apologies. I can no longer predict her behaviour. I would have expected her to wait in icy silence for us to make the first move, since we walked out on her."

I winced. My father would have caned me for being so rude. I stood up and dusted off my skirts. "Right. We can show her we can be decent, too. Let's go the Crystal Palace and do the grovelling first."

Jean said. "I beg your pardon? I have never set foot there. None but members of the Water Guild go there of their own free will."

"Then it's about time, isn't it? Let's go."

The dear man, who had faced armies of wizards without flinching, looked alarmed. "Surely you do not mean now."

Beorn laughed and whacked Jean on the back. "You're marrying her—you'd better get used to her running your life."

"Right now," I said, taking Jean's arm, "before I have time to think about it and chicken out."

We stepped out of the fire onto a stone causeway leading to an arched entry flanked by two guards. The guard on the right fainted.

Neither of us moved forward. A monstrous wave broke on rocks below and I flinched. Jean flicked a hand and the spray blew around us. I eyed him. He was looking at the towers overhead. The many windows reflected the overcast sky's dull grey.

"We are fortunate," he said, "not to view the Crystal Palace in its full, shining glory. It has never been kind to commoners."

I said, "It's unnerving me even without the sun on the windows. But you…"

"I feel the weight of its grim history, too, my dear."

"She walked into the Fortress like she'd done it every day of her life. Are we going to let a water witch show us up?"

"Of course not. Shall we?"

We walked past the guards and through the arch unchallenged. The guard still standing remained at rigid attention, staring through us, acknowledging our presence through a sheen of sweat and rapid breathing. The gate opened into a courtyard with a trio of water wizards crossing in front of us. They panicked and ran.

"We should have warned her we were coming," I said.

Jean sighed. "Yes, but it is too late now to retreat."

We crossed the courtyard towards an arcade through an inner wall, where the Frost Maiden, looking dazed, met us. We made stiff reverences and began to explain why we had come. Half a dozen pools of water welled up on the floor. Sorcerers and sorceresses stepped out of them and formed a protective circle around their leader.

A sorcerer in his fifties, bristling like an angry dog, stepped in front of the Frost Maiden. Water wizards aren't supposed to look dangerous. I took a step backwards.

Sorceress Eleanor plucked at his sleeve. "Charles—"

He said, "What's going on? We won't tolerate rudeness towards Her Wisdom."

The Frost Maiden said, "Charles, you do not understand. It is not they…"

Jean had gone rigid; his eyes glittered. I had dragged him into this mess—I had to do something about it. I stepped between him and the angry water wizard and curtsied. "We've come to apologise, sir. I took offense at something the Frost… something the Water Sorceress said and walked out of a meeting after hearing only half the story." I made another deep curtsey and held it. "The Fire Warlock showed us what you said, Your Wisdom. I'm sorry I was disrespectful."

Out in the courtyard somebody yelled something about the Fire Guild invading. No one in the circle of water witches and wizards moved or spoke. Curtseying has never come naturally to me, and having the Water Guild Council staring at me guaranteed I would wobble as I rose. I might have toppled over if Jean hadn't slipped a steadying hand under my elbow.

His bow was not his most graceful effort, either. "I, too, offer an apology, Your Wisdom," he said, in a tight voice. "The Locksmith and I have both been guilty of imputing insult when none was intended."

The Frost Maiden nudged the water wizard out of the way and made a deep and elegant reverence. No wobbles. "You are both generous, but I offer my own apologies. I did not and do not intend to offend. I beg your patience with me; a bad habit reinforced over a lifetime is hard to break."

"That is true for both of us." Jean's jaw clenched tighter. "I disparaged your proposal because you made it. I should not have; it is an excellent suggestion."

Colour rose in her cheeks, and she curtsied again without speaking.

There was a slight pause. The witches and wizards around the Frost Maiden displayed shock, relief, and confusion in equal measures.

"Lucinda, my dear," Jean said, resuming his smooth, urbane voice,

"You have not met the other members of the Water Guild Council. Let me introduce you, starting with the senior Water Mage, Sorcerer Charles."

The wizard who had planted himself in front of the Frost Maiden bowed. So this was the man who loved her. I studied him with interest. With the shock over, he looked more cuddly than dangerous, and made his own sheepish apology. "I beg your pardon, Your Wisdom. I know you better than that."

Jean accepted the apology with a tight smile. "Friction between the guilds affects even the Company of Mages. We are guild members first, mages second."

While Sorceress Eleanor continued the introductions, Jean pulled Sorcerer Charles to the side for a quiet conversation. I strained my ears, but all I caught was "Master Sven." They rejoined us in a few minutes, and after an exchange of inconsequential pleasantries that was a love fest by the standards of the usual Fire and Water Guild interactions, with the Frost Maiden saying little, we took our leave. Sorcerer Charles led us back out into the courtyard. Not a moment too soon—the arcade was as cold as my father's springhouse. If we had stayed much longer, my teeth would have started chattering.

The witches and wizards crowding the doors and windows overlooking the courtyard scrambled for cover when we reappeared. Jean expressed our regrets for our invasion of their stronghold, but the sorcerer made light of it.

"Once the news gets about that you two came to pay your respects, it will soothe the troubled spirits in our guild who don't understand the nature of the spell Lorraine was under and were offended that she made the first move. So no harm done. Although I admit to being taken aback that you could walk in with such aplomb. Few besides a pair of warlocks would have such nerve." He tilted his head at me. "By the way, I want to thank you for helping her maintain her dignity when she went to the Fortress."

"I beg your pardon? I didn't do anything."

"Perhaps nothing other than greet her warmly, but that was enough. She said she admires your sangfroid in walking under that portcullis. If you hadn't been there she would have been frozen, scared out of her wits."

Beorn was waiting for us in the Fortress's hidden practice room. He sat in one of the metal chairs with his feet up on the table, his hands locked behind his head.

I said, "Why don't you want Master Sven studying the spells in the Fire Office?"

Beorn's brows drew together. "Who said we don't?"

"Jean hasn't invited him to any of our sessions studying them."

Jean sank into a chair and massaged the back of his neck. "You have a mistaken impression. His scrutiny of my revisions would be invaluable, but the Fire Office will not allow us to show the spells to anyone not on the Fire Guild Council, or approved by the Company of Mages."

"But if he's named a mage…"

"Should have happened a year or more ago," Beorn said, "We can't get it past Flint because Sven is Jean's fair-haired boy."

"Oh. Poor Sven."

"I had hoped once I was dead," Jean said, "Flint would allow Sven's nomination. But now…" The corners of his mouth twitched. "I do not intend to die to pave the way for Master Sven's ascension. A bit of subterfuge is in order."

"Is that what you were talking to the water mage about?"

"Yes. Sorcerer Charles has proposed bylaw changes—ones I have already approved—but he will imply he is pushing through insupportable changes while there is no flame mage present. That should force Flint's hand."

Beorn grinned. "Good. I'm all for pulling the wool over Flint's eyes, so long as it's not me doing it. I have other problems on my mind. If not fixing the Water Office means civil war, with the commoners rebelling, and fixing it means civil war, with the nobles going berserk, how do we keep Frankland from tearing itself apart?"

Jean leaned back and closed his eyes. "There is a third possibility. A narrow and perilous path between two horns of a dilemma."

"Yes?"

"The nobles are a flock of sheep, gone astray because they have been leaderless for generations. If we can call the king to account, and convince him to take the Great Oath, the nobles will understand they have no choice, and will fall into line."

Had he gone mad? Even he couldn't make that wish come true.

Beorn's voice dripped sarcasm. "Pray tell, how do we do that, O great and wise one?"

Jean opened his eyes and smiled—the first whole-hearted smile I'd seen on his face in several days. "I do not know. Ask the Fire Warlock; he knows everything."

Beorn flamed him. With a sigh, I added my attack to his.

Some time later, Beorn signalled he'd had enough. He emerged grinning from the smoke. "Thanks. I needed that."

I pushed wet hair off my forehead and fanned myself. "What does the Frost Maiden do to release tension?"

"About that," Beorn said. "You heard what she said about being called the Frost Maiden. We ought to start calling her the Water Sorceress."

"Yes," Jean said, "I had on occasion wondered why she tolerated that pejorative title. Let us drop it, although it will be a hard habit to break. For all of us."

I said, "At least I didn't call her, Her Iciness."

"Tempting as it may be, that would be most undiplomatic. As to your question, she retreats to the far north, and sculpts ice."

Beorn gawked. "You're kidding."

Jean's eyebrows arched. "I am not. She is a talented artist. Her sculptures are quite lovely."

Ice? Lovely? I shivered.

We met in the Warren, and under Mother Celeste's calm influence, I followed a beacon of blue starlight through the maze of spells to reach the lock on the Water Office. The lock was identical to the one on the Fire Office, as was the power needed for release, but I did not panic this time.

After I reported what I had learned, and the potential dangers, the Water Sorceress said, "I am not surprised, given what we know of the earlier Locksmith." She cast me a piercing look. "Are you willing to pursue tapping into the volcano to release the lock?"

I said, "Do you still want to fix the Office, knowing that releasing it may kill you, too?"

"Yes," she said without hesitation. "I have seen far too many men and women dead or ruined because the Water Office has gone so badly awry. My own life is of little consequence in comparison. How could I live with myself if I could fix it, but would not out of cowardice? I only regret that to do so puts others in danger."

Why had I been angry with her at the earlier meeting? She had called me nosy and insubordinate, among other things, but those charges were true. At that moment I felt nothing but respect for her.

I said, "I will unlock it, Your Wisdom. No one else can." I would have to; my overactive conscience and the love of my life wouldn't let me escape it.

Sometimes, being a warlock stinks.

Among Old Friends

To most eyes, nothing changed. Jean recovered his good spirits, and we went on planning our wedding and honeymoon. He spent hours in the oldest parts of the library, studying the writings of the ancient warlocks, as one would expect of a mage, but also made time to go on picnics and engage in play of all sorts. He laughed often, but the unadulterated exuberance had leaked out of him. I grieved for that, and I would sometimes wake, trembling, in the middle of the night, from dreams haunted by flashes of lightning.

Those dreams I understood. The one that baffled me was about a beast in the shape of a man, but with teeth and claws and appetite as wicked as a lion's, stalking Claire in the shadows. If it ate her, it would be because I hadn't gotten there in time. I tried to call, tried to run to warn her, but my voice was muffled, and my limbs mired in quicksand.

I woke up, gasping. Thrashing around in my sleep had gotten my legs so tangled in the bedclothes I couldn't move them. I fought with the sheets and blankets until free, then flung the whole lot towards the end of the bed. They landed on the footboard, hung for a second, then slithered to the floor.

Why couldn't my sense of danger tell me something useful? A year ago, I had saved Claire from the lion on the challenge path. Dreaming about that monster now made no sense.

I hit the floor with a bone-jarring thump and heaved the bedclothes back onto the bed. It was early, but I didn't get back in. I'd had enough warning.

I was eager to see old friends, but I'd been away from Lesser Campton for a year, and the village was no longer home. I intended to visit my stepmother first, but as I crossed the commons, Danielle, the butcher's wife, screamed, "Lucinda's back! Look here, everybody! Lucinda's back!"

My proud new hat, emblazoned with the Fire Guild's dancing flames, elicited another shriek. "You are a witch—I knew it!" The news ran like wildfire through the village, and within moments I was mobbed.

For the better part of five hours, I told and retold my story as more old friends crowded in. Shrieks and whistles greeted demonstrations of fire magic; shudders and gasps accompanied encounters with the Fire Office and the Frost Maiden. But they met the revelation I had rescued and intended to marry the retired Fire Warlock first with dead silence and then with jeers and catcalls.

A debate over my sanity raged around me while I handed out wedding invitations, and the smith fetched the pastor from Old Campton. He read the invitations, doubling as passes through the Earth Guild tunnels to the Warren, and vouched that they agreed with what I had said.

The verdict was unanimous. They had, every single one, known all along I was a scorcher of a fire witch, and the village would come, en masse, to the wedding to inspect the warlock I was marrying. He must be a warlock as no lesser man would dare, but my delusion he had been the Fire Warlock must be a spell gone bad. Mine, his, who knew?

"Although," Mrs Miller said, "if you insist on leaving Frankland, it would be a mercy to know he really was the old Fire Warlock. It's dangerous out there, but you'd be safe with the Fire Warlock looking after you."

I took a deep breath, counted to ten, and let it out again. Tell them he was training me to fight like a male warlock? To call down the lightning? Might as well say, yes, we were both mad.

In mid-afternoon I escaped with a raw throat and trudged down the lane to my father's house. The garden had gone to seed; last autumn's leaves lay in windrows against the walls. A shutter swung loose in the breeze. I stood by the gate for several minutes before clenching my jaw and going in. I had been lying to myself in thinking I would come here first. If I had meant to, I would have skirted the commons and slipped down the lane behind the mill.

My stepmother opened the door a crack and peered through the gap, then flung the door open wide. She engulfed me in a hug worthy of an earth witch, and pulled me inside, with exclamations and questions coming faster than I could respond. Over biscuits and tea with lemon and honey, I croaked out my story, once again.

She said, "I'm so glad. You have no idea how worried I've been over you. I'll sleep better knowing you're marrying somebody who can take care of you."

"Right. Well." At least she believed me. "Tell me about Claire."

"She got sick, about three months after you left. I thought she was dying. Granny Martha said it wasn't anything she'd ever dealt with before. She took her through the tunnels to another granny in Gastòn."

"You didn't go with her?"

Mother Janet's breath came in gasps. "No...I couldn't. A city... Never..."

But your own daughter. I clamped my mouth shut and glowered.

"Besides," she said, "the Earth Guild never lets anybody who isn't on their deathbed through the tunnels."

"They do, if the person is accompanying an ill family member." I watched her fluttering hands, and fumed. "Go on."

"The other granny said it was serious, something she needed to keep an eye on, even after she got better, so Claire's been there ever since."

"Why? What did she have?"

"I don't know; they didn't say. I think she didn't want to come back. She's making some money—not much, mind you—doing piecework for a needlework shop."

Claire, working? "How can I find her? I want to see her."

"Oh, would you? That would be such a relief. I've been so worried about her. Bless you, dear."

She told me how to find Claire, and I should have gone then, but I could not abide the mess. While she rambled on and on, alternating between a year's worth of gossip and tears over the fat purse I was leaving her, I scrubbed, scoured, dusted, and mopped. I gave up after opening the door to Father's study. The bookshelves' stripped skeletons nearly made me lose my composure, but I held back the tears until I had said goodbye and was out of sight.

The next day I set out for Gastòn with butterflies in my stomach and a chill in my bones. My studies in self-defence had not armed me against glamour spells, and knowing one is at work does not make it easier to take. I'd almost rather face the unthawed Frost Maiden than Claire's glamour spell.

If it protected her from an unprincipled rogue, there could be some merit to it. She might lure a man into a marriage he didn't want rather than being lured herself into disgrace. But being stuck with him wouldn't be much of an improvement.

The Fire Warlock's gate opened into a busy square in the centre of Gastòn. Passers-by bowed and curtsied, showing proper deference to a high-ranking fire witch. No one panicked, no one ran, no one appeared in a hurry to avoid me, but I walked through the jostling crowd untouched. Within seconds the footpath was clear.

Except for one snarling nobleman—his attitude gave him away even before I saw the sword—who moved to stand square in the middle of the footpath. I would have to walk around him or smack into him.

Arrogant bastard. The nobles resented the talented as much as the commoners resented the nobles, but I'd not been on the receiving end before. I walked around him without otherwise acknowledging his existence. He called something after me. I didn't dignify his insult with a response, tempting though it was to flame him. It wouldn't teach him a lesson, and I would get into trouble.

Shame. The nobles would be a lot less obnoxious if the Fire Office didn't shield them from death or permanent injury. Whoever thought up those shields must have had cinders for brains.

Two blocks later, I was sweating. The commoners' deference had been heady, but even out of sight of the gate, my hat drew too much attention. I wasn't experienced enough to pick threats out of a crowd. I expected—hoped—that Jean was keeping an eye on me from the Fortress, but I came close to panic before the crowd thinned. Fighter training wasn't a bad idea, after all.

Mother Janet's directions led to a quiet street a long way from the centre of town. With few pedestrians about, I had relaxed by the time I found Mrs Wetherby's boarding house. Indistinguishable from its neighbours, its only oddity was a hex emanating from a sign saying, 'Women only.' I was searching for other protective spells when an eagle-eyed earth witch emerged from a sitting room by the front door.

"Morning, miss. I'm Mrs Wetherby. Are you looking for someone?"

"Yes, ma'am. I'm looking for my stepsister, Claire Nelson."

The woman's long face brightened. "You're Miss Lucinda, then? She talks about you quite a bit, and I'd gathered you were a fire witch, but I'm surprised she didn't mention you were a top-ranking one. Come in and have a seat. She went out for a walk. She won't be long."

I sensed no anger or jealousy. Were earth witches immune to glamour spells? I perched on the edge of the sofa. "You've gotten to know her well? I'm glad—I've been worried about her coming here by herself, with no one to warn her which men are cads and blackguards."

"That's what I'm here for. The girls listen to me—if they don't I give them the boot—and I take stock of every man who comes courting. If his intentions are bad, he'll forget where we are and never find his way here again."

A weight dropped off my shoulders, and I relaxed against the sofa. "You're using magic to conceal the women?"

"Of course. The Earth Guild provides safe houses for women on their own, and this is as safe a place as you'll find in this city. That's why I set up out here. Closer to the Earl's palace, with all those nobles about, would be dangerous. When one of my guests goes to the centre of town, she'll get a nobleman's attention only if she wants it."

"How do you do that? What spells do you use?"

Her lips pressed together in a prim frown. "Guild secrets."

"Fine." I shrugged. I would ask Hazel, later. "I'm glad Claire found this place. It was lucky for her."

"Wasn't luck. Granny Helene sent her here."

"Granny Helene?"

"The healer. She's been keeping an eye on Claire for months now."

That was all she would tell me.

Claire's shriek—Lucinda!—was as eardrum-piercing as Danielle's had been.

She looked thrilled to see me. Of course she would. That's how glamour spells work.

With my talents hidden by my lock and the Fire Guild emblem tucked into my pocket, we set out for the nearest inn. I treated her to a beef pie and cider, and we sat down to have a long heart-to-heart chat. Customers and staff in the inn turned to stare, ignoring me, gawking open-mouthed at Claire. She was, as ever, sparkling and golden. The waitress who brought us our food stammered and blushed, Claire made pleasant small talk, and the woman walked away smiling.

Claire insisted on hearing my story before she told me hers. I couldn't figure out what she wanted. She couldn't be interested. Had she acted this way in Lesser Campton? I couldn't remember. The last few conversations I could remember clearly were from years ago, before the glamour spell.

When I described unlocking my abilities as a warlock, she said with satisfaction, "That explains everything. I knew all along you were a witch. You had to be."

"I never said I didn't have an affinity for the Fire Guild, but—"

"Not that. You always acted like a witch—never admitting anybody else was your better, not being afraid of anything—"

"There are lots of things I'm afraid of."

"Like what?"

"Drowning, Storm King, lightning…"

"That's it, isn't it? Big things. Little things like spiders and dogs and broken arms never scared you. And you always acted like you were going to marry for love. Who else besides a witch or a rich man's daughter can do that?"

"I what? I did not."

"Of course you did. All those stories you told—your favourites all had the hero falling in love with a witch. The boys who came courting you— didn't I end up entertaining them after you got bored with them? You could've had them wrapped around your finger if you'd wanted to. And now you're getting married, and you're in love, aren't you?"

I felt as if I'd been sandbagged. "How do you know I'm getting married? I hadn't gotten to that part yet."

"Because if you weren't you would have started with, 'I haven't found a husband, but it doesn't matter because I'm a witch.' Go on with your story."

We finished our pies long before I finished talking. The crowd in the dining room thinned and the innkeeper brought us a pot of coffee, telling us we could stay and talk as long as we liked. Claire pulled a piece of embroidery out of her bag and set to work with a flashing needle. Claire, working?

The little I knew of glamour spells suggested it was unlikely she would have given it up, but I probed while I talked, and found no trace. I finished my story and asked about her. She waved that aside and peppered me with questions. Where would we live? Did I have a wedding dress? What could I do besides start fires?

She acted as if she cared. Could this be real, and not the spell at work?

"Marrying the Fire Warlock," she said, "sounds like something out of a fairy tale. And I said nothing much scares you—any other girl would run away, screaming. At least you know he can protect you from the wicked men out there."

Through clenched teeth I said, "I don't need anybody to protect me."

"Of course you don't, but you can't let him know that. A man wants to take care of his wife. How's he going to think he's a good husband if you don't need him?"

"I don't need him. I don't need anybody. I..." Less than three hours ago I had been hoping he was keeping an eye on me, to spot enemies in the crowd. I closed my eyes and counted to ten. "Claire, enough about me. How are you? Tell me."

"There isn't much to tell. I've made new friends, and met some nice men, and people like my embroidery enough to pay for it. Can you imagine? Getting paid to do something I would do for fun anyway."

True, she had sewn for pleasure even when she had been too lazy to do chores. "You've always had a good eye for colour. That whatever-it-is you're working on—"

"Table runner."

"—Is gorgeous."

"Thanks. I'd feel like a miser if I kept it to myself when someone else could enjoy it."

A year ago, she would have preened when complimented on her skills. But caring that it gave someone else pleasure? I wanted the change in her to be real. "Claire, I am so glad you stopped using that glamour spell."

She looked up from her embroidery, and stabbed herself with the needle. We both winced. She stuck her finger in her mouth, and I almost sucked on mine.

She said, "What glamour spell?"

Glamour

I gaped at Claire. How could she ask, *what glamour spell?*

She frowned for a moment, then shook her head. "I have to remember not to do that."

"Do what?"

"Frown. It makes wrinkles. I don't know anything about a glamour spell, but there is a spell on my bracelet—"

"What bracelet?"

"Don't you remember the gold and lapis lazuli bracelet I always wore?"

Of course. The spell, too powerful for Claire to use on her own, was on the bracelet. Jean had shown me that. How could I have forgotten?

"Granny Helene made me stop wearing it. She said it made me sick. I lay in bed for nearly two weeks, about to die, before I was willing to take it off, but then I got better at once."

"That's doesn't make sense. A glamour spell doesn't work like that."

"But I feel better—a lot better—since then. I want the bracelet back, but Granny Helene says I'm not strong enough yet, and maybe she's right. I see her every week—I trust her, I really do, but I want the bracelet back. She'll take it out and let me hold it, and she never seems to mind talking to me. She's given me lots of good advice about living here."

"Claire, when did you get that bracelet?"

"Oh, I've always had it. It was my grandmother's. I think. Or maybe not. I don't remember. It doesn't matter, does it?"

"Do you understand what a glamour spell does?"

"No."

"It coerces people into temporarily thinking you are the most beautiful and exciting person they've ever met, and that they're in love with you.

If you use it for too long, they resent the manipulation, and they'll attack you later, to avoid entrapment again. You used that bracelet with a glamour spell on it for years. That's why you have no friends left in Lesser Campton. That's why the Fire Warlock sent you back home, for daring to use a glamour spell on him."

Her eyes popped wide open. "Oh. Is that what he meant? I had no idea."

I slumped in my chair. "No idea..." After a moment, I said, "What about the men? Any good prospects?"

Her laughter, like liquid gold, was so contagious I laughed along with her. The innkeeper sported a smile as he wiped down tables.

"Oh, yes," she said. "There's a silversmith who is very sweet, and a handsome apothecary..."

She chattered away, describing half a dozen merchants and craftsmen who had all gotten Mrs Wetherby's grudging approval. My dreams about imminent danger must have been due to an overactive imagination.

I said, "Is there a leading contender? Which one do you like best?"

"I'm having trouble making up my mind."

That didn't quite ring true. "Is that all of them?"

"Isn't that enough? They've been keeping me so busy I wouldn't want any others."

Liar.

I stared at her with my coffee cup in mid-air. "There is someone else. Who is he? And remember, never, ever, lie to a warlock."

She reddened. "It's what, not who. I'm not like you, Lucinda. I can't afford to marry for love. I'll marry for money, and the nobles have it. I haven't gotten an introduction to any of them yet, but I will."

The unease Mrs Wetherby had dissipated returned, full force. I leaned forward. "Claire, noblemen don't marry commoners. Not often, anyway. A poor aristocrat might marry a rich merchant's daughter, but what could you do for a rich one? He'd only want you as a mistress. Haven't you heard the stories about pretty commoners being seduced, and then thrown away like old rags?"

"Of course I have. I'd have to be deaf and blind to miss them. Remember the girl from Old Campton everybody talked about a couple of years ago? I wonder where all those women come from who don't know any better."

I had wondered, too. Commoners laughed about the dim-witted bluebloods, but if recent stories were true, the half-witted girls in my generation would make the noblewomen look brilliant. The not-so-noble aristocratic men had no qualms about taking advantage of my silly sisters.

The girl from Old Campton had, like many other fools, been seduced and disgraced. But this girl had done the other ninnies one better. She had charged Baron D'Armond with rape, and demanded money for the child. The baron had not denied the baby was his, but denied the rape accusation. The penalties are so severe no one believed even our numbskull baron would do such a thing, and the girl and her family were the laughingstock of the district. The baron was acquitted, and the reparations the girl had to pay for slander bankrupted her family. The girl abandoned the baby and fled, no one knew where.

When the gossip started, I had not known what the word rape meant. I had heard whispers about what criminals—men whose lives were already forfeit—might do to an unaccompanied woman, but I hadn't understood those either. When Mother Janet evaded my questions, old Mrs Barnes, our neighbour down the lane, had taken pleasure in describing in detail what rape meant. Her cackle followed me as I fled for home, where I gave Claire a fumbling, abridged version of what she had said.

My face burned now, remembering. Mother Janet had been shocked at the girl's gall. I had wondered what appalling circumstances could drive anyone to throw away her own reputation by making such an accusation.

Claire said, "I'm not that stupid. Or desperate. I've been learning who's who in this city, and which men are good catches. I'll see for myself what the noblemen are like. If they're all cads, then I'll marry one of the merchants Mrs Wetherby says are decent men. But I'm not ready to do that yet."

She had as much, if not more, experience dealing with men as I had. She would make a better choice than many women would, but I couldn't shake my sense of disquiet.

"I want you to make a good match," I said, "but your father was a tailor, and left you penniless. Your stepfather was a scholar who didn't do much better. Why would a rich nobleman marry you?"

Some of her sparkle dimmed. "For love. I can make a man love me."

"Do you think you can keep a man charmed for decades when you don't love him?"

Her smile faded. "Other women have done it. Why can't I?"

"Just keep in mind," I said, groping for advice Mrs Cole had given me, "you'll have to live with him. If you don't marry for love, at least marry someone you like and respect. Promise me you'll be careful, and take Mrs Wetherby's advice."

"I will, and Granny Helene's, too."

"Good. Don't pass up a merchant you respect to marry a nobleman you can't stand."

She dimpled. "Especially if he's a rich merchant. Deal."

We finished our coffee, and I followed her to the needlework shop. As she conducted her business with the proprietor, I watched the crowds flowing past on the street. Two young men engaged in violent argument caught my attention. Even on a fashionable street a few blocks from the Earl's palace, they stood out, with brocaded waistcoats and layers of snowy lace peeking out at collar and cuffs of velvet frock coats. A glimpse of swords confirmed their status as high-ranking and self-important nobles. I sniffed.

Other pedestrians bowed and curtsied, and seemed relieved when the two men ignored them. My unease grew as the pair approached the corner where the needlework shop stood. It deepened into dread as they stopped at the entrance, still arguing. The older of the two, in his mid-twenties perhaps, was talking with fervour, but in a low voice, as if annoyed about carrying on an argument in public. The younger, in his late teens, didn't seem to care.

"Lucinda, I'm done. Let's go." Claire brushed past me and reached for the door. Horror solidified and dropped onto my shoulders like vultures.

"Claire, wait." I grabbed the nearest thing to hand. "I was admiring this, uh, cushion. Isn't it gorgeous?"

She beamed. "I'm so glad you like it. I made that. Would you like to see what else I've done?"

"Yes, please."

I listened and watched with half a mind as she sorted through a pile of embroidery. The rest of my attention was on the scene outside the door. The younger man snarled something and stalked away. The older one watched him go with his hand on his sword hilt, breathing hard. The younger man disappeared into the crowd, and the older one turned towards the side street. The vultures pulled out their talons and flew away.

I leaned on the table holding the cushions and trembled.

Claire reached for me. "Lucinda, are you alright?"

The shopkeeper rushed over with a chair. "Sit down, miss. You look as if you're about to faint."

I waved her away. "I'm fine—er, I will be fine. Sometimes being a witch stinks."

They fussed over me, but I refused the offered glass of brandy. All I wanted was fresh air. I walked out the door, and almost smacked into the nobleman who was still standing on the footpath in a brown study. Startled, he backed a few steps. I looked past him, searching the crowded street for the younger man.

The man in front of me doffed his hat and waited for a response. I gave him the slightest bob of my head, while still scanning the crowd. His head jerked back, and he gave me an incredulous stare.

My heart dropped. If I had embarrassed the Fire Guild...

He looked past me, and lightning struck.

He wouldn't complain that I'd insulted him. He wouldn't remember me. For all his sophisticated elegance, desire was as naked on this dandy's face as on the faces of the country bumpkins who had courted Claire in Lesser Campton.

She gave him the perfect curtsey one would expect from a rich merchant's daughter.

He made an elegant, deep bow. "Please, miss, may I know your name?"

She shook her head and walked around him. He quivered when I followed, blocking his view.

He lurched after us. "Wait, please."

Claire looked away, her nose in the air. "We haven't been introduced, have we, sir?"

We walked away without looking back.

The sense of danger that had overwhelmed me in the shop vanished. I watched Claire out of the corner of my eye. She looked at me the same way, wearing the expression of conspiratorial rapture that had made her my best friend a decade earlier. I grabbed her elbow and pulled her into a coffeehouse before giving in to the urge to giggle. Within seconds we were screaming with laughter, telling each other, "Stop! Stop! This is too much." We retreated into a dim corner, away from the staring customers.

"Claire, you look as pleased with yourself as a cat with a mouse tail hanging out its mouth. Why? Who was that?"

She turned a rosy pink. "That was the Earl of Eddensford's eldest son. Oh, Lucinda, this was just perfect. I am so glad you were with me. I must've been as thick as a plank not to see what being a warlock means, but your story was such a shock."

"What do you mean, what it means? Uh, that's not what I meant. Oh, God."

"It means they have to bow to you—"

"That's a relief—at least I didn't embarrass the Fire Guild by not curtseying to Earl Whosit's son. I get tired of bowing and scraping."

"When did you ever?"

"There wasn't any need before we left home. Do you think Baron D'Armond knows Lesser Campton exists? He's never set foot there."

"And if he had you'd've been more likely to spit in his eye than curtsey to him. I'm telling you, Lucinda, you always acted like a witch."

"I've been doing lots of curtseying lately—"

"Really? Who do you curtsey to?"

"The Earth Mother. The Frost Maiden—uh, the Water Sorceress, that is—"

"Oh, well. That's different. They deserve it. The point is—I've gone from being a nobody to being stepsister to one of the most powerful people in Frankland. You outrank everybody except the king and queen and the dukes. I guess you'll even outrank the dukes once you're married."

I gaped at her. "Claire, wait. Dukes and earls and their ilk don't associate with witches and wizards anymore."

"They don't marry them, you mean. But don't you see? That's what makes it so perfect. I'm not a witch, so they won't be scared of me. I can marry anyone I want. Even a duke would be glad to have me."

"But, but... If you're interested in Earl What's-his-name's son, why wouldn't you talk to him?"

"Lucinda, really. That wouldn't be proper. If I talked to him without an introduction, he'd think I was easy. I have to show I have self-respect."

"I have self-respect, lots of it, and I talk to anyone I want to, whether I've had an introduction or not."

"See? Only witches can get away with that."

"But I... Oh, never mind. Who's going to introduce you?"

"Oh, that's simple. If he's interested, he'll slip the shopkeeper a few coins, and she will. It will be better if he thinks he's chasing me."

"He's interested, all right. He followed us until we ducked in here."

"How do you know that?"

"I have eyes in the back of my head."

"Oh, for…" She clapped a hand over her mouth. "You probably do. I'm going to have to be careful."

When we left the coffeehouse, she turned north, for the outskirts of town and Mrs Wetherby's boarding house. I turned south, towards the city square, but not for the Fire Warlock's gate. I went to the Earth Guild house, and asked for Granny Helene.

Claire's bracelet sat on a table, a coiled scorpion ready to strike. I probed at it from across the room. Keeping my distance was silly, but I was unwilling to touch it. I detected the glamour spell without any difficulty, but could not read it.

"Only an earth witch can read the glamor spell," Granny Helene said. "There were other spells on the bracelet, including a forgetfulness spell, which I've already lifted. I'm glad to have heard your story. Someone seemed to have taken a serious dislike to your family. Mother Celeste and Warlock Arturos alerted Granny Martha and me to Claire's problems, but nobody said anything about Janet's problems—"

"Mother Janet? What's wrong with her?"

"She wouldn't leave Lesser Campton, even to take her own daughter to a healer. Claire shouldn't have been up and walking around by herself—"

"She really was sick?"

"What did you think?" the healer snapped. "That I would poison her to get her to give up the glamour spell? I admit, it did cross my mind, but my oath as a healer won't allow it. Granny Martha and I had been scratching our heads trying to figure out how to persuade her to come to me—I'm the closest specialist in curing curses—when we got lucky and she came down with a bad case of influenza on her own. I used it as leverage."

I stared at her. She turned red and looked away. "And made sure she didn't recover as quickly as she might have otherwise. Now, as I was saying," she went on in a rush, "after Claire was safe in bed with my assistant keeping an eye on her, I went to see your stepmother, and found a serious phobic spell at work on her. Its original intent was to stop her from going too far from home, say, ten miles, but as time went on it closed in on her until now she's terrified of even leaving the house."

"I had no idea. How long has she been under it?"

"It was one of the spells on the bracelet. From what you said, I'd guess the phobia was part of the plan to keep you from finding a husband. She was so terrified of leaving your village she couldn't approach the Scholar's Guild and ask for their help. I told the Earth Guild Council about it, of course, as it's their job to find out who did it, and got on with trying to undo the damage. I lifted the spell, first thing, but this is a tough nut to crack, it went unnoticed for so long. The distance doesn't help either, but I obviously can't convince her to come here."

My cheeks burned. How many times had I jeered at Mother Janet's panics? Once was too many. I, too, had lived in fear. I wouldn't wish that on anyone, and she had suffered on my account. I had not always gotten along well with Mother Janet, but she didn't deserve this.

Granny Helene continued. "I couldn't let Claire go back there either, as I need to keep working on her until she makes a complete recovery, which she will. From the glamour spell, anyway. The forget spell worked on her so long she may never remember about the glamour spell, no matter how many times I tell her."

"She is much more like her old self. She's still coming to see you?"

"Yes, that's why I haven't lifted the glamour spell yet. She'll keep coming back as long as I'm holding the bracelet hostage. At first, she came every day, and I had to send her away so I could tend other patients. When she doesn't come for a month, I'll let her have the bracelet back. With the spell lifted, of course. In the meantime, I reinforce the suggestion that her self-involvement was childish, and keep her focused on the good things she can learn from her experience."

"What good things?"

"How do glamour spells work?"

"They make the other person fall in love with you, temporarily."

"That's half of it. They also enhance the spell-user's ability to put the other person at ease, by encouraging small talk, good manners, and being a good listener. With many experiences of charming people behind her, Claire could become an extraordinary hostess. She would be quite an asset as a wife to some merchant, or a diplomat or noble who knows how to use her."

My jaw fell. I stammered something inane, and the earth witch laughed at me.

"Of course you didn't expect anything like that," she said. "But then who expected you to marry the Fire Warlock either?"

"I suppose a good hostess doesn't have to be smart. Oh, dear, I didn't mean…"

"Ah, well, as for that, you're judging her based on living with her and her mother while those malicious spells were at work on them. Those often have the side effects of dulling the mind and sapping the energy. By rights, neither is as lazy or dull as they've appeared for the last few years."

"I know. I shouldn't have said that. She ran circles around me today." I repeated our conversation about the earl's son, and she laughed.

"Lord Richard's not a bad sort. Claire is brighter than most of the inbred noblewomen this country is burdened with. If he married her, instead of the Red Duke's dim-witted and disagreeable daughter his father's been trying to pair him up with, he'd do the country a service. Besides, my impression is that Claire is quite hard-headed when it comes to men, and she wants to make a good marriage to support her mother. It would be a crying shame if Janet had to beg."

"I won't let that happen," I said. Damn the Chessmaster and his nefarious schemes that ruined people's lives willy-nilly. The lingering guilt I felt about sending him back to the Empire with my lock still hiding his talents evaporated.

Granny Helene picked up the bracelet with the tip of her wand, to put it away, while I mulled over the unsettling prospect of an earl for a brother-in-law.

"I suppose it is rather judgemental of me," I said, "to assume all aristocrats are shallow and selfish nincompoops. Although Mrs Wetherby seems to have a worse case of it than I do. I mean, it does seem insulting to the decent men to assume they're all lechers waiting to seduce any woman they can."

"Um…" she said, holding the bracelet poised in mid-air over its hiding place.

"Just as it's insulting to decent women to assume we're all so stupid we'll succumb to any nobleman who tries to seduce us. And thank God we live in a civilised country, unlike some wicked places I've read about that allow rape, and the woman has no recourse—her own family throws her out on the street as if she brought disgrace on them."

"Er…" she said, lowering the bracelet.

"I've taken enough of your time. I won't keep you from your work any longer." I left, too preoccupied to wonder why the earth witch was chewing her lip as she saw me to the door.

Family Matters

I sat at one end of the metal table in the practice room with two fire wizards arguing over my head. Jean listened with his arms folded across his chest and a frown on his face. René sat at the other end and sulked.

"Did the other Officeholders object to them leaving Frankland?" Master Sven said.

"No," Beorn said, "but they aren't used to thinking about people trying to kill them. I'm not saying the Empire's going to send an army after them as soon as they set foot outside the Fire Office's shields—"

"I should think not. The Empire would be stupid to start another war when they haven't recovered from the last one. The staff Quicksilver hired are all in the Fire Guild, all level three or four talents."

"Right, and except for Lucinda's lady's maid, they're wizards itching for combat experience. With that much firepower nobody's going to send less than an army against them, and they'd see that coming a hundred miles away. No, I'm not worried about the lot of them together."

"What are you worried about? A lone assassin?"

"Yeah. Jean can take care of himself. But Lucinda and René... Lucinda's aim is good, and she's getting faster, but not fast enough, and she's a puffball on the counterattack. A level three could swat her strikes aside like gnats."

René said, "What do you expect from a girl?"

Beorn scowled at him. "And you—you're dead-on perfect when you're paying attention, but when you're not—well, you're just dead. And you're barely a level four. You couldn't summon up a blast big enough to kill a shielded warlock, and you're the most likely of the bunch to wander off by yourself and get into trouble."

René resumed his sulk, glowering at Beorn.

Master Sven said, "And he can't yet jump through the fire, to get out of trouble."

"Right," Beorn said. "That's why I want everybody in that group studying the spells for searching out danger from a distance."

Jean said, "Teaching those spells will increase your own proficiency with them."

Master Sven bristled. "Yes, Your Wisdom. I am aware of that, Your Wisdom."

Beorn said, "Lucinda will have mastered jumping through the fire by the time they leave. If she keeps an eye on René, then even if Jean isn't paying attention, she can grab him and run."

René's head snapped up, fire in his eyes. "Warlocks don't run."

Beorn cuffed the back of his head. "They do when staying means getting killed. I don't want you coming back as ashes in a funeral urn."

"You know I won't. Quicksilver said I'm going to grow up to be a warlock."

I said, "He sure has a big head for a little runt. Who told him he was going to be the Fire Warlock?"

René's grin stretched from ear to ear. All three men turned on me.

"Nobody did," Beorn growled, "until now."

"Oops."

"Let me remind you," Jean said, "that you advised me to tell him he was destined to be *a* warlock."

"Sorry."

"And he can add two and two and get four," Master Sven said.

Beorn turned a gimlet eye on René. "Just because we know you'll survive doesn't mean they won't try. Maybe they'll burn you so bad you wish you were dead. Or maybe you're somewhere without Jean and you survive an attack that leaves Lucinda or some of the staff dead."

René's grin faded. "Wouldn't like that."

Beorn cuffed him again. "I sure as hell hope not."

"The staff wouldn't be at risk if René and Lucinda are safe," Master Sven said. "No one else is valuable enough to justify an assassination attempt. Bonds would be more effective. One between Warlock Quicksilver and Lucinda—"

"No." Jean and Beorn had spoken in unison.

Master Sven's eyebrows rose. "Why not? Many married couples develop bonds over time."

Jean and Beorn exchanged glances. Neither one looked at me. "If that happens naturally, that's one thing," Beorn said, "but too much togetherness, especially when you're just starting out, isn't healthy."

I didn't argue. Jean was already too much of a mind reader. Much as I loved the man, I wanted a little privacy.

René said, "I could have a bond with Lucinda." The three men turned to stare at him.

I groaned. "He's been badgering me about bonds ever since he read about them."

Beorn settled into one of the iron chairs and tipped it back until he was balancing on two legs. "A bond, huh? What do you know about them?"

René said, "They're magical links, like the ones between identical twins. You can read each other's minds. And they warn you when the other person is in danger."

Beorn fingered his beard. "That's not a bad idea."

Jean and I both said, "No."

Beorn gave Jean a surprised look, then turned back to René. "So why would you want one with a girl?"

"Because it would be like having a real—" He turned brick red and looked away.

"A real sister, huh? That what you want? A family?"

René surged out of his chair. "She already bosses me around like she's my big sister. At least she cares. You just want me to come back to be Fire Warlock."

The front legs of Beorn's chair slammed onto the slate floor. Sparks flew. "You think I don't care?" René took a couple of steps backwards. Beorn poked him in the chest and he took another step back.

Beorn shouted, "What do you think a family is?"

"Uh, a group—"

"People that care about each other. That's what you think, right?" Poke.

René backed further. "Yes, sir, but—"

"Sometimes they do. Sometimes they hate each other. 'Family' means they're stuck with each other, that's all. Got that?" Another poke, another step back.

"Yes, sir, but—"

"And I'm stuck with you. Like family. Since Lucinda let the cat out of the bag, yeah, you will be Fire Warlock someday. But not for years. Got that?"

"Yes, sir. I—"

"I'm not getting rid of you. You'll come back in a year or two and go to work as my assistant. And if I didn't care about you I could make your life hell. Got that?"

"Yes, sir. I—"

"Good." Beorn had backed René into the wall on the far side of the room, next to the door to the pantries. He bent down until his flushed face was inches away from the bug-eyed boy's. "And while you're gone, you'd damn well better not pull some cinder-brained stunt that gives you nightmares for the rest of your life. Got that?"

René nodded. Beorn pulled the door open.

"Good. Now go get some supper before I take a belt to your backside for being a halfwit."

René vanished. Beorn slammed the door behind him. "Frostbitten little—"

"Watch your language," Sven snapped. "There's a woman present." I rolled my eyes. Beorn glared at him. "Your Wisdom," Sven added.

"That's better," Beorn said. "Sorry, Lucinda. René's an idiot. Sven, go keep an eye on him. Nip that nonsense about us not caring for him in the bud."

"Yes, Your Wisdom." Sven gave him a sardonic smile on his way out. "But after that fine display of fatherly affection I don't think he'll give you much trouble."

Jean was laughing to himself. I tucked my hand into the crook of his arm. "Supper?"

"Soon. Beorn, my friend, you do need to be more careful in your choice of adjectives. Your encounters with the king and his advisors will not benefit from such rough language."

"Yeah, I know. Bad habit." He walked back across the practice room towards us. "A bond between Lucinda and René sounds like a good idea to me." He grinned. "In fact, I'd been trying to figure out how to suggest it without him gagging on the idea of a bond with a girl. Why'd you say no?"

My face burned. "I'm going on my honeymoon, for God's sake. Some things—"

Jean's eyes danced. "You are mistaken in how the bond works. You would share what you decide to share. Only imminent danger would override your control."

"Oh. That's not quite so bad then."

"But," Beorn said, "it takes a bit of practice to get used to. Don't wait till the day before the wedding."

"I didn't say I would do it. I'd be stuck with him for the rest of my life."

Jean said, "We are members of a small fraternity from which the only escape is death. He is part of our lives, magical bond or no."

Beorn said, "Like him or not, too. Like family. So why did you object, Jean?"

"It would increase the risk of them dying together. But perhaps I overreacted. The benefits of a bond are considerable. It would decrease the risk of either dying alone. They would monitor each other's safety, and could come to the other's aid, even though miles apart." He frowned at me, but it was from worry, not disapproval. "I do not want to see either of you in danger, but your safety is paramount."

I said, "But you've said, yourself, my sense of danger was fully developed. Wouldn't I know if rescuing René would kill me?"

"You might. But you have a gallant heart, and in the grip of strong emotion you might try to save him, even knowing the attempt could kill you."

There was silence for a moment. Beorn cleared his throat. "Maybe you should be asking yourself, would you be safer with a bond to René, or without?"

"With," I said, with no hesitation. I started. "How do I know that? But since you put the question that way, that feels like the right answer."

"Sleep on it," he said. "If the answer doesn't change, do it."

Jean frowned and shook his head. "Either choice worries me. I will trust your talent of prescience, and your judgement on this question, except for one final consideration."

"What's that?" I said.

"Strong talents, such as yourself and René, have, on several occasions, used such bonds to draw their bonded souls back from the very brink of death."

I goggled at him. "I didn't know that." Why should it surprise me? The Fire Office regularly pulled titled nobles back from the verge of death.

The arrogance that instilled—and in their mutton-headed unshielded cousins, too—was the root of one of Frankland's biggest problems.

Jean's sombre expression chilled me. "The four Officeholders have not let those stories become widespread. For every successful attempt, two or more have failed, and both in the bonded pair died." He gripped my shoulders and turned me to face him. "If you do establish a bond with René, you must promise me this—you will never, ever, follow him into the valley of the shadow of death."

My voice quavered. "I don't want to die, but..."

His grip tightened, and he gave me a hard shake. His eyes burned. "Promise me."

"I..." I swallowed and tried again. "I promise. But... But, Jean, sometimes I wonder, what's the point of being such a powerful witch? I'm more afraid now than I ever was in Lesser Campton."

"Very little of ordinary life ever had the power to hurt you, and you were not a target of Frankland's enemies in Lesser Campton." His tone was light, but there was a sadness in his eyes that made my own tear up. "If you had stayed there, hiding your talents under a lock, you would still be fretting after adventure, and the opportunity to see the world. Would you return to that quiet life?"

I shook my head. Life was better now. If I could get used to people trying to kill me.

After sleeping on it for several days, my answer to the question Beorn had asked remained the same—I would be safer with the bond than without. That answer did not relieve all my misgivings. René commented on my sweaty palms when we clasped hands to recite the oaths binding us together.

The bond was awkward at first. I started and dropped things every time René's voice—*hey, big sister*—echoed in my head, and forgetting to censor what I let him hear left us more than once with him in stitches and my face scarlet. Some of his revelations made me wince.

A week before the wedding, I cornered Beorn in the Fire Warlock's study for a private conversation. "Have you had any new visions about the future?"

He studied me for a moment, combing his fingers through his beard. "Why? Are you having bad dreams again?"

"Sometimes. Not often. It's more that I feel cold chills whenever the Frost— Whenever the Water Sorceress talks about being ready to fix the Water Office in five to ten years. Something is telling me that's wrong."

He nodded. "I've been feeling the same way."

"Oh. Damn."

"Right. I'd been arguing with myself over whether to say something to you. I'm glad you brought it up. In your place, I'd work on tapping into Storm King as fast as I could."

I nodded, not looking at him. "Even if I do succeed in calling down the lightning, there's still the Locksmith's hidden danger."

Beorn reached across the desk and gripped my shoulder. "Forget that. The lock is enough for you to deal with. Let me and Jean deal with the rest. It may not be too bad. We could be wrong—"

Both of us? I snorted.

"—So maybe you shouldn't say anything to Jean. Let him enjoy his honeymoon."

Most of that week I spent with our new secretary, dictating thank you notes for the gifts flooding in from all over Frankland. We were almost buried in an avalanche of precious metals and gemstones. I packed the more tasteful pieces for the state dinners we would have to endure on our trip, and shook my head over the vulgarity of the rest. But the ones that made me roll my eyes, and my secretary guffaw, were the necklaces and earrings from several of the more obtuse nobles.

Pearls, for a fire witch. What was wrong with these people?

I gave the pearls to Claire; she loved them. She came to the wedding on the arm of a wealthy wool merchant with impeccable manners, and my conscience eased on her account.

Jean and I exchanged our vows, without the dreaded word 'obey', in the Warren's Great Hall. It was packed to the rafters with members of all four magic guilds, scholars, friends from the Camptons, and a surprising number of nobles. Outside of coronations and royal weddings, it was the biggest party Frankland had seen in generations. We would have preferred a small, private ceremony in the Fortress chapel, but once Beorn and Mother Celeste heard Enchanter Paul's suggestion that an event including the Water Guild would help spread the news that the long feud was over, what we wanted had little bearing. It was exhausting.

After a week as the Earth Mother's guests in a secluded alpine cottage, we had recovered enough to return to the Fortress and collect René and our staff. Armed with letters of introduction from ambassadors and merchants, we set out to see the world.

During the two years we were away from Frankland, our retinue grew to include half a dozen young fire wizards. Calling themselves the Fire Eaters, they engaged in tournaments and practice duels with foreign wizards, becoming more proficient than most fire wizards in peaceful Frankland had been in centuries. A good thing, as it turned out, although it did not seem so to me at the time.

Our first stop, Thule, that land of fire and ice, treated Jean as a conquering hero. I had not expected such an enthusiastic welcome, but he pointed out their two warlocks, who could tap into their own volcanoes, had a better appreciation than anyone else of the degree of control he had needed to survive for so long.

Further, Frankland's victory against the Empire had dramatically reduced the pressure the Empire could apply anywhere—welcome news to the little countries on the Empire's edges. Jean intended to use that as leverage to persuade their Fire Guild to let us use their protective spells, but when he broached the subject, the younger of their two warlocks dismissed the idea out of hand.

He, like all Thule warlocks, had sworn to keep them secret. Jean should have known better than to ask, he said, and stormed out.

Jean watched him go with stony eyes. My spirits sank. If the decision to share the spells had to be unanimous, we were out of luck.

Our host, Warlock Mjöllnir, the senior warlock, took no offense. He shrugged off the other man's fit of temper and listened without comment to Jean's explanation of our need. When Jean finished, he sat for a while in deep thought, pulling at his moustache.

"Don't like it," he said. "Isn't right for a girl to master the lightning."

"I have to," I said. "There's no one else in Frankland—"

He held up a hand. "Didn't mean that. Wasn't right for your Great Coven to make those spells so hard to fix. Wasn't right for the gods to make the only one who could fix them a girl. But you're a warlock, so you'll do it, even being a girl. Duty first. Would help if I could. Can't. Sworn not to tell our secrets to outsiders."

"It is proper and justifiable," Jean said, "for Thule's Fire Guild's paramount concern to be Thule's protection. I do not want our mutual enemies drawing on volcanic forces either. But we are not asking you to expose your secrets to us, nor have we nothing to offer in exchange. I will tell you what I have learned over the years about calling down the lightning and suggest refinements to enhance the safety of your own young warlocks."

Mjöllnir's eyes gleamed in the light of the guesthouse fire. "Safer, eh?"

"In return, you will enchant a ring, and Lucinda will put a lock on it readable only by a member of the Thule Fire Guild. Your spells will be secure."

The glow in Mjöllnir's eyes faded. "Not for long. If you didn't guess right, you'll figure them out quick enough from what you see them do."

"I already know what they can do. If Thule will not or cannot help us, I shall recreate your protection spells myself."

"Get at it then," Mjöllnir said. "Have to start early, before the other ways sink in too deep. Another six months, year at most, and it'll be too late for that poor girl to learn."

Firepower

The Thule wizards' rejection of our request ruined my sleep, despite Jean's efforts to reassure me. "If we must," he said, "we will return to Frankland, and I will consult with the other mages to recreate those spells."

I said, "How will we explain that to our staff?"

"We may not have to. I still expect to convince Warlock Mjöllnir it is in Thule's best interests to help us."

Maintaining a cheerful façade was difficult when part of me said he was dreaming. The approaching tournament didn't help my peace of mind, either, but our wizards, eager to spar with new opponents, could talk of nothing else. Fools. During the battles with the Empire, Jean had fought an army of wizards, but then he had the Fire Office's backing and the Fortress's shields. In a tournament, the combatants would be out to score, not kill, but the Fire Office was no longer protecting him, or any of the Franks. The rules did not allow throwing lightning, but accidents, sometimes fatal, could happen. I had experienced enough injuries during childhood games of Soldiers-and-Wizards to frighten me away from this adult game.

My opinion counted for nothing. Several days after we arrived, we gathered in a large open valley for the first round. Soon the players were dodging through billowing smoke as thick as an ash cloud rising from Grímsvötn. Waves of magical energy shooting in all directions blurred and confused the magical signatures, until I couldn't tell which wizard was which.

Somehow Mjöllnir's flame-haired granddaughter, Hildur, kept track. I taxed her command of Frankish, demanding a running commentary while butterflies danced in my guts.

At least they weren't throwing flame at me. "No place for a woman," Jean had said. I did not argue. So why did the butterflies sometimes give way to steam? "You are not forceful enough," he had also said. Rubbish. I had more power to draw on than all but three of the men in the tournament; if war called for it, I could punch through a level-three wizard's shields as if they were paper. I shied away from that thought. No point in getting sick.

Despite my worries, searing pain exploding across my abdomen took me by surprise. I screamed and doubled over. A moment later, forcing myself upright, I jumped through the fire to where René lay on the ground, curled into a whimpering ball. Flame billowed at me and bounced off the mirror shield I slammed into place. I grabbed René and dropped him at the feet of a trio of resigned earth witches on the sidelines. We were soon in our guest quarters, with René sleeping off the effects of a bad burn, and me regretting my impetuous decision to bond with him. And praying Jean hadn't noticed I'd jumped into the arena without my shields up.

At the end of the day, the wizards still standing emerged one by one from the smoke, more or less singed. Most nursed several burns, some serious. Jean, untouched and unruffled, congratulated the other wizards on a battle well fought.

He assured me René had put up a good fight against everyone short of Thule's warlocks. They would not draw on the volcano in a tournament, but experience showed in other ways, and neither was inclined to pull their punches, even against a thirteen-year old.

"One cannot afford to let one's guard slip for an instant," Jean said, "when facing a lightning-wielder. Those two make me nervous."

I said, "I don't believe you."

His lips twitched. "You are a warlock, my dear. Would I lie to you?"

On the tournament's second day, I jumped into the arena with my shields up when René got burned. That evening I put my foot down. "You are done with this tournament. Fighting lightning-throwers is dangerous, and you can't keep a shield up for hours."

I glared at both him and Jean, daring one or the other to argue, but neither did. René seemed relieved, though he tried manfully to hide it.

"You were right," he said. "I can get hurt, even if I live through it."

"Good," Jean said. "I am glad you have learned that lesson. We must send you back in a few years for a refresher—you will hold your own very well by then."

René grinned. "I'll be able to jump through the fire by then. I'll get myself out of the fight. Lucinda won't have to do anything but watch."

I rolled my eyes. "Learned your lesson, did you? What makes you think I'd come back with you?"

"You'll have to. You think you can jump all the way across the ocean to Thule? You want to feel me get burned and be too far away to help?"

I glared at Jean. His eyebrows rose. I said, "Why did I think this bond was a good idea?"

The last day of the tournament, I stayed in our guest quarters and attempted to read, but René relayed Hildur's commentary on who scored against whom. I couldn't shut him out of my head. He was lucky I didn't torch his dinner.

That night, René cornered me with Matt, Jean's valet, and Tom, the secretary, in tow.

"I've been thinking about what Arturos said about you not getting better fast enough," René said, "and I've talked it over with Tom and Matt. Even if Warlock Quicksilver's letting you out of fighting, we're not. We're going to treat you just like one of the boys."

"What?"

"You're going to have to be ready for us to throw fire at you any time, anywhere, whether you like it or not."

"Why, you wretched little—"

"Just giving you fair warning."

"I'll get you for this, you—"

He danced out of reach. "Go ahead, flame me. I dare you."

I hit him square in the chest. He ducked out the door, laughing. Later, I asked Jean, "If tapping into the volcano is so dangerous, why do you want to teach René? He'll have the Token of Office someday. Can he handle it now? He's not a level-five yet, anyway."

"His lack of maturity does concern me, but with the protective spells he will not be in grave danger until he is a level five. When he is Fire Warlock, he will be in less danger the earlier we begin, and it will be easier on all three of us if you two learn at the same time."

"Yes, I can see that, but what will you tell him about why I'm learning, too—and why I'm in more of a hurry?"

"I will tell him part of the truth: that we intend to unlock the Water Office, and the lock is the strongest we have ever seen."

René, when told, shrugged. He was stirring the fire and didn't even look up. "I figured it was something like that. Otherwise you wouldn't have made us all work so hard on locks."

A week later, while we were making merry in the perpetual cool light of a far northern summer, Warlock Mjöllnir gave us two rings, one for me, the other for René. I put mine on and held out my hands. The simple gold wedding band on the ring finger of my left hand, the silver rune-inscribed band on my right—these were all the rings I needed.

"Wear it at all times," Jean said. "Do not ever go out in public without it."

"Sure," I said. "Easier to remember that way. But I am surprised. How did you convince them to do this for us?"

"These spells cannot be secret forever. I showed the Thule Guild Council that the Europan Empire has already recreated them. It is only a matter of time until there are other lightning-wielders."

I said, "They have? But…"

Jean smiled. "You surely do not expect me to ask them for help."

I didn't return his smile. "If they have them, why didn't they have half-a-dozen warlocks throwing lightning at the Fortress? Could even the Fire Office have stood up to that?"

The two men exchanged glances. Jean said, "There will never be that many of the highest-ranked warlocks in the Empire—the political forces within her will not allow it. Frankland is a thorn in her side, but not a threat to the emperor's hold on power. Any warlock who began the training without the emperor's permission would be executed by the emperor for treason or assassinated by any of a dozen competing factions."

Mjöllnir said, "Emperor can't learn—too old. Warlocks young enough to learn don't have enough clout to grab the throne when the old one dies."

Jean said, "A foolhardy emperor with dynastic ambitions might let his sons learn, but only one would survive the infighting. Relax, my dear."

The prospect of even one lightning-wielding enemy warlock fighting our Fire Warlock was nightmare fodder, but that problem, if it ever arose, was far in the future. We had more immediate problems to worry about.

"Empire's put a bounty on your head, girl," Mjöllnir said. "Big one. Boy's head, too, but not as big." He frowned at me for a moment. "Be careful. Even lightning throwers can be ambushed."

Mjöllnir took us to the rim of a volcano, miles from any settlement, and we began the long, hard work of building up the strength to channel the earth's fire on our own.

Jean said, "Now, and for years to come, you will draw as much power from me as you can handle, as quickly as possible. You will each learn your own limit, and go up to, but not beyond, that limit. With time, your limits will expand, and you must continue going up to the new limits."

René said, "If we're pulling through you, why is it dangerous?"

"I might mistake your limits, nor will I always be there to restrict the flow. Some day you will call the lightning on your own, else these exercises have no purpose. Before we begin, it will be instructive for you to experience the power flowing through me. Put up your own shields, and take my hand when ready."

As ready as I was ever going to be. I took his outstretched hand.

The crash blinded and deafened me. Scorching pain crackled up my arm. I snatched my hand away and screamed. I hugged my right arm against my chest with my left, my heart pounding. When my vision cleared, I wiped my eyes with my sleeve and flexed my hand. It was undamaged. "We don't have to do that again for a while, do we?"

"No, my love, not for many months. René?"

René stared at me, his eyes wide. He swallowed hard and took Jean's hand.

CRASH!

"Yow!" René jerked his hand back, as I had done. When he could speak again, he said, "Didn't you teach him a lock so he can't accidentally draw on Storm King? Would you teach me, too?"

Jean laughed. "Smart boy. Now, Lucinda, are you ready to begin?"

No. Not then. Not ever.

I massaged my arm and eyed his outstretched hand as if it were a viper. "How long does it take to learn to tap into the volcano?"

Mjöllnir shrugged. "Ten years—"

I yelped, "Ten years?"

He held up a hand. "Easy. We start as soon as he shows he's a warlock, but most are too hot-headed in their teens, so we stretch it out."

"How long will it take if I work at it day in and day out?"

He shrugged. "Five years, maybe, or four."

After my arm stopped aching, I took Jean's hand. He said, "Draw as much power as you can control, as fast as you can." Half again as much as the biggest blast I had made on Hooknose Ridge would be good. Heat like a blast from a blacksmith's forge flowed through me.

"A respectable start," Jean said, "but your experience with the lesser lock on the Water Office has stretched your limit. You can handle more than that."

"More?" I tried to pull my hand away. He wouldn't let go.

"Quicker, too." Mjöllnir said, "Timid now, pay for it later."

Timid, was I? We'd see about that.

"Do it now," Jean said.

I reached for more, much more. More than three times what I had handled on Hooknose Ridge surged through me. I reeled from his grasp and fell. Mjöllnir caught me and lowered me to lie on a flat boulder, pulling the heat away until I shivered. Spots clouded my vision, and I couldn't hold my head up.

The blood had drained from Jean's face. He pulled glasses and a pitcher of water out of thin air, and knelt beside me, propping me up to drink. I leaned against him until the spots faded and I could hold the glass without sloshing the water out of it.

Jean gave René a wan smile. "I would advise approaching your limit more gradually, and not coming quite so close. Ready for your turn?"

"No, sir."

René said that?

I said, "Sure you are. You can't be bested by a girl, can you?"

"Sure I can. I don't mind."

I turned my head and stared at him. He returned the stare with eyes as big as an owl's.

Jean said, "There is hope for him, yet."

"Just kidding." He took his time getting up. He made three blasts, each one larger than the previous. After the third, he swayed on his feet, and would have fallen on the rocks if Jean hadn't propped him up. Sweat poured off him, and he drained his glass of water in one long sustained breath. After a second glass he lay down on the boulder beside me, said, "I'm tired," and went to sleep.

The colour had returned to Jean's face. "I must be more careful what I order you to do. No more for today."

"Good start." Mjöllnir grinned. "Four years. Maybe three."

When I wrote to Beorn with what Mjöllnir had said, his reply was terse. "Too long. Make it two."

A Quiet Oasis

From Thule we hopped across the ocean to the New World via Ultima Thule. Jean's contacts were eager to talk with him for hours on end about governance, and he began a steady correspondence with the Frost Maiden, polite but cool in tone, describing the conversations in detail.

The discussions were enlightening, but I could not sit still for long with so much else to see and do. René and I often slipped out and went exploring with our staff while Jean talked. Usually, I hid the group's talents behind locks to make us less conspicuous. More than once we encountered robbers expecting easy prey. Our staff found these incidents comical. The robbers, not so much. We also fended off assassination attempts, amateurish and easily deflected. After several of these, Jean raked us over the coals for becoming complacent.

We settled into a routine for our practice sessions, jumping to remote locations twice a week; on the days in between engaging in ongoing but unsatisfactory exercises with locks, attempting to draw power from more than one person. Finding isolated places to practice was not a problem in the New World, but after we returned to the Old World, skirting the Empire, we often had to jump long distances to find a mountainside we could blast into heaps of charred rubble. I pushed myself as hard as I dared. Jean didn't forbid it, but reminded me the four Officeholders had agreed we had years to prepare. I eased up to reduce the danger of heatstroke only after getting pregnant. René tried his best but couldn't keep up, as he had not yet reached level five.

If I could have helped the competitive wretch along, I would have, because he made me pay for besting him. The Fire Eaters tormented me, and each other, day and night, until Jean stepped in and ordered them to slacken the pace before they drove away the mundane local servants. Not out of pity for me, I noted. If anything, he egged them on, pointing out that while René had the quickest reflexes, I had the best aim. When Tom or Matt attacked me as I rummaged for a snack in the middle of the night, Jean, drown him, slept through it. I confounded them by keeping a mirror shield on at all times—a feat none of the Fire Eaters could match—and the assaults became more cautious after I gave them each reason to be grateful my attacks were feeble.

As my belly expanded, I spent half my day shoving food in my mouth, eating quantities that amazed our staff and shocked our hostesses. I lost interest in seeing everything, choosing to stroll on Jean's arm through only the most interesting sites. The Fire Eaters saw everything; I listened to René's running commentary and waited for him to show me the most interesting bits in the evening's fire.

At the beginning of my ninth month, we stopped in a city built millennia ago around thermal baths, and I discovered immersing my gravid body in the water eased the strain on my back. I astounded Jean by going, night after night, to wallow in the tepid water at the shallow end of the pool in our host's seraglio, but there was nothing for even a fire witch to fear in water no deeper than a bath. I didn't remind him he had said the shields around the seraglio, particularly the ones barring men, were solid. Out of the Fire Eaters' reach, I could drop my shields, and rest my psyche as well as my aching back.

One evening, after a hard practice session on a remote mountaintop far to the north, all three of us were drained. Jean was dismayed when our host, an athletic warlock in his prime, announced he had arranged for a sporting event, of some aggressively bloody variety, to take place that evening for Jean's benefit.

I said, "You don't have to do anything other than watch, right?"

"True, but I would rather not. This so-called sport is less about skill and play than about instilling aggression in young men, with no proper outlet other than beating each other senseless. I have seen more than enough war; I do not approve of encouraging belligerence when not needed."

"Oh. Well." Pointing out that was how I viewed the tournaments would not be diplomatic. The endless hours of fighter training had one purpose: kill our attackers before they killed us. "I don't suppose there's any point in saying 'have fun'?"

He gave me a sardonic smile and left.

I shuffled to the pool and slipped into the water with a deep sigh. Perhaps there was some point in learning to swim. I looked up, jolted, and then relaxed. René had not overhead my heretical thought.

I lay like a beached whale on a ramp in the shallows, with my bugling belly rising out of the water. My headache intensified, and I recognised the signs—my sense of prescience was warning of trouble ahead. I cast about, checking with René, but he seemed in no danger. Together, we went over our plans for the following day, and found nothing there.

Jean did not respond to my call. As silly as it seemed to worry about him within the palace walls, Mjöllnir's warning—even lightning throwers can be ambushed—nagged at me, and I couldn't let it rest. I slipped in and out of René's mind with no effort, but my husband's was a stone wall. Whatever he had to hide was safe from me.

Of course he didn't have anything to hide from me. I refocused on the lamplight's rippling reflections on the surface of the water, but tonight they failed to soothe me. My lady's maid was sidling out into hip-deep water, looking pleased at her own daring.

"Katie," I said, "You're making me nervous. Don't go in over your head."

She turned a shocked face to me, then laughed at my joke.

"No, ma'am. This is as far as I'm going."

Few others were in the pool at that late hour: a pair swimming in deeper water, a giggling trio on the edge splashing with their feet, and an earth witch across the pool staring at me. I lifted a hand to wave, but I'd been mistaken; she was watching the swimmers.

I slid a little farther into the water with a sigh. Making friends is hard when you don't speak their language. My head throbbed.

I had slid farther than I had intended. The water was up to my neck. With a prickle of alarm, I tried to push myself further up the ramp, but my feet and hands found no purchase on the smooth tiles.

"Katie," I called, "Come here, please."

I was sliding faster. A weight on my shoulders, like someone's hands, pushed me further down. The water rose over my chin. I opened my mouth to yell, and got a mouthful. I thrashed about, but there was nothing within reach to grab.

Alarm blossomed into terror as I sank beneath the surface. In two feet of water, I was drowning.

The Honeymoon is Over

I flailed underwater and blasted out a silent scream for help. Instinct, reinforced by many hours' training, took control and poured fire at the weight pinning me down.

The weight vanished, but leaden limbs wouldn't obey my will, and I couldn't raise my head. My nose and mouth were full of water; my lungs burned. An eternity later, Katie yanked on my arm, hauling my head and shoulders up into a thick, roiling cloud of steam. Screams echoed around the tiled walls. Jean, the water boiling around his feet, grabbed and dropped us, dripping, on cushions in the guest quarters. He flipped me over and I belched out water while he pounded on my back.

I lay on my side, gasping, retching, and shaking as a drama I was barely aware of played out around me. Someone wrapped me in a blanket. Katie, engulfed in a man's robe too big for her, sat beside me, combing my hair, and hissing at anyone who came close. René curled at my feet, coughing and retching in time with me. Jean came and went, dealing with a stream of loud, angry voices. After far too long a wait, a tired and frightened healer appeared to soothe my lungs and still premature labour pains. The baby was unhurt, she reported, then ran away as if we carried contagion. Despite her ministrations, I could not stop shaking. Our entourage milled around, making such a din I couldn't understand what anyone said. Why couldn't they go away, so I could bury my face in Jean's shoulder and cry?

Mother Janet had been right. Thank God I had a husband powerful enough to protect me even from magical assassins.

Our host, the Sultan, appeared, and the racket in our quarters died. Neither he nor Jean raised their voices, but the younger fire wizards backed away, wide-eyed, from the white-hot confrontation between the two senior warlocks.

Our host left, and Jean shooed the awed wizards out of our bedchamber. "Thomas, William, Matthias, post a watch. Everyone else, pack, then sleep if you can. We shall leave in the morning."

René, looking much the worse for wear, stopped in the doorway. "Hey, Lucinda, if you ever nearly die again—"

"I beg your pardon." Jean reached for René with fire in his eyes.

The boy ducked the outstretched arm and disappeared. "—don't drown, okay?"

Jean sat down beside me, and I threw myself, sobbing, into his arms. He handed me a glass and insisted I drink. I gulped and choked, my throat burning. When, sometime later, I stopped shaking, I took another sip. "Where do you get this? I didn't think there was anything like it here."

"I drew it from Mjöllnir's cellars. I cannot evade the Fortress's defences, and I knew he had it because I gave it to him. I will make it up to him later."

"Why? That stuff is awful."

"This is one of the world's finest single-malt whiskeys, you heathen."

"You're wasting it on me."

He took a pull from the glass. "I did not fetch it for you, my love."

"I wasn't following the argument," I murmured into his shoulder. "Are we leaving in a huff, or did he kick us out?"

"It hardly matters, when the result is the same. Our departure is one of the few points we agree upon. I am unsure which he is most angry about—the imagined insult to the women at the pool, the damage I did on breaking in, or his embarrassment over discovering his concubine of fifteen years was a spy for the Europan Empire—"

"Wait, what? A spy? Who?"

"The earth witch who tried to murder you. Her existence was not our fault, and he may cease to blame us when he recovers his equilibrium, but the embarrassment of her public exposure will fester for a long time. It will be best for all if we remove ourselves and let him deal with the repercussions alone.

"Besides," he added with a growl, "I would find it difficult to maintain a polite façade towards a man who considers the attempted murder of a woman—even a witch of the highest rank—of less consequence than his

ENGINE OF LIES

own embarrassment and inconvenience."

"Give him a piece of my mind for me, will you? I don't want to ever see him again. But Jean, I don't understand. Why will he be embarrassed? There weren't many women in the pool, and anyway, they're all in purdah. Can't he keep it quiet?"

He started shaking. Startled, I raised my head. He was laughing quietly. His vivid eyes danced. "My dear, after all the work you have done towards calling down the lightning, you do not know your own strength. Everyone in the city heard your call for help—no, not a call, the demand of a terrified witch being murdered. The inhabitants of the seraglio converged on the pool. The palace's male inhabitants converged on the gates to the seraglio. Outside, a mob converged on the palace gates, nearly breaking them down. They do not know who you are, but they will not rest until they have heard every detail. This incident is the most exciting event this city has known in decades."

"Oh. Oh, no. I can understand why he's angry. Oh, dear."

"Oh, dear, yes, my dear." He laughed aloud, then sobered. "I should have been angry, too, in his place, but at the Empire and its spies rather than at my guests. I have offered my apologies to him and to his women for the imagined insult of seeing their bared flesh—I assure you I did not waste time ogling his harem—but I will not apologise for breaking in. The damage to his own household would have been much greater had I not."

"Jean, the spy—what's going to happen to her?"

He turned my face with his hand so I had to look at him. He regarded me with a slight frown, no laughter in his eyes now. "Lucinda, my love, tell me what happened in the pool."

"Somebody pushed me underwater. I flamed them, but there wasn't anyone there. And then you and Katie pulled me out. If you hadn't rescued me from the earth witch I would have drowned."

"And the cloud of steam?"

"You made the water boil, didn't you?"

He shook his head. "No, my dear. You did not need me to rescue you. When you flamed the earth witch holding you underwater, you attacked the real woman across the pool, not a phantom above you." The corners of his eyes creased into a slight smile. "You justified those hours of drill in the practice room, tracking a threat by magic. Your reactions were automatic and correct, but your attack was that of a warlock with deep

89

reserves, given added force by panic. The steam was your handiwork."

"The...the witch?"

"She is dead, my love. She died before I arrived."

"The other women?"

"Scalded, but healers reached them in time, and they will recover. I dispersed the heat, so no others rushing in were scalded. Only the spy died."

The shaking returned full force. "Jean, I didn't mean to kill her. I didn't mean to kill anybody. I wasn't even sure anybody was there."

His voice was a caress. "You defended yourself, my dear. Do not berate yourself for this night's work. If neither you nor I had killed her at the pool, she would still not have survived. The Sultan would have ordered her execution."

I gagged, and buried my face in his shoulder. I had tried to deny I had killed, but instinct would never let me wait for a rescue I could not be sure would come in time.

"Jean," I said, after a long time, "you said the damage would have been greater if you hadn't broken in. You mean, if you hadn't cooled things off, other people would have died?"

He drew in a long breath, held it, and released it without answering. I pulled away from him and sat up.

"Jean, I nearly killed a lot of people tonight, didn't I?" My voice rose, but I had no control over it. "The stronger I get, the more damage I can do. I don't want to kill innocent people. Maybe I should have drowned. Maybe I—"

"Stop this nonsense at once," he barked, grabbing my shoulders and shaking me. "We do not obey God's will by turning our backs on God-given talents, even dangerous ones. You must—you will—learn to respond to danger with dispatch and necessary force. You will overcome your childish reluctance to attack. You will attack, if necessary, to protect yourself or other Franks. It is your duty as a warlock."

I stared at him in mute shock. His expression was stern, his eyes hard. We could have been back in the Fortress, grim Fire Warlock and cowed supplicant rather than loving husband and wife.

His expression softened. "You did not hear what I said. You did well, remarkably well for someone who has known she is a witch for only two years."

I scrubbed at tears with the corner of the blanket. "Why? Why do I have to? I didn't want to be a warlock. I didn't even want to be a witch. I didn't ask for this."

"I did not ask to be Fire Warlock at the age of twenty-seven. Do you imagine I wanted to hold the Fire Office for more than a century?"

I tugged the blanket tighter around my shoulders, though the night was not cold. "No."

"I am sorry, my love. I cannot tell you all will be well on the morrow. You are a warlock, and must face the truth. To be a warlock means making life and death decisions. This evening's decision was simple—your life, or hers. You made the right choice—yours."

"But, Jean…"

"Yes?"

I couldn't meet his eyes. "If something like that happens again after the baby's born, and I react again with as much force, I could kill my own baby. I'd rather die."

He pulled me around, facing him. "Look at me, my love. Everyone has the right to defend themselves. Private citizens may decide not to exercise that right, but you are not a private citizen. You are a warlock, and a warlock's primary responsibility is Frankland's security. That duty trumps everything else: family, personal comfort, one's own life. You are one of the few indispensable people in Frankland's history. If your survival means my death, or our child's death, so be it."

I jerked away from him. "You are a ruthless, cold—"

"As cold-hearted as any Frost Maiden," he said. "Why do you think I survived as long as I did?"

I scowled at the merciless stranger—this man I thought I knew. "You can't order me to sacrifice my own baby."

Jean said, "One warlock cannot order another in matters of personal conduct, that is true. But the Fire Warlock can and does issue orders to other warlocks in matters relating to Frankland's security. You may recall that, as Fire Warlock, I ordered you to live long enough to unlock the Fire Office. That order still stands."

The Summons

Jean's severe mood vanished by the morning. He apologised for upsetting me, and I in turn admitted he was right; Frankland needed my talent. That knowledge had coloured my outlook for more than a year. Jean had expected to die for Frankland; it should not have surprised me he would be willing to sacrifice himself to ensure my survival.

That didn't mean I had to like it, or his willingness to sacrifice others.

He reassured me on that score. "You are no more dangerous to children than any other fire witch, and less so than many careless mothers, witches or not. If you were a danger, I would send the child back to the Fortress to be protected and cared for there."

I lay on the cushions, letting the warmth of his concern soothe me, and pondering my unasked-for responsibilities. Our staff bustled around me, getting ready to go. In the next room, the Fire Eaters congratulated themselves on having trained me so well in responding to attacks.

Still drained from the shock and a short night, I felt little emotion other than disgust—with the assassin, the sultan, and our own Fire Eaters—and annoyance with the little brat kicking, rolling, and dancing on my liver. I was almost sorry the healer had stilled my labour pains, but I didn't want the baby born here. As soon as we settled into our next stop, I planned to evict the little beast.

We travelled to Agra, and settled in for the winter. Our baby, a lovely little boy we named Edward after my father, duly arrived, and we added a nursemaid to our staff. René turned fifteen, and developed a sudden absorption in pretty girls. Dealing with his attempts to impress his current interest with his expanding powers kept us scrambling for months.

No longer constrained by pregnancy, I resumed pushing my limits as hard as I could, more than once collapsing from heatstroke. My ability to channel power expanded at the pace of fingernails growing, but sometimes we detected a change. I shouted in triumph the day we stood on a mountain high in the Himalayas, and Jean called down the lightning with my hand in his. I had not flinched. Or only a little.

René glowered, but did not volunteer to do the same. He was far behind and losing ground. Jean would not let him proceed as quickly, even when he reached level five.

The Fire Eaters, under Jean's orders, never went near the nursery, but resumed badgering me as soon as I regained my feet after childbirth. Jean remarked on my continued use of weak blasts in our mock battles, but I dug in my heels, pointing out I had proved I could be forceful when the occasion called for it. He frowned and shook his head, but did not pursue the argument.

All our staff showed signs at one time or another of homesickness, but I stayed too busy to indulge in it, or to brood over my near drowning. Sometimes, though, unresolved questions percolated through my mind and demanded attention. "Jean, why did that earth witch think she could get away with murder?"

We were resting between bouts on a snow-covered mountainside. I turned my attention away from the rugged landscape, and watched him consider my question.

He said, "You had hidden your talents. The assassin might not have understood your qualities as a witch."

"Yes, but you said either you or the sultan would have killed her if I hadn't."

"She would not have known I could break through the spells barring men from the seraglio." Jean smiled. "That was a nasty shock even to the sultan, who should have known better. Also, she had reason to believe the evening's entertainment would occupy my attention, and I would be slow to respond.

"As to the sultan…" He shrugged. "Perhaps she thought she could deflect the blame. Perhaps she thought in the turmoil following she could escape notice. Perhaps she seized an opportunity when it presented itself, without thinking it through." He shrugged again. "As she cannot explain herself, we will never know."

René pushed himself up from the boulder he had sprawled on. "What entertainment? The game the sultan talked about? You could've watched with half your attention. You do that all the time."

Jean gave him a sidelong glance. "Er…"

René and I exchanged looks. "Now you have to tell us," I said.

"Remember you can't lie to us," René said.

"You two are much too impudent," Jean said. "Disrespectful of your elders."

"Elders, bosh," I said. "You're so old that if we treated you with the respect due your age you'd be the loneliest man on the planet. Tell us, already."

His eyes twinkled. "Very well. The evening's entertainment was not, as you were led to believe, a game. Rather, he offered me the services of his concubines."

I breathed fire. "He did what?"

His eyebrows rose. "Does that surprise you, my dear? He appeared to feel sorry for me, having a single woman, and one heavy with child at that, to satisfy my licentious needs."

"So what did you do?" René asked.

I glowered. "He remembered his wedding vows, and that he's married to another warlock."

Jean smiled at me with devils in his eyes. "I suggested no other woman could survive my volcanic lust."

I flinched. And then snickered.

He sobered. "That incident lent impetus to our hasty departure. We exchanged angry words even before the murder attempt. I insulted him and his harem as much by declining as he insulted you and me by offering."

"Insulted them?" I said. "Rubbish."

René said, "I was there when the sultan told Lucinda he was taking you to watch that game. He said I should come along, too, but I was tired, and went to bed."

I turned my wrath on René. "I hope you are not suggesting you're sorry you missed such a sordid opportunity."

He grinned. "Would've been educational, and a warlock's got to know all kinds of things, right?" He rolled away from my outstretched fist. "But what I meant was, the sultan lied to us. Both of us. And neither of us noticed."

I stopped reaching for René and stared at Jean. "Did he change his mind after you left the guest quarters? He couldn't have lied to us."

There was no humour in Jean's face now. "He could. He did."

René's jaw dropped. I blinked at Jean. "But that's impossible. Lying to warlocks…"

"My dear," he said, "you want to believe the best of everyone you meet. This is one of your charms, but you are too trusting. You have already encountered conspiracy magic in the Fire Guild secrets. True, no one person can lie to you, bald-faced, without you knowing. But with magical backing drawn from many level five talents, the most outrageous lies will take both of you in."

A nasty knot formed in the pit of my stomach. How many secrets were there in Frankland?

René, in a very small voice, said, "We're not much good as warlocks if somebody can pull the wool over our eyes. Is there something we can do?"

Jean stared into the distance for a long moment before answering. "Your bond with Lucinda is a good start. Reading this will help." A book appeared in his hand, and he held it out to René. I read the title—*Engines of Lies: Conspiracy Magic*.

René asked, "Are there other secrets we should know about?"

Jean's eyebrows arched. "Would you trust any response I gave to your question?"

Hey, big sister, he's not going to answer, is he?

I didn't look at René. *He did answer. There are. And he's not going to tell us about them.*

Jean kept up his correspondence with the Frost Maiden throughout our travels. Without the hazards of face-to-face exchanges, the tone of the letters gradually warmed. He began looking forward to them, and I understood why; she and Jean discussed jurisprudence and thaumaturgy with a confidence and economy of expression no one else in our party, and few we met, could match. Each letter gave me fresh prickles of unease, and I abandoned my attempts to break the habit of calling her the Frost Maiden.

We encountered other powerful witches on our travels; many watched Jean with avid eyes and would have challenged my place at his side if they dared. He never gave me cause to doubt his commitment to his marriage vows, but he could not deny the attention was gratifying. I watched and wondered. After living alone for so long, did he feel hemmed in by marriage and family? I didn't ask. Despite my curiosity and Jean's insistence on warlocks facing facts, I had begun to learn not to ask questions I didn't want to hear the answer to.

Our staff wondered at times why I didn't exhibit homesickness with an infant in tow, but I was eager to see Cathay and Nippon, and news of growing unrest in Frankland did not inspire nostalgic yearnings to return. Beorn's letters grew darker in tone, and in private messages reiterated his goal: two years. Each letter was a new blow; the two years were almost over, and it hadn't been long enough. With more servants than I had ever imagined needing, I didn't have to spend time in the nursery, but rocking a colicky baby for hours soothed him and me.

The growing unease spurred me to renew my study of lock theory, and with the Orient's best theoreticians a short jump away, experiments and ideas flowed freely. René, always my willing victim, was most pleased with the yells and screams greeting his appearance after I made his head vanish. Jean vetoed René's pleas that I do it again, and I concurred. The blood pulsing in his neck's exposed arteries made my skin crawl.

With new insights, I cracked the puzzle of locks drawing on power from more than one person—my monograph on the subject should stand as the definitive work for centuries. I devised a lock Jean and René cast together, and even I, knowing the spell, could not unlock or break it. Either of them could relock the Water Office if I did not survive the unlocking.

How reassuring.

Without consulting Jean, René and I began on our own to work on locks against magic-backed lies.

I could not put a lock, any lock, on Jean. I hadn't dared try while he was the Fire Warlock, but afterwards, even with his cheerful concurrence, I could not do it. I would start on the spell, and his torch would burn through the words and overpower my candle flame. I didn't mind; the proof his defences were still strong was a comfort.

Jean noticed long before I did that neither the Frost Maiden's nor the Fire Warlock's letters gave more than the most superficial descriptions of events in Frankland. He began to worry, and then fret. When we left Agra in the spring, to that city's relief, and arrived in Cathay, he said, "After this we must turn towards home."

"But I want to see Nippon. Please?"

He studied me with a slight frown, but didn't respond. Events in Frankland took the decision out of our hands. News of disastrous revolts against two dukes reached us in Cathay. Hard on its heels came pleas from the Fire Warlock and the Frost Maiden for us to return to Frankland as soon as possible.

I would have lain awake half the night, crying, if Jean hadn't ordered me to sleep. I finally had to admit what he had known for months. I was homesick. And I was terrified of going home.

Homecoming

The messages summoning us home arrived on the thirtieth of June. We left the next morning. Most luggage we left behind, to be shipped home, but we still had a pile of bags and boxes. Our hosts watched with amazement as we linked hands and, with no apparent effort, Jean called up the fire to take eleven adults, a baby, and our baggage halfway around the world.

We didn't cover the whole distance in one jump, of course. That would have burnt out even him. We jumped nine times, with pauses between to let him cool off. Even so, it was an epic feat, and he was exhausted when we reached Frankland.

René lent a hand, but I was too wrapped up in dealing with a fussy baby, and in my own private terrors, to be of any help. Edward reacted to his mother's mood and cried harder as we got closer to home. The louder he cried, the closer I came to chucking him in a river to shut him up.

Our departure from Cathay was smooth and orderly; our arrival in Blazes was anything but. We landed in the town square in a drenching rainstorm—something guaranteed to make any Fire Guild member bad-tempered. Townsfolk poured into the square to welcome the returning wanderers. They tried to help by carrying our baggage in out of the rain, and mostly got in our way. Bags and boxes were shuffled around and misplaced, toes stepped on, and tempers lost.

Beorn had deeded to us his family seat overlooking the square—the last of his line, he had no use for it anymore. By the time our belongings were in our new house, our staff had disappeared, running off with or being dragged away by their own families and friends. The soaked bags we had carried home from Cathay were scattered willy-nilly on top of the crates of books we had shipped home from every city we visited. The pile took up most of the floor space in the kitchen, and looked as welcoming as Beorn's pet lion.

René dried the dripping bags, then curled up on the couch in the drawing room and snored. I paced up and down with the squalling baby, and barked my shin on a crate. I kicked it, earning a sore toe to go with the sore shin. I had to close my eyes and count to ten to stop myself from setting the box on fire.

Jean lay on his back on the settle. He was the only returning traveller who hadn't gotten soaked. The rain had sizzled off him like water droplets skating across a hot skillet. I glared at him.

A message arrived, saying the Fire Warlock needed to see us, now.

I said, "The frostbitten bastard can drown himself, and he's welcome to take the damned nursemaid with him."

Jean's eyebrows shot upward. "Is that so? Stop beating around the bush, my dear. Tell me how you really feel."

My cheeks burned. "Sorry." Neither the Fire Warlock nor the nursemaid deserved my anger any more than the box of books did, but I was ready to flame the next person or thing crossing my path.

Jean eased off the settle and relieved me of the howling infant. "You need food, rest, and Mrs Cole. Neither of us will get the rest we need, but we can arrange for the other two. Come, my dear."

Mrs Cole met us in the Fortress kitchen, and took Edward off our hands as if he were a cherub instead of a red-faced demon. "Of course I want to take him. I'll pretend he's my grandson, and when you're done here, I'll give him back to you and I'll take a nap."

"A nap," I said. "What a lovely idea."

She leaned closer and whispered, "If they talk for too long, lean back on the sofa pillows and close your eyes. They won't notice."

I started down the corridor. Jean called me back. "Sit down." He handed me a bowl of chicken soup. "Eat. I intend to. Mrs Cole's cooking will do wonders for you."

I had not eaten in hours, but my stomach was too tied up in knots to welcome food. I hadn't forced down more than three spoonfuls when Edward gave a tremendous belch and stopped crying.

Mrs Cole said, "There you go, you little darling."

I stared down at my soup, blinking back tears. That was all that had been wrong? I was a better wizard than I was a mother.

Beorn walked out of the fireplace and greeted us with bone-cracking hugs and thumps on the back. Naturally, he looked no older than I remembered, but tired, dispirited, and relieved to see us. I sipped my soup while he talked.

He said, "I'd like to hear about your trip, but not now. We have problems that can't wait. I let Lorraine know you were home. She'll meet us at the head of the stairs in a few minutes."

One of Jean's eyebrows arched. "The head of the stairs, you say."

"We cut a tunnel from the Crystal Palace to the Fortress."

Both of Jean's eyebrows soared. My head pounded. My choice of people to see on our arrival did not include the Frost Maiden.

"We've had to work together a lot lately," Beorn said. "She's still a pain in the arse, but she's gotten past slandering us every other sentence. We can get things done. If we didn't, we'd be in worse shape, what with the logjam in the Fire Guild Council. Flint's been fighting me every step of the way on using lower-ranking guild members to help keep the peace. He won't let me use them if I won't use him, and if I send him to stop a riot, I might as well burn the whole city down.

"Sven's a big help, but Sunbeam's backing Flint out of habit, and a mistaken belief that if a warlock jumps into the middle of a riot in a blast of flame he could cow everybody into cooling off and going home, and Frankland would be as peaceful as it ever was. As if it had been."

Jean said, "He has spent his life preparing to fight the Empire, and has never noticed unrest simmering under his nose."

"Yeah," Beorn said. "He means well, but he doesn't have a clue how to handle a civil war."

I dropped my spoon. Jean's eyebrows drew together in a frown. "Civil war? Frankland cannot have reached such a state so fast."

Beorn said, "I said the country would fall apart on my watch, and I was right, dammit. It's happening now."

We stared at him.

Both men said, "She's here," and rose from the table.

The soup smelled delicious. I left it behind with a sigh.

The Frost Maiden said, "Some day I would love to hear about your travels, but I cannot spare the time today."

Thank God for that. Her blue silk clashed with the red leather up-holstery in the Fire Warlock's study and set my teeth on edge. I closed my eyes and pictured her in the library. She looked outlandish there, too.

She went on, "You two look as if you would rather sleep than talk, so I trust you will forgive me for diving on in.

"The situation here has deteriorated far more quickly than I anticipated, and the bad news is an avalanche still gathering momentum. Madam Lock-smith, Arturos told me you have been working at channelling the lightning as quickly as you are able, based on premonitions both you and he have had about the urgency."

"Two years. That's what I've been telling her," he said.

I said, "And I've been telling you that wasn't possible."

"How long do you need?" the Frost Maiden said. "I regret asking this of you, but we—the four Officeholders, even Enchanter Paul—are agreed we must fix the Office of the Northern Waters as soon as humanly possible. The witches and wizards involved in rebuilding can be ready on a month's notice, perhaps two. How soon can you be ready to unlock it?"

A month? I stared at her with my mouth open. I clutched Jean's hand and looked at him for help. The colour had drained from his face.

He said, "Before we left we agreed we must fix the Water Office, but did not consider it so urgent. What has changed?"

The Frost Maiden started to reply but Beorn interrupted. "Better let me answer that." He took his time, combing his fingers through his beard. "It looks like the spark that set off the wildfire was Lucinda releasing that stinker of a lock on the Water Office."

I flinched as if he had struck me. If the Frost Maiden had said that, I would have flamed her. Jean, his face grim, gripped my hand so hard it felt as if the bones were grinding together. I cried out and he eased off. "I beg your pardon, my love."

Beorn said, "We aren't blaming you, Lucinda."

The Frost Maiden said, "Indeed not. At the time, we were all agreed it was for the best. I still believe so, but it has had consequences no one foresaw."

I couldn't manage a coherent two-word sentence. Jean asked the question. "What consequences?"

"With that lock's release," she said, "the Office became stronger. Not as strong as the Fire Office, but on a par with the Earth Office."

"Shouldn't that have helped?" I croaked.

She shook her head. "No. Most of my efforts, and my predecessor's efforts for half the Office's existence, have gone into restraining the Office's broken pursuit of justice. Now, even with the Water Guild Council's full support, I cannot hold it back."

Jean breathed, "Oh, dear God."

"Quite so," she said. "You understand."

"I don't," I said. "Explain it to me."

"You are too young to have seen the gradual changes in the severity of the penalties handed out. The Water Office is not as rigid as the Fire Office. The Water Guild members in the Great Coven understood that times change, and built in corrective measures, but those measures do not work as intended. Penalties the Water Guild hands out depend on the judgements handed down in earlier, similar cases. The precedences are a stream carving a channel deeper and wider, and once flowing in one direction we can no more redirect them than a mundane can redirect the course of a mighty river. The Water Office itself recognises its penalties have crossed the boundaries of common sense, but in trying to correct them, it makes them more severe."

Beorn said, "The Green Duke got a lot stricter about poachers. He's green in more ways than one, only been duke a couple of years, and didn't like his dad letting people get away with poaching rabbits and other small game, as long they left the deer alone. So he hauled a poacher off to the Water Guild to make an example of him, instead of dealing with the man himself. The Water Office froze the poacher's left hand off."

"A harsh judgement," Jean said, "but one it has applied in such cases for centuries."

"Right," Beorn said, "but it didn't stop other people from poaching. I wasn't surprised it didn't—the poor in that duchy poach to feed starving children, not for the fun of it. So, he hauled another poacher off to the Water Guild. All his neighbours thought well of this poor grunt, and as far as we could tell he'd been law-abiding up till then, but the duke had forced him and several other tenant farmers out so he could expand his hunting park."

I winced. "Ouch."

"He should never have been brought to your notice," Jean said. "A sensible duke would not have beggared a respectable tenant."

"A sensible duke," the Frost Maiden said, "would have accepted some blame when his gamekeepers caught the man poaching, and given him a helping hand out of the public's eye. A sensible duke would not have crippled a healthy and willing worker. But the Green Duke is not sensible, and the Water Office had to deal with the poacher. In its wisdom it attempted to show mercy." She turned away and stared out the window.

After a slight pause, Beorn coughed. "You know, Lorraine, used to be everything you said sounded sarcastic. Now I can't tell."

"I did not intend that as sarcasm. The Water Office did attempt to show mercy, but this is the area of most acute breakage. The Office recognised the standard penalty was overly severe, and it substituted a different penalty, but the new penalty was more severe, not less so."

After another pause, I asked, "So, what did it do?"

Beorn said, "It took off his hand and a foot."

The silence went on a lot longer this time. At length, Jean said, "And that triggered the uprising."

"Yup," Beorn said. "The common folk were already fed up with their ass of an overlord, and that was the last straw. They rioted. Fields, farms, and warehouses went up in smoke, and now there are a lot more unhappy, hungry people—and poachers—than there had been."

"And the next poacher brought to the Water Guild," the Frost Maiden said, "will suffer an even more drastic punishment, as the Office tries and fails to correct its past mistakes. This is but one example. There have been and will be others. The sluice gates have opened, and the streams of misery are becoming great torrents. The people are crying out for justice, and mercy. We must do something soon to rechannel those torrents, or dam them."

Beorn said, "The nobles are making things worse because they're scared. They've heard rumours from the guilds that we want to rebuild the Offices, and they know it isn't to help them. They have the upper hand now, and they're using the protections of the Offices to flush out troublemakers. They've set a backfire, and it's gotten out of control."

"Yes," she said, "They want to stamp out all dissent and unrest before the tide turns, and they are not hesitating to be quite brutal about it."

He said, "Starving homeless are drifting from town to town, and with the tenants gone, crops will rot in the fields. We're looking at a long hungry winter ahead. We'd already realised we were facing disaster, and I was going to send you a message asking you to come home, when we had back-to-back riots. Rumours are spreading across the country like wildfire. If nobles panic and start hauling people right and left off to the Water Guild, well…"

Jean said, "Tension must be mounting within the Fire Office, if it does not have a single enemy to focus on."

"No enemy at all," Beorn said. "Both sides seem true to Frankland, and it's…Let's say it's confused, and that's not good."

"You are not usually given to understatement, my friend."

"Huh. Anyway, we've all agreed to go ahead and fix her Office as best we can, as soon as possible, with the decisions we've already made. We may not get it right on the first try, but it'll be headed in a better direction. With the coven already familiar with the spells, and a less extreme lock, we can fine-tune it later, once we see how the fixes are working out."

"Or remove the justice-related functions." The Frost Maiden's mouth was set in a thin line. "Even I now accept that may be necessary."

Beorn said, "If we wait much longer, all we'll have left is a charred and smoking ruin."

I did not attempt to keep my voice from shaking. "At least now I know why I was afraid to come home. I'm not strong enough yet. I don't know how much it will take."

Beorn said, "We want you to take another look at that lock. Maybe you've stretched enough in two years that it won't look as bad."

I sniffed. Why dignify rubbish with a response?

The Frost Maiden said, "My dear Locksmith, please understand, you must not risk your life if you cannot open it. An attempt, too early, leaving the Office still locked and you dead would be disastrous. What we need is an estimate of how long we must wait."

Beorn said, "Yep. We're not telling you we're going to do it in a month, hurry up and get ready. You're going to tell us when."

The Newest Warlock

We walked to the guildhall in Blazes three hours later, with René in tow, for an emergency meeting of the Fire Guild Council. The nursemaid had crept back, apologising for abandoning us, and I had handed over my now-sleeping little angel. Jean and I had had time to eat, bathe, change into clean clothes, and inform René of the dire state of affairs, but we were bleary-eyed and on edge.

My eyes burned as if I had been awake for days. We had left Cathay mid-morning, travelled for ten hours, and arrived in Blazes before noon. I couldn't understand it. It should have been after midnight now, not early afternoon. Jean explained to René the theory behind the phenomenon—something about the earth's rotation—but my head throbbed. I couldn't take it in.

Warlock Sunbeam was waiting when we walked into the meeting room. He was, as always, cordial, and delighted to see René. "So, the predictions were true, and you've turned out to be a warlock? Excellent. I'm glad to know we have another wizard in line. As it seems Jean was right about the Fire Warlock being able to designate his successor, I'm sure Peter, when it's his turn, will be happy to—"

"Peter?" I said. "Who's Peter?"

Sunbeam's eyebrows drew together. "Warlock Flint, of course. He'll make the Fire Office skip you. As talented as I'm sure you are, dear," he said, with a graceful bow to me, "we will all sleep more comfortably knowing a woman won't be the Fire Warlock."

"Sure will," René said. "I'm a better fighter than she is."

"Er, right," I said. I didn't need Jean's wince and slight head shake to know not to argue. I would be ecstatic if it skipped me and went to René.

I would. Really. So why did I want to spit in the old man's eye? I turned my back on them and sat down at the conference table.

Beorn and Master Sven arrived together from the Fortress. Beorn grabbed René, wrestled him into a headlock, mussed his hair, and growled, "Haven't they been feeding you? You're as skinny as a new colt. And who gave you permission to get taller than Jean and Lucinda? Next thing we know you'll be as tall as Sven."

That was unlikely as Sven was a head taller than René, but the boy looked thrilled. "You think? I'm still growing."

Beorn let him go, tousling his hair again for good measure. "It's good to have you back. Too many fossils on this guild council."

While they were engaged in their manly salutes, Sven squared his shoulders and walked towards Jean and me, as if greeting us were a chore rather than a pleasure. He said, "Welcome back. You look, er, …"

"Dreadful," I said. "Don't beat around the bush. We should have been in bed hours ago."

"Let me reiterate my congratulations, Sven," Jean said, "on your ascension to the Company of Mages."

"Oh!" I said, "I'd forgotten. Yes, that's wonderful. You must be proud of yourself."

He flushed. After a curt "thank you," he turned on heel to greet René with obvious affection. The throbbing in my head intensified.

Was he still jealous of Jean? Or angry with me for forgetting he had been recognised as a mage? Didn't matter. His fit of pique, whatever its cause, was his problem, not mine. I stared out the window and cursed the knots in my stomach.

The last to arrive was Warlock Flint, giving off waves of anger like a blast furnace. His greeting was, "What's that fool boy doing here?"

Jean, his voice dangerously uninflected, said, "René is a full-fledged warlock, and as such is entitled to a place on the Guild Council."

"That's what you say. How do I know he's really a warlock?"

"Because I can do things—" René disappeared in a burst of flame. Flint rocked back a step. René reappeared carrying a large piece of cast-iron cookware. "—only a warlock can." The handle began to glow red.

"Put that down," I yelped, "before you ruin a perfectly good skillet."

The red glow disappeared, and he dropped the now-cold frying pan on the table. "Sorry." He grinned at me. Sorry, my foot.

Flint said. "Just because he can do that doesn't mean he has enough sense to be on the council. He shouldn't be here until he's eighteen, at least."

"I was on the council at sixteen," Jean said.

"Not helping," Beorn muttered. I snickered. Flint had been a late bloomer who hadn't proved he was a warlock until he was nineteen.

"The way I figure it," Beorn said, "is if I'm going to order him around, doing things only a warlock can do, then he has a right to a vote on the Council."

"What's the fuss about?" I said. "The Fire Office won't let you keep a warlock off the Council, will it?"

Beorn said, "We're wasting time. All in favour of René being on the Council—"

"Aye," René said.

"Nay," Flint said.

"—say aye."

Six ayes later, Beorn said, "Good. Now let's get down to business."

"Wait," Sunbeam said. "What's our new warlock's war name?"

Beorn blew out through his moustache. "That's not important. We have—"

"Of course it is. How can you expect rioters to disperse if you send them a warlock who doesn't have a proper name?"

René snickered. *And Flint doubts my judgement?*

At least he acknowledged your existence.

Beorn rolled his eyes at Sunbeam. "What's your suggestion?"

The old man looked taken aback. "I haven't given it any thought."

I said, "What about a—"

Flint's rough voice drowned me out. "Pest, nuisance, headache, aggravation, ..."

Two years earlier Jean had advised me to be polite but evasive with Flint, and let the Fire Warlock deal with him, but I didn't want polite treatment out of fear of the Fire Office. I would be a lightning-wielder someday. I wanted respect.

"Fervidus?" Sven suggested.

René winced. "Not Latin, okay?"

Sunbeam said, "Quickwit?"

I said, "The witches of Thule—"

Flint rode over me again. "Better make that halfwit. Moron. Imbecile."

Beorn and René glowered. Jean's eyes glittered. Flint was goading me, to get at Jean. Thought I was an easier target, did he? I readied a lock I had practiced on René, and began my suggestion again.

Flint interrupted. "Trouble, bother, plague…"

I snapped the lock on him. His mouth moved, but no sound came out. "As I was saying—"

He flamed me. An instant later Flint lay sprawled on the floor gaping at burns on his arm and chest. The other men surged to their feet, René shooting sparks from his eyes. Jean laid a hand on René's arm, pushing the boy's wand down, without taking his eyes off Flint. Beorn looked disgusted, Sven and Sunbeam looked shocked. Whether they were more horrified by Flint's actions or my quick reflexes and return fire, I couldn't tell.

Beorn jerked Flint to his feet by his unburned arm and shoved him into the hallway. "Don't come back until you're ready to apologise to Lucinda," he barked, and slammed the door.

I said, "Jean told me you couldn't keep another warlock out of the Council meetings."

"I didn't answer your question earlier because I wanted him to see he was outvoted, and not that I won because the Office overruled him. I can kick somebody out—temporarily. As long as I impose a condition the Office recognises as trivial to meet."

Sunbeam said, "Trivial for you or me, certainly. Perhaps not so trivial for our friend Peter. Did you remove your lock, dear?"

"Oh." I concentrated. "It's gone now, sir."

The old warlock's eyes twinkled. "I wonder what you do to Jean when you get angry at him."

Jean winked at me. "Angry? At me? Surely you jest."

The temperature in the room cooled with Flint gone, and my headache diminished. I might pay later for what I'd done, but I had been itching to flame something or somebody, and at least I had a good excuse with Flint.

"Go on, Lucinda," Beorn said. "What's your idea?"

"The Thule witches suggested we might use one of their names: Ari, eagle, or Hrafn, raven."

René shrugged. "Better than Fervidus."

Jean said, "I prefer another of their suggestions, a name that has earned some renown in Thule. Warlock Snorri."

René's eyes gleamed. He appeared to be holding his breath.

Sunbeam said, "Snorri? What does that even mean?"

"Attack," Jean said. "Onslaught."

Sven smiled. "How apt. In our exercises there always seemed to be three of him to the one of me."

"I don't like it," I said. "I don't want to be reminded day in and day out what a nuisance he is."

Beorn guffawed—the first laugh I'd heard that day from the normally ebullient wizard. "That settles it." He thumped the grinning boy on the shoulder. "Snorri it is. Now can we get down to business?"

Beorn and Jean parcelled out the competent fire witches and wizards, assigning the lower-ranking ones either to patrol the Green Duke's domain under Jean's supervision or Blacksburg under Sunbeam and Master Sven. Our Fire Eaters were paired with mature and trusted wizards, and would be sent to other hot spots, under Beorn's supervision.

My mind wandered, and my headache returned as I reviewed the confrontation with Flint. Jean was, as usual, right in his assessment that our reliance on the single Fire Warlock caused problems. An experienced warlock in his prime should never let a witch with only two years training catch him with his guard down. Sunbeam would be worse; everyone in the Fire Guild knew he was lazier than Flint. Even René, more alert and with better reflexes than either of them, would be in danger in the thick of an angry, rioting mob. Did Sunbeam and Flint believe they were invincible? I shivered.

Beorn started talking about René. Since he didn't look like a warlock, he would travel from place to place without guild emblems, as additional eyes and ears scouting for unrest.

"Lucinda, too," Beorn said, "only she's going to stay in Blazes or the Fortress, using the spells seeking out trouble from a distance. And she's going to see what the lock on the Water Office is like."

I opened my mouth to protest we already knew about that fiendish lock. The words I said were, "There's no point in making plans until we know what's there."

René's head snapped around. *Hey, big sister, I thought you already knew.*

I stared back, just as startled. *We do, but the Frost Maiden didn't want the news about the dangers to spread. She must have woven a spell around it to keep it a secret.*

So, I'm a part of a conspiracy? All right.

René looked thrilled. I found the idea unsettling.

Sunbeam looked unsettled, too. "I've heard wild rumours about plans to rebuild the Offices, but whenever anyone repeated the rumours to me, I've gone to great lengths to squelch such nonsense. Do promise me that's all they are—nonsense."

My headache returned full force. Jean broke the short silence. "The rumours are not nonsense. The Offices need repairs, and we would be irresponsible to not fix them."

"We're going to take the Water Office apart," Beorn said, "as soon as we can."

Sunbeam started up from his seat, shouting. "No, you mustn't. You can't. God knows I don't love the Water Guild, but wrecking any Office will destroy Frankland."

Beorn's gruff voice was almost as gentle as Jean's had been. "We won't wreck it. We're going to fix it before it destroys Frankland."

The light-hearted old gentleman's hands and voice shook. "But we've lost so much since the days of the Great Coven. They were so far beyond us in knowledge and power we can't possibly duplicate what they did."

Jean steamed. I put a hand on his arm. *Don't argue,* I thought at him, and met a stone wall. Why couldn't I talk with him mind-to-mind, as I could with René? He pursed his lips, nostrils flaring, but didn't speak.

Sven coughed. "I've been studying the Fire Guild spells in the Water Office for nearly two years, and there's nothing in them we can't handle."

Sunbeam turned a shocked face towards the mage. "Two years? You've been planning this for two years? Why haven't you told the Council?"

"Er..."

"Because I said so," Beorn growled. "Sit down."

Shock and bewilderment played across Sunbeam's face. He didn't move.

Beorn pushed him into a chair. "Sit down, I said. There's more."

A muscle in the old man's face twitched. "More?"

"Yeah. Jean's teaching Lucinda and René to call down the lightning on their own."

Sven blanched. Sunbeam gasped and sputtered, "My God, man, are you mad? Your own wife. You can't teach a girl to call down the lightning. That's… that's… that's murder."

I glared at the old stick-in-the-mud. Livid, Jean barked, "It certainly is not. She is more than halfway there."

"But why?"

Beorn said, "You've got to understand. If we can't fix the Water Office, we're going to need all the firepower we can get."

Seize the Night

Three days after our return, and feeling no more rested, I walked through the tunnel at the head of the Fortress stairs. Despite the July heat, I carried my winter coat over my arm, scarf and gloves clutched in my hands. Sorceress Eleanor met me at the exit and guided me through marble halls.

"Welcome," the Frost Maiden said, smiling, as we reached her study. "I trust we have given you a more hospitable reception than the first time you entered the Crystal Palace."

Her study was as plush as the Fire Warlock's, but his was a warm refuge, with carved wooden panelling and reds, yellows, and oranges in the carpet and furnishings. Hers had alabaster walls, an ocean of white carpet, and furnishings in blue and silver. Tall windows overlooked surf battering rocks on the edge of the North Sea.

"It's beautiful," I said. Claire would have loved it.

Both women wore sleeveless linen frocks. The Frost Maiden gestured toward a couch, upholstered in pale blue watered silk, with a neat stack of lap robes on one end. "The Earth Guild finds my home an uncomfortable place, I am afraid. Whether you will need those, or your own heat will keep you comfortable remains to be seen."

I donned my winter gear and her lap robes before diving into the thicket of spells making up the Water Office. An hour later, the cold had seeped into my bones, but we had reached the lock before my teeth started chattering. And once again, I asked what it would take to release it.

Two years of incessant training had worked its magic on me, and this time I did not flinch. Jean had called down lightning bolts greater than this, with my hands in his. Where once I had cowered before all displays of fire magic with killing power, I could now distinguish shades and degrees.

Given another year of training at the same pace, I could release the lock without permanent damage. Another two years, it would not hurt me. But now? I could release it, I was sure of that. I might even survive, but it would hurt like hell.

I had hoped my question would reveal a clear-cut answer—yes, I could handle it, or no, it would kill me—but it had not. I could not escape the burden of making up my own mind.

The Frost Maiden watched me with puckered brow. "I gather two years of practice have expanded your limits such that this lock is no longer certain death, but not such you are certain to live through it, either."

"That sums it up pretty well," I said. "I'd like to talk it over with Jean, if you don't mind."

"Of course. I understand." She rose. "Rather than returning through the same tunnel, may I give you a tour of Quays? It would be a blessing for more of the Water Guild to see us talking in a pleasant manner."

"Uh…"

She smiled. "Assuming you believe that possible. Perhaps if I entrust the commentary to Sorceress Eleanor?"

If she had offered a tour of the Crystal Palace, I would have begged off, but a tour of the town would take us out into the sunshine. I agreed, and they led me to the courtyard, where we climbed into an open carriage. Once through the gates, I shed my coat. Water witches and wizards watched our passage with wide eyes.

The one road through Quays carved a wide arc along high ground; most traffic was on the crowded canals. The front door of each house opened onto stairs leading down to a moorage. I did not express my view it was a ghastly way to live.

Two years earlier I would have held my breath and prayed each time we crossed one of the rickety bridges, but I had since learned to keep a polite face on with people I trusted far less.

That was an eye-opening thought. Sometime over the past two years, I, a fire witch, began to trust a water sorceress, and the world hadn't ended.

While climbing down from the carriage on the far side of town, I turned my head too far. The Crystal Palace on its hill glittered in the sun, dominating the townscape behind us. I froze, one foot in mid-air.

The coachman's assisting hand steadied me. "Look away, ma'am," he murmured. "Look down. Just one more step."

I finished the climb down, turned my back to the Crystal Palace, and raised my chin to the two water witches, but they were not laughing. Sorceress Eleanor's eyes were wide and staring. The Frost Maiden, smiling a moment ago, bore a strong resemblance to Jean at the end of the war: the look of someone reaching the end of his or her endurance.

"Now do you understand?" she said to the younger sorceress. "When the sight frightens a warlock, is it ludicrous innocent men must be dragged here in chains? Do you still wonder that they hate us?"

When I reported to Beorn on the lock, the big wizard sagged into his chair. He leaned back with his eyes closed, tugging at his beard.

"I had hoped," he mumbled, "you could do it without getting hurt. I should've known better."

"Even if I could handle the lock, there's still the Locksmith's warning. We don't know what her 'terror' means."

"Yeah."

I tucked my hands under my skirt. There wasn't any delicate way to approach this. I took a deep breath and dove in. "Beorn, you're a seer. Have you seen anything about unlocking the Water Office? Who lives? Who dies? Isn't there something you can tell me?"

He opened one eye wide enough to peer at me. Closed it again. "No. Not a thing."

I waited. After a while I stalked to the study door. "Fine. Don't tell me. Just remember you need my help."

"Come back here," he growled.

I stood in the doorway and glared at him.

"Sit down," he rumbled. "That's an order."

I returned to my chair and sat with my arms folded tightly across my chest.

He leaned towards me, hands on knees. "Look, Lucinda, foreknowledge is a curse, not a blessing. What do you think I could tell you? That you're going to die? You wouldn't want to hear that, and I wouldn't want to tell you. The only thing I could tell you would be you'll live through it."

"So tell me that—I'd like to hear it."

"The problem is those kinds of 'don't worry, you'll be fine' assurances have a nasty way of backfiring. If you know you're going to come through something just fine then you slack off, it's human nature, and you end up getting hurt worse than you would have otherwise. Maybe you get hurt so bad you think you'd've been better off if you had died. Or maybe you come through it fine, but everybody else involved dies, and you're mad as hell because I didn't warn you about that. But I wouldn't be able to warn you. The visions I have are always little bits and pieces—never the whole picture."

"But you're Fire Warlock now—doesn't the Fire Office help you see more of the future?"

"Not a bit. The Great Coven wanted decisions made on accurate information about current events and the judgement of experienced warlocks. They thought those were better than wild-assed guesses based on fragments. They built foresight dampers into the Office, not amplifiers. I've not had a single vision since I've been Fire Warlock."

I wilted. "So you weren't evading. You really don't have anything you can tell me."

"I can't begin to tell you how happy I am I've not had any visions. I'd rather trust your judgement."

"Beorn, I'm afraid. My sense of prescience is screaming at me not to do it. The future to me looks black—black as death."

He chewed on his moustache. "I'm not optimistic about anything right now either. Keep on working on calling down the lightning. I'll give you as much time as I can. Even if you weren't a good friend, I'd like you to still be here to unlock the Fire Office when this mess is over. Now, go home and sleep on it. Maybe it'll look better in the morning."

Sleep on it, Beorn said. Sleep wouldn't come. My sense of day and night had been out of kilter ever since we had come home. At four in the afternoon, I had to use magic to prop my eyelids open. At four in the morning, they wouldn't stay closed.

Others in the house were also restless. Jean was not in bed. I donned a robe and walked downstairs to his study. He looked up as I walked in and sat down across the desk from him. We studied each other in silence for a few moments.

I said, "It's no good. Either of us could write a textbook on locks more complete than that one. It's no help."

He grimaced and closed the book in his hands. "I know, love. I am not being sensible, trying to find something new in a text I have already read a dozen times, but scholarly research is comforting to me. It gives me the illusion I am doing something."

"Doing something? You've been doing a lot, haven't you? I've hardly seen you since we got back. Aren't things calming down?"

He shook his head. "No riots appear imminent, but the mood of the country is not calm. The charged tension is that of two circling swordsmen, each watching for the opponent's misstep. It is only a matter of time before a new disaster sets them lunging again."

I sat on my trembling hands. "Is it really so bad? I thought with you and René and our staff helping out, things would get better."

"Even with our return, the Fire Guild is stretched as thin as in any period in our history. The guards and most fire witches and wizards have been diverted from their normal duties to police troubled districts. The other guilds are assisting, but it is not enough. Another senseless Water Office action will undo our efforts."

I looked away from him. My throat felt tight. "It's up to me, isn't it? I was afraid, when I told you I could the release the lock, you would order me to do it."

"Order you? I am no longer the Officeholder. I cannot issue orders to another warlock. As your husband, I know you do not obey orders, even from me. I may persuade you to a course of action, but you will do what you believe you must, though the whole world stands against you."

I stared into the darkness outside the open window. I couldn't argue with that.

He said, "It is one of the reasons I love you. It is far more satisfying to have you follow my advice because you agree with me than if you obeyed orders you did not agree with."

"But you haven't tried to persuade me—one way or the other. How do you feel about it? Most Franks would never dream of letting their wives do something so awful."

He leaned his forehead on the heel of his hand and said heavily, "You have a right to be angry with me. I have been a success as Fire Warlock, and more recently as your teacher, but I am a failure as a husband—"

"I never said—"

"—because I cannot protect my beloved wife from danger."

The things my women friends had said two years ago came to mind, unbidden: they were glad I was marrying the retired Fire Warlock, he could protect me from all danger. I wanted to tell him he wasn't a failure, but the words stuck in my throat. I forced other words out. "You shouldn't have to protect me. I'm not defenceless. You've made sure I'm not."

"And I would not love you so dearly if you were. If I admired feminine helplessness, I would not have begun teaching you to call down the lightning. Tell me how you would feel if I ordered you to not consider unlocking the Water Office for another year."

The night was still, the silence broken only by crickets chirping and the clock ticking. The pendulum swung back and forth, back and forth. I'd been annoyed with Sunbeam for thinking a woman couldn't handle the Fire Office. Jean had more than once said a warlock's responsibility to Frankland's security trumped everything else. If Jean were the locksmith, he would not hesitate, even with a wife and young child. The Fire Guild would honour him as a hero, and ensure his family did not go without.

Did the Frost Maiden and Sorcerer Charles have conversations like this? They must have, and theirs would be no less difficult. Water witches and wizards have their own notions of duty, but are not indoctrinated from childhood to believe that duty involves giving one's life for one's country.

"I'd be angry," I said, "that you weren't treating me like a warlock."

The set of his shoulders relaxed a trifle. I walked to the window and gazed up at the massive Fortress looming over us, gleaming in the moonlight. Beorn was up there, getting some sleep, I hoped. Jean could not give orders to another warlock, but the Fire Warlock could. If it came to a choice between saving my life and saving the country, he would choose to save the country. As I would in his shoes.

I couldn't wait for Beorn to order me to unlock the Water Office. The magic would be stronger if I volunteered.

I said, "You believe warlocks must be prepared to lay down their lives in Frankland's defence. You'd be ashamed of yourself for putting family above country. You'd be ashamed of me for my cowardice. I'd be ashamed of myself." I turned and looked at my husband. "It would tear us apart, more slowly but just as surely, as trying and failing would. Wouldn't it?"

He managed a bleak smile. "You have confirmed my trust that you would understand. If we fail, and you are taken and I am left, all the years you have given me will be as bitter as ashes. But neither you nor I can tolerate inaction. The years will be as bitter if we do nothing."

"So, if you'd really wanted to take the decision out of my hands, and force me to agree to release the lock, you'd have ordered me not to."

His expression lightened. "I must be careful what I say to you. You are far too clever."

I reshelved the book on locks. "We should make good use of whatever time we have left. Stop this exercise in futility and come to bed."

"You are ever practical, my dear. I love that about you."

I said, "Especially since neither of us can sleep."

His mouth curved into a smile as he reached for the lamp. "I see. Carpe noctem, indeed."

Jean was right in that I could not stand inaction, but I still could not make a decision on how soon I would unlock the Water Office. He did not prod me, and I alternately blessed him and cursed him for letting me make up my own mind. I dithered and dawdled, and made myself frantic for the next day and a half over my own procrastination.

I had had enough. Action was called for. After a midday nap—mine, not his—I gathered up Edward and the nursemaid and set off to do what I'd wanted to do long before we came home: pour out my heart to a girl-friend.

Reunion

In the two years we were away, Mrs Cole had written several dozen long, chatty letters. Hazel, my friend in the Earth Guild, had sent nearly as many small packages, filled with advice and bundles of herbs for treating upset stomachs and other travellers' ills.

In that same time, Claire sent three two-sentence messages. The first, saying she was engaged, arrived while we were still in the New World. The second, coming soon after, said she had gotten married, and Granny Helene had returned her bracelet in time for the small, private ceremony. The third, reaching us in Cathay, announced the birth of a healthy baby boy and begged me to come see her when I got back home.

She must have married for love, after all. That was the conclusion I reached on arriving at the address included in the last message. The street was tidy, the houses and gardens well maintained, but it was a neighbourhood of minor merchants and craftsmen. Claire's was a narrow townhouse in a row of identical façades. Comfortable, but not impressive by anyone's standards.

I lifted the latch on the gate and stopped.

My nursemaid, a level-one fire witch, asked, "What is it?"

"There's magic at work here. Lots of it."

I sent my mental eye roving over the gate, the fence, the façade, and the roof with growing astonishment and suspicion.

"There are spells on everything—half-a-dozen at least I don't recognise, on top of the usual ones. They're Earth Guild protective spells, I can tell that much, and they're strong, but I can't make out what they're protecting against."

"That would be expensive, wouldn't it, ma'am?"

"Sure would. This much protective magic must be worth at least half as much as the house itself. Odd." Odd, too, that even with three messages from her, I didn't know her husband's name or occupation.

"Will they let us in?"

I opened the latch. "We'll find out."

Whatever they guarded against didn't include two fire witches and a baby. Not a whisper of resistance met me on walking from the gate to the stoop. I stood on the stoop for a moment, still suspicious, but unable to sense any threat.

The nursemaid said, "Are you sure this is the right place?"

"No, I'm not." I squared my shoulders and knocked.

A shriek of "Lucinda!" from an upper story window settled that question. A servant ushered us up the stairs into the nursery, and for a while, babies drove thoughts of anything else from my head. Claire's child, named Lawrence after her husband's grandfather, she said, was as adorable as Edward. They cooed and cried and spit up, and acted like perfect babies. Claire and I fussed and rocked, and she pelted me with questions about our travels. I talked about Jean, she talked about Richard, her husband, and we had a splendid time laughing about the wonders of married life.

Throughout, she evaded every question I asked about her husband's occupation.

Later, while both babies napped, she showed off the rest of the house. The furnishings were as out of proportion to the house and neighbourhood as the protective spells. Her bedroom was a feminine delight of satin sheets, feather mattresses, ruffled valances, and embroidered hangings. A duchess would not have turned up her nose at the gowns in Claire's wardrobe.

"Claire, how can you afford all this? Who is your husband? What does he do?"

She dismissed the question with a wave of her hand. "Never mind him. Will you look at the gorgeous deep blue silk in this skirt? The lighter blue underskirt is a perfect match."

"Stop it." I snatched the dress from her and shoved it back in the wardrobe. "I don't want to talk about clothes. I want to hear about your husband. How much time does he spend here? I don't see many of a man's things…"

Claire—the enchanting butterfly who never cried, raged, or even raised her voice—flushed a bright, angry red. "What do you mean, 'How much time'? Do you think he doesn't live here? I hope you're not suggesting I'm a kept woman. What kind of a woman do you think I am?"

"The kind with too hard a head and too much self-respect to throw away her life being somebody's mistress."

She tossed her head. "I should think so. I am married. I have proof."

"Then why do you need to argue about it? I didn't think you weren't. You're the one using the words, 'kept woman'."

The angry flush faded. She sat down on the edge of the bed with her hands in her lap, her head drooping. "That's what I feel like," she mumbled, not looking at me. "That's what people think."

I sat cross-legged on the rug and peered up at her. "Tell me. All of it."

The misery in her expression gave way to relief as the story tumbled out. "I married the richest bachelor—the best catch in the whole city. But he insisted we keep it a secret until his father dies. His father's very sick, and the healers say he won't live much longer. He wants Richard to marry the Red Duke's daughter. Richard's afraid of him, and thinks he'll be angry when he finds out Richard married a commoner."

"You married a nobleman? Which one?"

"The Earl of Eddensford's oldest son, Lord Richard. Do you remember, when you came to see me before your wedding, going with me to the needlework shop? We met him on our way out. I don't love him, but he loves me—I'm sure of it."

Could I forget seeing such naked desire in a man's face? "I remember. He followed us until we ducked into a coffee shop." I shouldn't have been surprised he'd pursued her, or that she had accepted his proposal. I was more sophisticated now than I'd been three years ago in Lesser Campton, and knew that desire often doesn't turn into love, or lead to honourable behaviour. Still, Claire was telling the truth. She believed her marriage was genuine.

A chill finger walked down my spine. "Claire, show me your proof."

She pulled a set of keys from a pocket, and unlocked a cupboard beside the bed. While she rummaged through it she said, "I didn't like it either. I wondered if he was already married, so I took him to see Granny Helene. She may not be an Earth Mother, but she's close, and she can tell when people are lying, like a Mother can. He swore up and down to her that he loved me, and he wasn't already married, and his intentions were honourable. She said she believed him, and he signed his full name and title in the book at the wedding. You know that's binding.

"And, she made him sign his name and title to a statement saying he'd acknowledge me and our children as soon as his father died, if not sooner. The Frost Maiden could freeze his hand off for not honouring that."

She could indeed. That relieved the worst of my fears, but the situation made my skin crawl.

I read the statement she handed me.

I promise I will make public my lawful marriage to Claire, daughter of William Nelson, tailor, of the town of Rubierre, and adopted daughter of Edward Guillierre, scholar, of the village of Lesser Campton, within one week of my father's death, if it is not already public by that time. I also promise to acknowledge any children born from this marriage.

Lord Richard Robles Bradford, eldest son of Robert Bradford, Earl of Eddensford.

Something about the acknowledgment of children nagged at me, but I couldn't put my finger on it. After a brief study, I shrugged. If it was important, it would come to me later.

"So, you've been living here for more than a year and a half, pretending to be a minor merchant's wife?"

"Yes. It was wonderful at first. He gave me a lot of money. I sent some home to mother, and had enough left to buy whatever I wanted for the house, and later, for the baby. He comes to see me two or three times a week—as often as he can get away. In between, I have servants to do the housework, so I can do whatever I want. I thought I would be so happy…"

Misery crept back into her expression. "But it's been awful. The neighbours know he doesn't live here. They think I'm his mistress, and they won't give me the time of day. The friends I made when I first came here give me the cold shoulder. Only Granny Helene and a few other earth witches believe I'm respectable." She waved a hand at the wardrobe. "I've got all those clothes, the kinds of clothes I dreamed of in Lesser Campton, but no place to wear them. I wear them for him, and he likes seeing me in them, but I want to show them off to other girls. Shopping's no fun anymore—the shopkeepers grovel for the money, but otherwise they'd treat me like dirt. I don't go anywhere—if it weren't for little Lawrence I'd be bored out of my mind."

I'd listened to this with clenched jaw and rising heat. "I don't understand. Two years ago, you said you could marry anyone you wanted—even a duke would be happy to have me for a sister-in-law. He shouldn't shunt you to the side like this. What's the problem?"

She picked lint off her skirt. "Richard saw you when we left the needle-work shop, and believed me when I said you're a fire witch. But you went off on your honeymoon, and I couldn't prove you existed. Whenever I tried to tell anyone Frankland's most powerful fire witch was my stepsister, they either laughed at me or accused me of trying to swindle them. Not even Richard believes you're a warlock."

I pushed the wardrobe door closed and slumped against it. "Oh, God. Of course not. I have trouble believing it myself. Claire, I'm so sorry."

"Well, you couldn't know, could you? But what bothers me the most..." She stopped, and let out a long sigh. "I've been watching the noblewomen. I've had lots of time to watch them. I thought at first I wanted to be like them, but the more I watch, the more disgusted I get." She laughed. "I behaved like one in Lesser Campton, before Granny Helene cured me of whatever it was I had. I suppose I should be ashamed to admit it. The Red Duke's daughter, the girl his father wants Richard to marry, is a selfish, whiny, spoiled brat with a tongue that could etch glass. I can't imagine anyone wanting to be saddled with her."

I forced a smile. "Your Richard should be grateful to you for letting him escape that fate."

"That's not the point. I watch the nobles, and they don't notice. I thought at first they ignored me because I'm a commoner, but it can't be that. I mean, I can go right up to a nobleman, almost walk into him, and he'll look right through me. It doesn't make sense. Men always notice me."

"Don't remind me. That sounds like witchcraft."

"That's what I think. And that's what bothers me the most." She looked away, her cheeks red. "Maybe Richard had someone put a spell on me so the other nobles can't see me. Maybe he's ashamed of marrying a commoner."

Flaming her husband would not help Claire. I pushed against the door of the wardrobe and sat up straight. "Claire, how many protective spells are there on this house?"

She looked confused by the change of subject. "Two, I think. The usual ones against fire and burglars. Maybe a couple against burglars."

"There are at least half a-dozen, and I can't make out what they're for."

"Considering how much I've spent on clothes and such, Richard might have thought the usual one wasn't strong enough."

"No, they aren't against burglary—I know those. I think you're right— Richard is hiding you."

Claire dabbed at her eyes, then dashed to the door. "I should check on the children." She came back, sometime later, with red-rimmed eyes. Tears threatened to spill over.

I said, "What are you going to do?"

"I have no idea."

"Then do this. Tell your Richard the warlock he doesn't believe in is burning up over the way he's mistreated you. I'll—"

"Lucinda, really, I can't do that."

"Why can't you? Well, fine, I'll write him a letter. I'll come back in a week. If you are not ensconced in the earl's manor by then, as his son's respected and honoured wife, I'll walk through the fire into the earl's bedroom and demand an explanation. If that scares an old, sick man to death, his death be on his son's head, not mine."

She clapped a hand over her mouth, her eyes wide. "Lucinda, you wouldn't." Then she laughed. "Oh, you would. Yes, you would. I am so glad you're back."

"Then why didn't you want to tell me about it?"

She resumed picking at imaginary lint on her skirt. "Because I'm ashamed I broke my promise."

"What promise?"

"Don't you remember? I promised you I'd marry somebody I liked and respected. I like Richard well enough, he's good company when he's here, but I don't respect him."

"Oh, Claire…"

"I don't understand why he's afraid of the earl. He's an adult, and he's never gotten into trouble with the Water Guild, so there isn't anything the earl could do to him, is there?"

"No, I wouldn't think so. If they weren't titled, the father could disown the son, but an earl has to keep the succession going. He can't disinherit his son without the king's approval."

"That's what I thought, and Queen Marguerite is Richard's aunt on his mother's side. He's her favourite nephew, and she can't stand his half-brother—so he says, anyway—so she wouldn't let the earl disown him. What's he afraid of?"

"I can't imagine. It would be next to impossible to kill him." I shook my head, once again, over the Fire Office's magical shields. If the titled noble and the next two in line, the heir and the spare, were subject to a bit of pain for their mistakes, there would be a lot less untempered arrogance on display.

Claire sighed. "I didn't really expect an answer from you. You're not afraid of anything."

I wasn't afraid? I understood then why I had sought out my oldest friend—to take my mind off my terror. I'd wanted to talk to someone who had never considered dying for her country. But I couldn't. The Frost Maiden's conspiracy spell wouldn't let me tell Claire the danger I was in. I might as well go back home. At least I'd done her some good by coming.

The heir and the spare. The nagging, amorphous worry took shape, the shape of a darling little baby boy. "You said your husband has a brother?"

"Lord Edmund. Half-brother by his father's second wife. I've not met him. He and his brother despise each other. With good reason, or so I've heard."

"Has Lord Richard told his brother about your son?"

She shrugged. "I doubt it. Is it..." The colour drained from her face. "Oh my God, Lord Edmund's not been shielded since Lawrence was born."

"Right. He could be injured, maybe even die, if he thinks he's shielded and he's not."

"Why did I never think of that?"

"You've not been getting enough sleep, you've had your mind on the baby, and you aren't used to thinking like a noble. Your husband must have thought about that months ago. He probably told his brother as soon as the baby was born." And if he hadn't, then, no, he didn't deserve Claire's respect.

"His brother's not nearby." She sounded uneasy, but colour crept back into her face. "He went somewhere up north several months ago. Over somewhere. Or after. Something. I forgot."

I ran through a hasty inventory of the northern Frankland map. "Abertee? Near the Crystal Palace?"

"Maybe. Wherever the White Duke lives. He was going hunting with the duke's son."

"Yes, Abertee. I'll send a message to the duke."

"Thank you. And I'll tell Richard tonight. I promise."

I sent the message on my return to Blazes and resumed wrestling with my conscience. Visiting Claire had not done me much good. Escaping for an afternoon had not resolved my quandary, and the pressure continued to build. I imagined myself balanced on the edge of a diving platform, looking down into deep water. The slightest nudge would push me in, over my head.

Two days later Hazel, my other best girlfriend, gave me that nudge.

News from Abertee

I was in the Fortress library, gathering an armful of detailed maps of Frankland, when a message arrived saying an earth witch was asking for me. I hurried home to find Hazel, accompanied by a gnarled individual she introduced as Master Walter MacLaren, blacksmith, of Abertee.

"Abertee? What are you doing in Abertee?"

"I took a post there after finishing my training as a healer. Why?"

I had never given the place much thought, other than finding it on a map, and now it had come up twice in a few days. Coincidences make me nervous. I shrugged. "Never mind. Go on."

"I'd love to hear about your travels sometime," Hazel said, "but..."

"But not today. You're not here on a social call," I said. "What's wrong?"

Master Walter, six inches taller than Hazel, had been trying to hide behind her. She pulled him forward. "Tell her."

He stammered something unintelligible and backed away. With Hazel's hand on his arm, his air of panic faded. He swallowed and tried again. "There's trouble abrewing in Abertee, ma'am, and the Blacksmiths' Guild is asking for the Fire Warlock's help."

"Good man. I'm glad the smiths have some sense." The smith beamed.

Hazel said, "Not everyone here seems so glad."

"What?"

"I didn't know how to find you, so we went to the Guild Hall. The clerk said the Fire Warlock was keeping you and Warlock Quicksilver busy, and to see Warlock Flint. He sent us away, saying Abertee would only get what it deserved."

I saw red and reached for my hat. There would be trouble, for certain. In Abertee. And right here in Blazes.

I came to my senses before I reached the door. Flint could wait. I apologised to Hazel and the wide-eyed smith for getting distracted, and led the way to Jean's study, where I reached for pen and paper. "What happened in Abertee?"

Hazel said, "The White Duke told a family of farmers—Douglas and Jessie Archer of Nettleton—that they had one week to move off their land, or he would burn them out. But he doesn't have the right to evict them. They're freeholders, not tenants. The whole district is up in arms about it. That family is as stable and law-abiding as they come, and if they're not safe, nobody is."

"If they're exemplars of good behaviour, why does the White Duke want to evict them?"

She smiled. "You and I would consider them fine, upstanding people, but a duke might not. Granny Mildred, the healer I'm assisting, says the Archers have been there as long as the White Duke, and are more respected than he is. They have a reputation for being outspoken, and the duke and his duchess don't appreciate it."

"Let me guess. The duke's a lazy idler, and the Archers remind him of his neglected duties."

"At every opportunity. Everyone in Nettleton is a responsible free-holder, and they don't like having an irresponsible overlord. So, they call him on it."

The smith said, "That's why it's called Nettleton, ma'am."

I laughed. And then sighed. "Oh dear. It really isn't very funny. Go on. The duke told them to leave. What happened next?"

Hazel said, "They didn't see that they had any choice, so they gathered up everything they could carry and fled. But not everybody in Abertee has as much sense. A group is gathering this morning to march on the duke, intending to pressure him into letting the Archers come back, but I don't see how they can force him."

"They can't. They'd only get hurt if the Fire Warlock had to step in on the duke's side. The rules keeping the magic guilds from stepping in to help are asinine. Murderous, even. We can see trouble coming from miles away, in a dozen places, but we can't force changes before things get violent, because that would be outside interference with the noble's relations with his own subjects."

I gave Hazel a sharp glance. Even suggesting to the smith that he come to us could get her in trouble with the duke.

She shook her head. "Master Walter knew to ask on behalf of the guild, so that means you can help, doesn't it?"

"Yes, that gives us the right to step in."

"What can you do?"

I chewed on my lip. "Good question. Is there anything else behind the unrest?"

My serene friend picked at the hem of her kerchief. Her freckles stood out against pale skin. I put down my pen and stared. She looked sideways at Master Walter. He gave her the same look in return. "You'd better tell, lass."

She said, "The White Duke didn't come himself to evict them. He sent another nobleman, an earl's son with a nasty reputation. He pawed the farmer's sister, and the farmer's brother, another blacksmith, hit him. Killed him. And he was shielded. So now the brother—"

Whatever else she said was lost in the roaring in my head. I sent out a strangled bleat to Beorn. The room rocked.

Sense returned, but not even Hazel's hand on my arm could calm my racing pulse and rapid breath. The smith yelled for a servant to bring whiskey. "Or whatever strong spirits ye keep in a fancy house," he muttered.

Tom shoved a glass into my hands. Other babbling staff crowded around, infected by my alarm. And then Jean strode out of the fireplace, barking orders. The staff huddled together, pale and silent, in one corner. The gibbering blacksmith backed into a different corner. I gulped brandy and watched the blood drain from Jean's face as Hazel repeated her tale.

"Impossible," he said.

Hazel said, "Granny Mildred and I both saw him, Your Wisdom. There's no question, he's dead."

"I beg your pardon, Granny Hazel. I do not doubt your judgement. But the Fire Office is not decaying. He could not have been shielded."

Abertee. An earl's son. I dropped the glass. Jean caught it.

"You're right," I said. "I bet he wasn't shielded. I shouldn't have panicked. Hazel, you said earl's son. The Earl of Eddensford?"

"Yes. What do you know about him?"

"He wasn't second in line any longer." I slumped in Jean's chair, limp from relief and alcohol, and explained about Claire's marriage and the baby.

Jean sent the relieved staff back to work. Colour had returned to Hazel's cheeks, but he was still pale.

"Nevertheless, this is a fresh disaster," he said. "The news that a commoner killed a purportedly shielded nobleman will be all over the country in a few days, while the explanation will take months or years to disseminate. If the nobles' faith in the Fire Office's shields is destroyed, they will lose any remaining semblance of rational behaviour."

I said, "I thought they already had."

"You are an optimist, my dear. Their behaviour can—will—degrade further. I will visit the White Duke, and make sure he understands. As for the unrest in Abertee, is there anything else we need to know?"

Hazel and Master Walter exchanged looks. He shrugged. She shook her head. "I don't think so, sir. What can you do about it?"

"I will send a fire wizard to escort the Archers back to their home, and I will tell the duke that if he continues with the eviction notice—which is unlikely, as he has no resolve and will back down when confronted—he must prove they are not freeholders, the burden of proof is on him, and he must present the evidence to the Air Guild for validation. If he does prove the Archers are tenants—also unlikely—he must give them a reasonable amount of time, say, three months, to settle their affairs and move of their own accord. Further, any additional threat of violence towards law-abiding tenants or freeholders will elicit further sanctions. That should be sufficient to relieve tensions."

"Assuming," I said, "the Fire Warlock agrees with your plan."

"Oh. True. I sometimes forget I am no longer Fire Warlock." His eyes focused in the far distance beyond Hazel's shoulder. We waited. When he refocused on her, he said, "He does, and will send Warlock Sunbeam to deal with the gathering hot-heads. Sunbeam can frighten them into dispersing without inflicting serious damage, and will enjoy the opportunity to show off."

"Thank you, Your Wisdom," she said. "The brother—the blacksmith that's on the run—had never been in serious trouble before. He's a good man, sir."

"One of the best," Master Walter said.

"Is there anything you can do for him?"

"No," Jean said. "That is the Water Guild's domain, not the Fire Guild's. Given the circumstances you have described, they will make no more than a token show of searching for the fugitive. If we attempt to help we will draw attention to him, forcing them to take action. It galls me to say so, but his chances are better without our help."

Hazel's shoulders sagged. "Yes, sir. I understand."

"I don't," I said. "If these Archers are such sensible people, why did the brother start a fight? He had to have known he'd come out the loser. It's stupid to risk being whipped within an inch of his life, or being crippled, or God-knows-what, to keep somebody from groping your sister. I mean, getting pawed isn't any fun for the sister, but some other things are a lot worse."

Master Walter came out of his corner, glaring. Hazel looked like I'd slapped her. Jean frowned at me. "Be careful about jumping to conclusions over events you have not witnessed."

I was taken aback. "Yes, sir, but—"

"And now, we must deal with Abertee's troubles. Thank you, Master Walter, Granny Hazel, for bringing this news." He bowed to them. "You have surely saved a life today, perhaps many." The smith nodded, mollified.

Hazel said, "And if we ever need to reach the Fire Warlock again, we'll come here first."

Jean shot a questioning glance at me. I said, "The clerk at the Guild Hall sent her to Flint. He told her to go away, they would get what they deserved."

"This is insupportable," he grated. "I will—"

"No, you won't." I jammed on my hat. "I will."

He frowned. "You are unlikely to have more success in changing Flint's mind than I have ever had."

I grinned. "I won't try. I'll tell the clerk and the manager at the Guild Hall what happened, and that you're furious." I waved at the maps I'd carried home. "And yes, the Fire Warlock is keeping me busy, dealing with exactly this sort of problem. If they direct visitors here to keep from angering the Fire Warlock, even Flint will have a hard time arguing with that, won't he?"

When I returned, Jean was scowling at images he had conjured up in the flames. I caught no more than a glimpse, not even enough to determine if the figures I saw were male or female, as he waved them away with a snap of his wrist.

I said, "I thought you were going to see the White Duke."

"I was acquainting myself with the earl's son, before approaching the duke. Forewarned is forearmed, as the adage goes, but I cannot say I am glad I did so." He grimaced. "Rarely have I had the misfortune of examining such an odious life, for all he was not yet twenty-one."

"Why? Show me what he was like."

"No. I cannot stomach it again. You would not stomach it even once."

"What could he have done that's worse than some things we saw in our travels? If you don't want to examine his life again, summarise it for me."

His eyes were cold. "It is unwise to do even that. Perhaps you are not yet mature enough."

Was he joking? His expression was distant and unreadable, without a hint of humour.

I set my jaw. "Beorn wants me to help him spot trouble brewing. It would help to know what a troublemaker could do that's so bad. Why won't you tell me?"

He shoved his chair backward and stalked into the fire. "Girl, you ask too many questions," he snapped, and vanished.

I stared into the fire with my jaw hanging open and my wand rolling on the floor. Jean Rehsavvy, the great Flame Mage, who encouraged curiosity and scholarship, thought I asked too many questions?

What could have led to such an uncharacteristic outburst? Some elusive memory nagged at me, but I could not drag it into the light. On the fourth or fifth time through the conversation with Hazel and Jean, the memory, triggered by Jean's comment I was not mature enough, finally surfaced.

Two years before, the Frost Maiden had refused to tell me the nobles' dirty little secret. My fists clenched of their own accord. I forced my hands open and wiped them on my skirt. Getting my breathing under control took a little longer.

Odd I should have forgotten. That unpleasant episode was the kind one tends to revisit, like picking at a scab, but I hadn't thought about it since... Since when?

Since Jean had worked magic on me to make me forget.

I ground my teeth and pulled my chair closer to the fire. Jean agreed with the Frost Maiden that I was too immature to handle some secrets, did he? Drown her. Drown him. I snapped my wand at the fire, and flames shot into the study. I snuffed fires in the hearthrug and nearest shelf, and forced myself to concentrate. Once I had the fire under control, I settled down in furious determination to uncover the secret they didn't want me to know.

Secrets

Three men on horseback, two wearing the White Duke's livery, trotted along a muddy path. The third man, Lord Edmund, looked ridiculous next to the two servants in their functional clothing. His fine garments had caught and torn in the gorse, and the mud the horses kicked up spattered his fashionable white trousers. I sighed, once again, over the idiocy of our ruling class.

Then I took a closer look, and was jolted out of the scene in the fire. I had seen Lord Edmund before. Two years earlier, in Gastòn, I had watched from the needlework shop where I waited for Claire, a palpable sense of menace growing with each step bringing him closer. I had grabbed the first excuse at hand to keep Claire from leaving the shop; I would have used her own embroidery to tie her up if I'd had to.

This menace had been Claire's brother-in-law? Oh, dear God.

Careful. I didn't know what he had done that could be so bad. Jean considered him loathsome, and if he came home and found me poring over Lord Edmund's life after he warned me away...

After locking myself in a guest bedroom, I wrapped the room in all the spells I knew against eavesdroppers before sitting down before the fire. And then I got up and went back to the library to collect the notes I'd made during our travels on locks against conspiracy magic. If a conspiracy was at work, I intended to not be part of it.

On a July day, the village in the Abertee hills should have been bustling with women doing chores or gossiping, and children playing, but not a woman or child was in sight. The only visible inhabitants were several men who drew together and glowered in silence as the three horsemen passed. The riders ignored them.

One of the lackeys pointed towards a farmstead a quarter mile from the village edge. "That's it. The Archer place."

Behind them, one of the village men said, "I'm going to fetch Granny Mildred. Somebody's going to need a healer soon."

The farm the riders approached was tidy and prosperous, with flowers in pots under the windows of an ancient stone house, and a yard hemmed in by a well-kept stone wall. On reaching a corner of the wall, Lord Edmund shouted, "Farmer!"

A mountain of a man walked out of an outbuilding, carrying a pitchfork, as the horsemen rode into the yard. Muscles bulged under the man's work shirt. I didn't need a description to guess this was a blacksmith.

Lord Edmund delivered his message. The smith, although obviously angry, made no aggressive move, only questioning the nobleman's authority to deliver the eviction notice. A grudging respect grew in me; he kept a better grip on his temper than I might have under similar circumstances.

Lord Edmund walked his horse around the yard, taking his time looking the place over. The smith watched him, with one cannonball fist clenching and unclenching on the pitchfork handle. Lord Edmund must have had the wit of a turnip. Even if the Fire Office had still shielded him, the blacksmith could have hit him hard enough to knock out all his teeth and make him see stars.

Lord Edmund said, "I hear you have a pretty sister. Where is she?"

The smith shifted to a two-handed grip on the pitchfork. "Gone fishing."

Lord Edmund dismounted and walked towards the house. "You're lying."

The smith bellowed, "You gave us the message, now get out. You've no right to do anything else."

Lord Edmund stopped with his hand on the door. "I will do as I please. You have no power to stop me." The smith, his path blocked by the two mounted servants, glared.

Lord Edmund said, "Don't you understand, simpleton? Or don't you know how to speak to your betters? Say 'Yes, sir.'"

"I know how to speak to my betters. You're not one."

The enraged nobleman ordered one of his flunkies to horsewhip the insubordinate cur. While they scuffled with the smith, Lord Edmund entered the house. I was still gasping at the wretch's barefaced cheek when he re-emerged, dragging a young woman by the arm. The smith pushed past the flunkies and charged for the house. Lord Edmund jerked the girl around and shoved her up against the wall, bringing the point of the sword to her throat. She stopped fighting. Her brother, an arm's length away, froze.

Tall and shapely, the girl would have been gorgeous if not for her expression of naked fear. Lord Edmund ogled her as if she was a tasty morsel instead of a decent girl from a respectable family, and sneered, "Perhaps this God-forsaken backwater is worth my time, after all." Lowering his sword, he stepped closer to her, and grabbed her breast with his other hand.

The blacksmith yanked him backwards. He fell in the mud, completing the ruin of his flamboyant clothes. He rolled to his feet and aimed a vicious, two-handed swing of the sword at the blacksmith's neck. The smith parried with the pitchfork, but the sword caught his arm and cut a long gash. As Lord Edmund came around for a second swing, the smith hit him, and he went down.

I blanked out the vision in the fire, and sat with my hands over my mouth, fighting down nausea. The fight was over. One punch, and Lord Edmund's head looked like a broken melon.

In spite of logic, I had been in total agreement with the smith and the terrified girl. I would have cheered the smith on if I'd been there in person. Lord Edmund had had no right to touch the girl as he had. Landing in the mud had served him right. There was no doubt in my mind either, that when he swung his sword at the smith, he'd intended murder. The Water Office might not agree, but the smith had fought back in simple self-defence.

But why had Lord Edmund said the visit might be worth his time? Groping the girl, as outrageous as that was, seemed insufficient compensation, and anything worse would have gotten him in trouble with the Water Guild.

After a few minutes, I picked up my wand again, to search for other episodes in Lord Edmund's life.

Lord Edmund and a servant rode into the yard of a small croft. The sweating servant said, "Ain't nobody there, milord. Ought we ride on?"

Lord Edmund said, "There is somebody here, or nearby. Look at the smoke from the chimney."

He dismounted and walked into the croft, which appeared deserted. He yanked a cloth off the table, sending crockery smashing on the floor, and revealing a young woman hiding underneath. He pulled her up by her hair and dragged her toward the bed. She screamed and fought, but he twisted her arm behind her and forced her down on the bed. I screamed with her, my body accepting what my conscious mind refused to acknowledge.

She clawed at his face. He beat her with his fists until she lay stunned, unable to fight back. As stunned as the girl, I watched as he yanked at her skirt, ripping it, and had his way with her.

I waved away the vision and vomited onto the hearth. After I got my stomach under control and cleaned up the mess, I curled into a ball on the guest bed, and lay there, trembling, while my disbelieving intellect reeled.

Only criminals and fugitives whose lives were already forfeit would dare take a woman, any woman, by force. For a man of wealth and position to commit rape? Unthinkable. That happened in less civilized countries, which didn't have the Fire Warlock protecting their women and children.

What a lie that was.

But Frankland didn't need the Fire Warlock for this. The Water Office handed out swift and severe penalties for rape, in one of the few times it sided with commoners. Everyone knew the tales from Frankland's early days where the Frost Maiden castrated noblemen, even dukes and princes, who had raped innocent young women. The penalties were less extreme for raping married women and widows, a fact that annoyed me, but even those were harsh enough to discourage all but the insane and desperate.

Why was Lord Edmund still aggressive enough to be groping the Archer girl?

I dragged myself back to the fire, certain there was more about Lord Edmund I needed to know.

Lord Edmund had been a snake of the worst sort, taking pleasure in other people's pain. He had bullied and tormented everyone he outranked, and had committed at least five rapes. Not all of young women either—in one case, when he couldn't find his intended victim, he'd abused her younger brother. By noon I had had all I could take of the wretched swine. I leaned against the footboard of the bed, heaving and retching, although my stomach had long since emptied.

That blacksmith had done the country a service. I would have executed Lord Edmund without qualms if he were not already dead. How had he gotten away with what he'd done?

Jean and the Frost Maiden were right. I wasn't mature enough for this. Maybe I never would be.

W hy hadn't anyone Lord Edmund abused lodged a complaint with the Water Guild? I returned to the life of the young woman I had first observed him rape. Shortly after he left, the Archer girl arrived, and found her still huddled in the corner, sobbing. The Archer girl took her to an Earth Guild house, and while a wizened earth witch treated the woman's injuries, the Archer girl said, "I stopped in to see Fiona on my way home from Crossroads. She hasn't stopped crying long enough to tell me anything."

"Fiona, stop that crying. Now," the old woman snapped.

Fiona gasped. Her tears dried.

"Who did this to you?" the witch said.

"It was the earl's son who's friends with the duke's son," Fiona said. "I was in town a week ago visiting my cousin. I saw him and asked who he was. My cousin said he was a dog making life hell for the duke's servants."

The witch had sagged at the words 'earl's son.' She mumbled, "I was afraid of that. The servants aren't the only ones he's making life hell for."

The Archer girl said, "What's his name?"

"Lord Edmund something-or-other."

"That'll do," the Archer girl said. She went to the door. "It's enough for the Water Guild to find him."

"Stop," the witch barked. "You can do that later. Right now, help me get Fiona into bed. She needs a good night's sleep as much as anything."

Fiona said, "I won't be able to sleep, Granny Mildred."

"Sure you will. When I tell you to sleep, you'll sleep. Got that? Now let's go." Granny Mildred led the way down the hall with a firm grip on the younger woman's elbow.

The witch and the Archer girl returned a few minutes later. The witch sat down by the fire and the girl went to the door.

"Come back here," Granny Mildred said. "You can't go to the Water Guild."

The girl stopped in the doorway, but made no move to return.

"I mean it. Close the door. Sit down."

The girl closed the door and sat down on the settle with her arms crossed, looking rebellious.

The witch said, "Now, then, Maggie, you think if you go to the Water Guild, they'll freeze his balls off, right?"

"That's what the stories say."

"That's the way it used to work. Mostly, it still works that way. I'm going to tell you a secret. It doesn't work that way anymore for nobles raping commoners. If Fiona goes to the Water Guild and accuses that louse of rape, he'll turn right around and accuse her of defaming him. He'll win, and every cent she and everybody else in her family makes for the rest of their lives will go to paying off the fine the Water Guild will slap on her."

Maggie and I both stared at the old woman in horror.

"You don't believe me, do you?" Granny Mildred said. "Let me tell you about Baron D'Armond's rape trial."

Once again I was jolted out of the scene in the fire. The things I'd already seen had made me sick, but this news was a new kick in the gut. Baron D'Armond was Lesser Campton's overlord. I remembered the gossip about the trial, and how everyone had laughed at the girl making the accusation.

I wouldn't listen to this second hand. With a shaking wand, I went searching for Baron D'Armond.

It was as Granny Mildred said. Baron D'Armond's history showed him raping the girl, but the rape was not shown at the trial; she was convicted of defamation and ordered to pay him one hundred franks for having the audacity to bring such a baseless charge. One hundred franks! An impossible sum for a family who counted their wealth in shillings and pence.

After the trial, the girl spent two days in a state of stupefied horror, seemingly oblivious to both her neighbours' jeers and her family's distress. On the third morning, she walked out of the house, through the fields, and straight into the river.

She didn't come out.

I lay face down on the guest room bed. All the certainties of Frankish life had turned into will-o'-the-wisps. There was no solid ground under my feet, only quicksand.

What would I have done in that girl's place? Of all the ways to kill oneself, drowning was the worst I could imagine.

Horizontal rays of sunlight struck the far wall. Hiding in the guest room wouldn't solve any of my problems. I was a warlock and had to face facts. Even facts the great Flame Mage Jean Rehsavvy didn't want me to face. I had lost my breakfast, skipped dinner, and had no appetite for supper. He would be expecting me at the aerie for the evening's practice, and I had no energy for it.

I flicked my wand at the fireplace, returning to the conversation between Granny Mildred and Maggie Archer. Tears slid down Maggie's cheeks.

The old earth witch said, "This is the big secret the magic guilds don't want you knowing. There's a lot of magic at work to keep commoners and noblewomen from finding out. I guess they figure law and order would break down if all the commoners knew. And the noblemen don't want their mothers, wives, and sisters finding out. There'd be hell to pay if they did."

Maggie said, "But you told me."

Mildred shrugged. "You and Fiona were going to find out one way or another. I reckon it's better you find out from me than from a trial, and I've got enough magic to let an occasional mundane in on it."

Maggie said, "What's to keep me from going and telling everybody else I know?"

"Won't do any good. The magic has caught you now, too, and you don't have the magic to expand the net. If you tell anybody that doesn't already know, either they're not going to believe you, or what comes out of your mouth won't be what you wanted to say.

"But why? How did it get this way?"

The old witch chewed on a thumbnail. "Damned if I know. A water witch told me what she thought, but I don't know if I trust her. It makes sense, and I wish it didn't. I like fire wizards more than I like water witches."

"What did she say?"

"She blamed it on the Fire Warlock. The one that just retired, that is."

An Honourable Man

I flew through the kitchen, grabbing bread and a chunk of cold ham. I was still forcing the food into my protesting stomach when I arrived at the aerie.

"Hey, Lucinda," René said, "Are you okay?"

"No. Leave me alone."

"But I—"

"René," Jean said. "It is time to begin. You first."

René looked affronted, but after another glance at me, shrugged and left me gnawing at my tasteless crust.

When it was my turn, I stood on the rim of the crater with my hands in Jean's, and struggled to focus my attention on getting through the practice session safely. It was hopeless. After all the pain I had witnessed and experienced that day, all I wanted to do was hurt someone.

Not just anyone. I wanted to hurt the man with me—the man who, at that moment, seemed a stranger, not my loving husband. Ignoring everything I'd learned about safety in the past two years, I pulled on Storm King as hard as I could. Harder than I'd ever done before.

Some jerk splashed water in my face. I sputtered and snarled. My eyes were dazzled, but I made out Jean and René leaning over me. I lay on the rocks, aching all over, as if I'd been on the rack.

"Wow, Lucinda," René said, "that was awesome. You made real lightning. Not like Jean or Beorn—it was just a little bit that didn't reach the ground—but it was real. I saw it."

Jean's eyes glittered. "Indeed, and almost killed yourself. If you had

147

done that on your own, rather than through me, you would have. Do not ever do that again."

I glared at him. He was uninjured. It wasn't fair.

They left me lying on the ground, and went on with René's exercises. After a while Jean came back and knelt beside me. "I sent René home. We are through for tonight."

I rolled over and pushed myself upright, ignoring his outstretched hand. "One more. I've only done one tonight."

"One was more than enough," he said, taking my arm. I grabbed his other arm and pulled on Storm King. The feeble spurt that was all I could produce in my exhausted state darkened my vision, and I fell. He caught and held me. I pushed against him, but he wouldn't let me go.

"Stop it," he rasped. "You should thank me for not letting you fall on the rocks, and from blocking a surge of power that would have killed you. Your reserves are gone. You cannot hurt me. You can only hurt yourself."

I sagged against him as he called up the fire to take us home. In our bedroom he steered me towards the bed. I grabbed the bedpost to keep from falling, and lurched towards the wall. Leaning against it for support, I staggered down the hall and into the guest bedroom. I locked the door behind me, and toppled face down onto the bed.

Jean had been wrong. A glance at his face had confirmed that. I had hurt him more in our bedroom than I could ever have hurt him calling down the lightning.

I woke from a muddled nightmare of Lord Edmund stalking Claire as a hunter stalks a deer, and lay for a time in a state of half-wakefulness, wondering why I was lying on the bed with my clothes on. I hadn't even kicked off my shoes.

Hunger forced me awake, and I shuffled towards the kitchen. At the foot of the stairs, lamplight streamed from the open door of Jean's study. I would have to pass the door to get to the kitchen. I retreated and descended the servant's stairs. A ham-and-four-egg omelette, several slices of melted cheese on toast, and half a pint of fresh strawberries comforted my body. My soul was not comforted at all.

The hall clock struck two. The lamp still burned in Jean's study. What could I say to him?

I sat down before the kitchen fire, determined to take my mind off Jean by answering a less important question. How had Claire, with a milksop of a husband, avoided Lord Edmund's attention?

"The wench was pretty, and I wanted her." Lord Edmund, aged about sixteen, was on his feet, sweating, before an older man in an upholstered armchair. "I wanted her so bad, I thought I'd die if I didn't have her."

"So why didn't you pay her?" the older man snapped. "Or even better, seduce her and have her for free? You're good-looking enough—why couldn't you do that?"

"I tried, but she kept saying she was respectable, like she thought she was somebody, but she was just a commoner. I got tired of her playing hard to get, so I offered her money, and she slapped me. I had to make her pay for that."

"So, you let a chit of a girl get you into real trouble. If you'd handled it better, it would have just cost you some pocket money. Now it's likely to cost me a purse full of gold to buy her and her father's silence. I should take it out of your hide, you ungrateful whelp."

The third man in the room, Lord Richard, listened to this exchange with hooded eyes. "Why bother?" he said. "Let them take him to the Frost Maiden. She'd teach him to behave himself, where you couldn't."

"No! Anything but that," Lord Edmund pleaded. He dropped to his knees and tugged at the older man's sleeve. "Please, Father, you will pay the hush money, won't you? I'll do anything you want, just don't let them—"

"Will you swear," Lord Richard said, "to never—"

"Shut up!" the earl said. "You are both damned fools. The stories about the Frost Maiden gelding gentlemen are nonsense—lies to keep the commoners quiet."

Lord Edmund gaped. "You mean I was worried over nothing?"

Lord Richard glared at his father. His father glared at Lord Edmund. "Not over nothing, fool. We have to keep this quiet."

"Why? What will happen if they take me to court?"

The earl shrugged. "You wouldn't even get a slap on the wrist. The girl would have to pay a trifle for slandering you, that's all. That keeps the Queen and the duchesses happy—if some tart has a duke's baby, the duchess will believe the wench seduced him, not the other way around."

Lord Edmund sprang to his feet, eyes alight. "Well, if that's all…"

149

Lord Richard glowered. His father grabbed a cane hooked over the chair arm and pounded it on the floor. "It's not all, you idiot. I'm trying to line up good marriages for both of you, but the girls' fathers know what goes on. The best families will cut us dead, the bastards, if they hear you've been through a rape trial. His grandfather—" He waved at Lord Richard. "—doesn't have a high opinion of you or me to start with. Do you think his cousin's fortune will go to you if the old man suspects? Get out of here. I don't want to see you again until this mess has quieted down."

Lord Edmund bolted with a grin on his silly face. His brother watched him go with a corded neck and bared teeth.

The earl tottered towards the door with his cane. "Come on, Richard. It's time you met my bastard nephew in the Water Guild. We'll send him to convince these troublemakers they don't want to press rape charges."

His elder son didn't move. "You owe me an apology."

The earl turned an astonished face towards his eldest son. "What for?"

"You could have summoned your nephew, and gotten him to extract a binding promise from Edmund that he would never assault a woman again. Instead, you gave him free reign to do as he pleases, knowing you'll pay to cover it up. And you called me a fool."

Two men faced each other, identical scowls strengthening the family resemblance. The earl, propped up on pillows in a huge bed, snarled at Lord Richard standing at its foot.

"Edmund's wedding to Lady Jane is off. You told your grandfather about Edmund, didn't you? Where's your respect for your family?"

His son said, "I have more family feeling towards my cousin Jane than I do towards Edmund. She's a sweet girl. I couldn't stand to see her in that brute's power."

"How will either of you make an advantageous marriage? You ruined your best chance by offending the Green Duke's daughter."

"You are mistaken. Edmund poisoned her affection for me."

"Nonsense. You blame all your problems on your brother."

"No, I blame most on my father."

The earl grabbed his cane and flailed at his son. "I'll teach you to be impertinent, you ungrateful whelp."

Lord Richard, out of reach, didn't budge. "And I'm not interested in your ideas of an advantageous marriage. The Red Duke's daughter Susan has a tongue like a whip, and Lady Margaret makes me cringe. I'll marry someone I won't mind coming home to, even if she is a commoner."

The earl dropped his cane. "I knew I shouldn't have let you spend so much time with your grandfather. He's given you some damned impractical ideas. Are you talking about a real girl, or are you dreaming again?"

His son flushed. "A real girl."

"A penniless nobody?"

"She has no money, but she's related to top-ranking members of the Fire Guild."

"I don't believe it. If she were, she wouldn't be penniless. Forget the wench—I won't let you marry beneath you."

Lord Richard walked away. "You can't stop Edmund's criminal behaviour. You'll not stop me from acting honourably."

"I could send Edmund to call on her. Would you still want her after that?"

Lord Richard froze with his hand on the doorknob, his shoulders hunched as if his father had struck him in the back. After a long pause, he spoke without turning around, his voice thick. "You win. I'll court Lady Susan."

The earl relaxed into the pillows. "Good. Make the girl your mistress. That wouldn't be a bad thing, if she's more pleasant than Lady Susan."

His son glared venom over his shoulder. "Fine. But remember this— my grandfather's opinion of you is much too high."

I was an idiot. I had made assumptions, and Claire would pay for my mistakes. Even with Lord Edmund dead, she would be in danger while her father-in-law lived. Any man wicked enough to threaten his son's sweetheart with rape would have other nasty tricks up his sleeve.

I owed Lord Richard an apology for the threatening letter I had written, but what could I say that wouldn't give away what I knew? Or that wouldn't make Claire feel worse than she already did?

Problems swarmed like locusts. I batted that one aside for the moment and went on watching Lord Richard.

"You would turn your own brother over to the Water Guild?" The water wizard gawked. "Have you considered what that would do to your family's reputation?"

Lord Richard looked as if he was sucking a lemon. "It would ruin it. I abhor such desperate measures, but he's a menace to every woman in Gastòn. Besides, he's making my life hell."

The wizard shook his head. "I'd love to make an example of him, but it won't work. The stories you've heard are true. We can't inflict any punishment on him, and a trial would make life unbearable for any woman brave or stupid enough to bring a complaint."

"Isn't there anything someone can do? If not the Frost Maiden, perhaps the Fire Warlock?"

"As long as he's only attacking women in your family's domains, the Fire Warlock can't interfere. If he attacked women in some other lord's domains, and if that lord complained, then the Fire Warlock could get involved. Those are a couple of big ifs, and I don't know what the Fire Warlock could or would do even then. King Stephen could stop your brother." The wizard shrugged. "But he won't."

The wizard leaned closer, his voice dropping. "You really want my advice? Hurry up and get married. Make a son as fast as you can, so he's out of the line of succession. If you think he's bad now, imagine how much worse he'll be if he's ever earl."

Lord Richard's long, thin face would tend towards the morose or melancholy even at the best of times. This was not the best of times. In his privileged life, few would have dared scold him, but he sat silent, head bowed, while the earth witch berated him.

"I don't like your kind. I don't like your brother. I don't like you. You're all the same, all you think about is sex, and taking advantage of poor women who don't have magic shielding them. If you can't get what you want for free, you take it by force, and turn the unlucky girl into a laughingstock for not being able to fight off somebody twice her size."

She flung open the boarding house door. "I'll not help you or any of your kind. Not with Claire; not with any of my girls. If the Fire Office wasn't shielding you, I'd put a curse on you for having the frostbitten gall to ask for my help seducing her. Go away."

Lord Richard didn't move. "My apologies, Mrs Wetherby. I did not explain myself well. I want to protect Miss Nelson, not seduce her, and you're supposed to be the best hand in Gastòn at the Earth Guild's protective spells."

The witch sneered. "Your manor is crawling with guards. You don't need my help to protect her."

"Those guards answer to my father. Without orders from the earl, they'll do nothing to protect her from my brother, my father's favoured and over-indulged son."

"So? All the more reason I should talk her out of having anything to do with you."

"And if you do, then what? Will she marry that annoying silversmith who's also courting her? If she marries a wealthy merchant or craftsman—you don't think she'll settle for anyone who isn't wealthy when she could have me, do you?—she'll live in the middle of town, almost under our eaves. Among the merchants we frequent. Don't delude yourself that my brother won't see her."

Mrs Wetherby's expression dissolved from contempt into horror. She closed the door, and dropped into a chair. "Go on. I'm listening."

"The only way I can see to protect her until Father dies, and the guards answer to me, is to ring her and her home around with protective spells like the ones you've put on this boarding house and your guests."

The witch growled, "Who told you about those?"

"It wouldn't be proper for me to tell."

"Why don't you talk the earl into sending your brother abroad for a few years? You can afford to let him tour the world."

Lord Richard's knuckles tightened. He stared out the window, away from the witch. "I don't know if that's enough. I've heard rumours about some of the other, lesser nobles. You would know better than I."

The witch stared at him through narrowed lids. "The spells you'd need for year-round, complete protection would cost you. A lot."

"How much?"

She named a figure that made me whistle. My estimate had been a mile low. Lord Richard didn't blink. "I'll pay it."

"Not so fast. I still don't trust you. If you want to convince me you're really trying to protect Claire and not just get on my good side, you'll pay in advance—"

"Of course."

"—regardless of who she decides to marry."

Lord Richard buried his face in his hands.

"And," the witch went on, "you'll pay for the spells' upkeep for ten years."

I had to strain my ears to hear Lord Richard. "I will pay for their upkeep for the rest of her life. Because, if she marries someone else, I couldn't bear to ever see her again."

Jean's study was dark. I sat down at his desk in the still-warm chair. A strong sense of his presence surrounded me in the quiet room.

Would sleep come for him? Probably not.

Were Claire and Lord Richard sleeping well? He might sleep better now with his brother dead, but his wife didn't understand what he had done for her. Not a good basis for a happy marriage.

I crossed my arms on the desk and laid my face down on them, tears seeping out unheeded. I wept for myself, for Claire, for all Frankland's women injured by this dreadful secret eating away like termites at the structure of our society. I even wept for Lord Richard, a decent, honourable, and intelligent man among a class I had had nothing but contempt for.

How many others had I misjudged?

How badly had I misjudged Jean? I had discovered about him…

What exactly had I discovered? That the Water Guild had spread a vicious rumour? Given the rancorous history between the two guilds, was that surprising? Why should I believe it?

I wouldn't believe it. I knew him better than they did.

He certainly knew me. Only a few days earlier I had acknowledged that if he had to force me to do something, he would order me not to.

As he had warned me away from Lord Edmund's life.

I raised my head, pulse quickening. By uncovering the secret on my own, with my locks in place, I was not part of the conspiracy. If he had answered my questions, the magic of the conspiracy would have trapped me, as it had trapped him.

I lit the desk lamp, and with a sense more of satisfaction than surprise, discovered the textbook on conspiracy magic lying in front of me. "Bless you, Jean," I whispered. "Sleep well. I love you."

I wiped my eyes, and opened *Engines of Lies* to the bookmarked page.

Cold Water

Dawn comes early in July. The darkness began to lift as I read at Jean's desk. The Fortress, a featureless grey wall in the growing light, dominated the view.

How tight was this conspiracy's hold on the Fire Guild? What would it take to break it, burn it, or cut through it?

I carried the book to the window and flipped to the spell I had read months earlier but had no use for then—a spell for making a conspiracy visible to the mind's eye: gossamer strands between members, gears, pulleys, and other couplings linking the strands, spinnerets extruding new lies. I cast the spell, and dropped the book.

The book hit my foot, but I didn't even swear. I leaned on the windowsill and rubbed my toe, unable to tear my eyes from the hideous tangle of wires and pulleys encasing the Fortress. No gossamer strands, these. Each connection was a cable thicker than Beorn's biceps.

I had delusions I could flick my fingers at that horror and it would disappear? I picked up the book and backed away from the window, trembling.

If the fifty-seventh Fire Warlock created that monstrosity, maybe the worst of it was here. I clutched at that mustard-seed of hope and walked through the fire to the bank of the Thames. I cast the spell again, and recoiled. The cables lay as thick here as on the Fortress. Strands of wire, thin in some spots, thick in others, spread out over London as far as I could see.

A park on a hill overlooking Gastòn provided a third vantage point. Again, cords entangled the whole city. I sank onto the dewy grass and wept.

My knowledge that the Water Office was broken had been intellectual, not emotional. Now I understood, with both heart and gut, why the Frost Maiden was willing to forfeit her own life to fix this cancer eating at Frankland from the inside. I could not abide this horror either. I had to act.

Despite the rising heat of a July morning, I shook from cold. If a conspiracy of this magnitude recognised me as a threat, and moved to silence me, I would stand no chance. Alone, I could do nothing, and had no one to ask for help. The older, wiser, and more powerful witches and wizards—Jean, Beorn, the Frost Maiden, even Mother Celeste—had known about this conspiracy for decades. They had not unravelled it. Had the men even tried?

With no conscious volition, I called up the fire, and stepped onto the causeway a hundred yards from the Crystal Palace. The glittering towers held no terror for me today.

The guards recovered in time to salute, and let me pass through unchallenged. Aside from the staff in the kitchen preparing breakfast, few were awake. I stood in the entrance to the Great Hall, waiting. The delay did not upset me, as I did not know what I would say, or even why I was there, except that I must see the Frost Maiden. I seized that thought and held on to it.

A groggy teenage water witch staggered into sight. I stepped in her way. "Excuse me…"

She shrieked and flattened against the wall.

I said, "I'm sorry. I must see Sorceress Lorraine as soon as it's convenient for her. Could you please…"

She jerked her head back and forth, sidled along the wall into a passageway, and bolted. An older, less volatile witch led me to the Frost Maiden's study, glancing over her shoulder every few feet.

A mirror in the corridor stunned me; I slouched and shuffled, my eyes were bloodshot with bags under them, and my face was blotchy from crying. I looked truculent and forty years old. No wonder the first witch had shrieked.

The Frost Maiden, alert and well rested, glided into the study a few minutes later, clad in a silk wrapper. With her blonde hair in braids over her shoulders, she looked seventeen.

She took in my appearance and started towards me with an expression of alarm. "My dear Locksmith, whatever is the matter? How may I help?"

She stopped an arm's length away, staring at the book I held. Expressions I could not read flashed across her face before settling into her usual cool detachment. A glance down showed *Engines of Lies* clutched to my chest with the title outward.

She took my arm and guided me towards a chair. "I see. No wonder you are distressed."

She understood. I collapsed into the chair she offered. I would not have to say anything that might alert the conspiracy magic to my outsider status. And I had made a decision. I had not known I had done so until that moment.

The Frost Maiden watched me in silence, her gaze giving nothing away. From her demeanour I could have been making a simple social call.

"Your Wisdom," I said, "How soon can the four guilds be ready to rebuild the Water Office?"

"Not less than six weeks. The end of August, or early September. Even then the Air and Earth Guilds will struggle, but we can live with, and repair later, mistakes in the spells they provide."

Six weeks. Not long enough. No, too long.

"Let's get it over with," I said. "Tell them I will release the lock on the first of September, whether they're ready or not."

Her expression altered, and she seemed as ancient as the sea. No excitement, no dread showed. Only acceptance, endurance, and relief. "I thought that must be why you came to see me. I am glad. Thank you."

I would have risen, but she stopped me with a touch on my arm. "A month and a half is an uncomfortable period, both too short and too long when one dreads an event at the end. You cannot spend all your time focused on releasing the lock, or you will go mad. When you are not at the Fire Warlock's beck and call, have you another task to occupy yourself?"

"Yes, ma'am, I'll—" I stopped, aghast at what I had nearly said. I hadn't admitted to myself until that moment my intention to dissolve the conspiracy. The room spun as I fought panic over how close I had come to disaster. It was madness to think such a thing—releasing the lock was dangerous enough, and I knew more about lightning than I did about conspiracies. It would be irresponsible to promise to unlock the Water Office, and then throw away my life on a wild goose chase.

I met her eyes, and gasped. The expressions that had flitted across her face earlier were back, and I read them with ease. Hope. Satisfaction. The room steadied as she held my gaze for a long moment. I would have traded my right hand for her advice, but the conspiracy ensnared her. I didn't dare ask. She wouldn't dare offer.

She said, "The Fire Guild has great power at its disposal, but your efforts tend to be abrupt and brief. Volcanic, one might say. Every warlock has a deep wellspring of anger, but it is not healthy for even the Fire Warlock to draw on that reservoir day after day, for weeks on end."

"Er, yes, ma'am."

"Undertakings requiring prolonged concentration and stamina tend to be the province of the Water and Earth Guilds."

During the war, Jean had held a besieging army at bay for months. Was she suggesting he didn't have stamina? Or that I didn't? I clenched my jaw. I would not lose my temper. Not before I understood what she meant.

"Frankland's greatest witches and wizards have been those, like Jean, whose temperaments span more than one guild. He is a torch, one cannot deny that, but there have been times when he seems made of the Earth Guild's marble. There is even a hint of ice in his soul."

Stung, I opened my mouth to protest. Closed it again, and steamed. I had glimpsed that ice, and been repelled.

"The coming month will be a hard one for you. You have extended the reach of your warlock's powers, but it is not enough. You need the Water Guild's talents of absorbing and soothing, or your outrage will destroy you before you can turn it on its proper target."

"Oh, right. You're suggesting I go down to the market in Quays and buy a water witch's talent? Assuming one was willing to sell."

"It cannot be bought and sold, or stolen. It must come from within, and be given freely. You, like Jean, have the ballast of cold reason and logic in your soul. If you did not, I could not offer you this gift." She held out her hands to me, water shimmering in her cupped palms. "The gift of cold water."

I stared at her hands, stunned. Was she trying to turn me into a water witch? Impossible. Would I end up in deep water? I might drown.

Nonsense. She was offering me power of a different sort than fire magic, and I would be a fool to turn it down. Dazed, I watched my own hands rise to clasp hers.

Even a warlock can die of thirst. I drank cool, sweet water—welcome relief after a trek through a scorching dessert. It soothed my hot face, my burning eyes. I did not understand it, but water flowed inside me, under my control, and I was in no danger of drowning.

When I had drunk my fill, I let go, clear-headed and refreshed. "Thank you."

She smiled. "It is a rare gift, not often given outside the Water Guild."

A gift with strings attached, no doubt, but one I would cherish. The sick dread that had plagued me for months had vanished. I was as serene as a mountain lake on a windless day.

I said, "I will do my best to be worthy of it."

"Your sleep will be less troubled, and you will be more patient. I do not know in what other ways the gift will help you; that is for you to discover, as it can only enhance what is already within you. The outer manifestations will fade as you fathom its depths."

Outer manifestations? I shrugged. The prospect didn't trouble me enough to inquire.

Intruder

The baked goods I started on my return from the Crystal Palace were almost done when the summons to an emergency meeting of the Fire Guild Council arrived just before noon. A middle-aged woman the footman announced as Mrs Schist arrived a few minutes later. A glance showed a drab mundane—not wide-eyed with terror, as most mundanes are on meeting a warlock, but nevertheless afraid. I had seen her before, but I couldn't remember where or when. I went on putting the final touches on the icing.

"Can it wait? I have a council meeting to go to."

She mumbled something. I said, "Speak up or step closer. I can't hear you."

She crept half a foot closer. "Yes, ma'am. I know about the council meeting. That's why Peter sent me. He told me to say he's sorry."

"What?" I dropped the spatula in the icing bowl and looked up. Marks on her shoulders and chest peeked out from the edges of her summer dress, but otherwise she was as ordinary a woman as I had ever seen. As if she worked at being anonymous.

She flushed. "Don't you remember? The Fire Warlock said he had to apologise before he could come back."

"He, who? Mrs Schist, what are you talking about?"

Her flush deepened. "My husband, Warlock Flint, flamed you…"

Aha. I had seen her before, many times, during the siege, but had never connected this mouse with Flint. I took a harder look at the marks on her shoulders. She had suffered serious burns, more than once. She tugged at her dress to hide the scars; more crisscrossed the backs of her hands.

So that was why Jean despised Flint. If I had not been under the water magic's calming influence, my blood would have boiled. Contempt must have shown in my face because the woman backed away, stammering.

I picked up the tray and walked towards the fireplace. "I'm not angry with you. I understand why he sent you rather than coming himself. Even he knows better than to lie to a warlock."

René was recounting the tournament in Thule to Master Sven when I walked into the meeting room with my tray of cinnamon rolls. Both spun around and backed away from me.

Master Sven said, "What the hell?"

"Lucinda, is that you?" René asked, in a voice pitched unusually high.

I set the tray down on the conference table. "Well, of course. Who else would I be?"

Jean's arrival forestalled an answer. He strode out of the fireplace and stopped dead. "Who are you," he rasped, "and why are you here?"

The hubbub of other warlocks arriving and reacting in a similar vein drowned out my protests. Flint and Jean, side by side, scowled at me. Flint shouted, "She doesn't belong here." Jean snapped, "Agreed." Both men did double takes, and recoiled. Jean blanched.

Ice gripped my heart. Typical fire wizard behaviour—reacting to an upset with anger. They were as obnoxious and overbearing as the Water Guild claimed.

Shocked, I backed out of the circle, and hit something solid. A pair of massive hands landed on my shoulders. "Shut up," Beorn bellowed over my head. "The Fire Office isn't fooled, even if you halfwits are. She's still a warlock. Lucinda, put your lock on."

"Yes, sir." I snapped the lock hiding my talents into place, and the noise died. Furious expressions gave way to relief and bewilderment.

Beorn said, "She's still our Lucinda, even if she does look like a water witch."

I twisted my neck to gawk at him. "I what?"

"Or, to be precise," Sven said, "our minds' eyes see a sorceress."

"A sorceress. Me?"

"Yeah, you," Beorn said. "Your warlock's fire looks like sunlight glinting off icicles instead of a flame." He shoved me into a chair at the table and sat beside me, one hand still on my shoulder. "Now let's have some of those goodies she brought. They'll prove she's still a fire witch."

I pushed the tray at Jean. "They're for Jean. You can have whatever he leaves."

He looked at it blankly for a moment. "Oh, I see. A peace offering? Thank you." He pulled apart one of the cinnamon rolls, and slid the tray down the table. "There are enough for everyone."

The colour was coming back into his face, but his expression was troubled. "I offer my apology, my dear, and an explanation. As Fire Warlock, I became so accustomed to seeing everything and everyone through my mind's eye it now dominates the physical one. Your physical form pleases me, but another witch could assume your appearance. Your magical signature identifies you, but it is so distorted I did not recognise you. A water sorceress's appearance in this Fire Guild bastion shocked me. I apologise for hurting you."

Except for Flint, the others around the table echoed his apology. The ice around my heart began to melt. Fire wizards do know how to apologise gracefully. They ought to, they have to do it often enough.

"She's showing her true colours," Flint growled. "I knew she didn't belong here."

Jean's glare would have intimidated anyone with any sense, but Flint began muttering a monotonous litany of insults. "Stinking fishwife. Empty boat for a brain."

I protested, "But you said a person's signature never changed."

"It does not change, no," Jean said, "but under a few extraordinary circumstances it may be temporarily distorted. This is one."

"But what is this?" A mouthful of roll muffled René's question. He ignored Sven's elbow. "What did she do?"

"It wasn't me," I said. "Sorceress Lorraine…gave me something."

"The gift of cold water," Jean said. "She has done you a singular honour."

"But what does it mean?" René asked. "And why?"

I drew in a deep breath. Several answers came to mind, none of them satisfactory.

Beorn's grip on my shoulder tightened. "That's why I called this meeting today. We got some God-awful bad news yesterday, so Lucinda and Lorraine put their heads together this morning. Come September first, whether anybody else likes it or not, we're going to take apart and rebuild the Water Office."

Flint and Sunbeam bounced to their feet, shouting. I looked to Jean for his reaction. He knew what it meant for me. He stared out the window, his expression unreadable.

At least I wasn't the centre of attention any longer. No one seemed to notice, or care, when I slipped away from the table and took a seat in a corner where I could survey the whole room.

I closed my eyes and once more worked the spell to see the extent of the conspiracy. I botched it twice because I knew I wouldn't enjoy the results. The third attempt worked, and the result was as bad as I had feared. Lies as solid as chain mail encased Beorn and Jean, almost blocking out the light of Jean's magical beacon and Beorn's bonfire. Flint was also shrouded, but to my astonishment Sunbeam was untouched.

That exasperating womaniser, who, as rumour had it, cheated on his long-suffering wife at every opportunity, didn't know about this?

Why should he? There were always women eager to throw themselves at a powerful man, even a married one. He had never needed to go hunting. There was no coercion in his good-natured soul. He had tried to flirt with me, before learning I was a warlock, and gave no indication of minding when I didn't respond.

But if I told him, he wouldn't care. I couldn't ask him for help; he wouldn't take the conspiracy seriously.

René, too, was free. He would help, but he had no more experience with conspiracies than I did.

And then there was Master Sven, Flame Mage. The entangling wires did not touch him, and his moral code was a good deal better than Sunbeam's alley cat ethics. He would take this conspiracy seriously, if anyone would, and would know what to do. I gazed at him, as enthralled as when I'd considered him a hot marriage prospect.

Beorn's bellow interrupted my silent prayer of thanks. "Too bad you don't like it. We're doing it anyway. Meeting's over. Get back to work."

René left first, through the fireplace, after giving me a long stare brimming with curiosity.

Hey, big sister, should we get you some pearls?

Don't be ridiculous. I'm still a fire witch, and if you don't believe me, wait until tonight. I'll blast your butt all the way to Blazes from the top of Storm King.

Yeah, right. Nobody answered my question. What did the Frost Maiden do to you, and why?

Later.

Later when?

We're meeting with Master Sven tomorrow morning for a session on spellcraft. I'll tell you both then.

Okay, but it better be good.

Better than you dare imagine.

Sven took the distraught Sunbeam by the arm and guided him towards the door. Sorceress Lorraine had spoken about water magic's powers of absorbing and soothing. Was there anything I could do to soothe the old warlock?

I went to him and took his hand, murmuring platitudes I'd learned at my mother's knee about fire wizards bringing change. He responded, his agitation diminished and flowed into me. Not to make me agitated, but rather to be absorbed into my reserves of power, to draw on whenever I needed.

Sunbeam squeezed my hand and thanked me. He and Sven left. I stood by the door in a daze.

Flint noticed me on his way out and checked. I snapped out of my daze. "It's your fault," he spat. "Women oughtn't to be warlocks. It's not natural. Or maybe," he said, shooting a sly look at Jean, "somebody who can do what you're supposed to be able to do, and I'm not saying you can, maybe that somebody isn't a woman."

"Maybe somebody who burns his wife," I said, "isn't a man."

He flamed me.

I saw it coming. I would have used my shields if I had not just had the experience with Sunbeam. But some other instinct took over, and I dropped the shields, letting him flame me unprotected. As with Sunbeam's agitation, the power flowed into me and I absorbed it.

I had no time to enjoy Flint's outraged stupefaction. Jean grabbed me and spun me around.

"Irresponsible idiot," he barked, giving me a hard shake with each word. "Where are your shields? Has your fighter training been for naught? When will you learn to protect yourself?"

I knocked his hands away. "It's the water magic," I said, in a voice a

Frost Maiden would have been proud of. "He didn't hurt me. He gave me power, and I could throw it back at him."

Jean was livid, his voice shaking. "Did you know that when he flamed you?"

"No, but I trusted the water magic."

"Fool." He turned away in a blind fury and slammed into the side of the fireplace. "A warlock cannot trust water magic, or a sorceress. Nor, apparently, one's own wife." He disappeared in a tower of flame so intense the room echoed with the noise.

The Warmth of a Warlock's Touch

In my ignorance, I had believed members of the Water Guild defective, lacking the natural warmth of Fire Guild members. Funny I had never noticed cold's defensive properties. Jean's fury, blocked by a wall of ice, did not hurt me. It wounded my pride a little, but that was all.

Cold reason argued Jean's anger was justified. I hadn't known what the water magic could do for me, and Flint could have roasted me. Cold reason also acknowledged it must have been a dreadful shock to see his fire witch wife transformed into a semblance of the water sorceress who had tormented him for more than a century.

Cold reason was cold comfort. Thunder rumbled from Storm King, and I winced. When the ice thawed, I would be a wreck.

I surveyed the conference room. Sunbeam's overturned chair. Jean's cinnamon roll, a single bite taken. The tray, still more than half full. Beorn sitting at the table, watching me.

"Where's Flint?" I asked.

"I tossed him out on his ear. Told him this time to apologise in person."

"He won't be back for a while, then."

"Years, if we're lucky."

I slid the tray along the table towards Beorn. "Have one. As peace offerings go, they didn't amount to much."

"Thanks," he said. "I like them, even if Jean doesn't. But I don't get it. You ought to be crying, or throwing lightning bolts, or something. What gives?"

I sat down across the table from him. The cinnamon rolls repelled me. I shoved the tray away. "It's the water magic, blocking things out. Or maybe I'm in shock. I'll cry, later."

"Looks like water magic to me. Now about that—"

"I know. I shouldn't have accepted her offer. It was a mistake."

"Like hell. What you did was damned impressive, and you're as cool as a water witch. If the Fire Office wouldn't throw a tantrum, I'd beg Lorraine to do it to me, too."

"Really? Why?"

"I could use some help keeping calm." He tugged at his beard for a while before continuing. "Lucinda, I've got something to show you. I showed this to Jean after you got back, but I figured you had enough problems then you didn't need to see it. I've changed my mind, and—"

I looked daggers at him. "I have less on my mind now?"

"No, and that's the point. When you're getting bad news, get it all over in one go. It's easier to deal with in one big steaming pile than a never-ending series of little piles."

I pushed away from the table. "I don't care. I'm sick of problems, and I'm sick of secrets. Keep it to yourself." I turned around before I was halfway to the door. "Forget I said that. I am a fire witch; I have to know."

He grinned and waved at the fire. "Atta girl. This was right after the riots. Watch."

An image of Beorn, the ruby in the Token of Office throbbing with red light, grew from the fire. He stepped out of a fireplace in the royal palace. King Stephen didn't give the exhausted Fire Warlock time to wipe the sweat from his face.

"What in God's name is happening?" The king's voice sounded an octave higher than normal, and shaky. "A mob killed the Black Duchess. Why weren't you in Blacksburg, protecting her?"

"I don't like what happened either," Beorn said. "But not even a warlock can be in two places at once. I was cleaning up the riot at the Green Duke's palace when the other one started."

"We're not supposed to have two riots at once," the king screeched. "We're not supposed to have any riots. You're supposed to be in charge of protecting the upper class and keeping the commoners under control. Why aren't you doing your job?"

Beorn's face, already flushed, turned a deeper red. He loomed over the king and barked, "Now see here. That's not my job. My job is protecting Frankland from its biggest threats. Right now those are idiots like the Black

Duke who wouldn't back down even after I chewed him out three times. If you want the nobles shielded you'd better start telling them to shape up, because the next time something blows up, I'll burn nobles as well as commoners."

The king screamed, "You can't do that."

"I can, if the Fire Office is convinced they're threats to the country's security, and after back-to-back riots it's gotten there. Besides, I'm sick and tired of protecting highborn halfwits."

"How dare you call my kinsmen halfwits? They're not responsible—"

"Damn right. They're the most irresponsible lot this country's ever seen, and shouldn't be in positions of authority to start with."

The king blinked at the Fire Warlock, his mouth open. "I meant they didn't cause the riots. You should find out who is responsible, and burn him."

Beorn and the king stared at each other for a long moment, nose to nose, before Beorn said, "Didn't your parents ever tell you to be careful what you ask for, for you will surely get it?"

The king looked unnerved. "What do you mean?"

Beorn's whisper was as hot as a glowing coal. "I mean, the unrest has been building ever since your great-great-something-grandfather stopped taking the oath to be the king for all the people of Frankland. You'd better reconsider what you just said."

"If things get worse," I said, "you think the Fire Office will decide King Stephen himself is the biggest threat to Frankland's security."

"Yep," Beorn said. "That's what I'm afraid of."

"Would that be so bad? Without Stephen, Crown Prince what's-his-name—"

"Justin."

"Yeah, him. He would become king, and he's too young to rule by himself. If we got someone with some sense—a mage, say—appointed as regent, things would get better, wouldn't they?"

Beorn shrugged. "Maybe. Maybe not. The nobles would only accept another noble as regent, and none of them other than the queen have any sense. But you're missing the point. What happens to Stephen?"

"We've put kings out to pasture before. Several went senile, and one went mad in his thirties."

169

Beorn shook his head. "The Great Coven made provisions for lunatics and simpletons. There's no way to force a king to retire, otherwise."

"But if the Fire Office makes you... Oh, no."

"Oh, yes. If the mandate to protect Frankland from its biggest threat comes into conflict with the mandate to protect the king, then what?"

My mouth went dry. The prohibition on making threats against the king was drilled into everyone in Frankland, from earliest childhood. No one dared risk the Fire Warlock blasting them to kingdom come for treason over a casual remark. Despite the July heat, I shivered, and shook my head.

"Well, then," he said, "If Stephen calls down the wrath of the Fire Office on his own head..."

I let out a gusty sigh. "Nicely put."

"These are Jean's words. He's better than me at figuring out what we can and can't say."

"Right. Go on."

"The opposing mandate may kill the Fire Office's agent for obeying the Fire Office's own orders."

I hugged myself until I stopped shivering. "But that's guesswork. We've never gotten into this situation before, so we don't know..."

"You sure?"

I jerked upright. "What? Well, of course. Even during the Scorching Times, when the records are most fragmentary, we have histories of the succession of kings. Most kings died of old age. There have been only a few that..." I stopped, mouth hanging open.

"That what?"

"The most recent Scorching Time started when the Fire Warlock and the king died together in one massive blast. We went through another pair of warlock and king before the Scorching Time ended."

"Yep. And since they didn't live to tell the tale, we don't know what led up to those blasts."

The water magic was helping me keep my temper, but it wasn't doing much for fear. I drew my legs up and curled into a ball. "Not another Scorching Time. Please, God, anything but that."

"Yeah, that's what scares me. Maybe we won't have to find out—it takes a hell of a lot to push the Fire Office that far. But when it does... I haven't named a successor."

"You should."

"René's only fifteen."

I said, "There aren't any good choices, are there?"

"No. René's powerful enough, but he's still a kid, and will be for years yet. Sunbeam can't understand how bad things are. He'd sit on his thumbs and do nothing until the Office forced him to burn the rioters or get charred himself. Flint…"

"He'd burn everybody he could, for the fun of it."

"In either case, law-abiding people die."

I said, "That leaves… He'll hate it."

"You got that right. If I weren't Fire Warlock, he'd torch me for suggesting it. I don't like it either, but there's no way around it."

"We don't know enough about the spells in the Fire Office's core. Will it work?"

"Of course it'll work. Jean named me his successor, and that worked."

"I meant, we don't know if I can wish him out of it a second time, when René's old enough."

"What? Oh, you thought… Forget it, Lucinda. None of the Offices will let someone serve a second time, unless there's no other qualified adult available."

"How do you know that?"

"It wouldn't take, when I tried to name him my successor."

"You what?" I yelped. "Damn you!"

"Whoa." He backed away. "Like I said, it didn't take."

"Good." Then the implications sank in. "Oh, no."

"There's nobody else, Lucinda. With a little ice in your veins, you'll be better at keeping your temper, and less likely to flame out than Sunbeam or Flint. And you'll have Jean around to help out."

The first time the suggestion was made that I might someday be Fire Warlock, I had fainted. I stayed upright this time. Fainting wasn't worth the effort.

He said, "When I talked to Lorraine this morning, she wouldn't tell me why she'd offered you the gift of cold water, but I figure she's trying to hold off the next Scorching Time, too. And she couldn't wait until you're Fire Warlock, because then the Fire Office wouldn't let her. I told her we owed her, big time. Never imagined I'd say that to a water witch."

"Can naming me your successor be revoked if—when—we get through this mess?"

He nodded, and I said, "Go ahead and do it, then. I'm so terrified of the unlocking, appointing me your successor won't make it worse. Odds are I won't live long enough for it to matter."

He intoned the magic words, then picked up his hat and walked to the fireplace. "I'm meeting the other Officeholders—we're going to tell King Stephen about your decision. You watch. From now on, keep an eye on all my dealings with him, so that you're ready, if it happens."

Fire bloomed in the middle of a courtyard, sending guards scattering. The Fire Warlock and Mother Celeste, arm in arm, stepped out of the fire. Behind them, Sorceress Lorraine and Enchanter Paul stepped out of a fountain. The quartet walked together in silence through an archway, past guards with rolling eyes, into an audience chamber where the king and his advisors waited. The stones in the Tokens of Office sparkled, sending flashes of coloured light bouncing around the room.

King Stephen sat on a throne on a dais with his advisors seated beside him. There were no other seats. The four Officeholders halted in a line before the dais. The king glowered. "You'd better have a good explanation for why the Fire Office shields failed Lord Edmund."

Beorn growled, "He wasn't shielded. Warlock Quicksilver and I showed you yesterday what happened."

Sorceress Lorraine said, "Your Majesty, an unshielded minor noble's death is of little consequence." She rode over the king's attempted interruption in her chilliest voice. "That is not why we are here. Both the Fire Warlock and I have warned you we intended to someday rebuild the Water Office. That day is upon us. On the first of September we will take it apart."

The king gaped at her. His agitated advisors cawed like a murder of crows. He waved them to silence. "You can't do that. This is Frankland. The whole world admires our stability. Nothing ever changes here."

Sorceress Lorraine said, "Your Majesty, change has already occurred. Two years ago, the Warlock Locksmith released a lock rendering the Water Office impotent. Now that it is stronger it is obvious to all the Water Office is broken."

"Then put that infernal lock back where it belongs. You, Fire Warlock, one of your witches released it. Make her put it back."

Beorn said, "No dice. The Water Sorceress and I can work together now, and it's better for the whole country. We're not going back to fighting each other."

The king snarled, "It's obvious why you don't want to. You're conspiring to steal power from me."

In her firmest parental voice, Mother Celeste said, "No, Stephen, this is not so. You, your father, and his forbears have given power away. The kings' greatest power came from the love and respect of his people. You forfeited that power when you abandoned the commoners."

The advisors' clamour grew to an uproar, with shouts about lies and nonsense. The king waved them into silence once more. He glared at Mother Celeste.

"You witches and wizards think you can make me take that damned oath, but I know better. I won't let your magic force me to do what you want. You still have to take orders from me. Your Offices demand it, even if you don't like it."

He leaned forward, teeth bared, staring at Sorceress Lorraine. "I order you not to touch the Water Office."

Her cool expression did not change. "This is not your domain, Your Majesty. The Office of the Northern Waters must be fixed, and I will do so."

"Then make sure you fix it so the riots stop," he screamed at her, "or the Fire Warlock will burn you and the whole Water Guild for threatening the country."

Beorn glared at him. Sorceress Lorraine shook her head.

The king leaned back and crossed his arms. "I order you to come to the royal palace when you're through with your so-called fixing, and show the nobles what you've done. Reassure them the country's not going to hell because of your tampering."

The four Officeholders exchanged glances in silent agreement.

Sorceress Lorraine said, "Very well, Your Majesty. But I warn you, an outcome that demonstrates the country is not going to hell may not be to your liking."

I turned back to the conference table and rested my head on crossed arms, fishing for any thought more pleasant than the problems lined up ahead.

My little boy. He was adorable, just learning to toddle. That cheerful thought didn't raise my spirits, because it was a shame he would soon have no mother. Even if I lived through the unlocking and destruction of the conspiracy, if I became Fire Warlock I'd have no time for him.

I must have slept, because the next thing I was aware of was Jean wiping tears from my cheek with a warm, gentle finger.

"My dear wife, once again I offer you my apologies. If you choose not to accept them I cannot blame you, but I trust in your generous nature to do so."

I turned my face away. "You said you couldn't trust me."

He stroked my hair for a moment before answering. "I was not rational. You should know a fire wizard's response to fear is anger."

"You've never said anything so cruel to me before."

"And I am ashamed of it. May I never do so again, but I have seldom been so frightened. The power you may absorb is limited. You do not know where the limit is, but I assure you at this time it is less than what Flint can throw at you. We are fortunate he reacted out of long-ingrained habit, and attacked with the feeble blast he uses for terrorising mundanes and lower-ranking members of the Fire Guild. If he had attacked with his full arsenal, you would be dead. Neither Beorn nor I would have had time to intervene."

Tears seeped from my closed lids and dribbled onto my arms. I was grateful for his touch. "I'm sorry."

"I worry more for your safety than I ever have for my own." His voice was as gentle as his hand on my hair. "I would protect you if I could, but to guarantee your safety I would have to confine you to the Fortress, and allow you out only in my company. You would never tolerate that lack of autonomy. To fulfil your destiny as a warlock, you must be responsible for your own well-being."

"Yes, sir," I sniffled. "At least you're still calling me a warlock. I was afraid you thought I'd turned into a water witch."

"Of course you are still a warlock. No water witch would have taken such a risk."

I sat up and scrubbed away the tears. Blew my nose. Studied his sombre face. "Thank you for coming to apologise."

His eyebrows lifted. "What did you expect?" The first gleam of humour I had seen in two days brightened his eyes. "How else could I reclaim my cinnamon rolls, with you standing watch over them?"

On Storm King that night we alternated calling down the lightning with probing for the limit on the power I could absorb. It seemed pitifully small, but Jean assured me it would grow with exercise. Little as it was, it stretched out my reserves, and I still felt fresh when Jean sent René home, nearly asleep on his feet.

At first Jean had seemed reluctant to touch me, but I must have imagined it, for he was in no hurry to return home. Holding his hands comforted me. Funny that in two years of marriage I had never noticed how warm they were.

We stayed at the aerie until long after the last glow of the summer sun had faded. Against the velvet blackness, relieved only by stars' diamond brilliance above and glowing lava pits below, I saw for myself a minuscule lightning bolt, like a baby dragon's belch, that I created.

When at last we went home, I was exhausted, but at peace. We were both pleased with my progress. The drama of the past two days seemed, for the moment, far away. I sat on our bed and began to undress. Jean watched me with a smile in his eyes.

I patted the bed beside me, as I had done many times before. "Help me out of my shift. It's a struggle by myself."

He didn't move. "I have seen you snatch that garment over your head with one hand. You do not need my help."

I dropped my hands into my lap and studied him. "What's the matter?"

He came closer, and cupped my face in his warm hands. "My dear, the outer manifestations of Lorraine's gift are still upon you. You are cold to my touch."

I reached up to grasp his hands. He pulled free. I said, "It doesn't matter, does it?"

"It does. I will keep my wedding vows, even in the midst of illusion. If I am startled out of sleep by a woman I cannot discern is my warm wife, my reactions may be instinctual and violent."

I flinched. His uncontrolled reactions had nearly killed me once; I had no desire to experience them again.

"Your safety is paramount." His lips brushed my forehead. "I pray you will understand. Goodnight."

He walked out and closed the door behind him. Only after the door of the guest room down the hall clicked shut did I lie down and bawl into my pillow.

Damn Lorraine. She never did me this much damage as my enemy. And this water magic was supposed to help me sleep, was it? Crying myself to sleep wouldn't be very soothing.

Racking sobs gave way to sniffles. The tears I shed merged with the trickles of tears other women hurt by their men had shed. The trickles became a rivulet, then a stream. The rippling water's music soothed me, and I relaxed towards slumber. The stream flowed towards the sea, where a boat lay in the shallows, waiting for me to step in.

I sat bolt upright in bed, yelling. "I'm a fire witch, goddamit. No boats. Anything but a boat."

Geez, big sister, what the hell was that? You scared the crap out of me.

I leaned against the headboard, panting. Stampeding bulls thundered in my veins.

Sorry, little brother. That was the water magic trying to rock me to sleep in a boat. God almighty. No wonder you yelled. At least that proves you're still a fire witch. Thank God for small favours. Go back to sleep.

I lay down and cursed at the water magic. How long before my pulse would return to normal? Would I ever get to sleep? I was red-hot, like a burning log in a kitchen fire.

And like a kitchen fire, I subsided as the magic banked the fire for the night, covering me up and tamping me down so I couldn't burn too fast. With a sigh, I let go of the anger, until only glowing coals and embers that would keep until morning remained.

I was asleep within minutes, and woke refreshed and alert after a night of uninterrupted, dreamless sleep. Sorceress Lorraine's gift had benefits, after all. I cast about with my mind's eye, and saw the household in good order. René sprawled half-on, half-off his bed as if he'd launched himself from the fireplace and fallen asleep before he landed. Servants sleepwalked through early-morning chores. The maddeningly pert nursemaid responded to Edward's cry for food. In the kitchen Jean wolfed down a plate of bacon and eggs…

I scrambled into a dressing gown and galloped down the stairs. "Jean, wait."

He mopped up the last of his eggs with toast and held out his mug. "I cannot stay, I am needed in Blacksburg."

I grabbed the coffeepot off the hob and poured. "I know, but I have a question. Yesterday, Beorn told me what else was bothering you…"

He had been about to swig the coffee, but stopped with the cup almost to his lips, eyebrows drawn together. "Did he? What did he say?"

"That you're worried about losing him. What would happen if…"

His expression relaxed, then became inscrutable.

I shouted, "What other secrets are you keeping from me?"

He drained the cup of its scalding contents and handed it to me, aiming a perfunctory kiss at my cheek as he passed, and bussing my ear instead. "Such a fervid imagination, fancying secrets everywhere."

The mocking laughter I heard as I hurled fire after him did come from my fervid imagination. He was miles away when the flames hit the back of the fireplace.

Brotherly Love

"Master Sven, I need your help with a magical problem," I said. "My help?" He grabbed a stack of books from a chair and shoved them onto a corner of his desk. "Please, sit down. Let me tidy up a little."

René moved books from the window embrasure to the stack on the desk and squirmed into the spot where they had been. I tipped the teetering pile of books and slid a penknife and a piece of chalk out from under it.

Sven reached for the penknife. "I thought we were meeting in the classroom, or I would have straightened up."

He should have straightened up his study years ago, but I held my tongue. "Yes, I need your help—yours and René's, I mean. I didn't want anyone to overhear us, so I thought your study would be a better place to talk. Do you mind if I use magic against eavesdroppers?"

There was no trace of foreboding in his expression. "Not at all. Go ahead."

I called up a barrage of spells and locks against eavesdroppers and conspiracies. For good measure, I even threw in a spell to baffle lip-readers.

René watched with growing excitement, Sven with growing alarm. "Good grief, Lucinda, what's this all about? Let me guess—you're confessing you really are a spy from the Empire who's stolen all Warlock Quicksilver's secrets?"

"Don't be silly," I snapped. "But it is about secrets." I paused and took a deep breath.

René said, "You're going to tell us why the Frost Maiden—"

"Sorceress Lorraine, you mean."

"Yeah, her. Why she gave you the gift of cold water. Is that the secret?"

"No. Er, yes. Maybe. It's to help expose the secret. Be patient, I'll get there. Sven, you're a mage—you do know something about conspiracies, don't you?"

Pride warred with caution and curiosity in Sven's expression. "A bit. I did a paper on them at university, and I've started or been a member of several."

The vision of that tangle stretched over London flashed before me. I recoiled. "You what?"

Sven's eyebrows rose. "What did you expect? They're fun."

"Fun?"

"Well, yes. At any time there are usually several running at the Fire Guild School."

I gave him a frosty stare that would have made a water witch proud. "If there are you should inform the school staff so they can put a stop to them."

He snorted. "The staff put up with them because they're good practice with theory-heavy magic. The conspiracies are usually childish attempts at hiding schoolboy pranks, like putting frogs in the housemaster's bed, or sneaking midnight snacks into the dormitory. The Guild Council always has somebody, right now that's me, keeping an eye on them so they don't get out of hand."

"Oh," I said, crestfallen. "I had no idea."

"Obviously."

René said, "I knew about them. Tom and Matt ragged on me all the time about the things I missed by not going to the guild school." He hefted his wand and began target practice on a line of roosting pigeons outside.

"They're safer, too," Sven said, "than the mundane variety, since they don't usually need to use violence to enforce keeping the secret."

I shrugged. "If you say so. They just don't seem like fun to me. I'd be happy to expose the one I'm a member of."

Sven's eyebrows rose again. "Really? You're in at least two. Which would you expose—the Fire Warlock's secret, or that you don't have to be a fire witch or wizard to use one of those diabolical weapons known as firearms?"

I shuddered. "Neither one."

"That's reassuring."

"I had forgotten both of those."

"So, what's the third one?"

"I can't tell you."

Sven looked smug. "Meaning it's one I don't know about. Giving me a challenge, are you?"

René thought at me, *You mean the one about the Locksmith's warning, right? Right.*

I said, "No. At least, I didn't mean to. That one isn't important, and I'm sure you could find out if you wanted to. It's obvious you know a lot more about conspiracy magic than either René or I do. I bet you even know how to expose one you're not a member of."

His smug expression deepened. "I do."

"That's why I need your help. There's a much more important, dangerous secret that I want to expose."

Sven looked sceptical. "Important? Dangerous? Why are you asking me for help instead of Warlock Quicksilver?"

I slipped crossed fingers under my skirt. "Haven't you seen how busy he is? He dashed out of the house this morning without even a peck on the cheek. I can't waste his time with this."

René, lounging in the window, gave first me and then Sven a sharp glance, before twisting around. Rapid bursts of flame led to a raucous chorus of angry bird screams.

Sven snapped, "Stop that infernal noise." He frowned at me, fingers drumming on the table. "What's the nature of the conspiracy?"

"I can't tell you about it until you promise to help."

"Nothing doing. I'm not buying a pig in a poke."

René flamed pigeons while I considered what would be safe to say. Sven was the most cautious fire wizard I knew, and I couldn't afford to scare him away, or put him in danger. But if he refused to help, I would be in a pickle. "The noblemen, the king, they don't want the secret exposed."

"What else?"

I wiped sweat from my face. "That's all I dare tell you without a promise."

René pivoted to face me. "I'll help. Promise."

Sven slammed his palm on his desk. "For God's sake, René, when will you learn to be more careful? It's dangerous for a wizard to make promises, and the higher-ranking you are the more dangerous it is. Nasty surprises can turn up anywhere, so a promise is risky even when you know what's involved. God help you if you don't."

René shrugged. "You just said nasty surprises can turn up anywhere, so it doesn't matter if I don't know what I'm getting into, does it?"

Sven glowered at him, nostrils flaring.

"Besides," René said, "Lucinda already told us she and the Frost Maiden—Sorceress Lorraine, I mean—want it exposed and the aristocrats don't. That's good enough for me."

I beamed at him. "Thanks."

"Interesting things happen around you. I don't want to miss out."

Sven looked apoplectic. I lurched to the window and threw a few blasts in the direction of the squawking birds, as an alternative to hugging and kissing the grinning boy. Behind me, Sven slammed books around and muttered to himself. I waited. Nothing I could say would improve matters, and curiosity would win—he was, after all, a fire wizard, and a mage.

"It's obvious you two naïfs need my help. You're both asking for trouble—serious trouble—without someone with sense keeping an eye on you. I will not make a blind promise. All I'll promise is that I'll help if, and it's a big if, it's important enough to run the risk for. And I'll decide, not you. Is that clear?"

"Clear and reasonable," I said, and kissed him on the temple. "Thank you. I'm happy to let you make up your own mind."

Sven didn't seem to find that reassuring. "Sit down," he snapped. "Stop looming over me. So, what is this conspiracy about?"

I hesitated, uncertain where to begin. "Before I tell you that, maybe I should tell you who else is involved, besides the nobility."

He shrugged. "Fine. Go ahead."

"To start with, there's Mother Celeste."

He gaped at me.

René added, "And Quicksilver and Arturos."

Sven choked.

I said, "Plus Sorceress Lorraine, Enchanter Paul…"

"Good God, woman," Sven exploded, "are you trying to get yourself killed?"

"No. That's why I'm asking you for help."

He glared at me, breathing heavily. After a moment he turned his scowl on René, still grinning in the window seat. "You two played me for a fool. You're in on it."

"Am not," René said. "She hasn't told me anything she hasn't told you."

"Then why did you say Quicksilver and the Fire Warlock?"

"Quicksilver too busy for Lucinda? Get real. And you've got a big head if you think she'd ask you first about something dangerous. She'd go to Quicksilver, then Arturos. She didn't, so she couldn't."

Sven half-rose from his chair and leaned across his desk until his nose was inches from René's. "So you figured that out, and still went ahead and made a blind promise to help her with this suicidal mission, whatever it is? I thought you were smarter than that."

"Look," René said, with the air of explaining something to a six-year-old, "Lucinda's going to do what she's going to do whether we help her or not. If she goes and gets herself killed, the whole country's done for. Do you want to explain to the Fire Warlock after she's dead you could have helped but didn't? I don't. I figure everybody's safer with all three of us in on it."

Sven sank back into his chair without taking his eyes off René. "Go on, then. I'm listening. Tell us the whole thing."

"Impossible," he said, when I was through. "I don't believe it."

"I do," René said. "Some of the things I've heard since we got back, when I've gone out listening for trouble, haven't made sense. There are families, and groups of women, here and there, burning with hate and fear. I couldn't figure out why. This explains a lot."

"I didn't think you would, Sven," I said, "and I won't convince you. This will." I unfolded the paper I had stuffed in my pocket and handed it to him. René left the window to read over Sven's shoulder. "It's a list of incidents in Lord Edmund's and Baron D'Armond's histories. Search for and watch them without me, because I'm not interested in losing my breakfast again. René and I will come back tomorrow morning. We'll decide what to do then."

"You go on," René said. "I'm going to watch, too."

I stopped with my hand on the latch. "You said you believed me."

"I do, mostly, but it's like learning theory without doing any actual magic. It's not quite real until you see it in practice, or do it yourself."

"You're too young for this filth. You won't like it."

"You can't stop me, now that I've read your list."

"Lucinda," Sven said, "Go away. I'll deal with them—the list, and René."

"I'd wish you a good day," I said, before I stomped out, "but you won't have one."

The Lady of the Manor

Claire's house was in an uproar, with servants running hither and yon, packing crates and trunks. Two servants collided in the kitchen, smashing china. Their mistress dithered about, fussing over boxes, issuing contradictory orders, and getting in the servants' way. I watched from a distance, waiting for an opportunity to step into an empty room. Sorceress Lorraine's magic must have had an effect, as I rivalled Hazel in outward serenity. Tapping my foot on the hearthstone seemed so gauche.

The nursemaid put Lawrence down for a nap, and left the nursery. I walked through the fire and bent to kiss his cute head. The nursemaid stepped back in, and screamed. My nephew cried. I picked him up and attempted to soothe him. The nursemaid retreated to a corner and watched with her hands over her mouth.

Claire came running. Her eyes grew enormous when she saw me.

"I'm sorry," I said. "I didn't mean to startle anyone. I waited until the nursemaid left before I walked through the fire—"

"You can walk through the fire?" Claire breathed.

The nursemaid gave another little shriek and blanched. With the air of one bearding a lion in his den, she crept closer, snatched the crying baby from me, and fled.

Claire would never do anything as unbecoming as the open-mouthed laugh I indulged in. She bent over with a hand on her mouth, wheezing and chortling. When I regained my composure I said, "You should commend her for having enough gumption to put Lawrence first even though she was frightened."

Claire wiped streaming eyes. "Yes, I'll do that. Oh, dear, it's such a shock.

But of course, you can walk through the fire. I should have realised. You can do anything."

"That's not so. There's plenty I can't do."

She waved a hand. "Unimportant stuff. You've always done anything you really wanted. Lucinda, I am so glad you're here. We're moving to the earl's mansion."

"I thought you must be. Lord Richard told his father about you?"

She shook her head. "You wouldn't know. You were right about Richard's brother being in danger. Before you sent your message, he had gotten into a fight up north, and the other man killed him. When the earl heard the news, he had a fit, and died a day later. Richard's the earl now."

"Oh," I breathed, and dropped into a chair. "Thank God," I added under my breath.

Claire stared down at her hands, her cheeks flushed. All traces of gaiety had disappeared. "Richard's upset, and from more than just his father dying, which he expected soon anyway. I think he believes it's his fault, and it probably is, that both his brother and father are dead, since he didn't tell Lord Edmund about Lawrence. Oh, Lucinda, I'm trying to be a supportive wife, but it's hard. I'm so ashamed of him. I'm dying to move out of this house, but I'm not sure moving into the mansion with him will be better. Maybe I would have made a better choice marrying the silversmith, or the silk merchant."

Earlier, when we had realised Lord Edmund was unaware his nephew had supplanted him, I had assumed his brother's lapse to be an egregious example of the self-absorption afflicting our ruling class. Now, I could not believe Lord Richard was oblivious. Had the absence of a warning been a ploy, a desperate gamble that someone, somewhere, would be angry enough with Lord Edmund to take a swing at him, and put a permanent end to his villainy?

An icy finger traced a line down my spine. I would not, could not, ever voice that question. I was not powerful enough to hide Lord Richard's answer from the Water Office. And damned if I wanted Claire's husband to suffer any more for his brother's wickedness, depravity the Water Office should have stopped years ago.

"Lucinda, are you listening to me?"

"Yes, I heard you." I took her hands in mine. "Claire, listen. I used magic to follow Edmund's life, and he was every bit as bad as Richard thinks.

Don't agonise over his death; Frankland is better off without him. And your husband is a better man than you give him credit for."

She gave me a polite, superficial smile. "Thank you for trying to cheer me up, but I know what you think of the nobles. Never mind. I'm glad you're here. Richard's coming soon to take Lawrence and me to the palace. I'm nervous. Would you come with us? I want the servants to know I'm related to a fire witch."

"Sure, but I should look the part. I'd better go home and fetch my hat. Back in a few."

I called a fire to life in the fireplace and walked through. In my last glimpse of Claire, her eyes were as big as saucers.

The dark red silk gown with gold stitching was one of the first I'd had made to order, when the Fire Guild gave me money to dress befitting my new station. I'd had some difficulty getting what I wanted, until Mrs Cole tracked down a costumer for a troupe of actors. The dress was not fashionable in the slightest. It was, in fact, a conservative cut in a style fashionable more than a century ago, when Jean was in his twenties. I indulged myself for a few minutes, remembering the gleam in his eyes when he first saw me wear it.

Ah, well, daydreaming wasn't doing either of us any good. I pulled off my linen frock and donned the red silk, then grabbed the hat with the flickering flames and returned to Claire's. She was in her bedroom with two maids helping her dress, all three chattering away. I walked in, and was met with dead silence.

I asked, "Will this do?"

Claire closed her hanging jaw. "Merciful heavens, no. This will be my grand entrance to my new home. I can't have you showing me up."

I snorted. "As if you're worried."

She dimpled. "Well, no, but I'd never thought that before. I beg your pardon for each and every mean thing I ever said about you not caring about clothes."

"They were mostly true." I eyed the impractical blue silk and white lace confection she wore. "I can't imagine wanting to wear that. You look like a doll."

"It's the current fashion."

"So?"

The arrival of Lord Richard's coach saved us from repeating that well-worn argument. We met him in the entry hall; he blanched and backed into the door. His Adam's apple bobbed up and down as Claire introduced me.

I held out my hand. "I'm glad to finally meet you, and I apologise for the letter I sent last week. After thinking about it further, it's just as well you didn't take Claire to live in the earl's mansion while your father was alive. It wouldn't have been a pleasant experience, living with someone who despised her."

The filaments of the conspiracy hanging from Lord Richard didn't stir. Claire gave me a reproachful stare, but he looked like a man given a reprieve from a prison sentence. The scenes in the fire had given the impression of a man suffering chronic melancholy, but within a few minutes he was as cheery as a man with a beautiful wife and a healthy income should be. His manners were faultless, and I warmed to him without reserve.

He inquired about our travels, and we carried on a pleasant conversation in the coach. Claire was pleased, but bemused. She watched me from the corner of her eye.

The earl's servants waited in neat rows at the mansion's front door. Eyes swivelled from Claire to me and back again as we alit from the coach. Claire gave me the faintest glimmer of a wink. If I had outshone her, we both would have been shocked.

The earl addressed his staff with, "It is my pleasure to present your new mistress, my wife of two years, Lady Eddensford."

I winced. Thank heaven it was a courtesy title.

"I also present her stepsister, the Greater Warlock Locksmith, wife of the Fire Warlock Emeritus."

Enormous eyes swivelled back to me. I pulled my hat brim a fraction of an inch lower, and they cringed in unison.

Lord Richard motioned towards the nursemaid and baby. "And finally, Lawrence, my son and heir." While we climbed the stairs, he directed the butler and housekeeper to give Claire a tour, but at the top she stopped him and turned back to the ranks of staring servants.

"Please, I want to say something first." Her only sign of nerves was fingering her gold and lapis lazuli bracelet. "The earl called me Lady Eddensford, but I'm a commoner, like you. You must know, or could guess, that's why he hid our marriage from his father, so there's no point in pretending otherwise. I want to be a good wife and a good hostess, but

I won't learn my way around overnight, and I will make mistakes. You know how to do your jobs—please help me learn to do mine. In return I promise to treat you as well as I know how. That's all. Thank you."

She smiled her most conspiratorial smile, the one that makes everyone believe she is speaking directly to them. Heads nodded, and a chorus of "Yes, ma'am's" answered.

The butler and housekeeper were eating out of her hand before we'd covered one floor. She responded to every story, and took the time to examine everything they saw fit to point out. She was acting, but no one short of a level five talent would have known. Lord Richard didn't know— he looked about to burst with pride at her delight in his home.

The house was lovely, more old-fashioned and comfortable than I had expected, less ostentatious than I had feared. Watching and listening with half a mind, I followed along behind. Did I dare tell Claire what her husband had done for her? At length, I decided against it, and turned my attention to Claire's bracelet. A probe confirmed Granny Helene had lifted the glamour spell. The earth witch had been right about Claire; she would be fine. She didn't need a spell to charm, or my help in handling her new household.

The butler would have ended the tour after the state rooms, family quarters, and guest rooms, but Claire insisted on seeing everything. I added my voice to hers—no house tour is complete without a glimpse of the kitchen. Besides, it was time I established my credentials.

Dinner preparations ground to a halt as the kitchen staff bobbed and curtsied and dusted themselves off. Had the lord and his lady never been there before? Mrs Cole would have taken it in stride and worked while talking. Claire and I exchanged looks, and after a cursory glance around, I expressed my thanks for the tour and announced I must be going. I walked into the fireplace and turned back, one foot in the flames.

"I'll come back after you've had a chance to settle in. When would be good? A week? A fortnight, or...?"

A dozen people stood frozen like statues. The fright on the earl's face mirrored the scullery maid's. Claire, bless her, looked as if she'd watched me step into the fire for years.

"A fortnight," she said. "Perfect. Come for tea."

"Lovely. See you then," I said, and walked through the fire.

Wishful Thinking

I arrived at Sven's study the next morning before René. Sven acknowledged my presence, then returned to staring grimly out the window. I checked that the spells I had cast the day before were still intact while we waited in silence for René.

When he arrived, he greeted me with, "You were right." He scrambled into the window embrasure, without the previous day's grin. "Is there any magic to unsee something you're sorry you saw?"

Sven shook his head. "If I knew of any I'd use it myself."

I said, "Forget that. The important question is, how do we expose this filthy conspiracy?"

"You're getting ahead of yourself. Are you—"

"I know," I interrupted, "you haven't agreed yet to help, but you will. You're a righteous man, and now that you know about it, you can't let it go on, either. You'd agree to help even if René hadn't already persuaded you."

Sven closed his eyes and looked pained. "Thank you for that ringing endorsement of my character, but that wasn't what I meant. Do you understand how it works? Are you sure this problem won't disappear when the Water Office is rebuilt?"

"Er, no. I hadn't considered… If it will, then why did Sorceress Lorraine get so excited over my learning about it?"

"I don't know. You may be right, but the point is, we don't know enough. We need to understand the conspiracy's limits and vulnerabilities. If we attack it now we might get lucky but more likely it will swallow us."

"We," René said. "You are going to help, then?"

"Of course I am," Sven snapped. "But don't tell the other mages I've lost an argument to two neophytes who've never even been to university."

René's grin reappeared. "We won't tell. Besides, if you bring this secret out into the open, won't it seal your reputation as a mage?"

"It will. I'll be the go-to man for conspiracies, secrets, and anything of that ilk. Don't think I'm not aware of that."

I said, "Thanks, Sven. Let's stay on track, please. How do we find out more about it?"

"We can probe a bit from the outside, but we'll make progress faster if we probe from the inside. Talk, that is, to someone who knows something about it."

I glanced at René. He looked baffled, too.

"How do we do that without giving away that we're not part of it?"

Sven's grim expression relaxed into an echo of René's grin. "Simple, and maybe even fun. We start a counter-conspiracy."

The Earth Mother's amber chamber was stifling. I'd arrived minutes before, and already wanted out. I leaned my head against the chair back and closed my eyes, too enervated to glare at Beorn for calling this meeting on the hottest day in July. If I had known how many more meetings I'd have to go to as the Fire Warlock's apprentice, I'd have told him to go jump in a lake.

"Believe it or not, and I'm not sure I believe it," Beorn said, "the king and I agreed on something."

I pried an eye open. He had warned me to keep an eye on his dealings with the king, and I'd missed the first one. Must have been while I was with Sven and René. If he asked where I'd been, we were in trouble.

"It is what one would expect," Sorceress Lorraine said, "given your close friendship."

Mother Celeste snorted. "I don't believe. Tell us."

Beorn said, "That jackass Lord Edmund is causing trouble just by getting himself killed. Every aristocrat who hears about him panics, and somebody has to go calm him down and explain what happened. Paul's been getting the worst of it."

"They have been trying my patience sorely," Enchanter Paul said. "None of the guilds has spare staff to spend handholding these nervous ninnies."

Beorn said, "The king already sent out the summons calling the nobles to Paris in September for the demonstration of the rebuilt Water Office.

I said make it more urgent, and tell them to get there like I was prodding their fat little butts with a fiery wand. When they're all there, which can't be until the end of August anyway, we gather them together and show them what happened to Lord Edmund. Stephen agreed it was a good idea."

A good idea? Making the new Earl of Eddensford look like a first-class self-centred ass in front of the whole country? Claire would be devastated. I straightened up, but strangled a protest. The four Officeholders weren't concerned about my discomfort, why would they care about hers?

"That's not a bad idea," Paul said, "but rumours will continue to spread, and we'll still have to deal with panicked nobles until then. Perhaps we should use conspiracy magic to curtail the rumours?"

Beorn bristled. "Hell, no. We've got too many of them now, and we shouldn't encourage people to keep secrets."

"Peace, friends," Jean said, "The news is already too widespread to easily contain, even with magical backing. Dealing with upset nobles is, I agree, frustrating and time-consuming, but letting the news spread may have benefits that outweigh the costs."

"Benefits?" Enchanter Paul's voice rose. "What benefits?"

"The nobility is too complacent, believing nothing will ever change in Frankland. Fear may spur them to come to terms with the changes forced on them. If they go to Paris expecting Frankland to fall apart, and there find how little has changed, they will be relieved and more willing to accept it."

Beorn pulled at his moustache. "Soften them up, eh? You've got a point."

Mother Celeste said, "Every one we can persuade to go along with the reforging is one we won't have to strong-arm, but unless we can convince the king, do we have any chance of that?"

"Queen Marguerite," Sorceress Lorraine said, "is the key. She is the one we must convince, because she accepts the myths that the administration of justice is even-handed, and the nobility are privileged because they are more virtuous than the commoners. King Stephen knows how human his kinsmen are, and privilege matters more to him than justice, but he values her good opinion. If we demonstrate to her virtuous commoners being wronged by the courts, and reprehensible nobles going unpunished, she will give Stephen no peace until he accepts our reforms."

Beorn and Paul eyed each other. "Sounds like wishful thinking to me,"

Beorn said. "She's never stood up to him before, why would she start now?"

"She has never disagreed with him before on anything that mattered so much to her own psyche," Jean said. "If we convince her of the need for reform, and she fails to act on it, she will have no peace, as in her own mind she will be no better than a commoner. I, too, may be guilty of wishful thinking, but I agree with Her Wisdom. There is more steel in Queen Marguerite than is apparent on first glance."

Lorraine flashed him a brilliant smile. I glowered.

"If you can convince her, which I doubt," Paul said, "that some nobleman is a scoundrel, she might only demand the king strip the reprobate of his privileges for sullying the honour of her class."

"If she does only that, and King Stephen agrees," Sorceress Lorraine said, "I will rejoice. Such a precedent will be impossible to deny when the next scoundrel appears, and the next."

Too bad Lord Edmund was dead. Too bad this conspiracy hid his crimes. If ever a noble deserved to be stripped of his privileges, it had been that reprobate.

"Finding an aristocratic scoundrel will be easy," Mother Celeste said, "but a commoner even a queen considers virtuous will be harder. The only case I can think of straight off is—"

"Stop!" Sorceress Lorraine held up a hand. "Do not tell me your suggestion."

"But you said—"

"We need a test case in September, but if you bring someone to my attention now, the Water Office may force me to act against him before the reforging."

"Oh. Oh, dear."

"Yes, you see the difficulty. If I had no conscience, I would bring a test case to the nobles in August, to shock the ones who, like the queen, believe the myths. But I do have a conscience, and I will not do so for a capital crime, although those are the ones most in need of reform. We must wait until after the reforging, and compare the new judgements with what might have been."

"But," Jean said, "if the other guilds identify exemplars of virtuous behaviour at odds with the Water Office, the Fire Office can protect them, on the basis their continued existence is vital to Frankland's security. That will trump the Water Office's claim on them."

Sorceress Lorraine shot him a cold glare. "You need not sound so pleased about that."

Jean's eyebrows arched. "I beg your pardon?"

"Never mind. Are the other Officeholders willing to take this on?"

Mother Celeste, Beorn, and Enchanter Paul exchanged glances, and nodded.

Beorn said, "You betcha."

Enchanter Paul said, "It will be a pleasure."

They went on to discuss other matters, which I listened to with half a mind, as an idea took shape. The king wanted a demonstration, did he? We could give him one, beyond anything he had imagined.

Claire might never forgive me.

Maggie Archer

It would be fun, Sven said, to start a counter-conspiracy. Fun, my foot. He looked like he hadn't slept in the three days since. Only René was cheerful, but he was not the scout testing our counter-conspiracy's viability. If it wasn't sound, I would be trapped. Sven and René would watch my every move from Sven's fireplace, and could reach me within seconds, but their aid was not reassuring. The odds were we would all three become ensnared, our hopes of exposing the conspiracy dashed.

We watched the older earth witch give the younger one her final instructions, and, as one, breathed a sigh of relief when the younger witch picked up her baskets and headed for the tunnels.

René said, "I thought she'd never finish telling the life stories of all those people I've never met and probably never will meet. What does it matter? Why couldn't she just say give Uncle Malcolm this liniment and Aunty Fee this salve, and be done with it?"

Sven tut-tutted at him. "It matters to an earth witch. She needs to spot new problems, not just deliver medicines for existing ones."

I said, "I'm glad she's out of that guild house. The traces of the conspiracy made my skin crawl."

"She's in the open air now. My supposition was correct; she's too young to be deeply entangled. There are less than half-a-dozen filaments clinging to her. If we've done it right, it should be easy."

"If," I said, without moving. "Are you sure we've covered everything?"

"We've been over this a dozen times," Sven said. "You're dealing with a single member of the conspiracy. You'll be fine."

"You're stalling," René said. "Move."

He ducked my fist as I stepped through the fire and out onto the Abertee hillside. Below me houses clustered around a tunnel mouth. "Hazel," I called.

She turned, startled but not panicked. Surprise gave way to pleasure. "Lucinda, what a nice surprise. What are you doing here?"

"Checking up on Abertee. Do we need to still keep an eye on the White Duke? If you're making your rounds would you mind if I tag along?"

"Not at all. If word spreads that the Fire Guild is still keeping an eye on us, that will help keep tempers under control."

From a distance, Hazel had looked as serene as always. Face to face, I saw shadows under her eyes and traces of distress not there before. "You're still worried," I said.

"Oh, yes. Abertee looks calmer since the duke let the Archers come back, but it's deceptive. All around me, I sense short tempers and deep-seated resentment. If he tries again to push the Archers or any other freeholders off their land, the pot will boil over again. Or if they capture the fugitive blacksmith. He's a good man, and means a lot to people here. Everyone I've met claims to be either his cousin or his best friend. If the Water Guild executes him for killing Lord Edmund, an angry mob will march on the White Duke, Fire Warlock or no Fire Warlock."

Her first patient could hardly see, but still-sharp ears and mind latched onto the news that she had a fire witch along. While Hazel spread salves on the old man's arthritic joints, he lectured me on the Fire Guild's failings in keeping the peace and protecting the rights of the commoners. Mindful of Father's admonitions to respect my elders, I listened with clenched jaw and murmured polite acknowledgment whenever he paused for breath. Concurring with everything he said didn't make it any easier to take.

The next patient gave me a similar earful. When we left, I said, "I understand now why Abertee yeomen have such a reputation for being troublemakers. Neither of them seemed the slightest bit awed by either of us."

Hazel smiled. "They were awed, but they're too proud to show it. It drives their overlords nuts. I love it—I feel at home here."

As we walked towards the tunnels, I studied the black strands of the conspiracy draped on her. They hung limp, unaffected by the copper-coloured filaments of the counter-conspiracy we three had created. Just as Master Sven had predicted. I probed, as he had taught me. They seemed undisturbed—again, as he had predicted. So far, so good.

He had drilled into me what I needed to say, and when and how to say it. I would start the script after we emerged from the tunnels, if no one else was within earshot.

We stepped through. A tall beauty entrapped by the evil filaments sat on a rock wall beside the tunnel mouth, sniffling over her knitting. Hazel gave her a warm hug.

I blurted, "You're Maggie Archer."

Both women blinked at me. Maggie wiped away tears. "Aye. Who are you? I've never seen so many flames on one hat before."

"You probably never will again," Hazel said. "This is the Warlock Locksmith, the highest-ranking fire witch Frankland has had in decades."

"Really?" Maggie breathed. "Wow."

A girl after my own heart. "You have an affinity for the Fire Guild, don't you?"

"Yes, ma'am. I can boil a cup of water by holding it in my hands." She blushed. "That's nothing next to you, I'm sure. It's not enough to make me a witch, I know, but—"

"Nonsense. Can you bake?"

She gave me a blank stare. "What?"

"Do you bake?"

"I make the best bread in this valley." It was a flat statement of fact, not opinion.

"Then you're a fire witch, even if the guild won't accept you. At least that's what the retired Fire Warlock would say."

She smiled, her tears forgotten. "But how did you know me?"

Sven's script flew out of my head. "I, uh, that is, after Hazel brought the news, I searched in the fire for what had happened. I watched Lord Edmund paw you, and your brother hit him. And I…I'm sorry about your brother."

Tears again filled her eyes, and she turned her head. I looked at Hazel. "And I take back what I said in Blazes. He did the country a service by getting rid of that wretch."

Hazel's shoulders slumped. The filaments surrounding her and Maggie came to life and reached towards me, questing like blind snakes. She said, "You know the secret now, don't you?"

The copper-coloured strands surrounding me rose, and sent black ends to meet the black strands. Hazel was almost an earth mother—I didn't dare lie. My hands trembled, and my heart raced. I said, "Yes, I'm afraid so."

"Lucinda, what's the matter? What did I say that upset you?" She grabbed my arm and pulled me towards the rock wall. "Sit down. Talk to me."

The black strands writhed, thickening, and danced away from the strands of the counter-conspiracy. The contrast between my gentle friend and the loathsome cords surrounding her agitated me further.

"I see the engine of lies," I blurted, "and it appals me." I parroted René's voice in my head. "I don't want to say the wrong thing and pull somebody else in. I want to understand what I've gotten into, so I don't make it worse. Can you help?"

The strands stopped writhing, but remained poised in mid-air. I sat on the wall next to the staring girl and practiced deep breathing, exhaling slowly.

Hazel said, "Shouldn't you talk to Warlock Quicksilver?"

"No. I'd have to admit I found out after he warned me away."

Maggie said, "You're talking about what Lord Edmund did, and the secret around it, aren't you?"

The black ends of the copper-coloured strands reached the black strands and coupled. I shivered.

Hazel chewed on her lip for a moment. "It's a hideous secret, and I'm sorry you found out about it. I can tell you what I know, which isn't much. It was started a long time ago by the Fire Warlock called Old Brimstone—"

"The fifty-seventh."

She shrugged. "Could be. As far as I know, the conspiracy stops the truth about a rape from being shown in court, even if everyone knows what happened. The Water Office will never convict a nobleman, because it won't see the truth. That's all I've heard." The strands relaxed and thinned. I began to breathe more easily.

Maggie jabbed a knitting needle at me. "She said you're the highest-ranking fire witch in Frankland. What are you going to do about it?"

The filaments soared. "Me?" I bleated.

René yelled, *Get away from her.*

She glared at me. "Somebody has to do something. It doesn't sound like anybody else will."

I scrambled to my feet. Hazel grabbed my arm. "Maggie," she said, "you don't understand. She can't. The only one who can expose a conspiracy from the inside is the one who started it, and he's long dead."

The strands stopped writhing. They hung motionless in mid-air. I sat down again on the rock wall and bent over, my head in my hands.

Maggie said, "You mean we can't ever get rid of it? That's horrible."

Neither of us answered. Hazel put an arm around her shoulders. The strands relaxed once again, returning to their limp, lifeless state.

Maggie's tears splashed onto her knitting. "I don't want anyone else to go through what Fiona went through. I wish I knew what to do. I'd do anything to get rid of it."

Hazel and I looked at each other over her bowed head. I said, "Be careful what you wish for, Maggie."

She raised her head and looked me square in the eye. With a jutting chin, she repeated, "I wish I knew what to do. I'd do anything to get rid of it. Anything."

Master Sven's fingers drummed a soft tattoo on his desk. "Hides the truth from a trial, does it? That wasn't what I wanted to hear."

"Yeah," René said, "because it means Lucinda's right. It's not part of the Water Office, so it will keep on working the same way after the Water Office is fixed. If we don't break the conspiracy, high-born slime will still get off scot-free."

"Yes. Despite my misgivings I have to admit you two may be right—we have to expose it."

I said, "How do we do that?"

"There are three ways to destroy a conspiracy. The best, and easiest way—"

"Is not open to us," I said. "Old Brimstone died more than two hundred years ago, and he wouldn't have agreed to stop it anyway. Next?"

"The second preferred method is to overpower it with stronger counter-magic."

"Oh, yeah, sure," said René.

"With the four Officeholders, most of the Water and Earth Guilds, and Warlock Quicksilver in on it," Sven said, "no, that option isn't open to us either. A conspiracy draws its power in direct proportion to the strength of the magic talents involved, so—"

"That's why you can't expose a conspiracy you're a part of, if you aren't one of the creators, right?"

"Right. It's a vicious cycle—the harder you struggle against it, the more power it sucks from you, and the tighter its grip."

"Ugh," René said. "What's the third way?"

"Expand it until it includes so many mundanes it collapses under its own weight. The higher the ratio of mundanes to talents, the harder it is to sustain. Besides, once it reaches a certain proportion of the people who might care, what's the point?"

We considered that in silence for a few moments. Comparative silence, anyway. Master Sven's drumming escalated to a hard rat-a-tat-tat. I put my hand on his. "Stop that. I can't hear myself think."

He snatched his hand away and crossed his arms, tucking his hands in against his chest. "If you weren't so bright I'd tell you to do your thinking somewhere else. Drumming helps me."

René said, "Is the third option any better? With so many witches and wizards already in on it, we'd have to tell nearly everybody in the country. There's no way we can do that."

Sven's eyes unfocused and he resumed drumming softly. "No way? What an interesting challenge. The Air Guild can—disseminating news, edicts, et cetera is part of their domain."

"Yes," I said, "but they do a lousy job of it. Any news we want propagated across Frankland takes forever to get out. Only the news we don't want spread, like Lord Edmund getting himself offed, sweeps the country in a matter of days."

"That's true," he said, "but the fact that bad news travels so fast shows it can be done." He dug a clean sheet of paper out of a stack and started scribbling. "I have some ideas. I'll do some research, and let you know what I find."

René said, "The Fire Warlock's asking where I am. Got to go."

I rose to follow René. Sven said, "You. Sit down."

He jotted down a few more lines, then jammed his pen in the inkwell. "I couldn't say this in front of René, but it's time you told me everything. I can't help you if you don't trust me."

"What do you mean? I've told you all I know."

"Look, Lucinda, you know I respect Quicksilver. He's the best Fire Warlock we've ever had, but…"

"But what?"

"And I don't like prying into what goes on between a husband and his wife, but..."

"Sven, what are you talking about?"

"You interrupted me when I started to describe the easiest way to destroy a conspiracy."

"I did?"

"You did. Tell me, what is the easiest way?"

"You convince its creator it's no longer needed, and he undoes the spell."

Sven's voice grated on my ears. "He, or his successor. Any Fire Warlock after Old Brimstone could have undone it. Quicksilver had a hundred years—"

I barged to the door, sending a stack of books toppling. "He couldn't have."

"A hundred years to undo—"

"I'm not listening to any more of this." I yanked on the door so hard it slammed against the wall. More books tumbled over. I didn't pick them up. I fled without troubling to close the door.

Braided Locks

"I protest," Enchanter Paul said, "most vehemently. We do not need to go underground. I am not budging."

Beorn growled, "Didn't you hear what Jean said? This amber box we're in is great for blocking eavesdroppers, but it couldn't hold up to a serious display of fire magic. Celeste wouldn't appreciate us burning her furniture."

"Furniture? Who cares about the furniture? What about the prospects of burning us?"

My stomach knotted. I should never have implied the fire magic might get out of hand. Sorceress Lorraine sat silent and unmoving, her eyes closed, her hands strangling the chair arms.

Jean's eyes flashed. "The risk is not great, but one cannot use powerful magic without risk. You should know that."

Mother Celeste said, "I know you don't like being shut up in small places, but from the description of the practice room, it sounds more to your liking than this room. And it is extraordinarily generous of the Fire Guild to take outsiders into such a protected place."

"It's much bigger," I said, "with a higher ceiling, and skylights."

"But it's underground," Paul said. "I barely tolerate being shut up in this box, even though it is above ground, with nothing but a ceiling and roof over us. I could break out if I had to. Furthermore, Warlock Quicksilver indicated the only way to get there is through the Earth Guild's tunnels. That is what I object to the most."

Mother Celeste's expression soured. "There's nothing dangerous about our tunnels, and we're all going together, so you couldn't possibly get lost."

"Madam, I have not been in one of your d—, er, dark tunnels since I developed my powers as an enchanter, and I do not intend to start now."

Sorceress Lorraine turned an imperious stare on the Enchanter. "Paul, stop this nonsense at once. You are as terrified of being buried alive, and rightly so, as a warlock is of drowning, or a sorceress is of being burnt. But none of those will happen today. The Locksmith is adept, and the tunnels are safe. If the Locksmith loses control, I am more likely than you, Paul, to be burnt, but I am going. No, we are going." She grabbed Paul's right elbow, and nodded at Celeste, who grabbed his left. The two women marched Paul, still protesting, towards the tunnels.

The three of us from the Fire Guild followed. With the Fire Office demanding his attention, Beorn marched as if he were an automaton. He had shrugged off my apologies, but this exercise was an imposition.

I had already spent a week preparing, working with each Officeholder in their strongholds to ensure I could draw on their power for the braided lock. Beorn gave me no trouble; one tug, and I had a cable of fire. But even with the best of intentions and Jean's coaching, the others did not find it easy to lower the innate barriers guarding their magical reserves and let someone else—from another guild, no less—draw on them. Sorceress Lorraine had the hardest time—we made dozens of tries before I pulled from her a line of blue as fine as spider's silk—but she would not give up.

Working with her had been exhausting, but I admired her perseverance. Enchanter Paul could have used some of the Water Guild's patience. He would have given up if Jean and Sorceress Lorraine together had not bullied him into line.

Paul circled the practice room, examining each narrow shaft under the skylights and chewing on his lip, while I lined the others up and explained the exercise.

"We are practicing locking and unlocking braided locks, like the one on the Water Office, so everyone will be ready when the time comes. We'll start with hiding a teacup. I'll deal with the lock, you don't have to. All you have to do is let me draw on your power.

"It will be easier the closer together we are. Sorceress Lorraine and I will sit, with my hand on her Token of Office. The rest of you can sit or stand with your hands on my head or shoulders. Understand?" Nods all around. "Then let's do it."

Even with the hours of preparation separately, the four Officeholders had difficulty letting down their guards in the others' presence. Enchanter

Paul, who had as bad a case of fidgets as René ever exhibited, roused in me a desire to wallop him. I came close to screaming from frustration, but finally I succeeded in drawing strands of energy—red, green, blue, and white—of about the same weight from all four Officeholders. The teacup disappeared with a satisfying little pop, and reappeared a moment later.

Expressions of relief and pleasure followed. With that success behind us, other small locks came more easily. A caged bird, followed by a candle flame, disappeared and reappeared in due order.

"Now we will try something a little harder," I said, and a fire sprang to life in the fireplace.

Enchanter Paul breathed a low, "Uh-oh."

Sorceress Lorraine forced a smile. "I did not realise you had such a dry sense of humour."

"The lock for this is small compared to the Water Office."

She winced. "I understand. Proceed when you are ready."

"Fine." I wrapped a mental fist around the four stands of power and yanked. The fire disappeared, hidden from our mind's eyes as well as our physical ones.

"Oof!" Enchanter Paul grunted. Mother Celeste twitched. Sorceress Lorraine's eyebrows rose.

"Are you all right?"

"Surprised, that's all," Mother Celeste said. "No harm done."

"Unlocking will take more power. Shall I go ahead?"

"How much more?" Enchanter Paul asked. "Twice? Ten times? A hundred times?"

"Er, maybe four or five times as much, but still less than a level three is capable of."

They exchanged glances and shrugged. Mother Celeste said, "Any level five could give you a hundred times as much. We aren't used to someone else demanding it, that's all."

"Get on with it," Paul said.

Keeping a careful grip on the four threads of power, I twisted them together, and ordered them to become cords. My mental candle flame raced backwards along the words in my mind's eye, reached the end with a loud crack, and blazed like a torch.

Mother Celeste cursed and snatched her hand off my shoulder. Enchanter

Paul staggered backwards, gasping. Sorceress Lorraine became a fountain.

I goggled. Lorraine had gone white and rigid, eyes squeezed shut. Water poured from her, splashed on my skirts, and pooled on the floor. I yanked my feet out of the way, but my shoes were already soaked.

Beorn tugged at his beard. He and Jean exchanged a long look, frowning at each other.

"What happened?" I said. "That was no more power than I've drawn from the level three wizards on our staff."

Enchanter Paul said, "Even a level three fire wizard has shields against fire magic that we don't have."

"You felt the blast from the release? I thought I was the only one affected." I looked at Jean. The worry lines around his eyes did not soothe me.

He said, "I am not altogether surprised."

"What?" I said. "You never said anything to me."

He said, "We practiced braided locks only with fire wizards. We could not be sure of the effects on members of the other guilds."

Enchanter Paul snapped, "You should have figured that out before asking us for anything."

Jean's nostrils flared. "And what foreign wizards should we have trusted to practice with?"

"Your problem, not mine. We're through for today." Paul was halfway to the nearest door. I started up to run after him, but Beorn pushed me back in my chair.

"Don't listen to him. You did fine."

"Paul, you fool, wait." Mother Celeste hurried after him. "That's the wrong door. You'll get lost."

Sorceress Lorraine pushed wet hair from her face. "I beg your pardon. Summoning water was a reflex action to protect myself from burns." The water drained out of her dress and hair, a line dividing dry fabric from wet sliding down her torso. In seconds we were both dry; the pool shrank and disappeared. Beorn sighed. Wet, her filmy silk dress could have been painted on.

I said, "I can't protect myself from the lightning yet; how can I protect anyone else?"

Beorn gave my shoulder a squeeze. "You don't have to. Leave that to Jean and me." He looked a question at Jean, who nodded.

"We must experiment further," Jean said, "but we do not need you."

"Good. I have other problems to see to." Beorn disappeared into the fireplace.

Sorceress Lorraine said, "Do not let Paul upset you, Lucinda. We are so unfamiliar with locks no one knew what to expect." A weak smile came and went. "I cannot claim eagerness for more, especially in the Warlock's Fortress, of all places, but I will devote as much of my time and energy as is needed to make this unlocking come to fruition. What do you suggest, Jean?"

Jean said, "Lucinda, my dear, if you draw on the four Officeholders through me, perhaps I can shield the others from the heat."

I considered the idea. "It might work. Worth a try, anyway."

Lorraine said, "Can we convince Paul to return?"

Jean shrugged. "We will experiment without him."

Mother Celeste returned, and we arranged ourselves with Jean seated beside me, and her hand on his shoulder. René, standing in for Beorn, had a hand on my shoulder. Sorceress Lorraine faced us across the table with her hand outstretched. Jean put his hand over hers, and I laid mine across his, touching the great sapphire in her Token of Office, without touching her.

"Ready?" I said.

"One moment," she said. The healthy pink in her cheeks faded into alabaster translucence; even with Jean's hand between us, I felt her skin cool. I suppressed a shudder. I had experienced the defensive power of ice; her armour demanded my respect even as it repelled me.

"Now," she said.

The strands of power appeared in my mind's eye as three cords, two of them on the far side of Jean's lighthouse beacon. I reached through the beacon and pulled, twisting the three strands together into one cord. The lock snapped closed; the fire disappeared. Another few seconds, and the lock popped open. Once again, the heat from a furnace rolled over me.

Something—pain? fear?—flitted across Jean's face, too quickly for me to identify. Lorraine smiled. Mother Celeste kissed us both on the cheek. "Well done, both of you," she said. "I felt a tug, and that was all. No heat this time."

After they left, and I was alone with Jean, I said, "Jean, what happened? Were you hurt?"

His eyebrows rose. "Do you believe such a trifle could harm me?"

"No, but I thought... I guess I imagined it."

He laid a comforting hand on my shoulder. "Think no more of it, my dear. When the time comes, you must concentrate only on releasing the lock. As Beorn said, let protecting the other Officeholders be our problem, not yours."

The Fire Guild's Reputation

Sven glared at me across his desk, his lips set in a thin line.

I returned the glare. "Couldn't you be mistaken about any Fire Warlock having the authority to abolish the conspiracy? You said there were variations in how they are created. Maybe when Old Brimstone set it up he put some twist in it so only he could destroy it."

Sven shook his head. "He couldn't. Yes, private individuals can, and often do, but when that happens the conspiracy dies with them. The Fire Warlock can't. I've spent most of my time over the last two years studying the spells making up the Fire and Water Offices, and I have a clearer picture now how they work. The Fire Office would have forced the creator to be seen as the Fire Warlock, not as Old Brimstone."

I didn't ask if he was sure. If he wasn't, he would have said so.

"Face the facts," he said. "Warlock Quicksilver didn't expose the conspiracy when he could have. That makes me want to vomit."

I turned to stare out the window at the pigeons. "There's some other explanation." I couldn't blame Sven for being angry, not even for hating Jean. I did when I first learned the secret. But I had calmed down. Sven was getting angrier.

He said, "We'll have to fight him when we expose it. We'll never be strong enough."

"Nonsense. Jean wants me to expose it. If he could have exposed it himself, he would have. He didn't, so he couldn't. That's all there is to it."

"Are you sure?"

I swivelled to face him, lifting my eyes heavenward. "No, of course not. I've only studied the man's every move for three years. I have no idea what he thinks about anything."

"Okay, okay, forget I said that. But maybe, and I'm not saying this is certain, you could be so indignant over what's happened to these women, that you overlook the idea others may have different concerns they judge more important."

I leaned on his desk and breathed fire. "What could be more important than protecting Frankland's women and children?"

He retreated as far as the clutter would allow. "You know that isn't the Fire Office's prime mandate."

"Yes, that's so, but Jean does care. And there's no mandate dependent on this conspiracy."

"No, but…"

"But what? Sven, you're beating around the bush. Why would a Fire Warlock, who can't take advantage of it himself, and who has no love of the nobility who can, keep this a secret?"

He edged further away. "To preserve the Fire Guild's reputation."

"To preserve… Sven, tell me you're joking."

"You do realise, don't you, that when this is exposed it will give us a black eye that will take decades, maybe centuries, to recover from? You know Warlock Quicksilver cares what people think of the Fire Guild."

"Yes, but not that much. I will not listen to any more of this unless you come up with a better reason than that."

He shrugged. "We don't have time to talk now anyway. If we don't hurry we'll be late for the meeting of the Reforging Coven. Let's not discuss it in front of René, either. Let him enjoy his hero worship."

"René doesn't… Oh, never mind." More than two years of daily, sometimes intense, contact with Jean had stripped both René and me of the worst excesses of hero worship. René respected Jean, to be sure, and loved him as one loves a grandparent or a revered teacher, but he idolised Beorn, not Jean.

No, Sven was the one displaying the anguish of a man whose hero has turned out to be human. I believed Jean couldn't expose the conspiracy, rather than wouldn't, but it was a matter of faith. Neither option was palatable for Sven.

I let the matter drop, but couldn't quell the sense of disquiet. We would revisit the question, I was quite sure, whether I liked it or not.

"We have covered, in broad strokes," Sorceress Lorraine said, "everything that must be readied for the reforging, but much detailed work remains. We must continue this meeting, and many more over the coming weeks, but only the mages need stay, as the problematic spells are those spanning guilds. The rest are welcome to stay if they choose."

The younger air witch, Enchantress Winifred, bolted for the door before Sorceress Lorraine finished speaking. Sven watched her go with a look that might have been either relief or disappointment. The older enchantress murmured polite thanks and followed with as much haste as dignity allowed.

Beorn said, "Celeste and I have problems we've got to deal with, and I need Jean's help. Sven can handle everything for the Fire Guild. Right, Jean?"

"Certainly," he said, and followed Beorn out the door. Sven's head snapped around. He stared at the closed door long after they were gone.

Besides the other mages and the two sorceresses, Lorraine and Eleanor, that left René and me. René sat with his head down, doodling on a scrap of paper.

With the enchantresses gone we wouldn't be held up waiting for one of the more patient mages to explain everything, twice. I settled into a more comfortable position, eager to listen to these learned men argue minutiae. I might learn as much in an hour as in our earlier meetings combined.

We made good progress until Enchanter Paul, the sole air mage, got into a wrangle with the senior earth mage, Father Jerome. I had trouble following the esoteric details, and asked questions. Eleanor mouthed a thank you at me. My questions drew satisfactory answers from Jerome, less satisfactory, and increasingly curt, answers from Paul, until finally, he said, "My dear Madam Locksmith, I know the Fire Guild has other pressing matters which require your attention. As Her Wisdom said, you don't need to stay. We won't think less of you for not understanding every jot and tittle in every spell."

For two seconds there was dead silence. Eleanor stiffened, her eyes widening. Sven's lip curled. My wretched face burned.

"Lucinda and I," René said, without looking up from his drawing, "are under orders to learn everything we can about the Water Office. Arturos and Quicksilver said that will help us understand the Fire Office."

Paul's eyebrows rose. "Do they expect two near-novices who have never been to university to keep up with the mages?"

Sven said, "Yes." The other mages turned to stare at him. He flushed. "They didn't say it would be easy. Just that the effort would be worthwhile."

"Is that so? Then it would be better," Paul snapped, "if René paid attention."

René looked up, eyes blazing. "I was listening. Father Jerome used Lucinda's questions to clarify his thinking, and refine his arguments. If you—"

"Enough." Sorceress Lorraine at her chilliest commanded attention. "Neither the Locksmith nor Warlock Snorri need justify their presence here. The Locksmith has earned our respect, and the right to have her questions answered. Even frivolous questions, which these were not. Shall we continue?"

With a murmur of 'Yes, Ma'ams', and a rustling of papers, the other mages struggled to hide smiles or raised eyebrows. Enchanter Paul harrumphed and went on doggedly with his losing argument.

You were about to insult him, weren't you, little brother?

All I was going to say was that if he followed Father Jerome's example he wouldn't sound like such an airdick.

All? Calling him names, and comparing him unfavourably to an earth wizard? If that's not an insult to an air wizard, I don't know what is.

Hey, I'm a fire wizard. I have a reputation to uphold.

Oh?

You know, the Fire Guild's reputation for speaking the truth, even when it hurts.

I thought you meant our reputation for being obnoxious, tactless wiseasses.

Same thing, more or less, isn't it?

Be careful, little brother. Your mouth will get you in serious trouble someday.

"Given the size of this conspiracy," Sven said, when we next met in his study, "we'll have to use both the second and third approaches. That is, bring as many mundane commoners in on the secret as possible to dilute it, before we put pressure on it from outside to break it."

"So how do we reach all the commoners," René asked, "when the Air Guild can't do it, and it's their business?"

Sven's lip curled. "They haven't made a serious effort. I have friends in the Air Guild—"

René said, "Like that enchantress you've been flirting with?"

Colour rose in Sven's cheeks. "I have not been flirting with Enchantress Winifred."

René hooted. I said, "She's been flirting with you. In case you hadn't noticed."

Sven's blush deepened. "I had noticed, but those coven meetings are serious business."

Hey, big sister. He won't marry an airhead, will he?

Not likely. He values intelligence too highly.

Sven said, "As I was starting to say, before I was so rudely interrupted, I respect a few members of the Air Guild, but most seem stuck in the tenth century. Their idea of spreading the word is to magically make a few hundred copies of a song or story and send it to the lower ranks, who travel from village to village telling the news. They ignore the printing press because they didn't invent it, and it's non-magical, so it doesn't count. To them, anyway. But I'm not a mage for nothing. I have connections in the printing business. We could print thousands of copies of a broadsheet and blanket the country with it."

"Will that help?" I asked. "Out in the countryside most people can't read. More in the towns and cities are literate, but—"

"Even out in the country most are within a few miles of someone who can read—a pastor, a retired scholar, a professional letter writer— somebody. If we put copies into their hands, the news will spread."

"Yes, but fast enough? In Cathay, the air wizards create notices that read themselves out loud."

Sven's eyes went round. "Wow. How do they do that?"

"No idea. But if we could figure it out, that would help."

"You bet."

"And we'll light a fire under the Air Guild by showing them up." René's impish grin was contagious. "Make them do a better job of pulling their weight."

"And make a few enemies, too," I said.

René's grin widened. "Do I care? How soon can we do it?"

Sven said, "Good question. It has to be synchronised with exposing the secret to the noblewomen. It's the queen and her ladies that matter."

I said, "We need to do it at the end of August—before unlocking the

Water Office—when all the nobles are gathered in Paris." I described my idea.

René laughed. "That'll serve the king right. Let's do it."

I said, "Sven?"

Sven frowned, tapping on his desk. "Might work."

René said, "What can I do?"

Sven said, "Find out which witches and wizards aren't members of the conspiracy. We'll recruit the ones that would be sympathetic."

"I'm on it," he said, and bounded into the fireplace.

"Sven, you're worried," I said. "Why won't it work?"

Sven continued his relentless tapping. "It can work. But what will happen if it does?"

"What do you mean?"

"You brought up the subject of making enemies. Remember what I said about giving the Fire Guild a black eye? There are guild members who don't give a farthing about the lives of mundane women, but will be pissed off at you—us—for making the guild look bad."

"Why should I care about such reprobates?"

"Warlock Flint, I expect, will be one. He's attacked you more than once already, with little justification. What will he do if he has justification? You live in Blazes, not in the Fortress. Can you be on your guard against him, day and night, for weeks on end? And not just for yourself. Who will protect little Edward when you and Quicksilver aren't at home? A level three lady's maid and a level one nursemaid are no match for a warlock."

The room spun. The next thing I knew Sven was bending over me, pressing my head and shoulders down to my knees.

"I'm sorry," he said. "You look ghastly."

I pushed him away. "I won't faint. I just hadn't... I mean, I said the conspiracy was dangerous, but I didn't..."

"No, you don't expect your neighbours to hurt you, do you? What normal, sane person does? Maybe I'm exaggerating how Flint will react..."

I shook my head. I'd seen evidence of Flint's mean streak, and he wasn't the only one in the Fire Guild with a vindictive nature. My obligation to protect Frankland's women fought with my primal urge to protect my family. Jean had been right in making me learn to fight. When this was all over, I would have to apologise for my stubborn streak.

Sven said, "I don't have a family to protect. Maybe you've already done all you needed to do. René and I can let you out of the counter-conspiracy, and we'll carry on without you."

"Aren't you..." I stopped. Sven wouldn't lie to me; I shouldn't ask a question he wouldn't care to answer. Sven, in his own way, was as good a model of a fire wizard as Jean. Like Jean, like Beorn, he would do what he had to. Even if, like me, he was afraid.

Jean's words, from months earlier, echoed in my head. A warlock's primary responsibility is to Frankland's security. That trumps everything else: family, personal comfort, one's own life.

"No," I said. "You can't do it without me."

"If that's the way you feel," he said, "then let's get on with it."

Counter-Conspiracy

Days passed with lightning speed. I moved in a blur of activity, taking no time to brood on the rapid approach of the first of September, or on the empty shell my marriage seemed to have become. Even after the superficial effects of the gift of cold water wore off, Jean did not come back to my bed. He was seldom home for dinner, and often left the house before dawn. We spent hours together holding hands on Storm King—every night, now that Sorceress Lorraine's gift let me absorb power and rebuild my reserves—but it was work, not pleasure, and he bore more resemblance to a slave driver than a lover. Aside from the practice on Storm King, we neither touched nor talked.

It is not accurate to say we didn't speak. We exchanged greetings and inconsequential pleasantries in passing—the kinds of things any two people sharing living quarters must say to each other to maintain a façade of civility. No one watching us would have guessed we were anything other than happily married and quite busy.

But we never talked about anything that mattered. If asking for his advice and guidance would not have given away our counter-conspiracy, I would have grovelled, begging for his help. I didn't dare mention any subject connected to it, and everything other than our house and Edward seemed to touch on it. I volunteered nothing. He asked no questions.

I had never imagined a married woman with a child, in daily association with dozens of people, could be so lonely.

The meetings with the mages went from twice a week to every other day as we struggled with the overlapping spells. Jean was politeness itself in the meetings, but paid me no more attention than he paid anyone else. He encouraged everyone to ask Sven the questions concerning fire magic, and stepped in only on the most arcane points. On those, sometimes even the other mages dropped out, leaving Jean and Sorceress Lorraine, the two oldest, arguing details that went over everyone else's heads. They were as far beyond me as Master Sven was beyond that silly air witch, Enchantress Winifred, and both exhibited pleasure at debating someone who did not need every other word explained. Sven glowered at them. I watched through hooded eyes, and loathed them both.

When not in the Warren's amber room or Sorceress Lorraine's chilly study, I held court in our drawing room in Blazes, listening to a lengthening queue of witches, wizards, and commoners reporting abusive nobles. I dealt with some problems until Beorn chewed me out for putting myself in danger and ordered me to stay home in Blazes to direct less essential personnel in handling wayward nobles and tracking fugitives. Any accused criminal the Fire or Earth Guild could locate, a warlock grabbed and dropped over the border with a nudge towards New London. A steady stream of hints from Sorcerer Charles about fugitives' movements helped. Each exiled fugitive meant one less contentious trial for us to grapple with, our neighbours' growing ire over the influx be damned. Only Enchanter Paul, whose jurisdiction included trade and diplomacy, minded.

As I got better at the long-range spells for communication and information gathering, I kept Sunbeam and other experienced members of the guild hopping, only calling on the Fire Warlock when a situation threatened to ignite. We dealt with new problems before they erupted into open violence, but knew we straddled a powder keg.

Sunbeam never complained, but looked exhausted and a decade older. He would fall asleep within minutes of sitting down in any chair with a back. René didn't bother with the chair. He would collapse onto the hearthrug and snore. Sunbeam's wife came to protest I was overworking him; she stayed for an hour, fussing around me like a mother hen, pouring chamomile tea, and insisting I lie down and take a nap.

I was grateful to Beorn for ordering me to stay home, as being close to my son helped assuage some of the anguish I felt about the prospect of leaving him motherless. If I had not been in the next room when the nursemaid yelled for me to watch him taking his first steps, I would have been heartbroken. Sometimes I gave in to morbid curiosity and wondered who would take up the mantle of mothering him when I was gone. Not that I expected Jean to remarry. He had lived alone for so many years, the demands of wife and child must test even his phenomenal self-control.

Any witch and wizard entering our doors to report a problem exited a recruit in the counter-conspiracy, if they did not already know the secret. The growing power of the counter-conspiracy bolstered René's optimism, but reliving the horror of comprehension with each new recruit took a vicious toll on my spirits. Every time I could snatch a free moment to work on the paper we planned to have printed to spread the word, I cried over it.

Sven and René did most of the legwork on the counter-conspiracy, and I covered for them, assigning them tasks only when no one else was available. I kept looking over my shoulder, expecting at any minute for Beorn to come roaring out of the fireplace, ordering me to stop favouring them and berating all three of us for not doing our share. That order never came, but waiting for it did nothing to calm my nerves. Thank God he didn't notice when I disobeyed his orders and left Blazes, each time recruiting a critical player in our counter-conspiracy.

"I hope you don't mind having tea out in the garden," Earl Eddensford said. "The house is an oven. Up on this hill we may catch a breeze."

"If there are any. Too bad I'm not an air witch."

Claire handed me a fan. "Pretend you are one. That's what I do." She snapped her fan open with a delicate little flick I didn't try to imitate.

"Of course I don't mind sitting out here, as long as we're in the shade. Your gardens are lovely." And they weren't heavy with strands of deceit, like the drawing room.

I itched to dive straight to the point, but was reluctant to put a pall on the conversation from the outset. Precious minutes ticked away as we made small talk. When I couldn't take it anymore, I said, "When are you two leaving for Paris?"

The earl flinched. Claire stiffened. "He's leaving tomorrow," she said. "I'm not going—not on this trip, anyway."

Her husband's lugubrious expression reminded me more of a little boy about to receive a whipping than a ranking nobleman. "Traveling in the summer heat would be too much for her. Besides, this is not a pleasure trip. She would be bored."

"Bored?" I said. "In Paris? She would find ways to amuse herself, and she's wanted to see Paris for, well, as long as I can remember."

221

Claire said, "Richard promised me we'll go next spring for a holiday. I can wait until then."

"Umm-hmm. And how are things here? Are you two settling into your roles as the new earl and his lady?"

Smiles returned at the introduction of this safer topic. "It isn't much of a change for me," he said. "I've handled most of my father's responsibilities for several years. I have been introducing Claire to the city's prominent citizens, and they've all responded most cordially."

She said, "His cousin threw a dinner party for us last week. It was fabulous. Let me tell you about the food…"

She rattled on, making my mouth water. If I hadn't known her so well I would have imagined she didn't have a care in the world, but for all her delight with the things she had seen and tasted, I sensed the party had upset her.

The earl excused himself, giving us time together for girl talk, before I had come up with an excuse to send him away. When he was out of earshot, I asked, "Are the people you've met really treating you well?"

"Well enough. Better than I expected, given that I'm a commoner." She shrugged. "I don't care if it's curiosity, or wanting to get on the new earl's good side, or what, as long as there aren't any obvious snubs. You remember I wondered if Richard was ashamed of me? I must have been mistaken. He's acting as proud as a duke."

"So you've gotten over being angry at him?"

She tossed her head. "I was never angry. You're making me forget what I wanted to tell you about the party. You should have seen what the hostess was wearing…"

While Claire talked, I threw all the spells I had used on Sven's study onto the hill. Keeping my concentration was easy—all I had to do was nod and say the occasional "oh, my," and "my goodness."

Odd. Even at her most conceited, Claire had seldom been boring. Was she blathering on to keep me from asking questions? She had already answered the one that concerned me most, and she hadn't lied.

Of course she hadn't. I had asked the wrong question. I would have been angry. Claire had been hurt and ashamed, and still was. Time to fix that.

The last spell, the one against lip readers, took more concentration. I closed my eyes.

"Oh, Lucinda, I'm so sorry I'm boring you. I've been talking about that party all this time. Tell me what life is like in Blazes now that you're back."

"No, no, not now. As much as I'd like to, I can't stay long, and we have to talk about the trip to Paris—"

"Oh, that. Richard should have gone yesterday, but he's been dragging his heels. He was upset when the second summons came, saying he had to go earlier. He wouldn't be ready to leave tomorrow if I hadn't told the servants to hurry things up."

"Claire, Richard is going to need your help. When he leaves for Paris, you are going with him."

Recruits

"Richard needs my help?" The scone Claire had been nibbling made a slow descent to her plate. "I know you witches and wizards are going to rebuild the Water Office. Richard told me the king wants to be sure it still works, and that's what the summons is about. But what does that have to do with him? Or me?"

"That's only part of it. Before that, there will be a meeting where the Fire Warlock shows the nobility what happened to Lord Edmund. And that's—"

"Oh, no." Claire seemed to crumple. "You mean the whole country will know. That's awful."

"Yes, but that's not the worst of it, and this is why you have to go with him. See, when—"

"What could be worse? I'm sorry, Lucinda, but this is why I let him off with a promise to take me later. I don't want to go. I don't want to be there when the Fire Warlock embarrasses him in front of everybody."

I stopped fanning myself long enough to stare at her hard. "He told you what the king has planned?"

"No."

"But you're not surprised."

She studied the roses downhill from us as if they were in full, gorgeous bloom instead of parched from the heat. "What happened to Edmund was the only thing anybody wanted to talk about at that party. Well, not the only thing. They talked about the magic guilds rebuilding the Water Office, too, but nobody knows what that means, and it just confuses them. Edmund dying upset them a lot more. They didn't say anything directly to either Richard or me, but I heard whispers. And then, when the second message came from the king, Richard was more upset. A lot more. So, no, I'm not surprised."

"I don't blame you for not wanting to go with him, but you have to. No, wait, don't interrupt. You didn't let me finish earlier. The king ordered the Fire Warlock to show the nobles what happened to Lord Edmund. He doesn't know we're going to give him more than he bargained for, and show them how Lord Edmund lived, and why he died, not just how he died."

She abandoned her scrutiny of the roses, and stared at me. "Lucinda, what are you talking about?"

I gripped the hard edge of the wooden bench. "Claire, I'm going to tell you a secret. The secret the noblemen, including your husband, don't want you to know." I described Lord Edmund's crimes, and the noblemen's secret. Baron D'Armond's trial, and Mrs Wetherby's boarding house. Maggie Archer and her friend Fiona.

I paused. Claire stared into the far distance. Her fan had fallen into the grass, but she made no move to pick it up.

"I know this is hard to believe," I said. "I can show you what I've seen, but we'll need a fire. We'll have to go in the house, to a fireplace."

"No, I believe you."

"Wait, what?"

"I believe you," she repeated, focusing again on me. "This explains so much. I ought to have guessed. People say one thing but everything I've seen since I came to Gastòn tells me another. Have you freed me from a spell?"

"I suppose you could say that."

"I should have known."

"Don't be hard on yourself. With magic involved, you couldn't have known."

"But I've known something was wrong, only I didn't know what. Some of the men at the party were just horrid. I've had men undress me with their eyes before, and I despise it, but this was worse, like I was a roast they couldn't wait to stick knives into. I can only imagine what that poor girl in Abertee felt when Edmund—and I'm not going to call him a Lord any longer, so help me God—when he was pawing her."

"Thank God he never got the chance to paw you."

She paled. "He would have. He was my brother-in-law. We would have met, sooner or later."

"Not while your husband had any say in the matter." I told her then, what he had done for her—the spells he had paid Mrs Wetherby for, his attempt to turn Edmund over to the Water Guild, his father's threat, and the son's defiance.

Claire had bent her head; I couldn't see her expression, but a tear splashed onto her plate. "Oh, Richard, I didn't know. I'm so sorry."

"So, you see, if ever he needs an understanding wife, it's now. He doesn't know what's coming. He expects to look like a self-centred coward with no family feeling—which is bad enough, since none of it's true—but when it's over, his brother and father will look much worse. The Eddensfords' reputation will be in shreds."

And it was my fault. The knowledge Frankland would be better off didn't make me feel much better.

Claire put her face down in her hands. "Can't I warn him?"

"No. I've made you a member of the counter-conspiracy now, and the magic won't let you say anything to him until the conspiracy is exposed."

"What should I do?"

"Go to Paris with him. He'll be in shock, and he'll need you to prop him up. I'll tell him he has to take you, and he's not likely to argue. Not much, anyway."

"What will you tell him when he asks why?"

I grimaced. "I'm still working on that. I had planned to say it wasn't fair he'd been to Paris many times and you'd never been once, but you snuffed out that idea."

She picked up her fan and tapped my arm with it. "Never mind. I'll tell him I've changed my mind and want to go. He'll take me."

"You changed your mind? I was at least trying to think up a reason. I'll make it an order if I have to."

Claire walked down the path at such a rapid pace I had to hurry to keep up. "Don't," she said. "I changed my mind, that's all. Let me do the talking. I'm going up to my room to fetch something first, then we'll talk to him."

She came downstairs empty-handed. For a moment I could not see a change, then spotted the lapis lazuli and gold bracelet. I chewed on my lip. Did she remember Granny Helene had lifted the spells on it? I shrugged. She knew better than I what it took to butter up an earl.

We found her husband in the drawing room, listening to a servant report on the arrangements for his trip. He brightened and waved the servant away. "I'd much rather enjoy the company of a pair of lovely women than listen to any more of that. Let's talk about something more pleasant than going to Paris."

"We came to talk about that," Claire said, "I've changed my mind. I'm going with you."

The earl shook his head. "Any other time, my dear, I'd love to have you along, but not this trip."

Claire took his hands in hers. "That's what I thought you would say, but won't you please reconsider? I want to do this for you. You don't want to go. Wouldn't it be easier, knowing I'll be waiting for you in the evenings when the business is all done?"

I strolled away to let them have a private conversation. From across the room I watched him melt, his hangdog expression slowly changing to acceptance, and then to relief.

They reached a decision, and walked arm-in-arm towards me. The earl smiled, but seemed a little dazed. I glanced at Claire and did a double take. Out in the garden she had, as always, been a beauty. With golden hair, fine white teeth, regular features, and porcelain skin, she must be one of the most beautiful women in Frankland.

But the radiant angel approaching would eclipse every other woman in Europa. I was as dazzled as the earl.

He said, "I've changed my mind about Paris. I just can't go without Claire. It's an imposition to ask such a favour from her at the last moment, but she agreed to come with me."

Claire said, "We need to tell the servants."

"Of course." He patted her hand. "I'll take care of everything. There are things I need to see to; I don't know why I've put them off for so long." He wished me a good day, and walked away, humming.

Claire was once again merely gorgeous.

I said, "How do you do that?"

"Oh, it's easy. He'd take me to the moon if I asked. Paris, that's nothing."

"Were you using magic?"

"Yes, of course."

"What magic?"

"How should I know? I thought you did. You're the one that told me about it."

"I did what? When?"

"Two years ago. Don't you remember sitting in an inn and telling me you're a warlock? You told me about my bracelet, too. I don't know what spells are on it; I just know that when I'm wearing it, I can convince anyone of anything."

Master Sven and I waited at the tunnel entrance for Hazel to finish seeing to her patients in Nettleton. I wiped my hands on my skirt. Sven wiped his brow for the second time.

It had to be the heat. Sven enjoyed conspiracies, and he was a mage. If anybody could do this, he could. No reason for the butterflies wreaking havoc in my stomach to afflict him.

He wiped his brow for the third time. If he did it again, I would flame him.

Hazel came out of the croft, and started towards us. Her pleasure at seeing me was displaced by the normal female reaction on seeing Master Sven for the first time: wide eyes and a faint flush. But that was all. After greetings and introductions, she turned back to me with no apparent regret. "I didn't expect to see you again so soon, Lucinda. Is anything wrong?"

Did she have a beau? She hadn't told me. Thank God, she didn't simper.

I said, "Yes, we have a problem, and need your help. Is there someplace we can go out of earshot?"

"We can walk further along this track, away from the village. Will that do?"

"Sure. While we walk, tell us everything you can about the White Duke."

Her forehead wrinkled, but she shrugged and started talking. I listened as we walked, nodding and making prompting noises whenever she paused, but most of my attention was on the filaments draped over her. One by one, Sven worked on each strand, cementing her connections to our copper-coloured counter-conspiracy strands; tying off and snipping the others, until only one connected her to the larger engine.

This was too tedious. We couldn't free more than a few people this way, and it would never work on the ones most entangled.

The last strand was tied off, waiting to be snipped. If Sven's spellcraft wasn't solid…

He made a face at me. I nodded. He snipped. The black filaments draped on Hazel flashed copper. The loose black ends shrivelled and blew away.

Sven let out a gusty, "Whoosh!" I sat down, too hard, on a rock. Hazel's head swivelled between us.

"Our problem doesn't have anything to do with the White Duke," I said, rubbing my bruised rump.

Sven explained about the counter-conspiracy and our plans. Hazel listened with a widening grin and gleaming eyes.

"What can I do?" she said.

I said, "Help us recruit Maggie Archer."

Sven said, "Come in, Lucinda," without looking up. He hunched over my paper, scowling. Red ink from his annotations and corrections obscured the black from my pen.

"Is it that bad?" I asked.

"Bad? No, it's worse. Worse than I imagined."

"Can I fix it?"

He frowned at me. "You? Of course not."

I would never claim to be as fine a writer as Master Sven, but this was a bit much. I leaned on his desk with my hands on my hips. "Tell me the truth. I can take it. If you need to rewrite it, that's fine."

"Rewrite? Oh, this paper. No, it's fine for a first draft. Of course you can fix it." He shoved it at me, and it fell over the edge. I grabbed it before it hit the floor.

"Sorry," he said, "I didn't mean that. I have other things on my mind."

"Like what?"

"Nothing I should bother you with. Forget I said anything."

"It's about the conspiracy, isn't it?"

"Uh…"

I brought my face down level with his. "You gave me grief when you thought I was hiding things from you. You'd better not hide things from me either."

He glanced sideways at the door. I blocked him in and leaned closer. "Give," I said.

"Back up," he said. "We're going down to the practice room."

Baffled, I followed him. I sat at one end of the iron table; he stood at the other.

"That's better," he said. "There's nothing flammable here. You remember I said I intended to find out how widespread the knowledge is among the noblemen? My research traced who each learned it from. If I drew a chart it would look like a tree, going back to a single trunk. That would be Old Brimstone, if I traced it all the way back. I haven't. I didn't need to—it narrowed down to half-a-dozen men, much sooner than that."

"When? Go on," I prompted, when he stopped and stared at me.

"A little over a hundred years ago."

"You mean during the last Scorching Time?"

He walked towards the door leading to his study. "No, I mean about five years after Quicksilver became Fire Warlock. He's responsible for spreading the secret."

A Warlock's Closest Friend

Anger, it has been said, is a warlock's closest friend, dearer to him than parents, wife, or children. Perhaps that is so. Anger was never far from me that August. If Sorceress Lorraine had not given me the gift of cold water, I might have behaved like Warlock Flint. Even with her help, my self-control shredded daily, if not more often, as tempers, not just those of the Fire Guild, flared all around me. The scramble to be ready for the unlocking, the hysteria among the nobles, and an epic heat wave took a toll on everyone.

Sunbeam was determined to stop the rebuilding effort. He got into shouting matches with everyone on the Fire Guild Council, Mother Celeste, and Enchanter Paul. His discussion with Sorceress Lorraine only avoided shouting because she froze him in place and walked away in a huff. The healer in Blazes had to appeal to the Warren for help; she had never before treated anyone for frostbite.

The nightly thunder from atop Storm King troubled the sleep of many residents in Blazes and the Fortress. Jean's answer to everyone who complained was a polite but evasive, "It will end soon." When a delegation complained to Beorn he told them to go to hell, and had guards escort them back to Blazes.

Flint attacked Jean in the guildhall's common room. The confrontation ruined three unlucky travellers' holiday, and turned the building's south-eastern corner into a heap of smoking rubble. When Flint, pale, bald, and scarred, came out of hiding a week later, the Fire Warlock ordered him to test and report on the defences of all Frankland's Fire and Earth guildhalls, a task that, if we were lucky, would take weeks. Blazes breathed a collective sigh of relief. My joy was short-lived; the Fire Warlock handed me the roster and ordered me to track his progress and warn the healers he was coming.

Sven developed a fixed scowl, and snapped at people wishing him a good day. We avoided discussing Jean, but our conversations sounded like two hissing cats with arched backs.

Hazel cried at the least provocation, or no provocation at all.

For several days René stormed in and out of the house, slamming doors and snapping at me as if I'd pissed him off, but he wouldn't tell me why. I got fed up and hit him with a blast hard enough to knock him across the town square and singe his eyebrows. He acted more like his normal, cheerful self after that. Too bad that method wouldn't work on my other friends.

Sven and Enchantress Winifred appeared to have moved beyond mere flirtation. They sat with their heads together, whispering, at the meetings of the full coven. I was trying, without success, to view it in a positive light—a little romance might reduce the tensions between the Fire and Air Guilds—when she snatched up her papers and stormed out of the room without asking leave. We turned to stare at Sven. He glowered, red-faced and thin-lipped.

Enchanter Paul said, "I hope you will have the decency to apologise for whatever insult you offered her."

Sven's colour deepened, even his ears turning red. "How can a mage's offer to tutor someone who isn't a scholar be construed as an insult? I'm offended she rejected my offer to help."

Enchanter Paul stiffened. "The Air Guild has its own, fully qualified theory teachers."

"Indeed," Sorceress Lorraine snapped, cutting off Sven's retort, "and I will expect you to ensure she uses them. Shall we proceed?"

I began to hate the many meetings, and rarely left one without a headache. Even the meetings with the mages, which I should have enjoyed, became distasteful. The discussions grew frantic as September first approached, and I resented the constant reminders. The smaller meetings, with Jean, the Officeholders, and their apprentices, were no better, with arguments between the best of friends. I walked into the amber chamber one afternoon on the heels of the two sorceresses. Beorn and Mother Celeste were growling at each other.

Mother Celeste said, "…safer in the Warren," before they noticed us and cut off the argument.

Sorceress Lorraine snapped, "Will you please continue this discussion some other time, when I do not have to listen to it?"

Beorn and Mother Celeste mumbled apologies, but Lorraine was not cool and calm. She looked like a fire witch, with nostrils flaring, lips tight. Sorceress Eleanor didn't look any happier.

Afterwards, I followed Beorn to his study, and tackled him alone, on a subject he'd already insisted he didn't want to talk about.

"Beorn, you had visions before you became Fire Warlock. Isn't there anything you can tell me about the future?"

He glared at me with his arms crossed. "If I told you something you liked you might not work so hard, and if you didn't like it, you might give up too easy, so I'm not going to tell you a damn thing. Get out of here. We've both got work to do."

I stomped to the door, annoyed the thick carpet muffled my footfalls, and swore at him all the way down the stairs.

On the twenty-second of August, I woke with terror crawling down my back like an itch I couldn't reach. An hour with the trouble-seeking spells provided no information to either confirm or dispel my fears, but the itch grew stronger as the day crept on. I was short with the queue of people reporting problems, and lost my temper so thoroughly with Katie that she fled, mumbling curses. After several snappish exchanges with René, he called me a first-class old hag and refused to talk to me any longer.

By late afternoon, I abandoned any pretence of working on the Fire Warlock's behalf and demanded Sven come down from the Fortress and deal with the queue. Tom kept his distance as I huddled over a small fire in the study. The house and its surroundings, the streets in Blazes, the royal palace where Beorn was arguing with the king; I searched them all for any sign of immediate danger.

Jean was in London. I scoured the crowds, Mayfair to Shoreditch, looking for the threat. After two hours, half blind with tension, I abandoned Jean for René, and found him in a crowded inn, ignoring rising anger as he coaxed information from a trembling serving girl. Black death reared behind him, from two directions. I dove through the fire, shot flame, grabbed an ear and an arm, and yanked. We fell out of the fire onto the floor of the study. The screaming girl landed on top of me with her shoulder to my middle. I shoved her off and rolled into a ball, clutching at my stomach.

René, swearing, brought the fire to a full roar and opened a window into the chaos in the inn we had just left. Two men, one by the bar, the other less than an arm's reach away from where René had been, blazed like torches. Other men and women, close to them or to where I jumped out of the fire, beat at burning clothes. Howling bodies surged for the doors and windows.

I scrambled to my feet and fled into the garden, retching. When my stomach was empty, I crept back into the house and peered around the study door.

Jean was calming our staff and the hysterical serving girl. Tom was pouring himself a glass from a bottle of our best brandy. René, wan and quiet, choked down more of the same.

I slunk away and climbed the stairs to my bedroom. I dropped down beside the sleeping cat on the bed and buried my face in her fur. The startled cat hissed, swiped me with her claws, and stomped away with her tail in the air. I lay face down, and sobbed.

When Jean came to the door some time later, I didn't raise my head. "How many people did I... How many died?"

"No one died, my dear."

"No one? But... I watched them burn. How..."

"The inn had burn cloths on hand, and the Earth Guild house is directly opposite. The two would-be assassins survived, as did the young women trampled in the panic. No one will even carry scars from the burns."

I took a tighter grip on the pillow. Still staring at the far wall, I said, "So you've come to scold me for not being forceful enough."

"No, my love, I have come to offer an apology for not trusting your instincts. You used the force needed to thwart the attack and save René, and no more. Your control, your aim, your timing were perfect. It was a superb performance for one so young. I could not have bettered it."

I rolled over and stared at him. "You're not angry."

"Not at all." He came closer and looked down at me, alarm in his eyes. "What happened to your face?"

I explained about the cat. He winced, summoned a jar, and spread ointment on my scratches with gentle fingers.

"I don't understand," I said. "You've always said to kill an enemy so he doesn't get another change to attack us."

He sighed and studied the jar in his hand, capping it before answering. "Our enemies, yes, but these men are not our enemies. They are, they believe, virtuous men protecting other Franks they admire and respect from tyrannical and unjust treatment at the hands of the Water Guild. They do not understand what René and the Fire Guild are doing for them, and are confused and frightened when they see the Fire Guild now hand-in-hand with our, and their, old enemy, the Water Guild.

"Beorn corrected their misunderstanding. He chastised everyone at the inn for not cooperating with the Fire Guild's efforts to keep decent men out of the Water Guild's clutches, and informed them they were lucky you were so soft-hearted you didn't kill the attackers on the spot. The two men will recover with a proper respect for a fire witch, and no desire to ever again draw the Fire Guild's attention.

"It is fortunate, indeed, you did not kill them. The already-frayed trust the mundanes have for the magic guilds would have deteriorated further. I regret not trusting your instincts regarding the use of force. As you have pointed out, you have shown you can be forceful when necessary.

"To kill when it is not necessary is…" He stopped, groping for words.

I caught his hand and held it against my cheek. "Is a bad idea."

The corners of his eyes creased into a smile. "Indeed. You have been wiser than I in this aspect of your training. I have been concerned for so long with fighting foreign warriors I did not consider you might need different weapons against domestic opponents."

"Or what you've been harping on for all our training—avoid acting as if we always need more power when we've got Storm King to draw on."

"Guilty as charged, madam. Indeed, if you had responded with greater force, innocents would have burned, perhaps died."

The knot of tension around my temples unravelled. "You haven't trusted my sense of prescience either. I know when I'm in danger. Or when somebody I care about is."

He resumed his study of the ointment, turning the jar over and over in his hands. "I apologise for that also. I seldom trust talents not under one's conscious control."

We talked for a while longer before Jean left with a promise to tell René and the Fire Eaters how pleased he was with my actions. I slept, woke refreshed, and went down to supper in a better mood than I'd been in for weeks.

René, still subdued, was making short work of a midnight snack the size of a field hand's dinner. He mumbled his thanks around a mouthful of sausage, and without looking up, added apologies for making fun of my fighting abilities.

"About time you noticed I'm not helpless," I said. "Although I'll never be a warrior like you."

He looked up and smiled. "That's all right then."

"Of course it is. Where's Jean? Why didn't anyone wake me?"

"Gone back to Blacksburg. He gave orders to leave you alone. Said you'd earned a rest today."

"Nice of him. Why was he home at that time of day? He must have walked in just after it happened."

"I called him," René said. "Figured he'd want to know."

I lowered my fork. "You did? How?"

René gave me a blank look. "I just yelled. In my head. Like I do talking to you. And he answered."

The blue and white pattern in the dining room's wallpaper took on a distinct red cast. I clenched my knife and snarled.

René scrambled out of his chair. "Sorry. Uh, for whatever." He grabbed a hunk of bread and scarpered.

My dear, loving husband let a fifteen-year-old boy into his head but threw up walls against his own wife? Bone of his bones, flesh of his flesh, was I? I'd show him. I'd make him regret ever telling me my attacks should be more forceful. I'd...

As if any attack I could throw would hurt Warlock Quicksilver, Frankland's greatest Fire Warlock. Compared to him I was...

I shoved my untouched plate away and retreated to my bedroom, locking the door before flopping onto the bed and bawling. Compared to the great Flame Mage, Jean Rehsavvy, I was nothing. A mere beginner, hardly fit to be in the same room with him, let alone demand his attention. How tired he must be of my naïve questions, my simpleton's nattering.

Especially with Sorceress Lorraine reminding him daily of the pleasures of matching wits with a mind as well furnished as his own. Far too polite to ever say so, he must bitterly regret letting himself be tied to a neophyte like me.

I thrashed about for hours, unable to sleep, until enlightenment made me jerk upright and stare out the window, unseeing, unmoving.

A bond, like the one I had with René, or the one I wanted with Jean, had its own dangers. Two years earlier, Jean, afraid of losing us both, made me promise never to attempt to draw René back from the brink of death. If Jean had a bond with me, he, hero that he was, would feel obligated to draw me back from death's grip, even knowing the odds against success. But if there was no bond, he couldn't try.

Paris

The stars vanished; the sky lightened. The breath-taking blaze of light when the first rays hit the aerie did not move me. My anger had died, leaving me hollow, numb.

What had Jean said three years ago, while fending off the Fire Office's demand he kill the spy in the Fire Guild stronghold? Something about not being averse to sacrificing himself, but there was no point if it did not improve the overall outcome.

My head called him sensible. Frankland needed him. Why risk losing his life, too, if I was doomed?

My heart called him traitor. Maybe Sven was right. Maybe this man I loved, that I thought I knew, had other secrets that would horrify me. He was as cold-hearted as any Frost Maiden. He had once said so himself. How else had he survived for so long?

For the next few days, I avoided him, hiding in our bedroom whenever he was home. The rest of the household avoided me. I refused to go up on Storm King with him. Without asking for or giving an explanation, Beorn took over and we continued our exercises with him. By the twenty-eighth, I was counting minutes until the meeting in Paris, when I would have a suitable target to blast to bits.

"As long as Maggie Archer is inside the circle, she's not in danger, right?"

Sweat beaded on Sven's forehead. René pushed the windows of Sven's study open further, but no air moved.

"We've been over this before," Sven said, "but if it makes you feel better, let's go through it again. Most magical conspiracies aren't dangerous, since they use magic to keep the secret. It's the mundane ones that use deadly force to prevent exposure."

"Except for—"

"Yes, except for the magical conspiracies, like this one, hiding criminal behaviour. Those can turn violent when under attack from outside. That's why Miss Archer has to be in the circle; we can't take chances with our star witness's life. Does everyone in the counter-conspiracy know what to do?"

"They ought to," I said. "We told them where to go, and when the time comes, to hold hands, because we'll be stronger that way."

"As long as we're not overpowered, Miss Archer will be safe. Make sure she knows. Once the attack begins, we won't have any time or power to spare for her." He drummed on his desk. "And we need both of you in it. One level-five talent isn't enough."

"Sunbeam will help. We warned him to be on the alert, and told him what to do. He doesn't know what it's about, but he'll be thrilled to show off in front a large audience."

"Good, I guess." Sven looked sceptical. "What did you warn him to be on the alert for?"

René grinned. "Conspiracy magic trying to silence an innocent and very, very pretty girl."

Sven snorted. "I should've thought of that. I must say I'll be grateful for his help."

I said, "I'm grateful Flint won't be there." Beorn had deputised him to stay at the Fortress while we were at the royal palace. For the first time in my experience, Flint had looked happy—happy, I supposed, to avoid a boring royal audience, and to have an opportunity to officially blast anyone making trouble.

René said, "I wonder how angry he'll be when he realises he's missed the day's fun."

Sven groaned. "Did you have to say that?"

"He's a problem only if we live through it," I said. "Stop worrying. It's time to go."

I ran through the tunnels to the Warren, to meet Hazel and Maggie in an empty classroom. Maggie was chewing her fingernails down to the quick.

"You look good," I said. "Real good. You'd pass for a guild member."

She ought to, wearing a red silk gown I'd worn to an endless succession of state dinners on our honeymoon. Hazel had added a flounce at the bottom to hide several inches of leg, but otherwise, with a couple of judicious tucks in the waist and bodice, it fit her well enough.

"I put a glamour spell on her," Hazel said. "Even the Fire Guild will think she's one of you."

"Good. The fewer questions, the better." I handed Maggie a sash embroidered in gold thread with fire guild symbols, and told her to knot it around her waist. "This will protect you from the fire. When the flames start flying, stay in the circle of witches and wizards. We'll protect you, or die trying."

"I trust you. I'm not worried. Not about that anyway."

I did a double take. That had not been bravado speaking. "What are you worried about?"

She clasped her hands behind her back and piped, "That I won't be loud enough for anyone to hear me."

Hazel smiled. "You just talk. I'll make everybody in the whole frostbitten palace hear you."

We waited at a side door to the ballroom until the procession started, then slipped like shadows into spaces left vacant on the end of the second row, beside Master Sven. He gave us the barest of nods. Behind us, Matt ogled and Tom mouthed a whistle at Maggie. From the front row, beside Sunbeam, René winked at me.

I glared at him. *You're enjoying this, aren't you, you little beast?*

Sure am. If I'm going to be Fire Warlock someday then I'm not dying today.

The procession advanced. The four Officeholders, plus Jean, as the only living retired guild head, took their places on the right of the dais, facing the witches and wizards down on the floor. Beorn glanced at us and winked. Jean didn't look in our direction.

The galleries overflowed with commoners and lower-ranking witches and wizards. Three years ago, in my previous trip to the royal palace, I had been up there. I had covered a lot of ground since then. If the next two years were as eventful as the previous two, would I be on the dais at a royal audience?

I shuddered. Any event impelling me to a place up there with, or as one of, the Officeholders was one I'd rather not consider.

The dukes took their places on the left, facing the rows of nobles. I craned my neck and saw the Earl of Eddensford. Golden hair at shoulder height beside him confirmed Claire was with him.

The royal family processed in. I ignored them, and worked the spell to show me the engine of lies. The dais disappeared, hidden behind a black, knotted mass dense enough to throttle every soul in the ballroom. It blotted out the flashes from the four Tokens of Office. It even blotted out Jean's lighthouse beacon. Grey filaments covered the walls, ceiling, balconies, and seated audience. I trembled.

Cut it out, Lucinda. What'd you expect, with everybody who's anybody in Frankland here?

I knew it would be bad, but not—

It's getting better.

Is it? How can you tell?

Watch the edges.

I was about to tell René he was nuts when I saw strands on the balconies and ceiling stirring, like cobwebs in a breeze.

The royal couple, with their twelve-year-old crown prince, reached the thrones on the dais. Finally, we were allowed to sit.

My mind's eye roved. Pamphleteers spread across the city, as Sven had promised. On street corners, someone—an urchin here, an old man there, somewhere else a young woman with a baby on one hip and apron pockets weighted down with papers—called out to passers-by to take a pamphlet and learn the nobles' secret. Knots of people, blocking the footpaths, clustered around anyone with a copy. Young men listened, then ran to spread the news. Innkeepers climbed on chairs and tables to get their customers' attention. Similar scenes would be playing out in other cities.

The conspiracy, under attack from many directions, began to pull apart. A tangle by a window disintegrated, strands drifting outwards. Coils of dark magic twisted this way and that, seeking a target—someone, anyone, to attack, but there were too many. The conspiracy was balked.

I settled back in my chair and breathed a heartfelt prayer of thanks. The conspiracy was dangerous, but it was a mindless thing, and Master Sven had predicted how it would act. We'd taken the necessary precautions. Things would go according to plan.

They might, indeed, have done so, if I had not, once again, underestimated the Earl of Eddensford.

Engine of Lies

Sorceress Lorraine strolled across the dais, gesturing at the large mirror hanging behind the thrones. "My lords and ladies, with their majesties' leave the Water Guild installed a magic mirror, in which you may witness the events leading up to Lord Edmund's death. Your Majesties may watch without leaving your thrones in these smaller mirrors." She handed each a mirror the size of a schoolboy's slate.

Beorn strode to the other side of the dais. He explained what everyone would see, and then the argument between Lord Edmund's father and brother played out over our heads, loud enough for everyone in the hall, and possibly the crowds outside listening at the windows, to hear. The scene gave no hint of Edmund's criminal behaviour—no surprise, that—as the father's threat against his son's sweetheart became instead a threat to withhold funds.

The scene in the mirror faded, replaced by Claire's private wedding to Lord Richard, with only two witnesses. The onlookers' first glimpse of Claire was at her most radiant. A gasp went up, followed by whispered conversations as we watched them leave the church. Lord Richard bent to pick jonquils beside the footpath, then handed them with a flourish to his glowing bride.

The murmur of voices grew as the next scene, an exemplar of domestic bliss, showed Claire, clearly pregnant, stitching beside a warm fire. She smiled at Lord Richard when he entered and kissed her. He stood in front of the fire, warming his hands, and talking about news of a blizzard in the northern districts.

A glimpse of an infant followed, and finally, my conversation with Claire. The scene did not, as I had dreaded, divulge Claire's opinion of

Lord Richard. It merely showed the end, where we realised Lord Edmund had lost his shields, and a message must be sent to warn him.

"That was the sixth of July," the Fire Warlock said. "She sent the message that afternoon, but it was too late. It arrived at the White Duke's manor after Lord Edmund Bradford was already dead."

He waved at the mirror, the images shifted, and we watched Lord Edmund and his henchmen ride into the Archer's yard.

I looked away from the mirror, and surveyed the room with my mind's eye. The black mesh was breaking up, much faster now. Clear sections grew overhead and in the balconies, but the massive knot on the dais appeared untouched. Despair shook me. Even with two years' experience drawing on the power of Storm King, I couldn't do it by myself. It would kill me. How had I ever imagined our tiny counter-conspiracy, with only two level-five talents, could overcome conspiracy magic backed by all four Offices?

Because Beorn would come to my rescue when he realised how far the news had spread.

I eyed Sven. He stared straight ahead, knuckles white on the hand gripping his wand. Sven had gone along with my plan, despite his misgivings. He must believe in them, too.

It was too late to reconsider. The printers and pamphleteers had done their best; we couldn't let them down.

Beside me, Maggie hissed. In the mirror, we looked over Maggie's shoulder as Lord Edmund groped her. Her brother pulled him away.

Maggie quivered, as tense as a bowstring. "Wait," I said.

A clamour of protest from the nobles turned into a collective gasp as the smith hit Lord Edmund and he went down. No one spoke. No one moved. The noise from the crowds outside, unable to see what had happened, was loud in the sudden silence. The earl leaned forward with his head in his hands. Claire put her arm around her husband's shoulders.

"So you see," Beorn said, "it wasn't magic. He wasn't second in line anymore, and the Fire Office didn't shield him. He got into a fight, and lost. That's all there is to it."

"All there is to it?" the king screeched. "That commoner had no right to fight him over some halfpenny whore. He's a murderer. Why hasn't he been brought to justice?"

"Now," I hissed, but Maggie was already on her feet.

246

"Lies," she yelled, her voice carrying through the hall and echoing out in the courtyard. "I'm a maid, not a whore. My brother saved me from a man who'd already raped five women. There are lies all around us. The magic folk can see them."

"And so shall you," I thundered, my voice as loud as hers. My wand and Sven's swept arcs across the ballroom, exposing the murky tangle to all eyes. The inert mass came to life, recognising, at long last, its attackers. Gears cranked, pulleys spun, strands lashed out at our group of witches and wizards, only to jerk away, burning, from the copper strands of the counter-conspiracy.

For a few moments, the spectators seemed spellbound, too confused or scared to react. Only the king seemed oblivious to the black horror surrounding him. "Guards," he yelled, "evict this impudent hussy. Who does she think she is, slandering one of her betters?"

From the corner of my eye, I saw Earl Eddensford rise, Claire beside him with her hand on his arm. How the magic worked I do not know, perhaps her touch freed him, because he said, in a ringing voice, "Let her be. She speaks the truth. Edmund was—" A wire whipped around the earl's neck and tightened. He stopped with a strangled gasp and fell, his hands clawing at his throat.

Men yelled, women screamed. Witches and mundanes, noble and commoner alike bolted for the doors or cowered in their seats as the roiling tangle searched for other threats.

A stiletto of a voice—Sorceress Lorraine's—soared over the commotion. "Mundanes, conspirators, freeze!"

Only the members of the counter-conspiracy, gathering closer to concentrate our power, were still free to move. Men, women, and children stopped dead in their tracks. The prince, diving from the dais towards his cousin, the earl, was caught in mid-leap. Claire, an angel come to rescue a poor sinner from the jaws of hell, stooped over her husband, golden hair haloing her face against the vile blackness.

A wire whipped around her throat, and tightened.

I yelled at René, *Help them.*

He ran, slashing a burning path to the earl's side with a fiery wand. Sunbeam saw Claire, and bounded after René, leaving Maggie exposed.

Cords lashed at her. She shrieked and dove for the floor. Tom vaulted the chairs and fell on her, knocking her flat and taking the brunt of a dozen scourging strands on his own back. He screamed. Other witches and wizards scrambled to fill in the gaps and tighten the edge of our circle.

Come on, Beorn, undo the spell.

The engine of lies, aware now of the gravest threat, abandoned the pamphleteers. The room darkened as gears turned, pulling in power, building an impenetrable mesh around its core. A bubble of fire formed around us where black strands met copper. If René and Sunbeam hadn't created a similar bubble, God help them. I couldn't.

Beorn, help. Now would be good.

Sven and I sent blast after blast of flame, hot enough to melt glass, shooting into the conspiracy's dense core, but it barely made a dent. I would use all the power I had, and it would not be enough. Even my rising anger, a battering ram of fury against the two warlocks on the dais refusing to help, wasn't enough.

The black mass pressed down on us, crushing our bubble. We squeezed together, a dozen witches and wizards crowding round me with their hands on my arms and shoulders. A thrashing cord broke through our defences, slashing a wizard across the face.

The copper strands of the counter-conspiracy wavered, and other whipping cords broke through. Witches and wizards around me flailed, screamed, clawed at my arms and skirts.

And then I discovered aid coming from an unexpected direction. Lorraine was freezing cables, sucking the power out of them. All around her, they fell to the ground and shattered. If there were just two of her...

The tightness in my chest disappeared. At long last, I understood what she had done. I threw back my head and laughed. Power, more than enough, surrounded me, and the gift of cold water made it mine for the taking,

I yanked my arms free and stretched them out to the thrashing tangle. With one hand I drew in power from the attacking cables, with the other threw it back out as flame. For ten long breaths, light and darkness seemed evenly matched, and then, at a pace befitting a king's funeral cortege, the diabolical engine began to destroy itself.

My arms shook from the strain before the jet of fire sizzling through the murk punched a path all the way to the dais. Jean's beacon flooded back in a glorious golden blaze, burning the hole wider and wider. In seconds, he pushed his way into the circle. Our burning bubble expanded, and encompassed more of the room. Terrified men and women stood frozen in place, forced to see and hear a battle they did not understand. Beorn, still ensnared, watched. René whooped and pumped a fist when our bubble swallowed his and Sunbeam's smaller one.

The bubble reached Beorn, lighting him up like a bonfire. He jumped off the dais with a roar and reached for me over Hazel's head. "What took you so long?" he said, grinning.

The black tangle disappeared in a dazzling burst, leaving the room clear. I followed the circle of fire with my mind's eye as it expanded further and further outward, sweeping all of Frankland and burning away the last remnants of the conspiracy.

Beorn let go, and we were back in the royal palace, facing a ballroom full of frightened and bewildered people. That was all I saw before I pitched forward into my husband's arms.

⸺ ❧ ⸺

I regained consciousness in our bedroom, to hear Jean barking orders at our flustered staff.

"You wonderful, wonderful witch," he said, punctuating each word with a brisk but fervent kiss. "Eat. Sleep. Rest here until you have recovered." Another solid kiss, and he disappeared into the fireplace.

I ate. I slept. I woke, still confused over Jean and Beorn's reluctance to help, but warmed by Jean's praise. The anger that had been my constant companion for weeks melted away. I had been a fool to let fear and jealousy cloud my reason; he did still love me. Hadn't he called me wonderful? Late in the afternoon, when neither Jean nor René had returned, and no word had come from Paris, I scraped together the last of my reserves, and called up images in the fire of the day's events.

The ballroom would have been a maelstrom of screaming people if the spectators had not still been frozen in place. The few moving were the counter-conspirators, and Mother Celeste, scrambling down from the dais to lay healing hands first on Earl Eddensford and Claire, half-strangled, and then Tom with his flayed back, and other unfortunates gashed by whipping wires.

While she worked her healing magic, Beorn provided an account of what had just happened. It was the most polished speech I ever heard him give. As if he'd spent hours practicing.

Only then did Lorraine lift her spell. The din the shuffling audience made died quickly as they strained to hear the shouting king. Whether he was too dim or too self-absorbed wasn't obvious, but he had failed to grasp Beorn's explanations. He was still raging at Maggie Archer, claiming she had defamed Lord Edmund, and demanding a trial.

I leaned forward, not wanting to miss Lorraine's sarcastic response.

"Certainly, Your Majesty," she said. "Here and now. This afternoon."

I almost fell into the fire. Maggie Archer on trial? Never once had I considered that possibility. Facing the Water Office was far worse than facing a magical conspiracy. Until this morning, the conspiracy had not tried to kill anyone.

Why were the hairs on the back of my neck standing on end? Maggie was in no danger. The Water Office didn't freeze slanderers. And it wasn't slander to tell the truth. With the conspiracy destroyed, the truth could be told at the trial. Maggie had nothing to worry about.

Then Lorraine's words from weeks ago came back to me. "I would bring a test case to the nobles in August, to shock them..." Ice water flowed through my veins. We had handed her a test case, made to order, for her to demonstrate just how broken the Water Office was.

Maggie in the Balance

Thank God I missed the legal manoeuvrings. Sitting before the fire in my bedroom, I flew through that tedium. Only a few things caught my attention: Tom and Matt facing down the king's men-at-arms over custody of the distraught girl. The crown prince, to his father's fury, regarding René with something close to hero worship. Lorraine boxing the king into a corner when he demanded the noblewomen leave the ballroom—if the allegations were falsehoods, nothing could offend their delicate sensibilities, could it?

A water wizard delivered a large silver balance to one side of the dais. Jean and Lorraine huddled with the king's advisors, while the royal family and nobles left for their midday meal. Despite the August heat, most commoners stayed, packed into the upper tiers, unwilling to give up their vantage spots for the coming show. Our pamphlets appeared, passed from hand to hand, amidst a rising tide of angry muttering. More spectators packed in the already crowded balconies until I feared they would collapse under their weight. Outside, commoners converged on the palace from all directions, blocking traffic in the streets, and climbing trees and fence posts to see. Far too late the guards attempted to close the gates, but the crowds wouldn't let them.

The nobles trickled back in. Tom and Matt escorted Maggie onto the dais, and saved her from falling when confronted with the silver scales. The royal family returned, and the trial began.

Over the past few weeks, I had grown accustomed to thinking of the head of the Water Guild as Sorceress Lorraine, a woman with heart under a cool demeanour. But the woman presiding over the trial was without doubt the Frost Maiden, with an alabaster complexion and a voice as sharp as the north wind.

That made two of us suffering from overactive consciences, but her armour was better than mine.

I had already had my fill of Lord Edmund. I flicked through the presentation of the first rape, noting with relief it did not show the woman's face, and nearly missed the interruption.

"Stop this! Now!"

The mirror clouded over, and I searched for the source of the vehement order. Queen Marguerite leaned forward on her throne, her face and body rigid, with her hands clamped over the squirming prince's eyes. Her husband squinted at her as if she had turned into a scorpion.

"I will not watch any more of this filth," the queen said. "I will not have my son subjected to it either." She raked the line of dukes with her eyes. "I never imagined anyone from a noble family could engage in such heinous behaviour. It is obvious, Stephen, we have been lied to."

King Stephen's relief was palpable. "Yes, yes, my dear, that is so." He turned and glared at the dukes. Several of them returned the glare, but didn't refute the charge.

"I beg your pardon, Your Majesty," Lorraine said, "but may I remind you several dozen men and women risked their lives today to destroy a conspiracy that, they claim, masked Lord Edmund's true nature. It is inappropriate for children, but if we adults cannot view these events, how shall we know the truth?"

The king summoned a man-at-arms to escort the protesting prince from the ballroom. Then he turned to his wife. "My dear, you should leave, too. Your delicate constitution can't take this."

"Queen Marguerite's constitution, Your Majesty," Mother Celeste said, "is stronger than yours. She is healthier in both mind and body than some of the women Lord Edmund attacked. She is unlikely to suffer permanent damage watching what they had to live through."

The queen patted her husband's hand. "Sorceress Lorraine and Mother Celeste make good points. It's sweet of you, dear, to try to spare me from this, but what kind of a queen would I be if I ran away from every hint of bad news? I believe I must stay, on behalf of Frankland's women, no matter how dreadful it is. But if other women want to leave, please go ahead and do so."

A flurry of conversation followed as many noblemen encouraged the women with them to withdraw. No one moved.

The queen said, "Must you show us everything? Couldn't you skip over some of the, er…"

"Most disagreeable parts?" Lorraine said. "Yes, but I insist we witness enough to either confirm or deny Miss Archer's charge."

The small mirror in the queen's hand wobbled. She gripped it with both hands, raised her chin, and straightened her spine. "Very well, go on."

The images in the fire faded as I burned through the last dregs of my power. The trial hadn't finished. I ran for the Fortress and charged up the stairs to the tunnel ending in the royal ballroom's cavernous fireplace. I crept forward in the shadows under the balconies while the magic mirror over the thrones replayed the argument between the old earl and Lord Richard. This time it was as I had seen it, to the old earl's detriment.

Maggie saw me, and glared. I looked away. Jean gave me the barest shake of his head. I shouldn't have come? Too bad, I wasn't going to miss this show.

The counter-conspirators were a sorry-looking lot of sluggards. Some valiant souls fought to stay awake; others, like René and Sunbeam, gave up all pretence and snored. Master Sven leaned forward, forehead resting on the seat back in front of him. He raised his head and nodded when I slid in beside him.

He whispered, "I promised Miss Archer the Fire Guild would pay the fine, but the rest…" He shrugged. "I'll pay out of my own pocket if the Council doesn't agree."

"I'll split it with you," I said. "Seems like the least we can do. But what do you mean, the rest? All I remember from Baron D'Armond's trial is a fine."

"The Water Office has been increasing the penalties, remember? Sorceress Eleanor said the most recent suit ended with the girl having to pay a fine and go into service with the man who raped her."

"Frostbite," I squawked. A dozen nearby heads swivelled to throw shocked glances at me.

Sven glared. "Watch your language."

"Why?" I hissed. "Because there are women present? That word can't be as shocking as what you just said. What went wrong? The truth is out now. How can she be convicted of defamation?"

"Oh, be quiet. I don't know." He put his head down in his hands and spoke to the floor. "When the commoners hear the penalties imposed they'll go berserk."

Thank God Lord Edmund was dead. The new earl was a decent man, but Maggie had already lost her brother, and now the rest of her life would be ruined. And it was my fault.

In the mirror above, a young fop I didn't recognise said to Lord Edmund, "You've been fawning over Lady Susan lately. I didn't think you liked her."

"My brother thinks she's his. I'll give his nose a good, hard tweak if I steal her out from under it."

"He doesn't act like he's in a hurry."

"That's why she'll accept when I ask for her hand. She's tired of waiting for him. Besides, she's rich. I don't have to like her."

"I know, but still… She says every nasty thing that comes into her head. I can't bear being in the same room with her. I can't imagine wanting to take her to bed."

Lord Edmund's smile was more repulsive than a grimace. "I can. When she's mine, I'll pay her back triple for every vile thing she's ever said to me. She'll learn to keep a civil tongue in her head, and I will enjoy every minute of it."

An outraged voice interrupted the scene. "That's my daughter!"

Lorraine said, "What would you expect? That a man who rapes without remorse would treat his wife with respect? You are a fool, Your Grace." She gestured, and the magic mirror became, once again, just a mirror. "We have now seen Lord Edmund's true nature, or enough of it that matters. We arrive now at the crucial questions. Miss Archer has accused Lord Edmund of raping five women."

She gestured at the silver balance. Doll-like figures, one resembling Maggie Archer, the other Lord Edmund, appeared, one on each weighing pan. "We do not simply have her word against his now-mute testimony. The evidence we have seen upholds her charge." Another hand wave, and five faceless figures appeared on the pan with the figure of Maggie. "We charge thee, Water Office, according to Frankland's laws and customs, to show those assembled here a just verdict. Is Lord Edmund guilty—"

"Stop," the king roared. "Lord Edmund isn't on trial."

"Indeed, he is not. He has doubtless already been called to account at a higher court than this, and nothing we say or do here on earth can change that verdict. What do you fear, Your Majesty? Your advisors have already agreed he is beyond our reach."

The king chewed his lip without answering.

"Perhaps," she said, "I may rephrase the question to be more to your liking. Did Lord Edmund's actions justify Miss Archer's charge of rape?"

"I still don't—" the king said, but the balance arm was swinging, the pan with the women's replicas dropping. The arm was vertical when it settled. A definitive yes. A gusty sigh, mingling relief, regret, and rage ran through the audience, and then was stilled. The answer surprised few other than Sven and me.

I glanced at Sven. He shook his head and raised his hands, palms up.

Lorraine waved again at the scales, and the arm swung back to horizontal. The faceless dolls disappeared, leaving Maggie and Edmund again in balance. "A second question," she said. "Did Miss Archer have reason to believe Lord Edmund intended to rape her on his appearance at her home?"

The pan holding Maggie's replica dipped.

"And finally, the question at the heart of the defamation charge. Despite the revolting scenes we have witnessed revealing Lord Edmund's true nature, that truth has no bearing on the charge against Miss Archer."

Sven jerked upright. "Frostbite."

"The only question I am permitted to ask in determining Miss Archer's fate is this, Did Miss Archer's statement, and the resulting exposé, damage Lord Edmund's reputation?"

The weighing pan holding the figure of Lord Edmund dipped. After one shocked intake of breath, the watching commoners turned in an instant into a howling mob, out for blood. Hatred and revulsion battered me like stones, though I was not their target.

Beorn's bellow shook the walls and echoed from nearby buildings, overriding the howling. "Sit down and shut up. I'll burn anyone with a weapon, be they scullery maids or dukes."

The mob ignored him. Missiles flew from the balconies: shoes, ladies' purses, anything at hand. The shielded noblemen yelled back, shaking fists at the commoners above them. Witches, wizards, and noblewomen ran for cover.

Fire bloomed on the dais. Jean, with King Stephen, Queen Marguerite, and Mother Celeste in hand, vanished. Lorraine stood like a pillar of ice at the edge of the dais. René, white-faced and wide awake, grabbed me and we ran for the dais with Sven on our heels.

Jean reappeared in a blast of flame and grabbed my hand. He lunged for Lorraine; she tried to shake him off, but she was with us when the noise died an instant later. So was the rest of the human chain we had reached for: René and Sven, Maggie, Tom and Matt. Jean let go and disappeared.

He had left us in the Fortress's ballroom. A few feet away, the Earth Mother was calming the shaken royal couple. Lorraine glided past them towards the mirrors on the inner wall. I followed.

She waved at the mirror, and I recoiled as the howling resumed. The mirror showed the royal ballroom from the dais. In dead centre, a duke charging towards the balcony stairs with sword in hand flamed like a human torch. I wheeled, slamming into René and knocking him down. He could pick himself up. I fled.

The Secret behind the Secret

By the time I conquered my nausea, the howling had stopped. In the Fortress ballroom, several dozen people Jean had plucked out of harm's way clustered near the mirrors. Most members of the counter-conspiracy sat on the floor and watched the seething mob with dull eyes. Claire and her earl, hand in hand, were talking to Lorraine.

Fortress staff carried in food, drink, and chairs. Mrs Cole waved a platter of bread and cheese under my nose and insisted I take some.

A survey from the windows of the ramparts below confirmed the Fortress was free of the hideous tangle that had dominated my vision and thoughts for more than a month, but it brought little comfort. What sort of grovelling apology was adequate for ruining Maggie Archer's life?

The girl huddled in a corner, crying. Hazel knelt beside her, stroking her hair, although she had no healing magic left. Sven brooded over them, absorbed in his own thoughts. René slouched beside him in charged silence, glowering at Lorraine.

I circled behind the royal family, out of the king's line of sight, to join Lorraine and Claire. The earl bowed to Lorraine and then me, and walked towards Mother Celeste. Claire spoiled her otherwise calm appearance by tugging and twisting her bracelet.

The Fire Warlock had regained a precarious control over the riot. In the mirror, sullen commoners streamed from the palace grounds under his baleful eye.

Lorraine said, "Five nobles and a dozen commoners are dead. Scores more on both sides have burns, some serious."

Claire asked, "What will happen now?"

"I do not know," Lorraine said. "The mob is dispersing, but it is still enraged, and will reassemble at the slightest provocation. Warlock Quicksilver has removed the targets of their wrath, and the Fire Warlock has beaten them into temporary submission, but the brutality of the Fire Office has inflamed passions, not cooled them."

I said, "What does the verdict mean for Maggie?"

"She must pay Earl Eddensford one hundred franks, and is bound to serve him for the rest of her life. If she leaves his domains without his permission, her feet will freeze to the ground. I have already informed both Miss Archer and the earl of the sentence."

Claire's bracelet winked at me. I said, "I wish someone could convince the king to approve of rebuilding the Water Office."

Lorraine said, "That would be a blessing, but I cannot hope for it. The broken Water Office preserves King Stephen's privileges, and this is all he understands. He does not grasp how much harm it does the noble class as well as the commoners."

I nibbled at my bread and cheese without tasting it. After a few minutes, Claire drifted away. My body ached. Time for bed. I turned to go, but Sven was walking towards me.

"We were wrong, Lucinda, dead wrong. If we can't fix the Water Office now, we've committed suicide." He stared past me at Lorraine. "The conspiracy was misdirection, wasn't it?"

"Yes," she said. "You understand. Lucinda, is there another room with a mirror? I have something to show you, but it is not for everyone's eyes."

"Yes, ma'am, there are dressing rooms at the end of the hall."

"Warlock Snorri, Master Sven, come with us. I owe you three an explanation."

Mystified, I led the way. As soon as the dressing room door closed, René erupted. "What the hell went wrong? We thought getting rid of that conspiracy would make things better."

Without taking his eyes off Lorraine, Sven said, "The conspiracy wasn't about rape at all. It hid a defect in the Water Office making defamation cases about appearances, not truth. If a commoner accuses a nobleman of a crime, the nobleman can turn around and charge the commoner with defamation. The commoner can't win."

"Exactly," Lorraine said. "Neither can a lower-ranking noble. The ranking noble insists on the defamation trial being held first, he wins, and the evidence is ruled inadmissible in other trials. With no evidence, the other case is thrown out of court."

I said, "No wonder the Officeholders didn't want that to spread."

"Not even the others fully understood. I trust you searched diligently, but you could not have seen what I am about to show you. Events in the Earth Mother's amber chamber cannot be seen outside without a participant's express permission, and neither of us has ever given that before."

She gestured towards the mirror. "Watch."

An Earth Mother and an Air Enchanter I did not recognise watched an argument between Fire Warlock and Frost Maiden. Jean looked no different, only a subtle awkwardness bore witness to his youth. Lorraine, too, was younger, and angry. Fire witch angry. Frothing at the mouth angry.

"What have you done?" she shrieked at the Fire Warlock. "Who have you told?"

Jean's eyes glittered, but his voice was cool compared to hers. "I let several scholars and a few wizards in on the secret. I intend to abolish this abomination of a conspiracy, but I have had no success in finding the original spell. I have asked for help. Why should you object?"

"Why? Because it is not your conspiracy, fool. The king and the Frost Maiden started it. Keep your hands off!"

Jean stiffened. "But Old Brimstone—"

"Old Brimstone found a loophole and exploited it. That monster did not care if anyone else knew. I care. If Frankland knew, the country would break down in open class warfare and anarchy."

Jean breathed, "But then… Oh, no."

"Oh, yes, you dolt, you cretin." Lorraine was crying tears of rage. "You have let more people in on the secret. Do you believe they will keep it to themselves?"

She stabbed a finger at him, and he backed away from her, stumbling against a chair. "The great Fire Warlock, protector of women and children. What a lie," she spat. "When more lives are ruined, their blood be on your hands, not mine."

René's outrage echoed off the walls. "If it was your conspiracy, why did we have to go to all this trouble, and cause a riot that killed people, to get rid of it?"

"Because its time is over," Lorraine said. "If it continued after we rebuild the Water Office we would have accomplished nothing. I could not dissolve the conspiracy, even with the Fire Warlock's help. The king had to agree, and this king would not."

"Lucinda." Sven had to clear his throat twice. "I'm sorry."

I nodded, without meeting his eyes. I leaned against the wall, not bothering to wipe away the tears sliding down my cheeks.

Lorraine laid a cool hand on my arm. "Jean was young, and passionate. An older, more jaded warlock would have let well enough alone."

"He loved you," I said. "He thought destroying the conspiracy would please you."

"Perhaps he still did then, but that was long ago, and I was content to let the Fire Warlock take the blame. I am grateful neither of you bear grudges."

I raised my head and looked at René. *You, too, little brother. Don't hold a grudge. She did the best she could.*

He gave me a sullen stare. *I'll think about it.*

She had done the best she could. I wasn't even angry with her for using Maggie. I admired her sangfroid in seizing the opportunity when it presented itself.

Sven said, "But now the secret's been exposed, and the whole country will know about Maggie's trial. Given time, others will guess. We've pushed Frankland into the bubbling caldera."

I said, "You mean we don't have any choice any longer. We have to rebuild the Water Office." The words, "or die trying," stuck in my throat.

"Yes," Lorraine said. "You, Lucinda, and I, and Jean are bound together. We three have set this in motion, and we three will see it through."

A Loving Couple

We returned to the ballroom, and came to a stop behind the royal couple. An angel knelt before the king. Late afternoon sunlight streaming through open windows made a halo of Claire's hair, and struck fire from her bracelet.

"...and so, Your Majesty," she said, "Richard couldn't stand to have anyone else suffer from Edmund's devilry. That's why he stood up for Miss Archer. Please don't be angry with him for doing what he knew was right."

The earl looked delighted, but stunned. The king mumbled about the earl betraying his class.

Claire raised limpid eyes. "But, sire, don't you see? Richard didn't betray the nobles. Edmund did."

"She's right, dear," Queen Marguerite said. "We expect better behaviour from our kinsmen than that. If a man behaves like a common lecher, he should be treated like one."

"It's not only that, Your Majesty," Claire said. "Even a nobleman has to take orders from the people who outrank him. But Edmund disobeyed his father, and he was nothing but trouble for Richard. If he were still alive, he'd keep on causing trouble. Richard would have to keep guards around me, day and night, to protect me from his own brother. An earl shouldn't have to do that, should he?"

The king said, "No, that's not right."

"And what about Lady Susan? She has a mean tongue, but that doesn't excuse what he would have done to her."

The queen said, "She's a duke's daughter. Remember, dear? What he said was outrageous."

"That's true," the king said.

"So, there you have it, sire," Claire said. "If the Water Office can't deal with men like him, it hurts the nobles too. That's why I'm begging you, Your Majesty, to let them fix the Water Office. For Richard's sake. For the sake of all the other decent noblemen who don't want their wives or sisters or daughters at the mercy of men like Edmund."

I held my breath. Lorraine, one hand over her mouth, clutched my arm, hard enough to bruise.

The king threw up his hands. "Very well. Fix the damned thing."

Orders came from the Fire Warlock to house our honoured, noble guests in the Fortress's state apartments until the Water Office was rebuilt. The witches and wizards involved in the counter-conspiracy were invited to stay for their safety, but could go home if they wished. Except for me. I was not to set foot outside the Fortress until time to go to the Crystal Palace on September first.

I grumbled under my breath, and left Jean explaining to the irate king that if the royal family stayed in the Fortress, the Fire Warlock could pay more attention to protecting the other nobles. I staggered to my old bedroom and fell onto the bed. I dozed, fully clothed, waiting for Jean.

Moonrise flooded the room with light, and Jean had still not come.

The Fortress was quiet, the dark ballroom long since emptied. Lamps in the state apartments indicated sleep eluded our royal guests. Jean was stargazing on the terrace outside the conservatory. He did not turn when I stepped off the stairs.

"Could you not sleep?" he said. "You have worked wonders today." He waved a hand; a small table holding a bottle and a goblet appeared. "Would you join me in a celebratory glass? I have pulled a vintage you might enjoy from the cellars."

"A celebration, is it? Why didn't you come to my room with the bottle and two glasses rather than leaning on the balustrade with an empty whiskey glass?"

He raised the glass to eye level, considered it a moment, and set it down. "I have been reliving today's events, raging at my helplessness when the conspiracy threatened to engulf you."

"If you had tried to help, it would have made it worse. It would have fed on your power and used it against me. Isn't that how conspiracy magic works?"

"It is. Perhaps I am irrational, but I cannot forgive myself for failing you when you needed me. I did not approach you because I believed you would not welcome the hero you have discovered has feet of clay."

I crossed the terrace to stand behind him, and laid a hand on his shoulder. "That's what I thought for a while, but I was wrong. His feet are the same fine materials as the rest of him."

He gave me a quizzical look over his shoulder. I slid my arms around him. "Lorraine showed us you tried to expose the conspiracy, and what happened."

He turned to stare back into the darkness. "Then you know I have innocent blood on my hands."

"I knew that when I married you. How could there not be blood on the Fire Warlock's hands?"

"Fighting a defensive war against invading armies is justifiable. Spreading a secret that harms the very people I am pledged to protect is not. I was arrogant, and others have paid for my sins with ruined lives. Those women haunt me."

"But how could I respect you if you had known about it and didn't do anything? I hated that idea more. At least you tried. And you've been trying to make up for it, haven't you? Two years ago you figured out I could expose it, and pushed me in that direction ever since."

"It was a long shot, my dear, and I had serious doubts even your righteous outrage would be enough. This summer has been hard on both of us. I had not understood how lonely a married man could be in his own home. Many, many times I withdrew from your company, because if I had stayed I would have demanded you talk to me. I despise the secrets we have kept from each other."

A warm glow spread from the pit of my stomach, and I hadn't even sipped the wine. "With this over, we don't need to keep any more secrets, do we?"

"I cannot guarantee there will never be secrets we must keep from each other."

"But right now?"

"With this over, I know of no secrets I must hide from you. There are other conspiracies in Frankland you, as the Fire Warlock's apprentice, should know of, but both Beorn and I are free to tell you. No other is of the same magnitude as the one you destroyed."

"Thank God for that." I nuzzled his neck, and he smiled. "I'm glad you didn't insist on going up on Storm King tonight. I couldn't summon up enough power to walk through the fire."

"I am not surprised. We are done with our exercises. Between now and the first of September, you should use little magic, and rebuild your reserves. You must be well rested."

"Good, a break from all this frantic activity would be nice. Oh, wait, no. What will I do for the next three days to keep my mind off burning to death?"

"There is a way to free you from worries for a few days. I would not normally suggest it, knowing you detest the loss of control in being ordered to sleep. But it might be what you need now."

"What is it?"

"Earth magic. A healer can divorce your body from your mind in such a way that your body does not respond to what your mind recognises as threats. With no bodily responses, your mind passes over those threats, and focuses on pleasurable activities."

I nibbled at his earlobe while I considered this. "What's the drawback?"

"You may be a danger to yourself while under this spell. I, or one of the Fire Eaters when I am not available, would have to guard you at all times, even within the Fortress."

"Beorn would let you stay here to keep an eye on me?"

"Yes. He ordered me to be well-rested, also."

"Let's do it."

For three nights we made love like newlyweds, and danced by moonlight on a Fortress balcony, to the music of an unseen orchestra. When not eating, sleeping, or making love I read poetry, played peek-a-boo with Edward, and watched the pageant of the last hundred years' history in the fire, nestled against Jean's shoulder. Worries—about Maggie Archer, the Locksmith's warning, Frankland's future—flitted through my mind, and disappeared. The deep sadness that seemed to underlie all Jean's actions bothered me not at all.

September first dawned hot, humid, and still. My nightgown stuck to me, and sweat trickled down my back. The air felt heavy, full of the tension that comes before a thunderstorm. How appropriate for the day in which I would wield the lightning, and let loose a storm whose intensity we could only guess at.

Jean had already dressed and gone. For the first time in three days, I was alone. In a corner, something moved. I shot to my feet, fully awake. An orange streak dived under the bed. I leaned against the bedpost, my heart hammering. I had nearly torched the startled cat.

The spell had worn off. Of course it had. I had to be alert to unlock the Water Office.

Drown that fool witch and her hidden terror. I preferred the lightning bolt's explicit threats, as frightening as it was. Between the two dangers, how many people might die before this morning was over?

Snatches of heated conversation floated through my mind—an ongoing argument between Beorn and Mother Celeste always choked off when I approached. Imagine, me, a fire witch, not demanding to know what the argument was about. Obviously magic had been at work.

Only then, while I leaned against the bedpost, did the overheard whispers and random memories coalesce and arrange themselves into a clear picture. Should Frankland's top healers be close at hand in the Crystal Palace, where they might be in danger? Or should they wait in the Warren where they would be safer, but perhaps inaccessible, if the hidden danger blocked the tunnels? No wonder Lorraine had gotten upset, listening to this argument. If the hidden danger was potent enough to kill everyone in the Crystal Palace...

My God.

My knees buckled, and I sat down hard on the bed. "I am not a seer," Jean had often said. True, but he could imagine a future, and I, looking over his shoulder, thought I could see what lay ahead: a new Scorching Time. The Fire Office would burn through Beorn, then through Sunbeam and Flint, while he watched, helpless to stop it. After Flint, the Fire Office would come back to land on him again, as a better choice than a not yet fully-grown boy.

It would not land on me; I would be dead. Even René's sulks two weeks earlier now made sense. Beorn would have warned him of what was coming, and ordered him not to attempt to pull me back from death's grasp. They couldn't afford to lose both of us.

The unlocking involved all four Officeholders—Fire Warlock, Earth

Mother, Water Sorceress, and Air Enchanter. The Fire Office did not tolerate threats to even one of those four. If one or more died, the Fire Office would go berserk. It would order the Fire Warlock to kill the treacherous slime responsible—me. If he refused, it would leave a smoking crater where the Crystal Palace and the town of Quays had been.

Why had I not thought about this before?

Because Beorn and Jean had both ordered me not to. "Forget it," Beorn had said, with his hand on my shoulder. "The lock is enough for you to deal with. Let me and Jean deal with the rest."

How, in the name of all that was holy, could they handle a problem like this?

The answer that came sent ice water flowing through my veins. They could minimise the danger to the other Officeholders by walling them off. I had to be in contact with Lorraine's ring; I could not avoid the hidden terror. And I would draw power through Jean. He, with all his shields up, would present an impenetrable wall sheltering the others, but the blast and the hidden terror would be reflected back at me. I would have no escape. No wonder I had sensed death ahead. No wonder he didn't want a bond between us.

"A warlock's responsibility to Frankland's security," he had said more than once, "trumps everything else: family, personal comfort, one's own life." I would die, and my husband would see to it, with the full backing of my cherished friend, Beorn.

And what then? Jean would hold the Fire Office a second time, until René was mature enough to handle it. He faced ten or fifteen years of arduous labour, struggling to keep Frankland from tearing itself apart. Ten or fifteen years of loneliness and defeat, his wife dead from his own hands, his dreams of reforging the Fire Office in ruins. A prospect grim enough to daunt the most heroic of men.

I might have pitied him, if I hadn't been angry enough to commit murder.

Anger Be My Shield

I swung between extremes, one second in abject fear for my life or anguish over abandoning my son, the next seeking an outlet for my blind fury. My target, the man who had lied to me so many times, had left the Fortress, and I could not find him.

Drown him. I broke off my search and went to say goodbye to my little Eddie, but stopped with my hand on the closed nursery door. He was laughing. Through my mind's eye, I watched him play for many minutes before I walked away, blind with tears. He would not remember, but he would hear the stories as he grew. Better he should hear that our last days together had been full of joy than that my distress had frightened him.

An Earth Guild charm hid my red eyes and nose. Master Sven didn't notice I'd been crying when we met at the stairs. We rode together to the Fire Warlock's study without speaking—to each other, that is. He buried his nose in his copy of the Water Office spell book and muttered to himself. Fine. I had never been less in the mood for small talk.

Beorn met us at the top. My glare would have scorched a lesser man. He responded with a bleak expression that gave terror the upper hand over my anger.

I brushed past him. "Let's go."

"Not so fast. In a minute or two."

"What are we waiting for?"

"René. He's coming with us."

"Why?"

"Because I said so."

"That's not a reason."

Beorn didn't bother to reply. René rocketed up the stairs.

Why are you coming with us?

He scowled and didn't answer.

Master Sven's brow creased. We ignored his questions and trudged through the tunnel in grim silence.

We arrived at the Crystal Palace on the heels of the Air Enchanter and his colleagues. Sorcerer Charles, hollow-eyed and ashen, led us into an open courtyard where the Water Guild Council and several dozen healers waited. My stomach churned. Mother Celeste must have called in all level four and five healers in Frankland. Hazel gave me a half-hearted wave. I clenched my jaw and turned away. What could they do for me when I was dead?

Master Sven studied the healers through narrowed eyes, chewing his lip.

Jean slipped into the rear of the courtyard. I kept my back turned on him.

The Frost Maiden walked out of a shadowed archway. Despite the heat of the day and my anger, I shivered. If only the outer manifestations of the gift of cold water hadn't worn off. Her armour was better than mine.

She said, "Thank you for being prompt. Some of you are confused and concerned about the number of healers gathered here today. They are here because we do not know what will happen when the lock is released, and we have reason to believe at least one, and possibly several, participants are in danger."

Sven's head snapped around. "What do you—"

She held up a hand for silence. "No one hearing this for the first time should be in danger, but since we do not know exactly what we will face, we determined to err on the side of caution and have our most talented healers near at hand.

"To reduce the risk, all not involved in the unlocking shall return to the Warren or the Hall of the Winds while the lock is released. It will take some time—half an hour, perhaps—for the Locksmith to work her way through the spells to the lock, but once she is there, the release will happen quickly. If our fears are unfounded, those of you in the reforging coven will return and the work will begin, and the healers will return to their guildhalls to go about their normal business.

"Do not berate your guild heads for secrecy; the decision to limit those who knew was mine and mine alone. If you have questions, my apprentice, Sorceress Eleanor, or the other Water Guild Council members will do their best to answer them. They will go with you to the Warren or the Hall of the Winds for their safety.

"Thank you for your patience."

The Water Guild Council began filing from the courtyard. The two enchantresses waited together, white-faced and rigid, as the healers queued behind the water witches and wizards.

Master Sven's raised voice made me jump. "Burn it, what's going on here? What danger? And don't tell me to shut up and go quietly—I want to know what this is all about."

Fighting terror with anger. Typical fire wizard behaviour. I would have kissed him if I hadn't been sure it would embarrass him.

The Frost Maiden said, "The warning of danger is in the words of the lock spell. 'Whichever power releases the lock, I swear, shall face my hidden terror there.' Master Sven, the warnings do not apply to you. Only the four Officeholders, Warlock Quicksilver, and the Warlock Locksmith should be in danger."

Master Sven swung around to stare at me. I fought down nausea, and nodded. Sven glared in turn at Beorn, and Mother Celeste, who both nodded in agreement.

He pivoted and shouted at Jean, "Why are you making her do this? Have you no decency? Look at her. She's terrified—"

I saw red and stopped trembling. Beorn grabbed Master Sven's shoulder and jerked him around, making Sven stagger.

"You don't know what you're talking about." Beorn punctuated his shout with a thump on Sven's chest. "Do you think any man in his right mind would make his wife do something like this?"

The witches and wizards who had already left the courtyard crowded back in to watch. I poked the two fire wizards. They kept shouting, without looking at me.

"Excuse me," I said, and spat fire like a young dragon.

Dead silence. Beorn and Sven goggled down at me.

"Nobody makes a warlock do anything." I eased off until the fire in my voice was only a small torch. "If he could, he would order me not put myself in danger, but he can't. Because a warlock's first responsibility is to Frankland's security, and that trumps everything else: family, personal comfort, one's own life. Everything. And I am a warlock, too. I beg you to remember that."

I turned to the crowd in the archway. "Move! Let's get this over with."

A mad scramble followed as the non-essential witches and wizards, including Master Sven, fled. Behind me Jean murmured, "Overcoming fear with anger. Typical fire witch behaviour."

Beorn grinned. Mother Celeste smiled.

"I don't know why you think it's funny. And you," I said, turning on Jean, "you are a cold, calculating, manipulative, ruthless son-of-a-bitch."

His face was as bloodless as an air wizard's. His lips compressed to a thin line, but he bowed. "Thank you, my dear, for the compliment."

"It wasn't one. You lied to me, you frostbitten bastard."

Beorn's hand came down heavy on my shoulder. "Don't blame him, Lucinda. He did it on my orders."

"I despise both of you." I shook off his hand and stomped into Lorraine's study. A line of crates made me stop short. I counted enough burn cloths to swaddle everyone in Lesser Campton, plus salves, lotions of all sorts, as well as tourniquets, splints, and bandages. An apothecary could have set up shop there.

Mother Celeste said, "I sent these over yesterday. Since we don't know what will happen, I brought everything I could think of. Most of the healers have gone back to the Warren, but Father Martin and Father Jerome are staying with us."

I shrugged and sat down on the sofa. Lorraine faced me. She laid her hand on the small table between us; I clasped it with mine and dove in.

We had met several times over the preceding weeks to review the path to the lock and to practice drawing power from both her and Sorceress Eleanor. I had no difficulty in finding my way. While I worked, Jean and the other Officeholders cast protective spells until the magic in the room was thick enough to chew on.

The lock unscrolled and I read it through once more, as if it were not already engraved in my memory. A fresh blast of fury rolled over me at the arrogance and short-sightedness of the original Locksmith, the breakage in the Water Office responsible for obscenities like Maggie Archer's sentence, and my husband's willingness to sacrifice me for Frankland's benefit. I nursed the anger. Anger might protect me, terror wouldn't.

Keeping a mental finger on the lock, I said, "I'm there."

Jean sat down beside me. I snarled at him and turned away.

He wrapped his arms around me and pulled me tight against his chest.

"Hush," he said. "It will be over soon." I lifted my hand, keeping a finger on Lorraine's sapphire, and he slipped his hand in between hers and mine.

Beorn and Enchanter Paul lined up behind us with their hands on Jean's shoulders, and Mother Celeste stood between the two seats, one hand on Jean and the other on Lorraine.

"Ready?" I said.

"Almost," Lorraine said. In a moment she glittered, rimed all over with frost. The frost thickened to a thin layer of ice. Jean shuddered. He clenched his jaw against my shoulder, but didn't pull his hand away.

Lorraine's armour complete, she gazed at me from iceberg-blue eyes. "Proceed when ready, Madam Locksmith."

"No matter what, I'm not stopping. We won't get a second chance."

"Agreed. Do it."

In my mind's eye the power from the four Offices appeared as four burning ropes in red, green, blue, and white. I reached through Jean's beacon to pull them into my own candle flame, twisting to make one thick cable, and bid it grow until it was enough to release the lock on the Water Office.

A glassblower's furnace blasted heat at me. Blazing light blinded my mind's eye, but the text hadn't moved or changed. With the power available from the four Offices, shoving was easy. Releasing the lock took mere seconds, and seconds were too long.

Lava gouged a channel up my right arm. Lorraine screamed. I clutched my anger, and shoved. With a deafening roar, my world exploded into a maelstrom of fire and blood.

The River

I fled, burning, through darkness. Nothing mattered besides the pain in my right hand and arm. If I'd had a knife, I would have cut it off. René ran with me, but couldn't put out the fire.

Jean was ahead, moving away from me. I sank a claw of charred bone into him, and wouldn't let go.

Help me, damn you. Put out the fire.

Nearby, a river held cold, inviting water. Jean pulled me towards it. Light streamed from the far bank. People I hadn't seen in years waited for me.

I lunged toward the river. That cold water would put out the fire. Drowning was easy. I'd nearly drowned once, and I knew. It would hurt a little, then it would all be over. No fire. No pain. No terror. No lies. No heartbreak.

René fought me, holding me back. I couldn't break free.

Let me go.

I can't. I promised Quicksilver I'd bring you back.

René dragged me, screaming, away from the river.

Knives stabbed at my arm. My hand throbbed in a healer's grip.

Earth Mother, why are you torturing me?

René, crying like a girl, pinned me down in the darkness. I fought him. The agony in my arm went on and on and on.

Jean, help me. I need you. Help me, or I swear to God, I'll make you wish you were dead.

There was no answer.

273

Lucinda, wake up. Big sister, can you hear me? Damn it, Lucinda, come back.

Someone called my name, over and over. The voice and the pain were driving me mad. Thoughts fluttered like moths against a glass door on a lantern. Jean had abandoned me when I needed his help. Where were the healers? Frankland's best had been nearby. Had they abandoned me, too?

Lucinda, can you hear me?

Telling René I hated him would take too much effort. Even the Fire Warlock's kiss had not hurt like this. My mental flame had vanished; I was as useless as a heap of cold ashes. I wanted Jean, and oblivion.

Jean, where are you? I need you.

Big sister, wake up.

A spark glimmered in the ashes. René's unreasonable demands fed my anger as breathing on a spark starts a fire. If I hadn't been dog-tired, I would have told him to go kiss the Fire Warlock.

The Earth Guild must have done something for me, after all. I could think again, and remember. I had released the lock. If only I cared.

Images René had seen floated through my mind. Blood, lots of it. A body sprawled on the floor, charred past recognition. No one could burn like that and live.

Big sister, talk to me.

Hell, no, you traitor. I'll never speak to you again.

A deeper voice joined in. "Lucinda, wake up. That's an order."

Hadn't I already done enough? The spark grew, became glowing coals. I snarled, "Go away and leave me alone, you frostbitten donkey, and take that nasty runt with you."

Beorn said, "That's more like it. I knew you'd come around."

I pried an eyelid open. Faces floated over me: Beorn, René, Hazel, an earth father, and some woman about a hundred years old. All were haggard, with blood-shot eyes.

They had wrapped me so tightly in Earth Guild burn cloths I couldn't have moved if I'd wanted to. Where was Jean? Keeping my eye open hurt. I closed it.

"I'm sorry, dear," Mother Celeste said, "but we won't let you go. Wake up and talk to us."

I opened both eyes and stared. The old woman leaning over me was Mother Celeste. Her face was a mass of wrinkles; the thick coil of grey hair had become thin, lank, and pure white. Her complexion was blotchy, as if she'd been weeping.

I said, "Did the Earth Guild let you down, too?"

"No, dear, but I understand why you feel that way. Someday, I hope, you will forgive us for what we are doing to you."

I said, "If you won't let me sleep, answer my questions. What are you doing to me? Where's Jean?"

Beorn's laugh, overloud and with a manic edge, hurt my ears. "All right, then. René, go get some sleep. Celeste, you can stop worrying. She's going to be fine."

"Humph. I don't tell you how to call down the lightning. You keep your fingers out of the healing arts, thank you."

"Someone died," I said. "Lorraine?"

"No, dear," Mother Celeste said, "nobody died—not yet anyway, but it was—is—a close thing."

The intensity of my relief surprised me. "I am so glad she survived. I was sure someone died. Was that her blood?"

"Yep," Beorn said. "The Locksmith's 'terror' was a black magic cutting spell."

Broken fragments coalesced into a clear image. I turned my head and vomited onto Hazel, sitting at my shoulder.

"Don't worry about that," she said, waving it away. "It's not the first time, and it won't be the last. You two suffered similar injuries. You were burned all over, with your right arm taking the brunt of it. The spell inflicted cuts all over Sorceress Lorraine, the deeper ones closer to her Token of Office. Her right arm was hacked to bits."

"Will she be all right? Can you regrow her arm?"

There was a short silence. Mother Celeste said, "She is very weak. Too weak, and too old, to tolerate treatment as painful as regrowing a limb is for an adult. We don't dare, not for days."

I said, "Isn't it better to do it as soon as possible, if you're going to do it at all?"

"Yes, that's so. By the time she's strong enough, it will be too late."

"That's a shame," I said. Painful, was it? An invisible blacksmith pounded my arm with a sledgehammer. The coals glowed a little brighter. "What are you doing to me? Are you regrowing mine?"

"Yes, dear," Mother Celeste said. "It was burned down to the bone—

burned so badly we cut it off and started fresh."

"Stop it. It hurts." I tried to pull away, but couldn't move.

Tears slid down her cheeks. "I am so sorry, dear, but the magic is almost done. It will take weeks to complete, but the worst is over."

Maybe that was so. The wracking pain that had driven everything else out of my mind had eased. It was now merely excruciating. It had been intolerable. Without René, I would have escaped.

"So, you're doing to me what you don't dare do to Lorraine? You bastards. I wanted to die. I can live without an arm. You should have given me a choice."

"No dice," Beorn said. "You have to stick around to unlock the other Offices. Jean said you had to be whole and healthy to call down the lightning."

Mother Celeste said, "Without an arm you'd always be off-balance. Even with the best of intentions you'd be unable to give the lightning the full-minded concentration it needs. We agreed weeks ago that keeping you physically sound was the prime concern for both the Earth and Fire Guilds. We planned all along to do whatever was needed, whether you agreed with it or not."

I spat at them, "You're both cold-hearted. As cold as a Frost Maiden."

Beorn said, "I didn't like it, Lucinda, but we had to."

Mother Celeste said, "It comes with being an Officeholder. It does something to you. You'll understand when it's your turn."

Beorn tugged at his beard and looked at me sideways. "Besides, years ago I had a vision that showed you with both arms."

"A vision?" The glowing coals flared into bright flame. "A vision? You... You... If I had any strength I'd drown you, you two-bit wizard with snowflakes for brains."

"Drown me, eh? I knew you'd be pissed off. Why do you think I'm telling you now, when you can't do anything?"

"You told me—"

"No, I didn't tell you. That's the point. Before you walked the challenge path, three years ago, I'd had a vision of you riding the moving stairs with a little boy, maybe four or five years old. I knew you'd survive. With both arms. I knew René would survive, too, or I wouldn't have sent him after you. We still nearly lost both of you. If I had told you or Jean you'd live through it, would you two have worked so hard?"

"If you knew I would survive, why was I so afraid?"

Beorn and Mother Celeste exchanged glances. She nodded. "She's strong enough. We won't lose her now."

"Because," Beorn said, "You misinterpreted the warnings. We made sure you did. They weren't about you."

I struggled to sit up. Hazel held me down with two fingers. "Jean wasn't in danger. He's channelled the lightning thousands of times."

"This was different. What did you think he did?"

"He protected the other Officeholders."

"Yeah, how?"

"His shields."

"Don't be an ass, Lucinda. You know better. That would have reflected the blast back onto you."

"But—"

"He let his shields down. He meant to absorb it all so you'd have a chance."

"No, no. That can't be. He never said anything."

Beorn shook his head. "We didn't want you screwing yourself up trying to absorb some of it. We, both of us, hid the danger from you."

"I don't believe you. Where is he? I have to see him."

"He's beside you, dear," Mother Celeste said, nodding to my right.

I turned my head. Father Martin and several other healers had their hands on a still figure shrouded in burn cloths.

I screamed, and thrashed about, trying to tear out of my own wrappings. The healers held me down, crooning. I wept for Jean, and for my own stupidity and self-absorption.

Beorn barked, "Shut up, Lucinda, and listen. He's not dead. Not yet anyway. It's still touch and go."

Mother Celeste said, "He is lost in the valley of the shadow of death. We don't understand why he didn't die. By all rights he should have."

Beorn said, "René says you did for Jean what René did for you—held him here by force of will. If that's so, then it's up to you. You have to help him find his way back, or let him go."

I sobbed, "He'll hate me."

"Too bad. Call him back. That's an order."

"Jean, come back, I need you," I called, beginning my own litany. "Jean, come home, Edward needs a father. Jean, can you hear me? Jean…"

Family Ties

Hey, big sister?
Pulling the blanket over my head didn't shut out René's voice. *Why are you bothering me when I'm trying to sleep?*

I want to make sure you're all right.

I'm not, but I'm not dying, either, if that's what you mean. I'm tired, and I hurt. Go away.

Is that the thanks I get for saving your life?

If I ever stop hurting, maybe I'll thank you. But right now, if I get my hands on you, you'll be sorry.

Hand, you mean.

Har, har. Go jump in a lake, runt.

As the bones in my arm extended, sharp stabbing pains alternated with periods of throbbing as muscles stretched, cramped, and worked into position, but the physical pain never overwhelmed the heartache I suffered. I drifted in and out of fog, each moment of clarity revealing a different healer at my bedside. Powerful ones: Mother Celeste. Hazel. Other earth mothers and fathers pumping life and health into me.

Until one morning I woke clear-headed for the first time in…days? Weeks? The earth witches and wizards were gone. My hand ached, but no worse than the muscle aches from strenuous exercise.

I dreamt of cinnamon rolls and apple tarts…

I rolled into my husband's arms. *Jean, I'm so sorry… Jean, you're nothing but skin and bones.*

You have none to spare either, my love. We have been living on our reserves for days.

I started with more than you did. As soon as I'm up to it, I'll bake anything, everything, you ask for. Jean, we're speaking mind-to-mind. I thought you didn't want...

Not at all, my dear. Mind-to-mind communication is convenient, and I am too weak to talk. I cannot now deny the bond between us, despite my efforts to ensure I did not drag you to your death.

But, Jean, you lied to me.

Did I? How so?

When you said, with this over, we didn't have any more secrets to keep from each other.

That was not a lie. Now that you have unlocked the Water Office, I have nothing to hide.

I pulled back to inspect him. He looked almost a stranger, with a burn victim's pink skin stretched tight over a bald skull, but the vivid eyes were the ones I knew so well. The tension and sadness, so evident since our return from our honeymoon, were gone.

But I meant the exposure of the conspiracy.

His eyes danced. *You would quibble over the meaning of the word, 'this'? I knew what you meant.*

What do you think you are, a lawyer? Hitting him with my pillow took all my strength. I lay, panting, against his rib cage while he chuckled. *Damn you. You weren't supposed to be hurt, damn you.*

Hush. If you had foreseen what I intended, my gallant wife, would you have let me? No. Never.

Of course not. But you were in danger, and I would far rather go in your stead, than do nothing and lose you. I have failed in other ways to protect you; forgive me for indulging my pride in this.

I beat feebly on his chest with my good hand. *Damn you and your obsession with being a hero.*

Stop. He caught my hand and held it. *I did not aspire to a hero's death. My motives were quite selfish, I assure you.*

What do you mean, selfish?

I lived without wife and family for more than a century. The prospect of living alone again frightens me more than the prospect of dying. I intend for you to outlive me. Am I not selfish?

I slipped my good hand under the collar of his nightshirt. *Oh, Jean, I don't know. Put that way, you sound very romantic.*

"Fool girl," he whispered, and kissed me.

Little brother, are you there?

Yeah, I'm here.

I'm sorry I told you to jump in a lake.

I'm not a runt anymore, either.

That's true. And, little brother…Thanks.

Well, big sister, I'm glad you're still here, but it damn sure wasn't my pleasure. It was bloody awful. Of all the ways to go, why did you try to drown yourself?

I had tried to drown myself? Memories swirled past, as distorted as images seen in misshapen mirrors. Then the memory of that cold river surfaced, and the pain that had driven me towards it.

Because sometimes living is harder than dying.

Just don't go there again for a good long time, that's all I ask.

Don't worry, I won't. Not while I have cinnamon rolls to bake.

The healers let us have visitors as soon as we had the stamina to sit up for ten minutes at a time. Master Sven, one of the first, perched on the edge of his chair, and looked everywhere but at me.

He cleared his throat twice. "I apologise for my behaviour in the Crystal Palace. I had no insight into the discussions you two and the Officeholders have had, and I jumped to unwarranted conclusions. I'm sorry."

I said, "Apology accepted."

Jean, with no rancour, added, "We regret you were unprepared, but the decision was not ours. We could not blame you for being disturbed."

Master Sven sighed and eased back in his chair.

I asked, "How is Lorraine? Can the Earth Guild regrow her arm?"

"No. She said she's grateful to be alive, losing it was a small sacrifice, and all she cares about is finishing the reforging. She doesn't need the arm for that."

"Couldn't the Reforging Coven finish it without her?"

He said, "Yes, and we did, mostly. We took it apart as soon as Mother Celeste could spare the earth mages. That was easy. We finished by mid-afternoon of the first day. It took several days to rebuild it. We made mistakes—"

I said, "You mean the Air Guild made mistakes?"

"All four guilds made a few. The Air Enchanter must have tutored

Enchantress Winifred, because the Air Guild made a better showing than I expected. As soon as Sorceress Lorraine is up to it, she'll inspect our work before René puts the new lock on. We should take advantage of her expertise since she's still with us."

"Very sensible of you," Jean said. "And the loophole Old Brimstone exploited?"

"Gone. We double- and triple-checked. That one won't bother us again."

"Thank God," Jean said, with deep satisfaction. "That alone is worth nearly dying for."

Sorceress Eleanor and Sorcerer Charles brought a gift, a necklace of perfectly matched pearls. I goggled at it, speechless.

"An inadequate token of our appreciation," Eleanor said.

"While you wear them," Charles said, "you cannot drown. Will you accept them?"

A lump in my throat prevented speech. I waved the box at Jean. He took the strand from me and fastened it around my neck.

"I believe now what I did not believe two years ago," he said. "The long war between the Fire and Water Guilds is over, and Frankland the better for it."

Our appearances shocked Claire, but after the first jaw-dropping moment, she hid her discomfort better than most witches and wizards did.

Their unease was their problem. We looked darned good for two people who should have been dead. Mrs Cole had brought an assortment of silk scarves, and after wrapping the one I picked out around my head, held up a mirror for me. Between the flowered scarf and the new, pink skin, I resembled a nun dipped in paint. The Earth Guild's best healers had ensured there would be no scars.

"Of course I insisted on coming," Claire said. "We're family. And being an earl's wife makes it easy to go wherever I want."

After summarising our ordeal, I asked her about Paris. Her face lit up. I listened to her description of what she had seen and done with some bemusement, as her recital seemed more about the wonderful time she was having with the earl than about the sights of Paris.

When she paused for breath, I asked a nagging question. "What about Maggie Archer? How's she doing?"

Claire's eyebrows drew together. "I don't know. I thought I would ask you."

"Me? Why? She's in your service now. Isn't she with you in Paris? Or did you send her on to Gastòn?"

"You don't know about Richard's orders?"

I looked at Jean for enlightenment. He said, "I am afraid we do not. What were they?"

"He didn't want her around, reminding us all the time of Edmund, so he ordered her to go home to Abertee and do whatever she wanted without bothering him again."

"Did he?" My guilty conscience sheathed its stiletto. I laughed. "That's noble of him."

Claire glowed. "Isn't it? I am so proud. The Earth Mother helped with the wording so he wouldn't accidentally jinx the girl, but it was his idea. The fine had to be paid through the Water Guild, but he gave your earth witch friend money to hand on to the Archers to pay it with. I am so lucky I married him."

"The earl is a fortunate man," Jean said, "to have a wife who loves him, and not just his wealth and position."

Claire shook her head. "But I don't..." Her eyes widened, and she laughed her merry, golden laugh. "I do love him. I didn't know, but I do."

Jean reached for my good hand. A warm glow spread through me. "A loving and forgiving wife," he said, "is a man's greatest treasure. Who knows better than I?"

End of Engine of Lies

The story continues in
The Blacksmith, Reforging: Book 3